BEYOND DESIRE

Felix Mendelssohn was one of the outstanding men of his time—the first half of the nineteenth century. In addition to his great personal charm, he had the good fortune to be a member of one of the wealthiest banking families of Europe; and so great was his musical talent that by the time he was twenty he was already famous as a composer and conductor. His full and active life provides the basis for this compelling romantic novel.

Beyond Desire is a story of love: Mendelssohn's love for the fiery Italian prima donna, Maria Salla, and for Cécile Jeanrenaud, his wife, who was one of the most beautiful women in Europe. But it is also the story of a different kind of love which became a dedication—his love for the music of his great predecessor, Johann Sebastian Bach, and his fight to restore that music to its rightful place in the world. It was a love and a conviction for which he was willing finally to risk his marriage, his career and his health.

Beyond Desire is also a broad picture of its time, with scenes in Berlin, London and Paris, and in the more provincial cities of Germany—Frankfurt, Düsseldorf, Leipzig and Dresden. Frederic Chopin, Robert Schumann, Queen Victoria, Richard Wagner, the Rothschild family and many other historical personages are woven into this warm and moving narrative, which shows the same skill in storytelling, the blend of pathos and comedy, passion and tenderness, that made *Moulin Rouge* a delight to millions of readers all over the world.

PIERRE LA MURE

BEYOND DESIRE

A Novel based on the Life of
Felix and Cécile
Mendelssohn

THE BOOK CLUB
121 CHARING CROSS ROAD
LONDON, W.C.2

THIS EDITION   1957

CONTENTS

Author's Note

This is a work of fiction, in which I have tried to portray the essential character of Mendelssohn and in particular his untiring efforts to re-establish the music of Johann Sebastian Bach. As Mendelssohn was dying he said these words, "*Should every note of mine perish, future generations will think kindly of me, for it is I, Jakob Ludwig Felix Mendelssohn, a Jew, who gave Christians their greatest music.*" In making this the subject of my story I have deliberately altered certain dates and events and taken certain chronological and dramatic licences to suit my purpose. In other respects I have adhered to history as far as it is known.

Prologue

THERE HE stood, a stocky old man in buckled breeches and shoes, wearing the big grey wig she had given him one Christmas, smiling at her the happy, vacant smile of the blind, and she said, " Yes, my Johann, it's all right," trying to control the quiver of her lips.

Usually she called him Johann Sebastian in full, but she thought of him as " my Johann," and sometimes it escaped . . . " It's all right," she repeated with a trembling nod of her coifed head. " You go and play the organ. It'll do you good."

It was mad, she knew, to let him go and play the organ at this hour of the night. It would wake up the whole school, bring down Herr Weinlick, the censor, who surely would send a report to Their Magnificences of the city council, and they would say that her Johann had gone mad as well as blind and that they couldn't keep such a choirmaster in a city school, and they would dismiss him. And where would they go, now that the doctor had taken their savings? Sweet Lord Jesus, what would become of them, with him blind and her too old to find work, and Gottfried sick in the head, and winter not over yet, and Leipzig still full of snow?

Panic widened her faded blue eyes in the thin parchment of her wrinkled face, yet she went on looking at him, trembling from head to foot, nodding stubbornly. She didn't know what would become of them, but she couldn't stand it any longer, watching him sit by the fire, his bib-knuckled hands on his knees, staring at the flames he could not see, counting the hours of the night by the watchman's call. She knew he was afraid of what was coming in the morning and he wanted to pray and ask God for strength, and making music was his way of praying. And so, even if His Magnificence the Lord Mayor himself sent them all to jail she was going to let him play the organ to-night and give him this last joy.

" Yes, my Johann, you go and play all you want." She stressed the last words with the unsure bravado of the poor challenging disaster. " Just don't play too loud," she begged softly, pressing herself against him. Then, in unaware contradiction, " And don't be too long."

" I won't."

His lips went on moving but no sound came from them. He just held her close to his chest as if he wanted her to hear his thanks directly from the beat of his heart.

9

The door of the bedroom opened, and Gottfried came in.

With a pang she saw that his reddish wig was askew on his head and he had forgotten to put on one of his stockings. The sight of him reopened an old wound, an instant forgotten. He did those things, she knew, because he was sick in the head, and the doctor had said he'd never get well, although he was a fine tall boy and sometimes he would sit at the clavichord and invent such beautiful music that even her Johann, who was very severe when it came to music, would listen to it with tears in his eyes. . . .

"Papa, may I go, too?" the simpleton asked, excited as a child. "I'll pump the bellows."

Johann Sebastian Bach nodded. "Yes, my son," he said gently. "We'll pray together."

From the doorway Anna Magdalena watched them advance uncertainly down the dimly-lit corridor, the blind man leaning on the arm of his son. Then she closed the door and stood motionless, her face buried in her hands. Now at last she could cry and crying was all she could do. She no longer asked questions or tried to understand why God sent them so much grief. Weren't they good people? Hadn't her Johann lost his eyes in His service, writing music by candlelight to praise His name and sing His glory? All those cantatas, those motets, that big Mass for which she had ruled the staves and that Passion, which was the thing he loved best, they'd all been written for Him. Hadn't He heard any of them?

She took her hands from her face and listened, straining her ear. He had begun to play and he was playing the Passion. She'd known he would play that because it was the story of Our Saviour Jesus and how they'd beaten Him and spat on Him and put a crown of thorns on His head and made Him carry His cross up to the top of the hill where they crucified the murderers, and He the very Son of God had endured it all without a word. . . . And now her Johann was playing the music he'd written about those terrible things so that in the morning he'd remember what Jesus had gone through for him, and he, too, would try to be like Him. . . .

She heard a sound of rushing steps outside and turned around to open the door. Yes, it was Herr Weinlick—and so mad he was sputtering to himself and in such great hurry he was more running than walking and hadn't even buckled his shoes.

"What's the matter with him?" he shouted at her from afar. "Doesn't he know it's past midnight? . . . Has he gone mad? . . . And who gave him the right to play the big organ? Only the organist has the right to play the organ and he's only the choirmaster . . ."

Better let him talk awhile, she thought, watching the censor approach, let him tire himself a bit . . . She'd learned that much

living all these years with a man. In the old days her Johann would
get himself into such passions he'd fling his wig across the room
and the only thing to do was to be quiet and let him rant and after
a while he'd calm down.

"A choirmaster, you hear, that's all he is." Herr Weinlick was
now only a few feet from her and panting heavily. "I'll send a
report and——"

Breath failed him and he had to stop.

"Come in, Herr Weinlick, and sit down," she said softly.

"I didn't come to sit down," he sputtered, following her inside.
"I came to tell you——"

Quietly she closed the door after him. The music didn't sound
so loud any more. "Sit down on this chair," she said with the
tranquil authority of women in their home. "And rest awhile."

She sat down next to him at the big dining-table. He wasn't a
mean man really, she thought, looking at him. Just poor and
afraid. Like her, like her Johann, like everybody that didn't have
any money. It was fear that made people cruel. . . . "You shouldn't
be running out at night like this without your coat."

"Never mind that," he barked, recouping his anger with his
breath.

"But you'll be sick. Look at you, all out of breath and
sweating——"

"I'm all right. I just warn you——"

Already she was rising. "I'll get you a little hot soup."

"I don't want any soup," he snapped, watching her bend over
the tureen hanging down over the fire. "I just came to——"

"And what will you do when you're sick?" she broke in, calmly
ladling soup into a plate. "You'll have to stay in bed and you can't
watch the boys any more and perhaps the rector writes to the
council he's got to have a new censor . . ." She walked back to the
table and set the plate of soup before him. "You eat this. It'll do
you good."

Noisily he sucked in a few spoonfuls. "I tell you this time he's
gone too far and I'll be obliged to send——"

"Eat," she said with withering finality.

For a moment he ate in silence, hurriedly, not daring to relax.
She leaned forward to him. "It's not his fault," she said and
pointed to herself. "I told him to go and play."

"You?" He was more surprised than angry. "What'd you do
that for?"

"He needed it. You see," now she was speaking as if he were
a friend, "the doctor's coming in the morning."

"For the operation?" The aggressiveness had ebbed out of him.
Instinctively he lowered his voice. "What time?"

"Seven. But his men'll be here first "—her voice strangled in a sob—" to prepare him."

For an instant the censor did not speak. He had witnessed the horror of surgical operations, and the mere recollection made him shudder. "I'm sorry," he said, placing his hand over hers. " I really am."

He strained his ears and realised that the music had stopped. " I must go," he said, springing to his feet, " and get the boys back to sleep." At the door he turned around. " You're lucky the rector sleeps in the back wing. He's a little deaf anyway."

"Then you won't write to the council?" she asked softly.

He shook his head. " But don't ever let him do that again."

" He won't," she said, but the words didn't reach him, for already he was rushing down the corridor in the direction of the boys' dormitories.

For a moment she remained seated at the table, gazing ahead. He had kept his promise, hadn't played too long . . . He'd be back soon. She rose, waited in the doorway. Soon she saw them approach, walking slowly, and she rushed to meet them.

"Thank you, Lena," he said softly.

The fear had gone out of his face. He had prayed and now he was ready.

Outside, Leipzig dozed in the stifling heat of the summer afternoon, but the room was dim and cool behind the sun-streaked shutters.

She saw he was asleep, lying peacefully in their high walnut bed, one hand on the coverlet, his head deep in the pillow. His breathing was quiet. At least he no longer moaned in his sleep as he had for weeks after the operation. . . .

Quietly she sat at his bedside and lovingly scanned his face. It was calm and white and still as a mask. Only his lips trembled faintly with each feeble intake of air. He was dying, she knew it and there was no use pretending or hoping or even praying any more. It was three months since it had been performed and it had failed. And he was slowly dying from the shock of it.

Oh, that operation—would she ever forget it, the monstrous, unspeakable horror of it! It had started with the doctor's "assistants," four burly brutes in blood-spattered aprons. No wonder decent people shunned them in taverns and in the streets as they did the hangman's helpers. Perhaps they had to be callous and foul and drunken to remain alive and be able to sleep at night. Many, they said, went mad from watching the things they had to watch and doing the things they had to do. Not a few cut their own throats.

They had brought a cask of some special liquor that was supposed to make you so drunk you didn't feel any pain and forced a half-gallon of it into Johann's mouth, laughing among themselves and saying dirty jokes, taking a few swigs themselves to steady their nerves, as they said. Then they had strapped him by the wrists and the ankles with leather belts on the big dining-table just before Dr. Taylor traipsed in, all spruced up and smelling of pomade.

And then the butchery had begun. Never, if she lived to be a hundred, would she forget the strangled gurgle that had come out of Johann's throat when the doctor had bent down, lancet in hand, over his eyes. Her knees had buckled under her and she had begged God for Johann and herself to die. His screams could be heard through the whole of Saint Thomas's School for a while, but little by little he had grown quiet, just moaning because he hadn't the strength to howl any more. She had stood during the whole thing, wiping the blood that sluiced down his cheeks from his eyes and the saliva that trickled down from the corners of his mouth. Once he had called her name, as if from very far and she had called his back to let him know she was there by his side.

And all the time that doctor didn't stop talking, telling of the wonderful cures he had achieved, especially in England.* Suddenly he had stopped, his lancet in mid air and shaken his head with a distressed clucking sound. " Dear, dear, the paralysis has set in," he mumbled to himself. She hadn't understood what he meant exactly, but at that moment she'd known her Johann would never see again. After that the doctor had quickly finished his work and departed promptly with vague admonitions about changing the bandages every two or three days and keeping the patient in a darkened room for at least a month. Two days later he had left Leipzig.

Now it was all over and Johann was dying quietly, day by day, as oaks died when shattered by lightning. And she was glad, yes, she was glad he was dying. It was better that way. If only she could go with him. . . .

She saw his head stir on the pillow. His lips moved, forming the syllables of her name.

" Lena," he mumbled.

" Yes, Johann?"

" Do you remember Cöthen?"

Cöthen was the place where they had met. How strange that he would think of that . . . " Yes, I remember."

The shadow of a smile drifted across his face. " Do you remember the little wall in the garden?"

* By a strange coincidence the same Dr. Taylor operated on Handel's cataract—with success.

"Yes, I remember." Gently she took his hand. "Don't speak, my Johann, don't tire yourself."

"You look so pretty . . ."

The words died on his lips and she knew he had relapsed into sleep.

Cöthen! . . . People said that just before you died your whole life returned to your mind and you recalled everything that had ever happened to you. Perhaps that's why he had mentioned Cöthen. Perhaps he was looking back a last time at his life on this earth . . .

Cöthen! . . . That was long ago, almost thirty years ago, but she remembered as if it were yesterday, a little town with a huge castle on the hill, its turrets gleaming in the summer sunshine and all a-flutter that day because it was the Duke's birthday. Flags waving in the courtyard, guests arriving, the Duke's guards at the gate blowing their trumpets each time a carriage rumbled through, lackeys in white wigs rushing hither and yon, like flustered hens. Yes, she remembered it all. She even remembered when she had seen Johann Sebastian for the first time. He was decked out in the Duke's livery, red-faced and fumbling with the handle of a carriage door. She had watched him from the servants' quarters, giggling to herself and thinking what a clumsy lackey he was.

That evening she had seen him again, this time in the servants' garden at the rear of the castle. He was sitting on a low stone wall all by himself and looking lonely. She had sat next to him—which was rather forward of her—but they had barely spoken that evening, except to say it was a fine summer night and wasn't the moon bright? The following night things had gone a little better. He had smiled when she told him she had seen him fussing with that door handle and he had explained he was the Duke's Kapellmeister and not a lackey really, although he was expected to give a hand with the service on special occasions. He wasn't much of a talker and there were long pauses, but no embarrassment, no uneasiness. Just the quiet pleasure of sitting there on that wall in the moonlight together.

The third night was her last night at the castle, for her father, a trumpet player, had been engaged for the three-day festivities of the Duke's birthday. This time they had talked a great deal. She had told him about herself, the little there was to tell, that she was twenty, unmarried, and lived in Weissenfels with her father, who was the town trumpeter. He had told her how all his life he had been consumed with a passion for music, copied music at night to learn how to compose, how at nineteen he had been appointed organist at Mühlhausen. After that his life had been that of any poor *Musiker,* eking out a living here and there, playing the organ in small-town churches, getting into trouble with the vestrymen because his music was too difficult, giving a few clavichord or viola lessons, entering the service of some rich duke, playing the organ during the Sunday service in the castle's chapel, conducting a small orchestra when His Highness gave a reception or a ball. That's what he was doing now at thirty-six at the Castle of Cöthen. He knew he would never be rich or famous, but his wife had died suddenly the year before and left him with several children and he was coming to this little garden at night to look at the stars and ask God for help and guidance.

She had understood him, for her father was also a *Musiker*, and neither rich nor famous. She knew you couldn't expect much from music, yet you could be happy just the same. During the following months Johann Sebastian had come to visit her at Weissenfels and in December they had been married. For a year they had lived at the Duke's castle, then Herr Kuhnau, the choirmaster of the Saint Thomas Church in Leipzig, had died and Johann Sebastian had applied for the post. And they had been here ever since.

How uneventful, yet how full a life could be! How monotonous yet how intense, how joyous and how sad! You felt deeper in tranquillity. In agitation you merely talked and gesticulated. The racing crests on the turbulent waves were full of nothing but foam. . . . In thirty years of quiet living with a man, you learned to know that man. If you were a woman you learned to know him better than he knew himself. With each passing year she had learned to love her Johann more and more. Not that he was an angel. Gracious, no! He could fly into rages—almost always about music—and once he had flung his wig at the organist because he wouldn't keep time; and he could be stubborn, stubborn as a mule. If he thought he was right he wouldn't give in to the Almighty Himself. No, he was no angel. But what woman had ever wanted an angel for a husband . . .?

He was good and tender and strong. His big brown eyes, his poor eyes now dead, could light up with gentle teasing and his broad shoulders shake with laughter. He could make jokes and write verses about his pipe, his long clay pipe that hung on the hood of the fireplace. He was all man and mighty was his manhood; no woman had ever been loved and caressed as she had. For a woman, what garments or gems are comparable to the delight of knowing she has remained young and desirable to her husband? His love was not of words but of deeds. How devotedly he had nursed her when she was sick with those fever's vapours that baffled the doctors! How many nights had he spent at her bedside, praying, holding her hand as she was now holding his. When she recovered he had bought her a linnet to divert her with its chirping and keep her company while he rehearsed the choir for the Sunday service or taught Latin in the classroom. He'd even written a whole note-book of simple harpsichord pieces especially for her.*

And with each passing year she had sensed his greatness more and more. She knew little about music but she was sure her Johann was a great *Musiker*. Often she had watched him at work, quill in hand, hunched over his little table, ruling his staves, writing his millions of little notes. She had seen him stop now and then, as if listening to some music no one else could hear. Then his face, his good, homely face, would glow as if touched by the sun and he was no longer of this earth but high in the sky, like an angel, where no mortal could follow him. . . .

She felt the feeble pressure of his fingers. "Yes, my Johann," she murmured. "I am here."

"Lena." He spoke so low she had to lean forward to hear him. "Lena . . ."

"Don't speak, Johann. Try to sleep."

"Lena," he said again and the word ended in a sob. She saw two lone tears roll slowly down his cheeks. "Forgive me."

Dimly he heard her voice begging him not to speak and so to please her he let the thoughts he would have liked to put into words expire unheard in his brain. Beloved Lena! How fresh and pretty she had looked, her blonde hair silvery in the moonlight, sitting next to him on the stone wall of the Cöthen Castle. . . . Poor Lena, now old and grey, her small face webbed with wrinkles by a lifetime of drudgery and secret privations. . . . She had given him herself as simply as one gives a pfennig to the poor. What would become of her now, now that the doctor had taken their savings? . . . Would she have to become a servant, go down on her knees and scrub floors, beg in the streets? . . . Every life had its hour of torment, its passion. His was over, but hers had just begun.

And all because of his music—this music that had taken his eyes and left them penniless—and which nobody wanted. . . . What would become of these reams upon reams of music he was leaving behind and which nobody wanted? Those cantatas, preludes, fugues, toccatas, the Passacaglia he liked, the Mass, and above all his beloved "Passion of Our Lord, According to Saint Matthew," into which he had poured his heart and his faith and the hope of all humanity in a better, kinder world? . . . Would they be dumped away like rubbish, or burned or swept away and left out in the rain? He did not know, he would never know. He was leaving them, as he was leaving his Lena, unwanted and unprotected.

* The manuscript of the *Little Clavier Book* for Anna Magdalena is in Berlin's State Library.

And all he could do was to pray to God to have mercy on them and place them in His Hand.

His lips moved imperceptibly. "Thy will be done . . ."

Aloysius Grumler shoved another bundle of music paper into his bag and turned to Anna Magdalena with an expansive flash of rotten teeth.

"Know what I think, Frau Bach?" he said, with the air of a man who cannot hold the joke a minute longer. "I think your husband wrote a lot of music!"

Frau Bach did not seem to hear and went on gazing out of the window, but the rubbish man appreciated to the fullest the hilarious humour of his remark. The grin in his stubbly face developed into a chuckle which rose to grating laughter which itself changed into a fit of violent and phlegmy coughing. At last his merriment dwindled back to a gurgle and finally subsided. With the back of his hand he wiped the tears from his grimy cheeks, swung the bag over his shoulder and shuffled out of the room.

Anna Magdalena did not move. She went on staring at the rivulets of autumn rain coursing down the window sill. This was the last time she would look out of that window, the last time she would see the trees in the park below with the rich Lungerstein Garden's houses at the end. How many times had she looked at those fine houses in which people lived who had all the thalers they needed, who didn't have to save pfennigs. Only two or three hundred yards lay between her and them, yet they seemed as far as if they had been living in another world. Well, she wouldn't see those houses any more . . .

She turned around and glanced at the empty room. How strange and alien it looked now, stripped of all furnishings, with its bare walls on which square patches showed where the pictures had hung. Slowly she refurnished it in her mind and saw it again as it had always been—the walnut bed in which Johann Sebastian had died, the engraving of Martin Luther over the kitchen table where he used to write his music, the oak chest stacked full with reams of music. Everything was gone. Only the music remained, dumped in a heap on the floor.

Oh, yes, she had tried to save it, she had asked friends if they would mind storing those manuscripts, but they had said their attics were full. And so finally she'd asked the rubbish man to come and take it away and he'd said he would but he couldn't give her more than a pfennig the bag, because it wasn't easy to sell old paper, especially all scribbled on with notes, and who in the world could possibly want it except shopkeepers to wrap things in it or *Hausfraus* to start the fire or line shelves and drawers with it. Now that, too, was almost gone. Another two or three bags and she'd be able to scrub the floor so that Herr Harrer, the new choirmaster, would find the place nice and clean when he came.

It was a good thing that her Johann was dead and couldn't see what was happening to his music. It would have broken his heart to see all his beautiful cantatas shoved by fistfuls into bags and carted away like rubbish. Perhaps he'd known all along it would turn out this way, and his music would be torn or burned or scattered to the four winds. The day before he died he had said, "Thy will be done." And that night he'd told her how we were all in God's Hand and we were to trust in His infinite Mercy. He'd been right. There was nothing else to do but put it all in His Hand and hope for the best. He was the Lord and could do anything. If He wanted her Johann's music to be heard again He would find some way to do it. It was up to Him.

But the Passion she wasn't going to let anybody dump into a bag and cart away like rubbish. No, she wasn't. She was going to keep it herself. That at least she could do. Because her Johann had loved it so she'd even tried to get it published, thinking how happy it would've made him. She'd taken the last folio of the manuscript, the end of the final chorus, and brought it to Herr Zeilach, the music publisher, but they didn't even want to let her see him because he was too busy. At last he'd received her in his office and spent half an hour telling her what a busy man he was and how he didn't have a minute to himself. Yes, he knew that her husband had died and he was sorry. A good *Musiker* he was, her husband, but his music had no popular appeal, and that's what music must have to sell these days—popular appeal. To please her he had taken the folio and said he'd look at it and to drop in next week and he'd tell her if he could do something with it. But the following week he was too busy to see her, and the week after he was away and when at last he'd seen her he was gruff and impatient. Yes, he'd looked over her husband's music and it was just like he'd said—too difficult. A double chorus —who could conduct a double chorus these days? Then he'd looked around for the folio and couldn't find it and he'd lost his temper and become annoyed with her for taking his time and he couldn't ransack his entire office for those confounded sheets of music. And so finally she'd gone away, empty-handed, and now the Passion wasn't even complete any more.

But just the same she wasn't going to let it go. All mangled though it was, she was going to keep it and protect it as long as she could. A bundle of old paper didn't take much room and it wouldn't be so lonely with it around. She'd look at it and talk to it and it would be a little like having her Johann with her in the room. She'd pretend he was out somewhere teaching or rehearsing the choir for the Sunday service and he was coming back in a little while. It took so little to make believe someone you loved hadn't died at all. . . .

Ten years passed. One morning, in 1760, a frail old woman was found dead on a pallet of straw in a Leipzig garret. Her sole possessions consisted of personal clothing and a few kitchen utensils. She was buried in the paupers' grave at the cost to the city of two thalers and fourteen groschen.

A few years later a road was opened through the Old Saint John Cemetery and many coffins had to be moved—among them that of a certain Johann Sebastian Bach, formerly cantor or choirmaster of Saint Thomas's School, a municipal charitable institution attached to Saint Thomas's Church.

The world took no notice whatever of these obscure and unimportant events. Great changes were taking place. In faraway America thirteen rebellious colonies were struggling for their independence. Thirteen years later, on a hot July day, the Bastille, a royal prison, was stormed by a howling and sweating mob. By nightfall the people of Paris found themselves launched into a revolution. Just as the last heads were falling from a guillotine a hungry long-haired Corsican lieutenant by the name of Napoleon Bonaparte entered the stage and swung into action. Thus the eighteenth century, the age of courtliness, gavottes and powdered wigs, ended amidst the roar of cannons, the rattles of wounded men and an avalanche of victory bulletins that lasted well into the following century. When at last the rumbles of the Napoleonic earthquake died away, Europe, stunned and bled white, turned to poetry to forget its sorrows and to music to sing its new hopes. Romanticism was flowering into its melancholy bloom.

Now it was almost a century since the blind choirmaster of Leipzig had died in his walnut bed. Somewhere, among the poor and nameless dead, he slept, forgotten by all—except the One in Whom he had placed his trust.

BOOK ONE

The Hand

Chapter 1

EARLY ONE September morning a blue cabriolet was racing through the narrow streets of lower Berlin towards the Hamburg stagecoach depot. In it two young men in beaver hats, cashmere neck-cloths, and mustard gloves sat side by side, swaying and bouncing in unison with every jostle of the carriage. One was Felix Mendelssohn, the banker's son; the other, his best friend, Karl Klingemann.

"And all because of a woman!" Karl muttered dejectedly. His wistful globular eyes gazed out of the carriage window and a sigh shook his fat clean-shaven jowls.

Felix laid a comforting hand upon his friend's sleeve. "Forget her," he said firmly. "Wipe that girl out of your mind," he went on with that inflexible determination we oppose to other people's troubles. "Soon you will be in England and safe."

These remarks produced no effect whatever. Lost in thought, Karl remained silent, his face turned to the window. Outside a new day was being born. High over the brick chimneys a joyous late summer morning was awakening in the lilac-coloured swaddles of dawn. Buxom *Hausfraus* in nightshirts and bonnets pushed open wooden shutters, cast loving glances at the flowerpots on the window sills and indulged in voluptuous yawns.

Karl steadied his beaver against a sudden jolt of the carriage and turned abruptly to his companion. "To think that because of a red-headed strumpet by the name of Anna Skrumpnagel," he said, with tremulous voice, "I am now fleeing Berlin in shame, in debt and in a hurry!"

"Courage," said Felix, feeling that a crisis was at hand.

Karl ignored the interruption. "And at this ungodly hour of the morning when young men of birth such as you and I should be going to bed!"

"Don't think of it," said Felix. "You'll see, you will love England. The girls there are very pretty."

"Girls!" Karl spat the word with wincing distaste. "Please oblige me and don't mention girls to me."

21

" You say that now, but in a month I wager you'll be head over heels in love again."

Karl Klingemann considered his friend with eyes full of reproaches. " How can you talk of love to me when I can barely afford sex!"

" Real love costs nothing."

Astonishment rendered Karl momentarily speechless. " Only a very young man would utter such abysmal nonsense," he declared. " Don't you know that virtuous women are the most expensive?"

" Not if they love you."

Karl did not appear to hear. Slowly he ran his bulging eyes over his companion. His gaze took in the lean patrician face with its lustrous brown eyes, the thin oval-nostrilled nose. " Of course," he sighed with helpless dejection, " if I were as confoundedly handsome as you, things would've turned out differently. The wench would've fallen in love with me and we'd now be fleeing together, clutched in each other's arms. Instead "—his voice rose to a throbbing pitch of self-pity—" the slut is now lolling in bed, probably not alone, while I am being exiled to faraway and fogbound England."

" On the contrary, England is a beautiful country. As a secretary of the Hanover Legation every door will be open to you. You will be dined and wined to death. I wish I were going with you. I was there last year—unfortunately with my father—and I met the most attractive young lady. Her name was Margaret. She had the face of an angel——"

" And the heart of a witch," finished Karl. He pressed an urgent hand on his friend's wrist. " Believe me, Felix, women are fundamentally evil. Their function in the world is to break men's hearts, empty their wallets and wreck their lives. They can't help it. The only thing to do is pretend they don't exist."

" I know. Anna was very cruel, but you must not grow bitter. All women are not like her. Some are very nice. Margaret, for instance——"

" Of course she threw herself at you, they all do!" Karl flung in a flush of enviousness. " You are the luckiest man alive. You are not an ordinary human being, you are a phenomenon, and exception to the laws of nature, a miscarriage of justice. You have everything —looks, talent, money."

" I shouldn't say that," Felix objected feebly. " My father keeps telling me we are paupers compared to the Rothchilds."

" My dear friend, everybody is a pauper compared to the Rothchilds."

" Every day he warns me we'll all end up in the almshouse if I don't settle down to work."

Karl Klingemann let out a derisive snort. "It must be a trait of our race, but all Jewish parents take their children for imbeciles. When my father got the bill for the sable coat I bought Anna, and some of my gambling slips, he wrote me a long windy letter giving me his malediction when all I needed was a letter of credit. He told me he was tottering on the very edge of bankruptcy when I knew perfectly well he had just opened a new branch in Munich."

"There are many things in life more important than money."

Karl shrugged impatiently. "Now you talk like an artist. Artists have their own peculiar brand of hypocrisy, and it is to pretend to despise money when they think of nothing else."

"I don't."

"Of course, but only because you have it. I told you you have everything. Two sisters who worship you, a fiancée who is both beautiful and rich."

"Nina isn't my fiancée."

"Everyone knows you two will get married one of these days."

"Only because we've been brought up together. Our parents decided we should get married when we were still in our cradles."

"And to crown it all you have genius—a perfectly useless thing to a millionaire. You are already a great composer."

"How do you know? You hate music."

"True. I was merely being polite. So far as I am concerned music is an unnecessary and expensive noise, but the fact remains you are famous." A look of admiring despondency came into his eyes. "The gods have been kind to you. Somehow you will have to pay for it. Perhaps you, too, will meet your Anna Skrumpnagel. Then you will know the torment of unrequited love. Believe me, Felix, give up women before it is too late."

As the cabriolet raced towards the depot, Karl pleaded with his friend to profit from his own unhappy experience and renounce women, all women—the good and the bad. The good ones were forever trying to reform men and merely succeeded in making liars and hypocrites out of them. The other ones were infernal creatures. They usually were also the most attractive.

With passion he denounced the woman who was the cause of his exile. "A lying, predatory wanton, animalish, selfish—and expensive—that's what she is. Even her name, Skrumpnagel, is an outrage. She has the morals of an alley cat, the ethics of a grave robber. She is a wallet-vampire, a heartless wench, but "—he stopped abruptly as memories flocked to his mind—" but how soft her hair, how deep her mouth! Her breasts are pure Delphic marble and much warmer."

For a while resentment and regrets seemed to dispute his soul. Soon, however, desire swept aside all other emotions. "She is a

slut, a creature of Satan, but I can't live without her." He gripped
both of Felix's wrists. "Do you hear? Somehow I must get her to
come and join me in London and you "—the grip tightened around
Felix's wrists—" you must bring her to me!"

"I!" exclaimed Felix, startled by the unexpected turn of the
conversation.

"There is no time to go into this," blurted Karl, now thoroughly
aroused. "You said a moment ago you wanted to come to London
and see your Margaret again. I shall move heaven and earth and
find some excuse for you to come to London in the spring, but only
on the condition that you bring Anna with you."

"But Karl, you just said——"

"Never mind what I said," shouted his friend. "I must have
Anna or I shall do away with myself and you'll never get back the
money you generously lent me. Go to see her to-night after the
show. Tell her I've forgiven her, assure her of my undying love, take
her to supper and keep my memory alive in her callous heart."

He was still giving last-minute instructions to Felix when the
cabriolet entered the courtyard of the Hamburg mail-coach depot.
Already the confusion of departures filled the air. The four mail-
coach horses fretted in their harness. Blue-bloused porters carried
leather trunks on wheelbarrows.

As the coach rumbled away Karl leaned out of the window.
"Remember," he cried, waving a mournful handkerchief, "the
Friedrich Wilhelmstadt Theatre! Go to see her to-night——"

That evening Felix had the pleasure of watching Anna
Skrumpnagel from the wings. A thaler to the stage doorman had
given him this privilege. The Friedrich Theatre had no strict rules
about the privacy of its entertainers. Its devotion to Art ran a
distant second to its need of making money. To this end the
actresses were encouraged by the management to mingle with the
audience, composed almost exclusively of men, and trained to
simulate a burning thirst which could only be quenched by the
more expensive beverages.

From his vantage point Felix assured himself that his friend had
been right. Anna was no great artist but she had remarkably
beautiful legs. She used them with telling effect. The applause
which greeted the end of each one of her songs was more a tribute
to their nimbleness than to her vocal artistry. Listening to her,
Felix couldn't help wondering how such a feeble and tremulous
voice could come out of this well-developed chest and this large
red-lipped mouth. The audience, apparently, had no such reservations. It feasted its eyes on the singer's sensuous face and magnificent body and had a strong, if not necessarily artistic, experience.

Sternly Felix reminded himself he was here on a mission of mercy. His was a noble and disinterested duty. He was rendering a last service to his friend now jostling and bouncing on the road to Hamburg. Loyalty was the cornerstone of friendship and he was full of loyalty when, a moment later, he knocked at the door of Anna's dressing-room.

A high-pitched woman's voice invited him in. As he entered, he remarked that Anna was sharing her dressing-room with another actress who, at this instant, was fastening a belt made of brightly coloured paper leaves and large pieces of glass, which seemed to constitute the main part of her costume. His presence provoked neither protest nor surprise.

" Fraulein Anna Skrumpnagel?" he asked, addressing himself to the red-haired girl.

" What do you want?" was the non-committal answer.

" I come on behalf of my friend Karl."

" Well, you can go straight back and tell him I don't want to see him any more." Her voice, feeble but sweet a moment ago on the stage, was now singularly rasping. " I never want to see that big fat face of his again."

" You won't," said Felix. " He left Berlin this morning."

For the first time Anna turned her slumberous eyes on him and she gave a start of surprise. " You're a friend of his?" she asked in a distinctly more amiable tone of voice.

" His best friend," said Felix with feeling. " We are like brothers. I've known him all my life. Before leaving he entrusted me with some important messages for you."

The clatter of the orchestra which consisted of a drum and three trumpets made conversation difficult. He had to raise his voice to make himself heard. " They are of a personal nature," he shouted, glancing meaningfully at the other woman. " I wonder if you'd do me the honour of supping with me after the show."

Anna's gaze remained fixed upon him and he gathered the impression she was forming a not unfavourable opinion of him.

" She can't," said the actress who had finally fastened her leafy belt around her waist. " We've got a double engagement, haven't we, Anna?"

Thus addressed, Anna seemed to awake from her speculations. " Tell them I'm sick, tell them anything." Then she turned back to Felix and gave him a slow disturbing smile. " Wait for me."

During supper Felix did his duty manfully. He was eloquent and persuasive. He praised Karl, elaborated on his qualities of mind, his sensitiveness, his appreciation of beauty, the generosity of his heart. Anna spoke little, gave him sidelong, lidded glances and put away a substantial meal. Only when dessert had been removed and they were sipping their demi-tasses did he broach the delicate subject of her coming to England in the spring. " Naturally he will defray your expenses, you can depend on his generosity."

She hesitated. " London is very far," she said. " I have to hear more about it."

It appeared that only in her apartment would she listen to the details of Karl's proposition. Felix had no choice but to accept her suggestion. His loyalty to his friend was now compounded with a feeling of genuine sympathy for this superb creature who looked at him with such tender eyes. They drove to her apartment which was located in a good section of town, but consisted of only one sparsely furnished room. Since she insisted on changing her clothes and slipping on " something more comfortable," he was obliged to stare at the wall while she did so.

A moment later she appeared in a filmy negligée which was surely very comfortable but also very transparent. A flush suffused his cheeks and his throat narrowed perceptibly, yet his loyalty to Karl did not waver. " You must go to England," he said, averting his eyes.

By now she had assumed a reclining position on the bed. " Come and sit next to me," she said languidly. " I want to look into your eyes and see if you really mean that I should go to England."

Apparently she intended to look into the innermost recesses of his eyes, for as soon as he had seated himself on the edge of the bed she coiled a bare arm around his neck and irresistibly drew him to her.

" Do you," she asked, speaking now in a barely audible whisper, " do you want me to go to England?"

He tried to disentangle himself, but he was off balance. With an ever so slight pressure of her arm she drew him nearer still. Their faces were now so close he had trouble focusing his eyes. Conflicting thoughts whirled through his mind. Was he betraying his friend or was he intensely loyal? After all, he had promised Karl to bring her to London and she seemed almost convinced.

" Yes," he repeated with strangled forcefulness, " you must go to England. You've been very cruel," he said with panting reproachfulness. " You've broken his heart."

Something like a smile drifted across her lustrous eyes. " I have only broken his bank account," she said. " And I am not cruel. I don't want you to think I am cruel. Do you think I am cruel?"

As he attempted to explain his feelings on the matter, she drew him still nearer to her. He felt himself sinking into a quicksand of warm flesh. His last conscious vision was that of Karl, pushing his round anguished face out of the window of the departing coach and waving a despairing handkerchief.

When he regained his senses, he found he was in bed with Anna nestled against him, her face buried in the curve of his shoulders in an attitude of absolute contentment. Outside the paleness of dawn gleamed in the silvery curtains behind the window panes. Soon it would be daylight. Stealthily he inched away from her and managed to slip out of bed. He dressed hurriedly and with little care. For an instant he stood by the bed watching Anna sleep, wondering whether he should wake her. He decided against it, silently opened the door and went out.

He had some trouble finding a *fiacre* at this hour. When at last he caught one, he flung the address to the coachman and leaned back on the worn leather seat. The long drive through the coolness of dawn refreshed and stimulated his mind. Again he asked himself if he had betrayed his friend. After a few minutes of specious argumentation he concluded that he had not. What else could he do, how better could he watch over her, persuade her to go to England? Her kisses and caresses he had accepted by proxy, so to speak.

He was in this cheerful state of mind when the carriage approached the family mansion. He instructed the coachman to pull in at the service door.

He let himself through the small gate at the end of the aisle devoted to the servants' quarters and at last reached through a side door the majestic entrance hallway. It seemed even larger and more impressive in the early morning stillness. Through caution born of habit he removed his shoes and in his stockinged feet climbed the wide marble stairs to the first floor where his apartment was located. Passing before his parents' bedroom he changed to a ghostly tiptoe and hurried by, unaware that his father was watching him from his bedroom doorway. Even in his bare feet, nightshirt and tasselled nightcap Abraham Mendelssohn managed to look like a banker, at this moment a very disgruntled and disapproving one.

"I'm pleased to inform you that *your* son Jakob is now at home," he said, regaining the conjugal bed. Abraham Mendelssohn persisted in calling his son "Jakob." On this point he was adamant and querulous. "You can call him whatever you like," he would remark, "but he was named Jakob Ludwig Felix and I see no reason why I shouldn't call him Jakob."

For an instant Leah Mendelssohn arose from the depths of slumber. "You see he is up with the sun," she said, the shadow of a smile floating over her lips. Then she relapsed into sleep.

"That's what comes of coddling him," he grumbled, slipping back under the blankets, "encouraging him with this foolish music business. Mark my word, nothing good will come of it."

He had said it often and he was prepared to say it again, but a speech requires an audience, and his wife slept peacefully. For a while he watched her through eyes tender with love. Dear Leah, wonderful wife, admirable mother. Somehow the sight of her lost in blissful sleep reassured him and quelled his alarm. He let out a sigh, shook his tasselled nightcap and turning on his side went back to sleep.

Late next morning Gustav, Felix's valet, entered his young master's room and, as he expected, found him sound asleep. Knowing from experience that nothing would waken him—in the old days he had to splash cold water on his face to get him to open his eyes—he began humming loudly to himself as he went about the room.*

He was sorting Felix's clothes when the door opened and Fanny Mendelssohn came in.

"Still asleep?" she asked without waiting for the reply.

The old servant nodded his shiny pate and went on with his work. Without hesitation the young lady walked to her brother, kissed him on the cheek; then, gripping his shoulders, proceeded to shake him with all her strength.

"Get up, get up," she commanded. "Come on, open your eyes. It's almost noon, and I've something to tell you. Something important."

"What is it?" The words came from another, infinitely remote world.

"I've received a letter from Wilhelm." This remark was accompanied by another bone-shaking jostle. "Johann brought it to me when he came back from the bank."

Felix let out a long-suffering moan and struggled to a sitting position. "What does he say? Does he still want to marry you?"

"Of course he does. He'll be back in the spring."

"I think he is after your dowry," Felix said with a grin.

This was a standing joke between them. For three years their father had opposed Fanny's attachment to Wilhelm Hensel, a poor art student, cutting short all discussions with an emphatic, "He is after my daughter's dowry." This remark had been taken by the Mendelssohn children as an expression of all-embracing, arbitrary and final disapproval. In the last two years the young artist had been living in Rome, attracting notice as a portrait painter. Only recently had Abraham Mendelssohn consented to a carefully supervised and censored correspondence between the two young people. Gradually he had become reconciled to the dismal prospect of an artist as a son in law, and a tentative betrothal date had been set for the following spring.†

---

* All Mendelssohn's biographers mention the almost cataleptic quality of his sleep.
† In addition to being outstandingly gifted as a musician—several of the songs included in the earlier editions of Mendelssohn's works were written by her—Fanny Mendelssohn was a talented water colourist. She had met Wilhelm Hensel at the Berlin Academy of Fine Arts.

"I suppose you're dying to read me the letter you've just received," smiled Felix. "Do you mind if I have my breakfast while I listen? One understands and sympathises so much better on a full stomach."

Fanny read her fiancé's letter with the blushing emotion of a young woman in love. Felix watched her with tenderness and envy while wolfing down his breakfast. This was love—pure, steadfast, complete. How wonderful it must be to be in love. . . .

As though reading his thoughts, Fanny rested the letter on her lap and said, "If you know how wonderful it is to be in love."

"What makes you think I don't?" he protested, his mouth full. "After all, Nina and I are going to get married one of these days and we're supposed to be madly in love with each other."

"But you aren't."

"How do you know?"

"Do you hear music, do you hear birds twitter when you kiss her?"

Felix pondered the question. "Are you supposed to?"

"Do you feel sunshine when it rains, do you walk on a cloud with your head in the sky? You'll see, it will happen to you when you meet the right girl."

"It'll be too late," he said, gulping down his coffee. "By then father will have bullied me into marrying poor Nina. He's got it into his head that if I get married I'll settle down and go to work at the bank."

At this point Gustav appeared in the doorway of the bathroom and informed Felix that his bath was ready. Once more Fanny kissed her brother on the cheek and went out of the room. This morning, as usual, Felix lingered in his shoe shaped brass tub and sponged himself abundantly while chatting with Gustav. They continued their conversation while he began dressing leisurely and fastidiously, as usual. Then slipping on a blue silk bathrobe, he passed into the room which he used as a study and, taking his quill from the elegant desk set, he proceeded to correct the proofs of the four hand arrangement of his C minor Symphony which his English publisher Cramer had sent him the day before.

For two hours he worked with total and serene concentration. His mind was swept clean of all irrelevant thoughts. Unaware of the chirping of birds in the garden, the rumble of carriages on Leipzigerstrasse, the occasional patter of footsteps along the corridor, he worked with effortless yet irresistible absorption. His handsome face, a moment ago so mobile, had set into a mask of unapproachable remoteness. Now and then his eyes wandered from the pages but they remained unseeing, turned on some inner vision.

The work done he let out a sigh of relief. His features relaxed.

Methodically he set the quill back into its stand; then he rose and pulled the bell rope.

"I'll be going to town in a moment," he told Gustav.

"Will you ride or drive in a cabriolet, Herr Felix?"

Felix cast a glance at the sky. It was too beautiful a day to be driving in a wheeled box. "I'll ride Juno. Please have her ready in half an hour."

Unhurriedly but with a perfect co-ordination and economy of gestures, he finished dressing, putting on the cream coloured, skin fitting riding breeches, the brown calf high boots. He hesitated a few seconds between a blue and grey riding coat, chose the grey, and flapping his silver knobbed riding crop he went to pay his respects to his mother. As he was about to knock on the door, he turned to Gustav. "Please put the proofs on my desk in the riding pouch, won't you?"

He knocked, waited for the familiar voice; then turning the door knob, he entered his mother's sitting-room.

Leah Mendelssohn spent most of her time in this room, sitting in her high backed wing chair, reading—she read Homer and Sophocles in the original Greek—or knitting endless woollen scarves for an orphanage she patronised. Yet her nearly invisible presence permeated the enormous house. She was the mainspring of the exceedingly complex mechanism that assured the smooth functioning of this oversized residential establishment. She possessed the executive quality of planning to the highest degree. Hers was the ability to command and obtain results. Her thin face framed in soft *bandeaux* of grey hair mirrored the orderliness of her mind. There was kindness but little sentimentality in her clear blue eyes. She had no patience with roundabout ways, shallow effusiveness and esoteric verbiage. She liked integrity, neatness and precision.

"I am glad to see you, Felix," she said, with a smile, giving him her hand to kiss, and resting her knitting on her lap. "Sit down and tell me what kept you out until six o'clock this morning." She smiled at his look of surprise. Two minute fans of thin wrinkles opened at the corners of her eyes. "I don't want to know her name or what she does. Merely whether it is anything serious or not."

Felix knew his mother too well to attempt hiding the truth from her. She detested lies, called them childish subterfuges and a waste of time. "No, Mother, it isn't anything serious," he said. "As a matter of fact it is a rather ridiculous affair. It came out of my promise to help Karl, but have no fear, I have lost neither my head nor my heart. I merely feel rather silly."

"That's all I wanted to know." Her tone signified that she had dismissed the matter from her mind. " Have you been working to-day?"

" I corrected the proofs of a piano transcription of the *Midsummer* Overture and a four-hand arrangement of the Symphony in C."

" From which publishers—Schlesinger or Breitkopf?"

" Neither. Cramer of London."

" Very interesting." She did not speak for a moment, the silence between them broken only by the soft clicking of the ivory needles. " The British appreciate your music so much more than we do here," she said at last.

" After all, the *Midsummer* Overture came out of Shakespeare."

" But the Symphony didn't. Neither did the Octet or the Quintet, yet they all had much greater success in England than here." She rested her knitting in her lap. " Have you ever thought of settling in England?"

" I wouldn't like it." The reply had been immediate, unhesitant. " You know how much I love England, but I am German. I think and feel like a German. My home is here."

" I am glad. I only wanted to know how you felt about it." Again he knew that the subject was closed, sorted and labelled in some cell of her mind.

For a while they chatted of various things. Her hand flexed against her cheek, she watched him, crouched at her feet, lifting his lean handsome face, speaking with the eagerness of youth. She knew him better than anyone, and better than anyone she understood the contrasts of his nature, the never-ending conflict between a prodigious and serene intellectuality and his restless emotionalism and morbid sensitiveness.

Of his talent—she distrusted the word genius—she was absolutely certain. Methodically she had buttressed her opinion with that of outstanding and outspoken musicians. Zelter, his gruff and exacting teacher, had told her, " Madame, I have nothing more to teach him, he could teach me a lot. His musical gifts are simply phenomenal." Cherubini, director of the Paris Conservatoire, a vain and brutal man, had been left speechless by his improvisations and his fugues. What could one say of a boy who at sixteen had written the *Midsummer* Overture, the Symphony in C at fifteen, and a quartet before he was twelve? She had watched him conduct professional orchestras with the tranquil assurance of superior knowledge, the authority of a seasoned conductor. His intricate but spotless orchestra scores left no possible doubt of the orderliness of his creative processes. And then a thousand times she had observed this phenomenal, almost frightening faculty of total concentration which had brought him success without apparent effort in any field he had chosen to engage. Casually, as if playing, he had learned six languages, passed his law examinations at the Berlin University with brilliance. The great Hegel himself had confided to her that he could easily have become an eminent jurist. With all that, he had found time to read and digest the masterpieces of ancient and modern literature. For good measure, he could draw superbly. What could one say before this over abundance of talents? No, his was no ordinary mind.

But his mind was only a part of him. He rode, swam, danced and skated beautifully. He beat his father at chess and was regarded as a champion billiards player.

Then where was the flaw? Where was the discord in this monotonous litany of perfections? She alone knew the answer, and as she gazed on his high-strung, handsome—almost too handsome—face, she felt a spasm of anguish and a secret premonition of the future.

" Are you riding in to the town?" she asked.

He nodded and got to his feet. " I want to show Herr Zelter the corrected proofs before mailing them back to England. And then " —he hunched his shoulders and made a wry face—" I'm afraid I must stop at the bank and get some money."

Both knew what it meant and they exchanged a conspiratorial glance.

" Perhaps you'll be lucky," she said. " Perhaps your father will be in conference and unable to see you."

Again he bent down over her hand. " Let's hope so."

But Abraham Mendelssohn was not in conference and he was most anxious to see his son. When the head cashier informed him that " Herr Felix " was at his desk with a request for two hundred thalers, the banker let out a grunt and said, " Send him in."

Felix received the message with fortitude. Squaring his shoulders, he entered his father's office, bowed courteously and stood waiting for the sermon that was to come.

To-day the banker leaned back into his leather seat, crossed his hands over his paunch and considered his son for a considerable amount of time. " I was deprived of the pleasure of your company at breakfast," he began at last. " No doubt you'd been working late and were enjoying a well-earned rest."

Felix was acquainted with his father's peculiar brand of irony and chose to remain silent. Next time he came home at dawn, he told himself, he'd slip into his room through the window.

The banker went on in his most mellifluous tone, " Your numerous bills which come to the bank for payment as well as your frequent cash withdrawals assure me you are attending to your material comfort." Then came the roar and the ritual slam on the desk. " When the devil are you going to start working and earn some money? Yes, money. This low contemptible thing you spend so easily. Do you know how hard it is to earn money? How much things cost?"

Then Abraham Mendelssohn launched into the history of the Mendelssohn family. Being of a logical turn of mind, he began at the beginning with the inspiring saga of the poor schoolteacher of Dessau, on the Elbe. With much pathos, the multimillionaire financier described his grandfather's hardships, privations and tribulations. This, Felix had computed, usually occupied five minutes; to-day it took more than ten. At last his father was ready to tackle the inspiring biography of Moses Mendelssohn, his father. This was the *pièce de résistance* of the lecture. Moses Mendelssohn was the family's great man and this time his son did unusually well by him.

At fourteen, Moses had already realised what his father, the poor and harassed schoolteacher, had failed to notice in an entire life-time, that the only thing to do with Dessau was to get away from it as far and as soon as possible. In his haste he had walked all the way to Berlin. There, for a time, things looked worse, if possible, than at Dessau. He knew no one. Of course he was penniless. He was a Jew, a distinct handicap in those days. He was uncommonly ugly. To crown it all, he was hump-backed. Most young men would have given up right then and there. Not Moses.

" My father had an iron will," Abraham Mendelssohn said, pressing a pinch of snuff to his nostrils. " Also exceptional intelligence and great resourcefulness."

Felix nodded in full agreement. Obviously, the grandfather must have had all three, for in less than a month, living on bread and water, he had managed to obtain employment as a book-keeper in a silk factory. This done, the astonishing young man proceeded to set an example of superhuman industry. After toiling the customary sixteen hours daily on his ledgers, he dragged himself to his garret and launched into several hours of really hard work. He read and wrote extensively on philosophy, philology, sociology, mathematics, metaphysics and other arduous subjects. When his grandfather slept, Felix had never been able to discover. He had thought it inadvisable to put the question to his father. The fact remained that on this regimen Moses had not only survived, but translated the Hebrew Bible into German—a Herculean task in itself—written several profound essays and a sensational best-seller called *Phaedon*.

Even more remarkable, he had found time to fall in love with a comely Hamburg girl, Fromet Guggenheim, who at first wouldn't even give him a glance. This obstacle he also overcame. He persuaded her that he was the man she had been waiting for all her life, and she married him, hump and all. At once he started building a large family, stopping only when he had six children—three boys and three daughters.

"I was the third child," remarked the banker, adding with engaging modesty, " my sole distinction having been to be born in 1776, a year made memorable by the Declaration of American Independence and Watt's experiments with steam, both events pregnant with incalculable consequences. So puny was I at birth, it was feared that I might not survive the difficult period of infancy."

Felix had some difficulty imagining that stocky square-chinned man before him as a puny infant, but he refrained from interruption. He merely shifted to another foot and stood ready for the second part of the lecture.

His father continued with the eulogy of Moses Mendelssohn. Now married and a famous author, Moses had acquired a partnership in the silk factory which afforded him a modest influence and the leisure to devote himself to the missionary tasks he enjoyed. An idealist from birth, he wrote prolifically on all sorts of lofty subjects. Celebrated as a thinker and a wit, he was sought by the most illustrious men of his time. He dined with Frederick the Great in Sans Souci and duly listened to his distinguished flute playing. He consorted and corresponded with world-famous philosophers, scientists and statesmen. He launched into a one-man crusade to improve the relations between Jews and Gentiles and did his best to tear down the wall of mutual prejudice and suspicion they had built between them. He reminded them all that they were God's children, equal under God's sun. When he died at fifty-seven, there was not a Jew in Germany who did not know about Moses Mendelssohn.

"My father left us a great name," commented the banker piously, "and therefore a great responsibility."

The only thing Moses had not left was money. Too busy to improve the world, he neglected to improve his finances. " I decided to change all that," said Felix's father with great simplicity.

From then on Abraham Mendelssohn was talking about himself. He did so with the relish and studied modesty of all autobiographers and, when necessary, with their lapses of memory and candid disregard of truth. He had learned the banking trade in Paris as cashier in Monsieur Fould's bank, and did his best to depict this short year of apprenticeship as a period of spartan asceticism and heroic privations. He did not elaborate upon his marriage to Leah Salomon. Realising the difficulty of labouring the fiction of crushing poverty after marrying one of Berlin's richest heiresses, he deftly switched to the theme of untiring industry. " At your age I had the responsibility of a large banking establishment in Hamburg and I was working night and day." Somehow, though, he had found time to purchase a delightful country home, Martens Mühle, in the most fashionable suburb. " I bought it for your mother who needed the fresh country air," he explained. " It is there that your sister Fanny, yourself, and your younger sister Rebecka were born. We were then at the peak of the Napoleonic maelstrom."

In due time the maelstrom had engulfed Hamburg and Abraham Mendelssohn had decided to move his family and bank to Berlin. No decision could have been more opportune. While Hamburg writhed under the Corsican's heel, the Berlin bankers were enjoying a period of great prosperity. Soon the Mendelssohn Bank was making more money than ever. A fourth child, Paul, had been born and the growing family required larger quarters. Abraham purchased a beautiful and spacious house on the Neue Promenade. The ground floor was given to the bank, the rest to the family. " My office was located beneath the nursery," the banker reminisced with a smile. " Sometimes the squeals of your laughter would come through the ceiling."

During the following years the bank had prospered steadily. Abraham Mendelssohn had known the rare and delicate pleasure of becoming richer and richer every day. While preaching the virtue of thrift, he indulged his own luxurious tastes. Every summer he took his family on a long journey to Paris, Switzerland or the Italian lakes, and his idea of modest and inconspicuous travelling was a procession of three coaches crowded with servants, secretaries, tutors, governesses and his personal physician in the train of his own splendid four-horse carriage.

His business acumen and integrity had rapidly placed him in the forefront of his profession. After the collapse of the French Empire he had been selected to represent Prussia's reparation claims at the Paris Conference, an important mission which he had discharged with ability and complete success. " There is no greater satisfaction than to serve your country," he remarked, modestly closing this glamorous episode of his life.

Felix nodded approvingly, knowing from experience that the lecture was drawing to a close. At this point Abraham Mendelssohn took a short breathing spell and gazed uneasily out of the window. Felix knew the signs. His father was about to explain how " a modest businessman " like himself had come to purchase the palatial establishment at 3 Leipzigerstrasse. The main building alone consisted of forty-two rooms, a stupendous marble stairway, a dining-room capable of accommodating a hundred dinner guests, a kitchen of appropriate size, an ornate music room and an immense ball-room. The garden consisted of seven acres of lawn, flower beds, marble basins and antique statuary. There was a bird sanctuary. There was a small forest full of tame and merry game. There was a theatre. There was a small observatory. There was a huge summer house where in summer Sunday concerts were given in the presence of two hundred guests and with the assistance of a professional orchestra hired for the occasion. The various buildings on the estate could have accommodated a fair-sized village and required a small army of butlers, maids, cooks, gardeners, grooms and coachmen. It was recognised as the most opulent private residence in Berlin.

Another man might have hesitated to attempt to fit this colossal evidence of wealth in a picture of modest affluence and rigid parsimoniousness. But not Abraham Mendelssohn. Like his father Moses he was a man of great resourcefulness. " Your mother and I had been married twenty years and I was shopping for some unassuming anniversary present in harmony with our moderate income when this house was offered to me at an incredibly low figure. Practically for nothing. I can truthfully say it was almost given away. Since it had a nice garden and your mother is fond of flowers, in a moment of weakness I surrendered to the temptation. But "—he raised a warning finger—" don't think I am a rich man. Nothing could be further from the truth. Compared to my friends, the Rothschilds, why, I am practically a beggar. This is why it is imperative that you should find some way to earn money."

Felix let out an inward sigh. The lecture was over. There remained only the familiar exchange of views on the unsoluble question of money.

" You know I'd like nothing better than to earn my expenses," protested Felix, " but there is very little money in music."

" That is why you should look upon it as a pastime and not as a career. Any profession that doesn't feed its man isn't worth the name."

" I'm watching for any opportunity. Perhaps some orchestral conductor in Munich or Cologne or Düsseldorf may be kind enough to resign or die, so that I may take his place."

" This is a long-term approach to the problem," declared the banker with an impatient gesture. " You may be an old man yourself before such a post becomes vacant."

The remark was so true that it did not call for discussion. Abraham Mendelssohn cocked a bushy eyebrow and glanced at his son. " Of course, you could work here as a lawyer. I always can fit in one more lawyer."

Felix let out a gasp. " You wouldn't want that, Father! I'd make a terrible lawyer."

" Not worse than the average," said the banker dryly. " You are not stupid." Thoughtfully he rubbed his chin and considered his problem child. "And Nina?" he asked abruptly. "When are you going to marry her?"

Although expected, the question always brought acute discomfort to Felix. "As soon as we are sure of each other."

"And how long will it take to be sure?" The banker was growing petulant. "You've known each other all your lives."

"That's just it. We are much like brother and sister. I don't think she has any romantic attachment for me."

"Romance! What has that to do with marriage? She likes you, doesn't she?"

"I am sure that she does."

"Well, that's enough. Mutual liking is all that's necessary for a good solid marriage. In my time girls did what they were told, but nowadays they are full of nonsense. They want romance, they insist on loving their husbands. Romance is to love what a picnic is to the business of eating. Look at your sister Fanny. Losing her head over a penniless painter who probably is a fortune hunter. Mark my word, nothing good will come of it." For a while he seemed to ruminate the bitterest apprehensions. Then he suddenly looked up. "When did you see Nina last?"

"I don't remember exactly, Father. Ten . . . twelve days."

"Go to see her this afternoon. And take her some flowers. Women like flowers. Three or four dozen roses." Hastily he corrected himself. "No. Make it one dozen, that should be enough. After that it becomes ostentatious."

"Yes, Father."

"And try to persuade her to marry you soon, will you?"

"Yes, Father."

There was a discreet knock on the door. The banker's secretary announced that Count von Steinmiltz of the Royal Treasury was outside. Abraham Mendelssohn nodded and rose from his leather chair. "Marriage is what you need," he said, walking towards the door. "It'll give you the proper perspective and a sense of responsibility. On your way out stop at the cashier's. He'll give you what you need."

"Thank you, Father."

Summer, that year, lingered through September. Then the first autumn rains came and the weather turned cold. From his window Felix watched the elms in the garden turn auburn and the leaves float down on the lawn. The summer-house concerts were discontinued and so were the garden parties that had been a pleasant feature of the previous months. Winter came early and with it the snow pads on the window sills, the grey slab-like skies, the huge logs burning bright in the fireplaces.

At 3 Leipzigerstrasse, life assumed its winter routine. Abraham Mendelssohn's sumptuous private coach was discarded and now the banker, bundled in furs, went to work every morning in an equally luxurious sleigh. Leah Mendelssohn hardly left her sitting-room and spent most of her time by the fireside reading, knitting and supervising the management of her enormous house.

Felix slept more soundly than ever. He wrote a considerable amount of music, did much skating and dancing, met his friends at fashionable cafés. He followed Hegel's post-graduate lectures at the university, attended the opera and the Singakademie concerts, sent flowers, bought a number of useless and expensive things and earned no money at all. He spent some pleasant afternoons with his fiancée Nina and many delightful evenings with Anna.

Faithfully he wrote his friend Karl, telling him how he was doing his best to persuade Anna to go to London in the spring. He didn't, however, think it necessary to go into details and describe the circumstances in which he exercised his persuasiveness. As weeks went by he grew rather fond of Anna. She was not, he found, the heartless and voracious woman he had been led to expect. She could be meek, tender, docile, and he learned how the same woman could be two entirely different persons to two different men. She had fallen in love and retracted her claws. Having shed her former self, she now revealed the pathetic defencelessness of those who love more than they are loved. For the first time in her life she experienced love's excruciating and exquisite pains. Her splendid cow-like eyes filled easily with tears—sometimes of joy, more often of longing and disappointment. She stopped mingling with the patrons of the Friedrich Theatre, with the result that her earnings dwindled to approximately nothing, which was the amount of her salary. Yet, when Felix insisted on making up the difference, she refused indignantly, revelling in the hardships and privations of love with the enthusiasm of a fakir for his bed of spikes.

Whenever Felix spent an evening with her she did her best to please him, and her best was very good. Anna's education left much to be desired, her table manners were sketchy, her mind had the sweeping vacuousness of the wide-open spaces, but in matters of love her knowledge was encyclopædic, her memory prodigious, her inventiveness surprising. She was born to love as a bird to fly. With stupefaction Felix discovered that this good-hearted sensuous girl would make someone an excellent wife and at times he pondered whether, instead of sending her to London, he would not do better to give her a dowry and send her back to her farm.

Thus winter passed. The snow thawed on the roofs and the streets became quagmires of mud. The Spree swelled and its ochre water churned and whirled around the stone pillars of the bridges.

And then it was April and all of a sudden the air was alive with the winged twitter of swallows. In the parks trees waited for spring, each twig green-nailed with buds. Children in velvet suits and lace collars yelled and ran and stumbled on the grass.

Wilhelm Hensel, Fanny's patient suitor, returned from Rome, and grudgingly Abraham Mendelssohn set the betrothal date for the end of the month. An atmosphere of excitement descended upon the house. There was to be a formal dinner followed by a short concert and a ball. Much had to be planned and organised. Felix plunged into the preparation of the festivities. He wrote special music for the occasion, rehearsed the orchestra.

At last the great day arrived. Early that afternoon he drove to town for some last-minute arrangements. As he was passing by his favourite flower shop he remembered he had not seen Anna for almost three weeks. He told the coachman to pull in and entered the shop.

An elderly lady walked to him with a welcoming smile. " We haven't seen you for a long time," she said.

He explained he had been busy with his sister's betrothal. Oh yes, she knew all about it. While she chattered he wandered about the shop, inspecting the display of flowers. The shop was in a dilapidated yellow brick building which at one time had known a short-lived popularity as a theatre and concert hall. Since then fashion had moved to another section of town and the antiquated hall with its tarnished decorations and worn plush seats had fallen on evil days. It was used for rehearsals, magic lantern shows, sparsely attended lectures and short-lived theatrical productions. Penniless concert artists rented it for their hopeful débuts, their comeback or farewell performances. It was a melancholy place, smelling of dampness and failure, gloomy with the ghosts of the artists whose hopes had died there.

That afternoon Felix's attention was attracted by the sound of a piano seeping through the back wall of the shop. He stopped in the middle of a sentence and listened. The music was unfamiliar to him, wild and caressing, unlike any he had ever heard. But there was no mystery about the manner in which it was being played; here was piano-playing at its superlative best.

" Do you know who is playing?" he asked the old woman.

" A young pianist, a Frenchman, I think. Anyway, he has a French name. I looked at him the other day while he was practising and he looked like he should've been in bed instead of playing the piano."

Felix raised a finger to his lips and walked to the rear of the shop whence the music came. For a while he listened, straining his ear. *Mein Gott,* how that Frenchman could play! He felt a spasm of enviousness. It was scandalous to play as well as that. At times the piano sang with the throbbing softness of a 'cello; at others he thought he heard two pianos with two pianists at each keyboard. He could not believe his ears. This was not keyboard technique, this was magic.

"He plays well, doesn't he?" the woman whispered. Then she added, pointing to a recess in the wall, "If you want you can get into the hall through that door."

Hastily, Felix gave Anna's address, dictated a tender message and slipped into the hall. The spectacle that presented itself was heart-rending. Less than twenty people sparsely dotted the first two rows. It was no longer a concert, it was a wake. On the stage a blond tragic-faced young man was playing with the abandon of despair. Lost in some mournful reverie of his own, he had long forgotten, Felix sensed, his handful of listeners. When he came to the end of the number he was playing, he did not even seem to hear the meagre applause. Without taking a pause, he raised his two arms, as if swept by some inner fury and with a motion of his whole body struck the thunderous opening chords of the Revolutionary Etude.

Felix had watched many thrilling pianistic feats, but never had seen or heard anything like this. In billowing waves of sound, vertiginous, chromatic, the Etude shouted the strident, dishevelled call to arms of a nation about to die. It was the musical shroud of a people going to its doom. When the piece came to its abrupt, shattering end, Felix sprang to his feet, frenziedly clapping his hands. At the keyboard Frederic Chopin seemed to awake from his trance. He wheeled around on his stool, surprised by this one-man ovation, and gave to Felix a slow exhausted smile of gratitude. Then he rose, gave a ceremonious bow to his pitiful audience and walked off the stage.

A few minutes later Felix wound his way through musty backstage corridors to the pianist's dressing-room. He knocked and the pallid young man himself opened the door. He was in his shirt-sleeves, sweat still glistening on his forehead and his bony clean-shaven cheeks. Damp strands of tawny hair clung to the sides of his face. He had removed his high stiff collar and his rumpled, ruffled shirt was open at the neck. In his hand he held a crumpled towel.

He recognised his hand-clapping admirer and smiled, "Oh, *c'est vous!*" he said as though he had been expecting him. "*Entrez, je vous en prie.*"

Felix entered the shabby dressing-room and introduced himself.

"Not the Mendelssohn of the *Midsummer* Overture?" he gasped, grasping Felix's sleeve. Felix nodded, smiling and the pianist let out a cry of incredulous admiration. "*Bohze Moy!*" he exclaimed, lapsing into Polish in his excitement. "I can't believe it! Do you know that you've written a masterpiece? Even as a piano piece it sounds wonderful. Have you heard it on the piano?"

Again Felix nodded. "I play the piano myself. Not like you, of course."

Chopin had forgotten his fatigue of a moment ago. He was shaking with excitement, nervously brushing back the wisps of blond hair that kept swaying across his face. "We must play it four-hands together," he said. "I'd like to ask your advice on the interpretation of some parts of it. By the way," he flung casually, "my name is Chopin, Frederic Chopin. But don't be misled by my name. I am not French, I am Polish. As Polish as can be."

"What!" It was Felix's turn to gasp and stare. "Then you must be the composer of the *Là ci darem* Variations? Do you realise that *you've* written a masterpiece?"

With the impulsiveness of youth they stared at each other, laughing, not knowing what to say. Then all of a sudden they began to talk at random, often at the same time. They had a thousand things to ask each other. They felt like old friends.

As Felix was complimenting him on his superlative performance of a moment ago, Frederic Chopin let out a grunt of abysmal dismay. "One more superlative performance like this one and I'll have to walk to Paris. I'd hoped this concert would bring me some money, instead it has ruined me. I'll be lucky if I can pay my coach fare."

"When are you leaving?"

"To-morrow."

Felix frowned with disappointment, then his face brightened. "Look, Frederic, my sister's getting engaged to-day and I must hurry back home. Why don't you come with me? You'll meet many people and we'll have a chance to talk. Do you like to dance?"

"Any Pole likes to dance."

"Good, because there's going to be a ball. Then afterwards when everybody's gone we'll have some music, just the two of us."

And now it was over—the dinner, the concert, the ball. It was late, very late. It was more than two hours since the last guests had departed in the blaze of torches and the rumbling of carriage wheels. Liveried servants had long snuffed out the sparkling chandeliers and the wall candelabra in the hallway and along the corridors. The huge ballroom, a moment ago so crowded and sparkling, alive with the swirl of hooped skirts, noisy with laughter and dance music, was now silent and dark, except for the blue shafts of moonlight slanting through the high arched windows and, in a corner, a small pool of amber glow from two silver candlesticks standing on the piano. Felix sat on the piano bench, one hand still resting on the keyboard. A few feet away Frederic Chopin, his legs crossed, was sprawled deep into a green plush arm-chair in an attitude of relaxed thoughtfulness. Neither of them spoke. They had talked too much, drunk too much champagne, laughed and danced and played the piano too much. Now they were tired, drowsy, a little sad, content to enjoy the silence of the night in each other's company, each lost in his own thoughts, letting the excitement of the day ebb away from their limbs and their minds.

All of a sudden Chopin spoke. "Your sister Fanny is the happiest girl in the world to-night." His brooding gaze remained fixed on the spot of moonlight in the middle of the room. "She loves and she is loved. What more can anyone want?"

Felix smiled. "Odd that you should say that. I was thinking the same thing."

"Wonderful, but very rare. Everyone loves someone, but seldom each other. This is one of the reasons why I left Poland. I couldn't stand any more to watch the girl I loved love someone else."

Again silence fell between them. Somewhere a clock chimed.

"Strange, isn't it," Felix remarked, "that milestones, even the happiest, make us feel the passing of time and think of the future. And when you think of the future you always end up by thinking about death." He straightened up on the bench and prepared to rise. "I'm getting morose. We'd better go to sleep."

"Just a few more minutes," pleaded Chopin. "God knows when we'll see each other again. Play one more of your compositions and we'll go."

"All right, but I'm going to play something that neither you nor I could have written." While talking he turned to the music cabinet at his side and pulled out a thin folio bound in rare leather. "It's a fragment of some oratorio or cantata by Johann Sebastian Bach."

"Dear old Bach!" Chopin smiled. "My teacher used to make me play his *Well-tempered Clavichord* until I thought I'd go mad."

"So did mine. I suppose everybody who plays the piano has had to struggle with those exercises. But this is something quite different. It is to the *Well-tempered Clavichord* what a Rembrandt is to a geometrical design. Personally I think it is the most magnificent music ever written."

"Why isn't it published?"

"Because, as I told you, it is only a fragment, the last four pages of a much larger composition. Where the rest is, nobody knows. Herr Zelter, my teacher, found those pages in an old music store amidst a lot of rubbish. How it got there nobody knows. Now shut your eyes and listen. Try to imagine a chorus, an organ and a full orchestra."

When he had finished playing he turned to his friend. "Well?"

Chopin did not reply at once, staring unseeingly ahead, as if in a trance. "It is shattering," he said at last. "Even Handel's *Messiah* doesn't have that sweeping grandeur." He turned to Felix. "How can it be? How can a work like that get lost?"

"How can the Venus de Milo remain two thousand years buried in a field? Answer me that." He replaced the folio in the music cabinet, rose and still talking handed one of the candlesticks to Chopin. Taking the other one, he started towards the door. "It does seem incredible, but if you stop to think of it, a great many masterpieces have been lost one way or another. Fire, wars, people moving away, or not appreciating the value of what they had. Why, for instance, do we have so little of Pergolesi's or Lasso's music? What became of the chorus music of the Greek dramas? The early Gregorian Masses?" They were now advancing through the echoing corridors, holding their candlesticks high above their heads, their shadows following them on the walls. "Same thing in painting. Do you realise that only seven or eight paintings by da Vinci are in existence? Now, isn't that strange? A man who lived to be over seventy and was still painting a few days before his death? And Vermeer? Why are there only thirty-seven Vermeers in the world?"*

They reached the second floor.

"Fortunately the Paris coach leaves only at four in the afternoon," Felix remarked with a smile. "I'll drive you to the depot. And don't worry about getting there in advance. Your place has been reserved."

Before his friend could utter a word, Felix waved to him and made his way to his room.

The following day Chopin left for Paris. Like Karl Klingemann, he leaned out of the receding coach and waved his handkerchief. Then he was gone, and Felix drove back home.

At 3 Leipzigerstrasse, life resumed its smooth, luxurious course. After the commotion of Fanny's betrothal the return to orderly schedules brought about a welcome relaxation. Outwardly, everything was as it had always been, but soon Felix became aware of a change in the atmosphere of the house. Fanny's engagement had shattered the dogma of immutability, the axiom that things would forever remain as they were. It marked the end of an era, the closing of a way of family life so happy and tenderly united that already

* By a dramatic coincidence, Mendelssohn's original manuscript score of his masterpiece, *A Midsummer Night's Dream* Overture, was lost in a London hackney in 1829 and has never been found. In 1906, a copy of the score came to light, but not in Mendelssohn's hand.

it assumed a legendary iridescence. It was the portent of other changes to come. The Mendelssohn family, one and indivisible, as it had fancied itself, was about to crumble and scatter. Already Fanny was engaged, soon she would go away. All departures are death-like and it made no difference that she should merely move away to some other section of the city. Fanny gone, the house would not be the same. The sound of her lovely singing voice, her garden bonnet hanging in the hall, her brushes and water-colour paints—all these things were part of the atmosphere, the soul of the house. Soon there would be other engagements, other marriages, other separations. One after another, the young Mendelssohns would go away. In a few years the princely mansion would be just another deserted house, a grand and melancholy shelter for two ageing and lonely people.

Everyone in the house, down to the humblest scullery maid, was aware of the approaching changes, but curiously it was Abraham Mendelssohn who most betrayed his secret anguish. At times at dinner his heavy-lidded eyes would travel around the table, stopping over each one of his children in turn, and sudden embarrassing tears would hang precariously over the rims; to main-tain his dignity he would clear his throat or blow his nose or make some querulous remark.

Felix tried to return to his pleasant, carefree existence and found that he couldn't. He, too, had changed. He was going to make his father happy for a change. Now that Fanny was going, he would show his parents that he was a real Mendelssohn, serious and hard-working. He would marry Nina if she did not mind and if it made his family happy. Why, he might even go to work at the bank.

Meanwhile, the first thing he was going to do was to end this ridiculous and hypocritical " proxy " relationship with Anna, give her a fair-sized dowry and send her back home. He wrote his friend that he was defaulting on his promise and in turn was releasing him of all obligations to provide him with a good excuse to go to London.

This done, he went to see Anna. He found her sitting on the edge of her bed eating sauerkraut with her fingers. To his surprise, she did not rush to kiss him, as had been her habit. He kissed her on the cheek, sat down at her side and informed her he no longer expected her to go to London. Again he surprised him by informing him she had never meant to go anyway. She went on to say she wouldn't be able to see him any more.

" No more," she said with a sad shake of her flaming hair.

During the past three weeks, she explained, while he was forget-ting her, she had done some considerable thinking. She had reached the conclusion that he didn't love her and never would. They just weren't the same kind. Recently she had met a man who, she felt, was very much her kind. You couldn't say he was handsome. He was short and bald and he had a paunch. A brewer, but not one of the rich ones. But he loved her enough to want to marry her—and she had told him everything—and since he was willing to take her as she was, she was going to make him the best wife a man ever had.

As she finished talking, emotion overcame her for an instant. Tears filled her beautiful eyes. " I've loved you too much," she said quietly. " It's no good. You get hurt all the time when you love too much."

She wouldn't hear of the dowry and Felix had no other recourse but to send her a magnificent and anonymous wedding present.

Thus, Anna Skrumpnagel vanished from his life.

In due time Felix received a letter from Karl. With relief he read that his friend had lost all interest in Anna since meeting Suzy Plunkett, a young English woman of the most inventive mind and intriguing personality. " I'm looking forward to telling you more about Suzy, for Sir George Smart, director of the Philharmonic Orchestra, is sending you an invitation to come here and give a concert of your compositions."

To Felix's astonishment his father read Sir George's letter without explosions of disapproval and prophecies of disaster. " Most flattering, indeed," he said, resting the letter on the desk. " Sir George says that all London is waiting for you but fails to mention money. I don't quite see how he expects you to get to England. Possibly by swimming . . . On the other hand, it is an undeniable honour for a youngster like you to be invited to conduct the Philharmonic Orchestra."

There was a gleam of pride in the old man's eyes which he hastened to conceal from his son by turning his gaze to the window. " Perhaps," he went on, musingly rubbing his chin, " this trip could even have some practical usefulness. I'm negotiating a loan for the Royal Prussian Treasury and trying to associate the various branches of the Rothschild Bank in this affair. I am already in full agreement with Nathan Rothschild, the head of the London branch. But James Rothschild, who directs the Paris branch, is somewhat hesitant. Now his wife, Betty, who incidentally happens also to be his niece, is a delightful lady very much interested in the arts, especially music. She has a great deal of influence over her husband and it just came to my mind that on your way back from London you could stop in Paris for a few days and strike up a friendship with her. As I said, she is most interested in music . . ."

" I think I understand what you have in mind, Father," said Felix. " I shall do my best."

When a week later, the paddle-ship churned her way out of the

Hamburg harbour, Felix stood on the deck, watching the wharf recede in the distance. Then he turned around, looked at the sky and took a long breath of salty air. It was good to be young, rich, famous, and to be going to England. . . . Softly he repeated to himself a sentence from Sir George's letter. " All London is waiting for you . . ."

He smiled.

Chapter 2

IN A flourish of trumpet blare, cracking whip and galloping hoofs, the Dover stagecoach burst into the cobbled courtyard of a Charing Cross inn. Amidst the joyous confusion of arrivals, luggage was unstrapped, porters piled trunks and coffers on their wheelbarrows and passengers alighted. With a lift of hooped skirts and a glimpse of pantaloons, ladies climbed down the folding carriage steps and plummeted into the arms of waiting relatives.

Felix spied Karl Klingemann, resplendent in a lilac frock-coat and flowery cravat. With surprising efficiency the diplomat attended to the transfer of his friend's luggage, and soon they were rolling through the shady lanes of St. James's Park.

" Of course you're staying with me," said Karl. " I won't hear of your going to a hotel. This town is waiting for you; you'd be eaten alive by admiring females which, incidentally, is my idea of a delightful death."

Abruptly, his round jovial face composed itself in a blend of mournfulness and sympathy. " I regret to inform you that your Margaret is now the wife of a dour and kilted Scottish earl. She lives in a crenellated and mouldy castle on some Godforsaken moor, buried in everlasting mist."

Felix gulped down his disappointment. " She had promised to wait for me," he said with a rueful sigh. " You just can't depend on women."

" Not even Englishwomen!" stressed Karl. " Take my Suzy, for instance. I dislike her intensely, but I love her to death. She'll break my heart, I know. Women were created for the purpose of breaking men's hearts and they enjoy doing it. Fortunately for us, we survive an almost unlimited number of heartbreaks."

Having relieved himself of these remarks, he expanded his broad chest and took a long cheerful breath. " Isn't this a lovely park?" he cried, waving at the budding trees and sun-freckled lawns. " Would you believe that at one time this was a stinking marshy meadow and without Henry the Eighth, dear old Henry the Eighth, who had it drained——"

The explanation trailed off in mid-air as he noticed that Felix was gazing at an approaching horsewoman in tight-fitting green riding habit, followed by a liveried groom. She rode side-saddle, her slender hips swaying rhythmically with the leisurely pace of her gleaming chestnut mare. She held her head high in an attitude of haughty aloofness. Even from a distance, Felix could see she was beautiful, and her beauty seemed to increase as the distance between them lessened. He was still staring at her as she rode by the carriage. Their eyes met long enough for her to give him a long-lashed appraising look, just as Karl lifted his beaver and whirled it in an elaborate salute.

"Who is she?" asked Felix when the horsewoman had passed out of sight.

"The Marchioness of Dorsythe, England's most beautiful widow and one of the Queen's ladies-in-waiting."

"A shame that such a beautiful woman should be so cold and arrogant."

"Beware of appearances," remarked Karl sententiously, as he pulled his snuff box from his citron-coloured waistcoat. "Of course she is cold and arrogant. This is expected of her. But I suspect her to be human. She takes frequent trips on the Continent, especially to Italy, and I've noticed that regularly at the same time a handsome lord or dashing officer of the Guards vanishes from the London scene, returning two or three days before her own reappearance." He pressed the brown dust to his nostrils and inhaled violently. "Mere coincidence, no doubt," he wound up with a chuckle.

The cab had turned into Green Park when Felix told his friend he wished to deposit his father's letter of credit. Karl directed the cabby to the Rothschild Bank.

"I'll just be a minute," said Felix when the carriage came to a halt.

The cashier examined the letter of credit over the rim of his spectacles. Then he disappeared, returning a moment later to inform Felix that Herr Rothschild was anxious to make his acquaintance. Felix was ushered into the banker's office and was greeted by the frog-eyed, pot-bellied gnome who was the almost legendary Nathan Rothschild.

"Our fathers were great friends," said the banker, waving Felix to a seat and taking his place behind his desk. "I myself entertain the most cordial business relations with him. I regret I was away when you came to London with him and I am delighted to have the opportunity of meeting you, especially on the occasion of your first concert in London." For an instant he rested his eyes on Felix and a curiously attractive smile softened his hard and ugly face. "Your father must be proud of you."

Felix smiled and made a deprecatory gesture, and the financier went on. "He'll change his mind after the concert, you'll see."

In a leisurely way he inquired about Felix's family, his plans. Finally he seemed to remember the letter of credit he held in his hand. "Quite a sizeable sum," he said. "Your father is a most generous man." He rose from his chair and escorted Felix to the door. "I don't think the Philharmonic Orchestra was ever conducted by anyone as young as you. Until now we all have known the name of Moses Mendelssohn, but I think I shall hear a great deal about his grandchild."

Karl was dozing in the cab when Felix joined him at last. "Forgive me, but Herr Rothschild wanted to see me. Those big bankers always seem to have all the time in the world."

"It's true in any field," observed Karl, coming out of his nap and flinging his house's address to the driver. "The higher you get, the more you have people doing things for you until finally you have practically nothing to do yourself. At the legation, our minister spends most of his time writing sonnets to his dead mistress. He couldn't stand her when she was alive, and now he weeps each time he speaks of her. A memory is easier to love than a person."

"If you ever start writing sonnets to your past mistresses," said Felix with a chuckle, "you'll be writing night and day. Tell me, how do you like being a diplomat?"

"I love it. I was born for it."

As the cab wound its way towards Bury Street, the portly young man extolled the charms and privileges of a diplomatic career. The work was interesting and light. So light, especially at the Hanover Legation, that everyone there had time for leisurely lunches followed by long restful siestas. Then there was the social life. Hostesses adored diplomats. Any diplomat—even a third secretary at the Hanover Legation.

But most of all it was the exhilarating sense of occult power attached to diplomatic status that Karl appreciated. "Suppose I'd like to have my landlord thrown in jail," he said with a cheerful beam on his round face, "I could do it in five minutes."

"On what grounds?"

"Anything." His tone implied he had only to choose among a variety of charges. "I could say we have secret information he is a secret agent. Or a dangerous revolutionary. This would be good for three or four weeks in jail until an investigation revealed that a frightful mistake had been committed. I explained this to my landlord one day when he was getting unduly anxious about the rent. He saw the light and became soft as silk."

He was still chuckling when the cab stopped in front of the small but decorous house at 39 Bury Street, where he lived.

During the next two weeks Felix was too busy with the preparations for his concert to accept the invitations that poured upon him. Everyone, it seemed, wanted to meet the young millionaire composer. The season was in full bloom and London was at its dazzling best. Everything about the town delighted him—the discreet

courtesy of its people so different from the oppressive Latin effusiveness, the shady parks, the houses, the shops, the streets. Even rain,
he decided, could have charm in London. The greatest singers in
the world—Sontag, Pisaroni, Donzelli and the fabulous golden-
voiced Maria Salla, who had just made a triumphant début—were
all in London at the moment. Yet Felix would refuse to go out and
hear them and his friend would grow indignant. " At least come to
hear Maria Salla," he would plead. " I tell you she is fantastic." He
would wag a prophetic finger under Felix's nose. " Some day, when
your grandchildren learn that you had the opportunity to hear
Maria Salla and you stayed at home with your nose in your scores,
they will say ' Our grandfather was an idiot '." Felix would accept
the rebuff with patient good humour and return to his work.

There was no time to lose. The date of the concert had been
set for May 25th, the programme had been selected. Besides the
inevitable *Midsummer* Overture, he was to conduct his Symphony
in C and a scherzo from his Octet especially orchestrated for this
occasion. Everywhere he had met with friendliness and co-
operation. Thomas Attwood, treasurer of the Philharmonic Society,
was kindness itself. Sir George Smart, conductor of the Philharmonic Orchestra, gave his whole-hearted support to his young rival.
He, in turn, was anxious to do his best. In Berlin his family was
waiting with bated breath for the outcome of " this British
adventure," as his father called it.

But mostly it was the formidable body of veteran musicians that
composed the Philharmonic Orchestra that he wanted to conquer.
With them, wealth, prestige of birth, social graces did not count.
Only competence, authentic mastery would do the trick. His heart
was beating hard when for the first time he stood on the rostrum,
baton in hand, feeling their sceptical glances. Even after the first
rehearsal, those crusty professionals did not give in. It was a long
arduous road. Yet daily he felt their increasing respect, their
gradual recognition of his right to lead them. Smiles appeared on
their wrinkled side-whiskered faces when, in courteous but firm
terms, he corrected some mistake which they thought would pass
undetected. After the final rehearsal, they rose in a spontaneous
gesture of tribute. He was so startled by this unexpected demon-
stration that then and there he wept, furious at himself for this un-
British display of emotion. But they understood, and a veteran
tuba player expressed their feelings in twangy cockney. " Cry all
you want. You're a fine musician, and you'll see, to-morrow we'll
play them off their seats."

The prediction proved true. At the end of the concert the
audience rose in ovation. This time Felix did not cry. He bowed
with impassive formality and turning to the musicians, now his

friends, he asked them to rise and share with him this moment of triumph. Afterwards, in his dressing-room, he knew the intoxicating impact of public acclaim at close quarters. In the eyes of women he read the tremulous admiration which already was an offer of love. He felt their hands grow limp under his formal kiss. Titled hostesses begged for his presence at their dinners. Sir George Smart pleaded with him for another concert. Herr Rothschild gripped his hand. " Good work, Felix. I'm sending a special messenger to your father." He tried to discount the fantastic praises, dismiss the superlatives, the absurd flatteries. He did his best to keep himself in hand. He bowed, thanked, muttered deprecating protests. But just the same it was thrilling to hear oneself called a genius by Thomas Attwood, who had been a pupil of Mozart's; acknowledge the bows of eminent critics, the congratulations of celebrated artists. It was difficult to refuse all this adulation, this spume of temptation. And when the Marchioness of Dorsythe, no longer cold, no longer arrogant, had purred in his ear an invitation to come to tea the next day, he had whispered " Yes."

" Well," asked Karl that evening when they were back in Bury Street. " how does it feel to have London at your feet?"

" Thrilling, but if I stay in this town another month I shall become a pompous, vainglorious, insufferable ass."

" Now will you come and hear Maria Salla? She's singing to-morrow in the *Barbiere*, and I tell you she is phenomenal."

" I thought you didn't like music."

" I don't. I go to look at her. Oh, those eyes, those lips! I'd even give up my Suzy for that girl. Which of course would be like falling from the frying pan into the fire from what I hear about her."

Felix covered a yawn with his hand. " She may be all you say, but still I won't go. I'm tired. I don't want to hear any more music, not even my own. I said so to Sir George, who wanted me to give another concert." He parted the sheets and slipped into his bed. " London is beautiful, its people are wonderful, Maria Salla is phenomenal and I love her, I love your house and I love you. I love everybody but I am tired and I want to go home. By the end of the week I'll be on my way."

Next afternoon he drove to the Dorsythes' mansion in Berkeley Square. It was a graceful Regency house standing, neat and square, on a carpet of lawn behind a forbidding iron fence. A liveried footman opened the carriage door. Another one took his hat, light spring cape and gloves; and still another one preceded him along a marble-floored corridor to a spacious drawing-room furnished with discreet opulence and decorated with family portraits of haughty ladies in medieval hennins, velvet toques and plumed hats and fierce and beefy lords in suits of armour, mail shirts, silk doublets, state robes and gold and scarlet uniforms. The Marchioness, he felt, had footmen and ancestors to spare.

Somehow, he had expected some small aristocratic gathering and was surprised but not displeased to find there was to be no other guest.

" I didn't ask anyone else," she said as if in reply to his thoughts, as she glided into the room in a rustle of grey silk, " because I wanted to have a chance to talk to you."

All arrogance had left her. If anything, her manner betrayed a certain embarrassed listlessness. She went on talking and sat down next to him on the narrow settee, averting her eyes, nervously crumpling the lace handkerchief she held in her hand. A fat white-gloved majordomo entered carrying a tremendous silver tray which he set on the table, and then he withdrew with almost unbearable solemnity. While the Marchioness poured, Felix made some casual complimentary remarks about the family portraits on the walls. She stopped, looked at them with a curious blend of pride and resentment.

" Some were my late husband's ancestors, some are mine," she said. " Our two families came to England with William the Conqueror."

Whereupon she plunged into an involved and tedious history of both houses, and again Felix was struck by the mixture of family pride and bitterness that crept into her voice. " Yes," she said at last, turning to him with an uneasy smile, " it is gratifying to possess a long and glorious ancestry, but if you knew how many dangers it creates, how much caution it imposes." Inadvertently, she rested her hand on his knee. " Especially when one is as lonely as myself."

It seemed incredible that such a delectable creature could be lonely in a city like London and Felix said so. The beautiful peeress insisted it was, nevertheless, true. She was very lonely. Oh, yes, her duties as lady-in-waiting, her solitary rides, a few social functions brought a semblance of fulfilment in her life, but deep inside she still felt lonely. Especially in the evenings did she become aware of a gnawing emptiness, a yearning for she didn't quite know what.

" A friend, that's what I need," she sighed, peering at him through the curved fronds of her lashes. The moment she had spied him in the park she had sensed they could be friends, great friends. After watching him during the concert, she was certain of it, and that's why she had invited him—to tell him what great friends they could be.

Her fingers, as she spoke, tightened over his thigh. He rested his hand over hers and gave it a gentle pressure. This innocent gesture sent a responsive shudder through her slender body. She drew herself closer to him and he felt the tender resilience of his new friend's breasts, as she nestled against him.

Yes, friendship, that's what she craved. Friendship with a great artist like him, sensitive and understanding. But in London, friendship was impossible. Everyone knew her. This was the price of being the Marchioness of Dorsythe, one of the Queen's ladies-in-waiting. Even in her house, surrounded by eighteen servants, she could not hope for privacy. Servants gossiped and their gossip seeped into palaces. But she knew where they could have the privacy friendship required. A sunny villa in Italy . . .

"It's near Rapallo." Now her lips brushed against his ears, her voice came in hot, gasping whispers. "Nestled in the hills among the olive trees . . . Oh, darling, that's the place for us . . ."

She would go first and he would meet her a few days later. There they would be alone, away from the harsh cruel world. There he would compose, they would go bathing in the transparent waters of secluded coves, lie side by side in the sun. And at night they would watch the gleaming stars, listen to their heartbeats and the cicadas.

Gently he disentangled himself from her embrace. Karl's remarks sounded in his mind. How many times, he thought, looking at her, had she gone through the same scene, spoken the same words? Yet he did not want to laugh. He felt sorry for her, sensing her inner conflict, the wrestling of her carnal hunger and her pride. Like a queen, she was prisoner of her station. She hadn't the right which humble people had, to sin. She was nailed to a blazon. Those family portraits on the walls had become her tormenting jailers. They had forced her, ardent and sex-starved, into the lone arrogant horsewoman he had seen in the park. They had made a hypocrite out of her, stooping to shabby stealthy Italian affairs. In time they might bring her to some tragic end.

"I'd love to join you in Rapallo," he said, "but I must be home in a few days."

He did his best to save her pride. He was kind, he held her hands. Never would he forget that she had chosen him for a friend . . . Perhaps some day in the years to come . . .

She was looking at him, her mouth slack. In her eyes there were tears of shame, disappointment and longing. She did not look as beautiful or young as a moment ago. There were little freckles and thin lines on her face he hadn't seen before. She didn't look like a cold and haughty marchioness in the bottle-green riding habit, she looked like a woman, any woman whose little bubble of romance had burst.

He took her face between his hands, softly kissed her lips and walked away.

That evening, with his friend Karl, he attended a reception at the Devonshire House and danced far into the night. Even the crushing formality of the occasion and the awesome splendour of the surroundings could not repress his high spirits. After the tension of the previous weeks, his pent-up boyishness asserted itself in fits of irrepressible hilarity. His youth overrode his fame, he could not cling to a pompousness that was alien to his nature. The job was done, the concert over, he wanted to have fun. And fun he had. He talked and laughed and flirted. Champagne blurred the faces, swayed the floor under his feet and swept away the last vestiges of his reserve. " Do you know you've proposed to six different girls?" remonstrated Karl as they drove home through the deserted streets. " Champagne was invented by a monk, it's a treacherous drink."

It was the same at Lansdowne House the following night. Karl's rebukes grew sharper. Felix was unrepentant. " When I feel gay, I behave accordingly," he said. Two days later, at the Prussian Embassy, he drank even more champagne and his spirits soared to new heights. With gaping mouths and raised eyebrows, dowagers watched the conductor of the Philharmonic Orchestra caper like a youngster and spin their daughters around the ballroom.

As they were walking home, Karl vented his disapproval. " How do you expect to impress people if you act like a schoolboy?" The sound of his voice broke the stillness of the moonlit night. " What would your Grandfather Moses say?"

" My grandfather was a philosopher. He'd say there's a time to be serious and a time to be foolish. This is the time to be foolish, and I say to hell with you!"

When they entered their apartment, they found a letter placed in evidence between two lighted candles. It came from Berlin and had been brought by special messenger. With a frown, Felix opened it and began to read. His face, a moment ago flushed with laughter and champagne, turned grave.

" What is it?" asked Karl.

" My Uncle Nathan, who lives in Silesia, has written my father about the terrible floods they've been having there. Hundreds of families are homeless. Now my father wants to know if I could give a benefit concert for those poor people."

The following afternoon he sat in Sir George Smart's office. Nothing remained of the capering youngster of the night before. His brown eyes rested anxiously on the elderly man who was reading Abraham Mendelssohn's letter.

"Well, Sir George, what do you think? Will the British public care about the plight of those people?"

Sir George rubbed his chin before replying. "The British can be very generous—especially if they get a little pleasure for their money. You can write your father he can depend on us."

"I don't know how to thank you," Felix said with feeling. "When can we give the concert?"

"Not before mid July, I'm afraid."

Felix gasped. "Mid July! But that's six weeks away!"

Sir George nodded. "I fear it can't be helped. Neither the Argyll Rooms nor Covent Garden will be available before then. Besides, there's going to be a great deal of preparation——"

He stopped as the door was flung open and a very beautiful, very agitated young lady shot into his office like a hurricane. Felix caught a glimpse of her eyes. They were light—probably grey or hazel, he couldn't decide—and this surprised him because her hair was jet black. But light they were and at this moment full of thunder and sparks.

She ignored Felix and started talking even before reaching the desk. "Signor Smart," she began, "you are a big *bugiardo*. You tell big lies. Until this day I think you are my friend."

Sir George received this declaration with perfect British *sang-froid*. "Have you met Herr Mendelssohn?" he asked graciously.

The young lady tossed Felix an impatient nod and Sir George had barely time to slip to Felix, "This is Miss Salla," before the visitor resumed her discourse in that peculiar Italian-studded English of hers. "When the other men lie, I laugh, because it matters not what they say." She spoke as though she meant what she said. "But when my best friend, *il signor* Smart he lies to me, then I feel very sad."

Dramatically her voice broke. For a moment she considered her erstwhile friend with the troubled expression of a disappointed child.

Sir George took advantage of this brief respite. "Would you mind telling me what this is all about, and how I lied to you?" he asked with patience born of a long-suffering experience with opera singers. "But first wouldn't you like to sit down or we'll all have to stand. And this," he added ruefully, "may take quite some time."

It did. It took Miss Salla forty-five minutes to state her grievance. She had been engaged by Sir George—who, in addition to his duties as conductor of the Philharmonic acted occasionally as director of Covent Garden—for a three-month season at the fabulous salary of two thousand guineas. Before giving in he had remonstrated that only Henriette Sontag, the incomparable German soprano, the greatest singer in the world, commanded such a salary, and to-day Miss Salla had learned that Sontag's salary was two thousand and *five* guineas! This she regarded as a betrayal, an insult both personal and national. Especially since the German singers, they sang from *la trippa,* the belly, and without feeling, while the Italian singers instead, they sang from *il cuore,* the heart, with much feeling.

All this came out in a torrent of *Madonna mia's,* imprecations of *Maledetto's* and the most astonishing display of histrionic talent Felix had ever witnessed.

Sir George was at a loss to explain the five guinea discrepancy. "It must be some clerical error," he suggested. This Miss Salla refused to believe. It was a machination, an affront to her artistry, her country. He tried to soothe her feelings, offered to make up the difference from his pocket. No, that wouldn't do. She wanted the correction made on the *contratto* or to-morrow she wouldn't sing Rosina in *Il Barbiere.* "The public it will wait and wait and wait," she hissed with superb timing, "but La Salla she will not be there!"

At the threat Sir George felt a ring of cold sweat around his brow. "Don't forget, Miss Salla," he warned severely, "that your contract contains a penalty clause of two hundred guineas. For one who argues so fiercely over five guineas this would be a rather extravagant revenge."

With a snort the singer leaped to her feet. '*Il contratto!*" She laughed at the *contratto,* spat on it! She had been cheated of five guineas and the *contratto* it was finished. So saying she veered around and started towards the door. In a flash Sir George was also at the door, grabbing her arm, pulling her back into the room.

"How could you do such a thing to me!" he cried in a heart-rending tone. "And how can you be greedy, so mercenary and heartless over a paltry five guineas when in Silesia people are home-less, cold and hungry!"

"What Silesia? What people?" she wanted to know, gradually returning into the room.

"Tell her!" said Sir George, turning to Felix.

Felix did. From imagination he described the murderous Silesian inundations, the sinking farms, the bellowing cattle, the mothers clutching their children in a last embrace as they drowned together in the muddy torrents. "We were just arranging the details for a benefit concert when you came in," he concluded.

A startling change had come over the singer. Her clear and slightly slanted eyes reflected her concern. "And the *bambini?*" she asked with dismay. What was going to happen to the poor little *bambini?* Abruptly she turned to Sir George. At once, this very minute, he must take one hundred guineas from her salary and send it to the poor hungry children. Also the five guineas she was entitled to and had been cheated out of . . .

"And you will sing to-morrow?" asked the baronet with an inward sigh of relief.

Of course, she would sing. And from the heart and not like La Sontag, who sang from the belly . . . Felix expressed his gratitude, thanked her in the name of Silesian children. This touched her very much. In the office the atmosphere was becoming dense with emotion. Sir George cleared his throat and declared that Miss Salla's heart was as large as the range of her voice which was extraordinary. Slowly the scene was drawing to a close in an exchange of mutual respect and protests of eternal devotion.

Miss Salla turned to Felix. "Maybe you drive me to the house, *si?*" Her eyes stayed upon him as she spoke. They no longer were full of sparks. They could, he observed, be strangely tender.

Downstairs her carriage was waiting, an open brougham drawn by two perfectly matched hackneys. They drove through the bustle of Oxford Street, chatting easily, enjoying the afternoon sunshine. She lived, she told him, at the corner of Half Moon Street and Bolton Row, in Mayfair. He remarked this was but a short distance from Bury Street. Why, they were neighbours. Well, almost . . . Then maybe he comes to see her, *si* . . . And maybe, some evening she cooks the *past' asciutta* or the *lasagne* for him, *si?* . . . She inquired how long he had been in London, and he said about a month.

"Then perhaps you came to Covent Garden to hear me, *si?*" she asked, her lips parted in a smile of anticipation. "Perhaps you hear me sing *Il Barbiere di Siviglia* or *Lucia* . . .?"

With some embarrassment he admitted he had not yet had the pleasure of hearing her beautiful voice. He saw her smile fade. Disappointment fell like a shadow over her face. Hastily he explained he had been too busy with the preparations for his concert.

"But I see in the newspaper you go to Devonshire House and Lansdowne House and the Embassy of Prussia," she retorted. Strange darting little lights were coming out of her eyes. "To go to those places you are not too busy, no? To dance with stupid rich girls you are not too busy, no? But to come to hear me you have no time."

They had crossed Hyde Park Corner and were entering Mayfair. He only had a few minutes to regain her sympathy, he told himself, bring the tenderness back into her eyes.

"Maybe you think opera is good only for stupid people," she persisted. "Not like the big symphonies."

"On the contrary, Miss Salla, I love opera."

"Then maybe you don't like me, you think I am *brutta,* ugly."

He burst out with laughter. "Ugly! Why I think you are the most enchanting——"

"Maybe you think I'm stupid because I make many mistakes when I speak?"

"I assure you nothing could be further from the truth."

"Then why don't you come to hear me sing?"

Her persistence exasperated him. "Dammit," he exploded, "I told you I couldn't. You didn't come to my concert either. Now did you?"

She gave him a look of hurt reproachfulness. "But I come to your concert," she said. "I hear you play the Overture and the big symphony."

He was staring at her, swelling with delight. She had come to his concert, seen him conduct the Philharmonic . . . "Why—why didn't you come to my dressing-room?"

She let out a contemptuous snort, as the carriage pulled in before a two-storied brick building. "Like all the stupid girls who makes eyes like sheep at you and open their mouths like sardines out of water?"

He helped her out of the carriage. With a wave she dismissed the driver. The trotting hoofbeats receded and faded away. In the approaching dusk Half Moon Street was quiet and lilac-hued.

Still talking she started up the few steps to the door. "And you give big smiles to everybody, kiss all the women's hands and make many salutations. That's why I don't come to your dressing-room." They reached the landing. "If a man wants me he must want only me."

Suddenly her mouth was upon his—full, soft and loving. Her fingertips dug deep into the back of his neck. He felt her jaw slacken and the tip of her tongue slide over his lips. Her body arched into his own and for an instant their hearts mingled their beats.

Then, as suddenly as it had come, it was over. The door opened, and she was out of sight.

That evening he told Karl about his encounter. "And then she kissed me," he said with an advantageous tug at his cravat. "It was a case of love at first sight, if I ever saw one."

The diplomat let out a moan of dismay. "Lust, you mean. There is no such thing as love at first sight, only lust at first sight."

"Whatever it was, it was delicious."

His friend took a few steps towards him. "Run, Felix!" he said with pleading urgency. "Forget the concert and the Silesian flood. Believe me, go away and don't look back."

"And give up those kisses?"

"You fool! Don't you see that kiss was a hook, and now you've swallowed it all—bait, hook and sinker. She has you at the end of her line."

Well, he finally was listening to her, and no mistake, she did have a phenomenal voice. . . . It was thrilling to hear that voice flow out of her throbbing white throat, soar like a jet of crystal-like sound to the upper galleries where sat the real connoisseurs, swell in steady crescendo until it filled every crack and cranny of Covent Garden. More thrilling still to watch her prancing about that enormous stage in her Spanish costume, swaying her hips, tossing her black curls, fanning the lust of every man in the audience. But most thrilling of all to know that she loved you. . . .

For she did love him, and no mistake about that either. Poor silly Karl with his " Run, Felix!" That kiss yesterday had the ring of true passion about it. She was his. Well, almost . . . To-night would see her final surrender. Exciting, wasn't it? Every man in London yearning for her, and he. the foreigner, picking her up like this, without effort . . . La Salla!

Strange, however, she had ignored him all through the performance. Yet she couldn't possibly miss him, the box was practically on the stage . . . On second thought it was better that way. This wasn't the Friedrich Theatre where Anna used to blow kisses at him the moment he came in. This was Covent Garden and all London was there. Restraint was imperative. Especially with Her Majesty sitting in the Royal Box and half the court watching. Restraint—yes, that was the watchword in this town. Just the same she could have slipped him a little smile.

The performance over, he hurried backstage, but, as was to be expected, there was a crowd in her dressing-room. He would wait outside, he decided. For a while he watched the usual after-performance confusion. Stage hands carrying cardboard trees, players still in their stage costumes wandering about. All right, by now they should have said their piece, told her she was a great singer. Why didn't they go home, why didn't she send them home? . . . She knew he was there. In the note he had tied to the roses he had sent her that afternoon he'd told her he'd come to see her after the show. Then why didn't she get rid of these people? It was rude to let him wait like this. He had a good mind to leave and teach her a lesson.

He was furious as well as hurt when the last visitors filed out of her dressing-room. More than an hour he'd been standing there, waiting . . .

He knocked.

A bony wrinkle-faced woman opened the door. She was shabbily dressed, did not even wear a maid's uniform. Very poor form, he thought, for a prima donna to have such a slattern around . . .

"The *signorina*, she says you wait," blurted out the slattern in an English on a par with that of her mistress. "In twenty minutes you come again, *si?*"

Before he could protest the door was shut softly but firmly in his face.

Outrageous! . . . Miss Salla had a magnificent voice, her kisses were in a class by themselves, but her manners were appalling.

"Appalling!" he repeated half-aloud to himself.

He was still debating whether he should go and teach her a lesson when the dressing-room door opened again. Maria Salla was standing before her mirror straightening the collar of her evening wrap.

"I am so-oo happy you come!" she cried over her shoulder, as though his presence came to her as a complete surprise. She spoke in that theatrical, insincere tone of welcome actresses reserve for perfect strangers. Absently she held out her hand for him to kiss, withdrew in a swift retracting gesture and returned to her mirror. "Next time you don't send roses, no? All the men they send roses. You send something else, *si?*"

The gall, the effrontery of that girl! . . . What made her think there'd ever be a next time? . . . But before he could think of a witty and scathing retort she turned to him, took his arm and with an enchanting smile said, "Now you take me to the dinner, *si?*"

Ten times that evening he wanted to rise, stalk away and never see her again. She had a way of infuriating him, pricking his vanity, scraping his nerves with an intonation, a mocking glance. Then she would give him a look of such caressing intensity, laden with such promise of love that his heart would skip a beat. It was maddening. Perhaps Karl had been right after all . . .

While they sipped their demi-tasses she led the conversation to the subject of athletics. The previous year the high-wheeled velocipede had burst on the sporting horizon and become the rage. She said how much she enjoyed her morning rides.

"Maybe you know how to ride on the velocipede, *si?*" she asked in that lazy drawl of hers.

"No, I don't," he said crossly. "And I am not planning to learn."

"Maybe you have the fear?" she purred, raising her cup to her lips and peering at him through the filigree of her lashes. "Many people have the fear of the velocipede."

"No, I don't have the fear, as you say," he snapped back. "I think it's a ridiculous contraption, that's all."

"Maybe you have not the ability?" she went on with that

unhurried persistence that he had noticed was an exasperating trait of her character. " Only very good sportsmen can keep the equilibrium on the velocipede. Maybe you fall with the face on the ground?" Her words trailed in a faint giggle.

" I would not fall with the face on the ground," he retorted hotly. There was nothing difficult about riding a velocipede. A lot of stupid people rode them. " And let me tell you," he added with barbed irony, " they look perfectly ridiculous."

She pleaded and coaxed, became insinuating, sarcastic and downright scurrilous. He remained adamant. He liked sports as well as anyone, he declared. He swam and rode rather well, he was good at croquet and all lawn games. " But I am not going to climb on one of those machines and nothing you can say will make me change my mind."

Next morning in a sunflecked deserted alley of Hyde Park, he still had not changed his mind. No, he hadn't and he was telling her so as she helped him climb on " one of those machines." She was a wonderful teacher. Patient, kind, methodical. Her eyes were full of tender glints and she never ceased praising his bravery, complimenting him on his equilibrium. Whenever he fell from the unwieldy vehicle she ran to his side, held him in her arms, smoothed his tousled hair into place and wheedled him back on to the saddle. By morning's end he could stay up in precarious equilibrium for brief periods of time, and they rode side by side, laughing like happy youngsters.

He saw much of Maria during the following days. She loved his company, she said, but all impulse to kiss him seemed to have gone out of her. " You are like a *ratello*, a brother, to me," she informed him. All her life, she explained, she had wanted a *ratello*. Her first day's kiss had not prepared him for this sudden twist in their relationship, but he did not dissuade her. She was, he had observed, a girl of many moods, and it was wise not to go contrary to them. Had she looked upon him as a father, he would have pretended to agree. He merely hoped she'd soon return to more rewarding feelings.

Her notions of brother-sister relationships were hazy, he found, and free from prejudices. Affection, she told him one day, was based on trust, and her trust in him was complete. During their drives home after her performances at Covent Garden she would snuggle against him, her sleepy trusting head on his shoulder. He would feel the gentle swaying of her body against his, now and then a jostle would tighten her arm around his neck. It took all his willpower to remain the brother she trusted him to be.

The days grew warmer. They went punting on the Thames, her hand trailing in the water as they glided alongside the shady banks. Twice they drove out of London in her blue victoria and picnicked in well-hidden sylvan retreats. After lunch they lay side by side on the grass, quiet and somnolent, gazing at the patches of blue sky through the foliage, listening to the twitter of birds high above their heads. She would fall asleep, cuddled against him with the abandon of a child, her lips brushing his ear.

As swiftly as it had come her sisterly mood disappeared one morning as they were riding through the Mall. They made a handsome pair and people turned in their saddles to watch them pass by. At a curve of the alley he found himself looking straight at the Marchioness. He immediately recognised the soft oscillation of her hips, the slight rocking of her upper body. As usual she was alone, aloof and arrogant, followed by a liveried groom. Their eyes met, hers strangely compelling in their fleeting glance. Time to salute—a lift of his shiny top hat, a bow, a smile . . . She gave him an almost imperceptible, furtive nod of acknowledgment, a flutter of eyelashes. Then she was gone. It had lasted only a few seconds. He turned around, aware of a laboured, angry breathing at his side. Maria was glaring at him through eyes that had become hard glittering stones.

" Maledetto!" she hissed under her breath. " You make the love with the look to that woman!"

" I? . . . Why, I merely——"

" And she makes the appointment with the smile . . . You think I don't see but I see everything . . ." She was trembling from head to foot, choking with jealous rage. Her eyes had turned amber. Panthers about to spring must have eyes like that, he thought. " You think I don't see your eyes go under her skirt . . ."

" But darling, I swear——"

" You swear big lies, like all the men. You are a pig! Yes, a pig!" she repeated. " A snake, a toad, a maledetto." The last word was sucked in a swish of her riding crop. Her horse reared with a neighing of pain and darted off at lightning speed.

He plunged after her in hot pursuit. Their mad galloping sowed panic in the sedate bridle path. Two dignified sportsmen in top hats toppled from their velocipedes at the sound of the thundering hooves. At last he managed to jerk the reins from Maria's hand and bring her foaming mount to a halt. She flipped him a glance of undiluted hatred, but they were both out of breath, drenched with perspiration and too angry to talk. They did not speak until they were back at her house.

As she entered into the drawing-room she flung her tricorn hat across the room, snatched a graceful porcelain from a small round table and hurled it at Felix, missing by inches.

" Are you trying to murder me?" he asked.

"Yes," she said through clenched teeth. Her roving eye stopped on a lovely Dresden candlestick. "I want to kill you." As she spoke the candlestick whisked by his ear and went crashing against the wall.

He caught her wrist as she was reaching for another missile. Brutally he pulled her to him. "I thought we were brother and sister," he said.

To this she replied by kicking his shin and biting his hand, all in one motion. They fell into a wrestle. He found she had neither training nor sportsmanship. She fought to hurt and did not care about ethics. Her hair had come undone, the bodice of her riding habit had burst open. With astounding speed she pinched, kicked and scratched, all the time spitting insults at him in an Italian dialect he did not understand.

Then suddenly she surrendered, pressed herself against him, sobbing. "*E perchè ti voglio bene*," she said in a whisper of shame, her cheek against his chest.

"What does it mean?"

"Because I love you." She looked at him through troubled eyes. "Never before I love a man. Always the man he loves me . . . All my life I have the fear to love because love gives much pain." She paused and her face winced with anguish. "Maybe it is better you go," she said, so low he almost did not hear. "Maybe it is better for you. Also better for me."

He smiled, patted her cheek with the indulgent tolerance of the man who knows himself loved. How could she speak like this, how could she suggest such a thing? He had a benefit concert to give. "Remember the poor little Silesian *bambini*?" he teased, kissing her hair.

Yes, she remembered them. She would give a benefit performance at Covent Garden. Much money it would bring, much more than his concert. She would give two, three benefit performances for the Silesian *bambini*. "But you go, *si?*" Now there was entreating urgency in her voice. "You go quick."

He chuckled softly, a little vexed by her remark about the money that her benefit performance would bring. Of course Covent Garden was much larger than the Argyll Rooms, and no doubt more people would want to hear her sing than watch him conduct the Philharmonic. But the concert had already been announced—July 13th, in the afternoon. "So you see, darling, even if I wanted to," he said, lifting her chin and leaning down, "I couldn't go away now."

An odd look flashed in her eyes. "Maybe you regret . . ." she murmured.

Like a red ripe fruit her mouth opened. She raised herself on

her toes and he felt her body grow tense and curve into his, as her
kiss rose from her heart to her lips.

With that kiss a new Maria came into being—a creature of
infinite complexity, seductiveness and deceit who seemed to have
flown out of Hell for the sole purpose of driving him mad.

Used to women's advances and eager surrenders he had come to
look upon the Game of Love as an amiable but monotonous
diversion. She proceeded to correct this misconception. In addition
to her spectacular physical assets, she possessed a genius for bewitch-
ment. She made full use of it. She initiated him into the exquisite
torments of love. With unerring skill she inflamed his desire to make
the denial of herself more cruel. He knew she could look like a
Della Robbia angel, he discovered she could also look like a whore.
Her limited vocabulary proved adequate to express her maidenly
protests as well as the most wanton suggestions.

The results of this strategy were prompt and devastating. From
being loved he became for the first time in his life amorous. He lost
his gift of restful slumber. His judgment grew foggy, his will-
power dwindled to naught. The hairshirt of unrequited desire kept
him in a permanent state of restlessness. He was both happier and
more miserable than ever in his life. He had reached the stage when
the victim adores his tormentor. Hating Maria he could not bear
the thought of giving her up. He found his new condition exciting
as well as exhausting.

He found it also extremely expensive. Apparently Maria had
made up her mind to wipe out his sizeable balance at Rothschild's
and leave him penniless even before his concert, barely three weeks
away.

It began with a horse. They were riding through Hyde Park one
morning when she declared that his horse had the tired and stupid
look of all rented horses. She felt much shame, she went on, to be
seen with a gentleman who rode such a tired and stupid-looking
horse. Especially when the gentleman happened to be the famous
Signor Mendelssohn, who, as everybody knew, was very rich.
Feebly he remonstrated that it seemed rather extravagant to buy a
horse for the short time he still had to remain in London. To this
she replied that far from being an extravagance, the purchase of
a horse was a shrewd investment.

"You see, *carino*," she explained craftily, "you save the hiring
money."

In his depleted mental condition this argument appeared to
him irrefutable. He went to the bank, withdrew a substantial sum
of money and bought a horse. The dealer confirmed everything

Maria had said. " I know, sir, it seems like a good bit of money,"
he said, patting Rosina on the neck, " but in the end the best is the
cheapest. You won't have any trouble selling her when you leave.
Probably make a handsome profit, too."

When she saw Rosina, Maria declared that the horse looked
fine, but now it was about Felix's clothes that she felt shame.

" Really?" he said, taken aback. " They come from the best
tailor in Berlin."

That was just it. In Berlin they knew not how to cut the clothes
for the men. " Only here," she said. She no longer could be seen
with a gentleman in such ridiculous clothes. Besides it was not a
useless expenditure since the London fashions for the men they
were the best everywhere. " Even when you are back in Berlin you
look good in the London clothes."

Karl gave him the address of his tailor. He had refrained from
further reproaches or warnings. Now and then he would look at
his friend with a baleful, hopeless expression in his bulging eyes,
but he kept his thoughts to himself. " Here it is. He is expensive
but good. Don't mention my name, if you please."

In Savile Row Felix was duly metamorphosed into a London
dandy. He stood a long time before a full-length mirror and learned
that lapels were a little wider this year and puce was the season's
colour. Boots were square-toed and beavers came a trifle lower.
He felt rather awkward when he appeared in his new English
clothes. Maria gasped, clasped her hands—and talked of something
else.

At the bank the cashier glanced at his balance with visible concern but silently counted the money out. The night before, Felix
had written his father, explaining the exigencies of London's social
life. Surely he'd understand.

" How's your money lasting?" asked Karl several days later.
He read the answer to his question in Felix's dejected look. " No
letter from your father yet?"

" No. Perhaps he's written directly to the bank," said Felix with
little hope.

" Parents are notoriously callous towards their children's money
problems." A silence fell between the two friends. Then Karl let
out a sigh. " Most women put an exaggerated value on their virtue,
even those who have practically none at all."

" If you're alluding to Maria, you're wrong," said Felix. " She
isn't mercenary, merely extravagant. She loves me, I think—but
she's struggling with herself."

It was true. Many times she had seemed on the verge of surrender. Her eyes softened, her mouth clung to his. She turned limp
and acquiescent, then by a supreme effort she caught herself and

B.D.   C

sent him home in the paleness of dawn, dazed and aching with unsatisfied desire.

"Some women have been known to struggle with themselves for years," said Karl with wry sympathy. "For your sake I hope passion gets the upper hand—soon."

Yes, soon, Felix echoed in his mind. Time was growing short. The benefit concert was scheduled for the following week. With a spasm of regret he recalled her silly "sister" period, the innocent picnics, the happy leisurely June days that could have been filled with love and had been wasted.

"I don't understand women," he said with a defeated shrug.

A slow smile, both ironical and wistful, slid over Karl's face. "That's what I say each time a woman declines to do what I'd like her to do. But cheer up, Felix. Nobody understands women. The greatest minds have tried and given up. Perhaps there is nothing to understand."

Felix saw little of Maria during the following days. She was rehearsing a new opera, and his time was taken up with rehearsals. It was good to be once again among musicians, to forget Maria for a moment. Music did not hurt. It cleansed and comforted. The love of music brought peace and light into your soul and made you forget the other kind of love that could be so cruel. Yes, Maria had taught him a lesson. She had bruised his ego, deflated his cockiness. For this he was grateful to her. Never again would he think that love was just an amiable, monotonous game. This was about all he would bring back from his journey to London. A lesson—and a scar.

He stopped at the bank in the forlorn hope his father might have sent another letter of credit. Perhaps he might be able to negotiate a loan. After all, Herr Rothschild was a friend of the family, he had been enthusiastic after the first concert. And he seemed such an understanding man.

At once he was introduced into the banker's office.

"I've just received a letter from your father," began Nathan Rothschild.

Felix's face brightened. "Really? . . . I thought he might write directly to you. I explained the situation to him. Living is so expensive in London."

"It is, isn't it?" said the banker, a teasing glint in his searching eyes. "And horses do eat like horses, don't they?" He took the letter from his desk. "Would you like me to read what your father says?"

Something in the banker's tone warned Felix. His heart sank. "You needn't, Herr Rothschild. I can guess. My father tells you that I am an incorrigible spendthrift, that he gave me ample funds and asks you not to advance me a single penny."

"You have remarkable insight into your father's mind," said the banker. "I should have been delighted to advance you money, but——"

"I understand and I thank you just the same," said Felix, getting up. "Parents sometimes forget they too were young once . . . It's all right. I'll manage somehow."

"One always does at your age," said the banker with a wistful smile.

On the even of the concert Maria asked Felix to take her to supper after her performance at Covent Garden. And because she had not seen him for two days and he would soon be leaving, she suggested they take a private dining-room. Once this suggestion would have sent his heart leaping in his chest, now he merely accepted it as another of her caprices.

It was a small thickly-carpeted room with the dining-table in the centre and. in a corner under a potted palm, an unusually large divan. The champagne was superb, the service unobtrusive.

They spoke little during dinner. Never had she looked so beautiful or so desirable, and again he marvelled at the endless variety of her expressions. Around her neck hung a single emerald of extraordinary size and beauty he had never noticed before. In the candlelight her eyes were chartreuse. He thought he read in them some secret plea, a regret for things that could have been.

"Some day you understand," she said, taking his hand.

"Understand what?" he said, pretending surprise. "I had a wonderful time."

"You tell big lies," she said quietly. Her whisper barely rippled the silence of the room. "Soon you marry a fine girl, you have fine children——"

"I know. Like the poor Silesian *bambini*." He laughed.

His attempt at gaiety did not succeed. Her eyes remained soft and grave, her voice unchanged. "Then you see it is better that way," she said.

"Fine. Let's drink to that." He raised his champagne glass, took a sip and leaned forward across the table. "By the way this is a magnificent stone," he said, squinting at the emerald.

"I buy it in Milano when I make the début at La Scala," she said. "You know Milano?"

Did he know Milano? . . . Of course he knew Milano and its wonderful Duomo that seemed made of tattered lace. And Florence and Naples and Amalfi and Rome . . . Why, he knew Italy better than his own country. He'd even had his portrait painted in Rome by Horace Vernet at the Villa Medici. He loved Italy! The narrow *vincoli*, the bare-footed *bambini*, the beggars, the old churches, the grand *palazzi*. The dirt, the sunniness, the beauty, the timelessness that was Italy. . . .

"You like Italian cooking, no?" she asked when he finished talking.

"Of course, I do!" Everyone loved Italian cooking. *Pizza, past' asciutta, risotto*, he loved it all . . . But Italian cooking was tricky. It called for great ability, great *savoir-faire* . . .

Patiently she waited, knowing he was prattling on to relieve the tension of his nerves, escape a moment his resentment, his dejection at the disappointing denouement of their relationship.

"Maybe to-morrow I cook Italian dinner for you, *si?*" she said. "When I see you the first time I say maybe I cook for you some day, remember? . . . To-morrow, after the concert, you come to my house and I cook Venetian dish for you, *si?*"

When Felix came home that evening he noticed a strip of light under Karl's door. Noiselessly he peered in and was met by a melancholy sight. In his nightshirt and tasselled nightcap the third secretary of the Hanover Legation was sitting up in bed, mournfully staring at the coverlet.

"Why aren't you asleep?" asked Felix, sitting on the edge of the bed.

Karl let out a lugubrious sigh. "You're looking at a man in the throes of emotional and financial debacle," he announced with solemnity. "This morning my banker informed me that my account was overdrawn above and beyond all reasonable limits. Then this evening Suzy, the woman I love, expressed the wish that I stay away from her. Preferably for ever. Although not a surprise, this came nevertheless as a great blow to me." He took a long wheezing breath and turned his bulbous eyes on his friend. "But let's not discuss my sorrows. How's the elusive prima donna?"

"She was very sweet to-night," said Felix quietly. "I've never seen her look so beautiful. She wants me to spend my last evening in London with her to-morrow. She's going to cook an Italian dinner for me."

"How touching!" cried his friend with emotion. "Women are wonderful! You ruin yourselves for them, then they cook a plate of spaghetti for you and call it even! To-morrow, when every duchess in London will be panting to have you at dinner, you'll be struggling with a heap of greasy, slimy, slithery *tagliarini* in the company of a pretty girl who's made a fool of you."

He reached for his snuff box on the nightstand. "Cheer up, Felix. You are not really in love with her. It's your pride that's hurt. I was like you but after a few times you get used to it. You'll see it hurts less and less. Amazing how alike two women of the same age can look with their faces buried in the pillow . . ."

" You are a cynic," said Felix, getting up. " Good night."

" Oh, by the way," Karl called after him, " you know of course that she has a lover, don't you?"

Felix froze in his steps, then slowly turned to his friend. " I don't believe it. It's not true," he said in a toneless voice.

" But it is," said Karl, pressing the snuff to his nose and brushing tobacco specks off his shirt front. " He came to see me this afternoon. Awfully nice chap. Frightfully rich. He gave her an emerald."

It was towards the end of the concert, as he was conducting the last movement of his symphony, that Felix decided that Karl was right. One shouldn't take women seriously. Since learning about Maria's deceitfulness, every hour had been a claw of time bedding itself into his flesh. Now he had enough of it. All this pain, this bewilderment, this agony of jealousy—all this was ridiculous. Maria was a vixen with the morals of a minx, incapable of love, truth or common decency. She had lied to him from the very first, toyed with him and cost him a lot of money. The thing to do about it was forget it all and never, never again believe another woman. To-night, after dinner—the famous home-cooked Italian dinner—he would take her in his arms and tell her he'd known all the time about her lover and her lies, and then with a light kiss and an amused chuckle he would bid her adieu.

The clatter of applause brought him back to the reality of the concert, the Argyll Rooms, the distinguished and enthusiastic audience. During the short reception that followed he forgot the haunting thoughts of Maria. He smiled and bowed, he expressed his thanks and kissed ladies' hands, declined numberless invitations and promised to return to London the following year.

In the coolness of the late afternoon he drove home with his friend Karl. " More than three hundred guineas will be sent to the Silesians," he exclaimed as they were nearing Bury Street. " It is a great satisfaction to work for charity."

" Perhaps you could give another concert for my benefit?" ventured Karl. " My condition is as desperate as that of any Silesian."

" Where's your pride?" said Felix in a tone of rebuke.

" Nowhere at the moment. But give me some money, and I'll be the proudest of men."

Felix had started packing and was giving him instructions for the sale of Rosina when there was a knock at the door. Karl's manservant ushered in a tall side-whiskered gentleman of impressive mien.

"Herr Mendelssohn?" he asked with awesome formality.

"Yes?" said Felix who somehow mistook him for a creditor.

"Herr Felix Mendelssohn?"

"Yes. What is it?"

The gentleman frowned. With the same Olympian unctuousness he gave his name, declared his titles and informed Felix that Her Gracious Majesty wished to see him.

"Now?" gasped Felix, aghast. In two hours he was due at Maria's.

"Now," nodded the court messenger with inexorable finality.

During the brief ride in the royal-crested carriage to Buckingham Palace, Felix inquired how long Her Gracious Majesty was likely to require his presence. In a tone of astral condescension the gentleman let fall from barely moving lips the information that Her Majesty's time was of such incalculable value, her occupations of such utmost importance that royal audiences rarely lasted more than a few minutes.

At the Palace's entrance Felix was entrusted, like a delicate parcel, to a white-stockinged, red-and-gold liveried footman of almost pontifical solemnity. Through deserted, oppressively gilded and mirrored saloons he was led to a small, almost intimate room where the young queen sat bent over her needle-point, chatting spiritedly with her ladies-in-waiting.

As the door opened, she raised her cornflower eyes and looked smilingly at Felix. Her smile enchanted him, it had a unique quality of shyness and regal dignity. She held out her hand and apologised for "abducting" him. His presence, she explained, afforded her ladies and herself an extreme pleasure, but it would be a delightful surprise to His Royal Highness, who was an ardent music lover and a great admirer of his. His Royal Highness was not at the Palace at the moment, but would soon return. She then introduced him to the various ladies of her entourage. As he bowed his way among them he sent a silent prayer that His Royal Highness would soon come home. The Marchioness of Dorsythe flitted him a careful smile as he bent over her hand and he caught a swift but eloquent flutter of her long lashes.

"And now, Herr Mendelssohn," said the Queen, "won't you please play for us?"

He did. Each short piece was greeted by the most flattering comments. Requests became more pressing and numerous as time went by. With a smile he obliged, glancing with growing uneasiness at the ornate clock on the chimney mantel. Still no Royal Highness! Where, oh, where could His Highness be? . . . Lights were brought in, and in the flicker of candles the room grew more intimate. So did the Queen and her ladies. They now sat in a circle around the piano, smiling, admiring, insatiable. The clock chimed seven, then eight. Felix still played on, but his mind wandered away from the music. Maria would be beside herself . . . This was torture. Would His Highness ever come? Hadn't Her Gracious Majesty anything better to do than listen to music? No prime minister calling on urgent business, no official function, no threat of revolt anywhere in the Empire? . . . On the mantel the clock dripped raindrops of time . . .

At long last Prince Albert came in. With him was a tall gentleman of great distinction and several years his elder. Both were in civilian clothes. At their entrance the ladies-in-waiting rose and performed expert curtsies. With consummate grace the Prince kissed the Queen's hand, bowed to the ladies and expressed his delighted surprise at finding Herr Mendelssohn. Felix was then presented to the other gentleman who had been watching him with smiling interest and turned out to be His Majesty Friedrich Augustus the Second, King of Saxony.

"Perhaps you will come to Saxony some day?" said the King with a gracious smile. "Have you heard of the Gewandhaus Orchestra of Leipzig?"

"Of course, Your Majesty."

But already Prince Albert was breaking in. "Herr Mendelssohn will perhaps conduct the Gewandhaus Orchestra some day," he declared, rubbing his hands. "but now let's have some *goot Musik*."

Everyone seemed to be in the highest spirits. The impromptu musicale was an unexpected diversion from the dull routine of court life. With leaden heart and flying fingers Felix galloped through several of his compositions. Then the Queen announced she would sing one of Herr Mendelssohn's songs. But somehow the song could not be found. It had already been packed for her forthcoming sojourn at Windsor Castle, she was informed. "Well, have it unpacked," she commanded in a tone of sudden withering authority. For a while the Palace was a-flutter with footmen rushing in all directions. At last the song was produced. The Queen sang in a slight but pleasant voice. Felix did not dare look at the clock any more.

Finally the concert came to an end. Her Majesty inquired if Felix wished to be driven back home.

"Only to Half Moon Street, Your Majesty. I am to meet a friend of mine there." For good measure he added, "An old friend of my family. We went to school together."

The Queen was about to order a carriage when the Marchioness remarked that Half Moon Street was on her way home. With the

Queen's permission she would be glad to drive Herr Mendelssohn to his old friend's home.*

It was one of those summer nights when the sky turned deep purple instead of black. A soft breeze trailed over their faces like an impalpable yet caressing hand. They drove in silence for a while, then the Marchioness took his hand. Why didn't he want to come to the Italian villa? she asked in a trembling whisper. "You'd love it there . . ." No doubt he would, he replied. The olive trees, the secluded coves, the cicadas—he would love it all, but important business awaited him in Berlin. He had stayed too long in London. . . .

As the carriage entered Half Moon Street, she crept closer to him. "At least give me one kiss," she murmured. Again he felt that apprehension of disaster he had already experienced in her house. He leaned down to kiss her and felt himself sinking into a vortex. Her arms tightened around his neck, her lips clamped to his like hungry leeches. It was a long, unhappy kiss. Dimly he heard a clatter of shutters furiously slammed shut and became aware that the carriage had been standing still under Maria's window. Swiftly he extricated himself and leaped out.

Cautiously he waited for the clip-clop of hoofbeats to fade away before climbing the stairs. He pulled the bell, but no sound came from the house. He rang again. The clapping sound hammered the night a few times, then died. He ran down to the street. Light filtered through the shutters of her room. She was upstairs . . . He called her name. Softly at first, then more loudly.

A sudden blind rage engulfed him. She wasn't going to let him explain, she wasn't going to tell him good-bye. He would leave London without seeing her. His rage swelled into fury. She had lied to him and made a fool of him and now she was going to let him go without a word. She would even cheat him of that silly dinner she had promised. Strangely this hurt him most of all. He didn't mind the horse, the trunkful of clothes, but he wasn't going to let her swindle him out of that dinner. He wanted nothing else from her, but he wanted that.

"Maria!" he called a third time. "Please, Maria . . .!"

As his cry rose to the window he knew she would not answer. He stood there panting, craning his neck, seeking some means to get into the house. In a flash he remembered the door under the steps. Already he was there turning the knob. In a gust of rapture he felt the door slide open. He rushed inside, ran through the basement, climbed the stairs three at a time. As he neared her bedroom he heard the muted scuffle of her footsteps rushing towards the door, shoved it open before she could lock it.

* On this occasion the Queen gave Felix a ring which he wore all his life.

She stood there, as if nailed to the floor, glaring at him with a rage equal to his own.

"Maybe you think I am a fool?" She spat the words through clenched teeth. "Maybe you think I don't see you kiss that woman?"

Yesterday he would have stopped, tried to explain. To-night he did not care what she thought, what she had seen. He gripped her shoulders, pulled her to him. His mouth found hers. Again she fought with unskilled fury, her face contorted behind the swinging, dishevelled hair. He did not feel her blows, shielded by his anger. Again and again he kissed her, bruising her into submission. Locked in hostile embrace they stumbled over to the bed. In gasping spurts he told her about playing for the Queen, being delayed against his will. She did not care about that. Only the kiss, that kiss downstairs in the carriage. "You cannot lie this time . . . I see you with my eyes . . ."

Suddenly he was laughing. "And what right have you to be jealous?" Yes, what about her lover? And the emerald? . . . "Bought it in Milano, didn't you?"

"You know?" There was relief, almost joy in her voice. "I am glad . . ." He felt her body soften, almost deliquesce into his arms. Now it was her mouth that sought to cover his own, breathing the words on his lips. "To-morrow I tell everything . . . We laugh." Then in a sigh of surrender she said, "*Tu sei troppo orte . . .*"

"Speak English," he said, shaking her angrily.

"You are too strong," she said. A smile drifted across her face. Her limbs turned limp, relaxed into acquiescence. "Long time I fight because I have much fear of love . . . But now I fight no more."

Then all was silent in the room. On the round small table the candle flame pulsed and throbbed at the end of the wick.

A week later Felix awoke in a cheerful maple-furnished bedroom of a country inn, somewhere in Surrey. In the open window hung a pale blue sheet of sky. Now and then a puff of breeze wafted in, billowing the organdy curtains, bringing the perfume of yellow climbing roses and the call from the world of sunshine and green foliage outside. It was like awakening in Heaven, some rustic suburb of Heaven for lovers only.

Maria lay at his side sleeping with one side of her face pressed against his bare chest, like a figure in a bas-relief. The rest of her was spread hither and yon. Although they fell asleep, limbs entwined and clinging to each other, by morning he always discovered her like this. She unfurled in her sleep like those flowers that open at night. This was one of the things he had learned about

her since they had fled London and said good-bye to the world of
conventions, contracts and common sense.

He also learned that she awoke swiftly, bright-eyed and full of
mischief. Her sensuality was, like her faith, total, naïve and
unorthodox. Towards God, the angels and the saints she observed
a respectful, distant reserve. But with the Virgin, represented by a
small coloured plaster statue of the Madonna della Salute, she was
on terms of the greatest intimacy. The figurine was her most
treasured possession. Often she held it in her hands, speaking to it
in pleading whispers or angry reproachful tones, according to the
mood of the moment, and always in the liquid, almost unintelligible
Venetian patois.

Gently he caressed her hair, trailed his fingertips over her bare
shoulder with the tranquil assurance of undisputed ownership.
She was his, she had told him a hundred times, his to do with whatever he wanted. For instance, he could beat her, if he felt like it.
That was perfectly all right. In Venice, where she was born, a man,
if he was loved, had the immemorial right to slap the woman he
loved. No argument about that. He could also take her whenever
the urge was upon him, whatever the place or the hour. He was
the *padrone*, the master. She had explained this to him at great
length. She belonged to him and her mission was to keep him
happy. On the other hand, if she gave him pleasure and kept him
in good spirits, then he must be sweet to her, give her many kisses
and words of love and let her have her way about most things.

This arrangement had proved enormously successful. She had
kept him happy and he had let her do whatever she wanted. And
the first thing she wanted was to get out of London. She told him
so that first morning in her bedroom at Half Moon Street. "You
and me, we go away and never come back, *si?* she said, kissing him
somewhere around the chin. Dimly he remembered that she had a
contract and that his place was reserved on the afternoon coach to
Dover. "Besides," he sighed, kissing her throat, "I haven't any
money. I've spent it all and my father will not send me any."

She shrugged with scorn. "Money!" she snorted. "I have
money. Plenty."

He protested that never would he go to the country on her
money. It was undignified, it was ungentlemanly. She looked at
him with surprise. What was this business about being "ungentlemanly?" *Maledetto!* . . . He was the man she loved, *no?* Well,
then that was enough. She cared nothing, less than nothing, whether
or not he was a gentleman. But he did; he was a man of honour,
and a man of honour didn't go to the country on a woman's money.
Then she hit on an idea. "In the country you write an opera, *si?*
I sing in the opera you write. We earn much money, thousands of

guineas. Then you give me back the money." At once everything seemed clear and proper. An advance on the opera he was going to write—a perfectly legitimate business transaction. If Rossini could write *Il Barbiere di Siviglia* in thirteen days, he, Felix Mendelssohn, could certainly dash off an opera in a few weeks. With Maria in the title rôle it would be a triumph. Money would pour in, and wouldn't Father be surprised? "But, darling," he said, remembering her contract, "how can we go to the country? You have signed a contract with Sir George." She shrugged. When she signed the *contratto*, she explained, she hadn't been in love. Now she was in love and therefore the *contratto*, it was broken. That's all there was to it. "The love is like death, it always comes first." Feebly he spoke about honour, the respect of the given word. Again she looked at him in wonder. Honour? What was this foolish talk about honour? She was in love, she wanted to go to the country with him, no? When one was in love, the honour it disappeared. Besides, *il signor* Smart, he was such a nice man, he had such a big heart, surely he would understand it was more important for her to be with the man she loved somewhere in the country where the birds sang and the flowers bloomed than at Covent Garden singing some stupid opera . . . While speaking she stippled his face with little puckering kisses. By the time she was through he was convinced.

Karl, of course, felt somewhat differently about the whole thing. But he merely shook his head. "Oh, the madness of it all . . .!" he sighed enviously. "The disarming absurdity of youth, the divine idiocy of love! . . . So you're going to write an opera!" But he understood. He even managed to scrape fifty pounds together. Good, wonderful Karl!

And so they had fled like two criminals and come to this little inn where they had spent a week of heavenly bliss. And now another happy day was waiting for them.

With a smile he looked about the room. His eyes rested on the table near the window. It was stacked with the reams of music paper she had bought for him. Enough paper for several operas. He hadn't as yet written a single note, but soon, very soon, perhaps to-day, he would settle down to work.

Maria stirred and he saw that she was awake. "Good morning, darling." He was smiling. "And stop tickling me, will you?"

Then her lips were close to his, her eyes staring into his own—clear, wide, already coaxing. "I love you," she murmured. "You love me, no?"

"Of course I do."

"Then why don't you say? Love is like a plant, it must have water. The words of love are the water for such a plant."

And so he told her he loved her and she asked how much and he said very much and she asked why and he said he loved everything about her and she said he was a liar. He said he wasn't and she said he was and they argued. As they argued, blood started racing in their veins, and the debate degenerated into a mêlée of lips and hands. Then after a while she said, " To-day I go and look for the house."

" What house?" he protested weakly. " We don't need a house, we're perfectly happy here."

Yes, but there were other people at the inn, and how could he write the music for the opera in such a place? No, no, he couldn't . . . He thought he could but she knew he couldn't. So she would go and find a little house where they would be all by themselves. There he would write the opera. No, she did not want him to come. She wanted to surprise him.

Late that afternoon she returned, a smile of triumph on her face. She had found the house. It was big, old and very cheap. More than that she would not say. He must see it for himself.

A moment later they were rolling through shady sweet-smelling lanes. In the sky clouds were turning pink. Over the countryside hung the stillness of sunset. At the turn of the road they came upon it.

" There!" she said, waving at Carrington Castle. " You like it, no?"

Carrington Castle was smaller than Windsor, but not much. Built in the eleventh century, it had kept the pristine beauty of its original architecture. A fortified town more than a mere castle, it consisted, besides the huge main house, of a jumble of turreted dungeons and crenellated towers, bastions and demi-bastions, merlons and casemates, barbicans and baracoons—all built of tremendous hand-hewn stones, now mossy with age and specked with narrow Gothic stained-glass windows. Around the whole thing ran a wide moat filled with stagnant glassy water, deep green in colour, that reflected the high rampart wall. The sole entrance to Carrington Castle was by a draw-bridge held over the moat by massive rusty chains.

" It is only two hundred guineas the month," she explained as Felix remained silent and slack-mouthed, as if struck by lightning.

In a rush of words she explained how she had come across such a bargain. Before leaving for Florence twelve years ago the Earl of Carrington had placed the castle for sale or rent. Strange as it may seen, no one had yet come forth to pick up this pearl of medieval architecture. This explained why Maria had been able to rent it for so little money. And for only two hundred more guineas a month they could have the skeleton staff of thirty-two servants that assured the barest maintenance of the manor.

"Here you have the inspiration for the opera," she said excitedly. "Here you write beautiful music."

And they could move in immediately. She had attended to all money matters, but being naturally cautious, she had rented the castle for three months only. With the staff, naturally.

He looked at her, shaking his head in speechless astonishment. Twelve hundred guineas! She had paid twelve hundred guineas for this miniature Carcassonne.

A silence fell.

Suddenly she was clutching his arm, looking at him, tears rushing to her eyes. "I see on your face you think I am very stupid," she said in a trembling whisper. "You think I am *un asino*, a donkey. But you don't understand. In Venice when I am a little girl, very poor, with no shoes, I always think of some day I live in a big castle with my prince . . . I have my prince——"

"And now you have your castle." He smiled, leaning down to kiss her. He understood. She was living a childhood dream and the castle was part of it. "We'll be very happy in our new home."

They moved in the next day. They slept in a large baldaquined bed in which almost every Queen of England had slept at one time or another and which had seen much history. The castle being devoid of any kind of plumbing, heating or lighting, Felix grew used to the hardships of medieval living. For his study Maria had selected the banquet hall. It was dim, damp and about the size of a small cathedral. An irremovable stench of stale cooking and rancid tallow hung like a fog, bringing the memory of feudal and riotous feasts. The gigantic crested fireplace gave out enormous billows of smoke and no heat at all. Since the windows were opaque with dust and too high to provide any light, Maria stole two huge *cierges* from the chapel and set them on Felix's working table, but their flames were six feet above the table and proved of small practical use. Felix, shivering in a bed blanket, declared his study perfect and announced he was ready to go to work.

As for Maria, her enthusiasm was a joy to behold. Every day she started on some new exploration through the castle, returning with thrilling stories of new dungeons, new secret passages, new mysterious culs-de-sac. One morning she got lost and inadvertently locked herself in the prison. Her howls pierced through the yard-thick walls and reached Felix who was running about his study to keep warm. It took him two hours to locate and rescue her. When at last she was in his arms, she sobbed from relief. Both had been much shaken by this episode and to release their inner tension they sat down on the pallet of straw. It was late in the afternoon when they came out of the jail.

She lost her taste for adventure and henceforth spent more time with him. They spoke about the opera he was going to write. One serious difficulty, he pointed out, was that he had no libretto.

"The libretto in all the operas it is always stupid," she observed. "So you write your own libretto."

He thought this an excellent idea. Now, for a subject . . . Here Maria proved most useful. Together they ransacked history, ancient and modern, mythology and the folklore of many nations. For a while he waxed enthusiastic over Fredegonde, Queen of the Franks, a beautiful and wicked servant woman who had filled King Chilperic with such uncontrollable lust that at her suggestion he had repudiated his first wife Audovera and strangled his second, Galswintha. Maria thought it would make a fine opera. One day she entered the banquet hall wearing a helmet and a mailshirt from the Carrington collection and peering over a heavy oversize shield, also from the castle's armoury. He burst out laughing, she burst out in tears. They wound up in each other's arms. Fredegonde was discarded.

A few days later she appeared as a very fetching Saint Genevieve on her way to call on Attila. She looked mightily seductive in her very plain, very filmy robe. This time he did not laugh. He pulled her to him, as Attila might have done, and they sang an impromptu duet—she pretending fright, he bellowing in a harsh baritone, rolling ferocious eyes and running dexterous hands over his visitor. Saint Genevieve, Felix's opera, died with this performance.

During the following fortnight Maria appeared successively as Catherine of Russia, the man-eating empress, Cleopatra, Helen of Troy, Joan of Arc, and Santa Barbara, the young and very attractive martyr. Felix did not write his opera, but they laughed a great deal. At times sudden flashes of sanity tore the veil of their rapture. They saw the absurdity of their predicament, the fragility of their love affair. Then they hugged each other with greater passion.

Meanwhile the thirty-two members of the staff wandered about the castle, invisible, their presence unfelt but for the amount of food they consumed. They kept out of sight, an easy matter in the castle. They kept out of sight even when Maria wanted one of them. In vain she rang the bell cords that hung down here and there on the walls. One day in desperation she rang the bronze bell which in the days of chivalry had called the Carrington men to arms. No one appeared. Careful inspection of the grounds and the castle proved fruitless. Carrington Castle was deserted except for a ninety-year-old retainer who was too weak to walk. In a voice trembling with age he revealed that the cook had taken offence at Maria's sharp bell-pulling and had left, taking with her all the valid members of the staff.

Bravely Maria prepared dinner that evening. It was not very good, but Felix pretended to enjoy it. For a few days she attempted the impossible and tried to keep house in the castle. Refusing Felix's help she carried pails of water from the courtyard well, gathered wood for the kitchen stove, puffed her cheeks and blew her precious breath to start a fire. Unsuccessful, she grew short tempered, then tired, then dejected. Watching Felix chew stoically and force one of her meals down his gullet, she would look at him across the table with big apologetic eyes and fight back her tears. Both lost weight. They did not lose their gaiety, but it became apprehensive. The veil of rapturous nonsense that enclosed their lives was now torn in many places. She grew pale and her nerves deteriorated. During a storm she burst, wild-eyed and dishevelled, into Felix's study crying that a ghost was running after her. Finally she admitted that perhaps it had been a mistake to rent Carrington Castle. Gently he agreed.

The evening before they left they went out for a walk on the crenellated parapet. The moon was full and cast pale silvery beams over the machiolation. After a while they sat on a granite slab. They remained silent for a long time, holding hands, feeling close and chaste, very small and a little lost.

Then for no reason she started talking and told him about her childhood in Venice.

It was a banal and pitiful story of poverty. Her father, Vittorio, was a gondolier. At fourteen Maria sold flowers at the corner of Palazzo Ducale, a favourite spot among tourists. Now and then one of them would take her as well as her flowers to his room, and that day she would bring home more money. Desperate poverty asks no questions and no questions were asked. " Mamma she looks sad but she says nothing. Papa he says nothing also but he goes to the *trattoria* and he drinks much wine."

One day as she was carolling her wares she was approached by an elderly gentleman. He had kindly eyes in an ugly face and asked her whether she would like to become a singer. She said yes and went with him to Milano. He was a famous singing teacher and for three years carefully trained her magnificent voice. Her sensational début at La Scala was his last joy; he died a week later. Abruptly she found herself rolling in money, the toast of Milano. She sent for Romola, a distant cousin of hers, who became her maid. She sent money home, thus unwittingly hastening her father's death. Paddling his gondola on a foggy winter night, Vittorio, drunk on his daughter's money, forgot to duck one of the innumerable Venice bridges. His head struck the stone with such an impact that he reeled back into the black waters of the canal where he quietly drowned. The gondola went on its stealthy way and was found three days later floating over the Adriatic in the direction of Trieste.

Henceforth Maria had lived an enchanted, wandering life, going from triumph to triumph, engaging in short-lived love affairs, squandering vast sums and pinching pennies, bewildered, uncaring, and secretly awaiting and dreading the coming of love.

"That is why I find you so hard," she said, turning her face to him. "I feel much fear because I see I fall too much in love with you."

"Is this why you made me spend all my money?" he asked with a teasing smile.

"Yes. I think perhaps you become angry with me and go away. But every night I pray the Madonna you stay."

"You little minx . . ." Their gaze caught in smiling embrace. "By the way," he said, breaking the spell, "how about the emerald? Who gave it to you?"

She laughed. "When I come to London I rent the house on Half Moon Street and in this way I meet him."

One of those chance encounters that could shatter a destiny . . . The owner of the house was a retired merchant, a wealthy sedate family man. By the time he finished showing her the house he was head over heels in love. Nothing like this had ever happened to him before. It showed in the flush of his cheeks, his glance, the embarrassment of his manner. She saw it, smiled, felt sorry for him. For one month he had possessed secretly, stealthily, the most desired woman in London. To her it meant nothing, to him it was heaven and hell, one of those middle-age passions that convulse a man's life. Then she had met Felix and instantly dismissed her lover. Dismissed him as casually as she had taken him. To the elderly man it had been nameless agony. Finally she had consented to see him once more and had seen the degradation that passion can inflict on a man. He had wept, begged, knelt before her. She had taken the emerald he was holding out to her and given nothing in return. He had walked out of the house, a broken ashen-faced old man.

"You must return that emerald at once," Felix said when she finished. "Do you hear, Maria? At once."

"The emerald?" She stared at him with that look of astonishment he knew so well. "I sell it before we leave London."

He looked at her, finding nothing to say. There was no trying to understand her . . . She was as she was. She had sold the stone so they could flee to the country together. The emerald had paid for the Carrington folly . . .

He felt her hand on his sleeve. " You still love me, no?" she said in a whisper of anguish.

Slowly he drew her to him, held her face between his hands. Yes, she was as she was and she loved him . . . Somewhere in London an old man was broken-hearted. She didn't care, she had forgotten. She was here, humble and tense with love, her lips waiting, already parted for his kiss . . . "Yes, I still love you. But I'm glad we're getting out of this place."

They were lucky. A few miles from the castle they found the cottage of their dreams. This time Felix approved. It had a thatch roof, a broken fence, a brook. And it was cheap, really cheap. He had finally settled on Esther as the subject of his opera and planned to work seriously. Maria plunged into an ecstasy of house cleaning. She scoured and she swept and she scrubbed; she performed with a song on her lips the most menial tasks. Because she was happy in her work she wanted him to share in both. " Please, *carino,* you help me move the bed, no? . . . Light of my heart, I can't reach the shelf of that cupboard . . . *Mio piccolo Felix,* maybe you give me the hand with the curtains, *si* . . ." Never had he seen her so happy, she was like a bird in spring. When she did not sing, she talked. Her mind, he discovered, had no bottom—anything that came into it fell on her tongue. He learned that the peace of the country did not necessarily mean peace at home.

Abruptly she remembered she was an opera singer. If she was going to sing Felix's opera she must practise. The air became alive with trills and vocalisations. He admired her singing but found it a deterrent to composing. Tactfully he mentioned this to her, and she was hurt and offended. " The people they pay much money to hear me sing, but you pay nothing and you are not content." For the first time she made some barbed remarks about composing. Of all the arts it was the most demanding and the least glamorous. A concert pianist—ah!—there was a mate for an opera singer. Both travelled, both performed. They were gipsies, happy nomads in the realm of art. A composer—pah!—he only sat and wrote. Anything—even beautiful singing—disturbed him.

It was their first quarrel and it ended in an orgy of remorse, self-reproaches and promises. To celebrate their reconciliation they walked down by the brook and made love on the grass.

Slowly, like a full-sailed caravel, summer was sliding by. Already the evening had an autumn languor. Maria kept her word. She not only stopped singing, she stopped talking. She tiptoed about. Occasionally he caught her eyes resting on him. If he suggested a walk she replied that nothing must take him away from his work. She would sit by his side, grimly silent, her hands on her lap.

" Come on," he would smile, " don't look so glum."

" I am chained to a composer." She would sigh and give him a houndlike long-suffering look. " All my life I stay like this."

Seeing no one, going nowhere, they had little to say to each other. They were talked out. As a substitute to conversation they made love. This side of their relationship was still intact. As they became aware that their foolish world of romance was crumbling about them, they sought shelter in the sombre fastness of sex. Their love-making grew more brutal, it assumed a quality of despair, an undertone of farewell. They emerged from their embraces only to find themselves farther apart, strangers with nothing in common but their desire. Like all unhappy lovers they soon discovered the sexual stimulus of quarrels. They squabbled for no reason but to make up and make love. Without gaiety they seized each other, bruised each other's flesh only to relapse into their respective alien worlds.

" I am not good for you," she said softly one morning. She looked tired. He knew she had cried during the night. " I give you pleasure but not happiness. That is bad."

He was about to protest, say words he no longer believed. She pressed her fingertips to his lips. " You don't talk," she whispered. " If you talk you tell lies."

That day she had a long mumbling conversation in Venetian with the little plaster statue of the Virgin. Later in the afternoon she went out. When she returned she was, he noticed, deathly pale.

It rained that night and the following, a furious October rain that came in splashing sheets against the windows. But the morning after, the sun rose in a cloudless sky, glistening the dripping leaves.

" To-day you go for a walk, *si?*" she said almost gaily. He protested that he didn't want to go out, but she insisted. " It is not good for you to stay in the house all the time."

Besides she wanted to clean the room while he was away . . . Grudgingly he gave in. When he stood in the doorway, about to close the door she ran to him. " I love you always," she said in a panting whisper. She kissed him softly. " Now you go." She almost pushed him out of the house.

When he returned that afternoon he found Karl sitting on his chair, munching an apple. His throat tightened, his palms went damp with sweat.

" Where did she go?" he asked in strangled words.

" I don't know, and I wouldn't tell you if I did," Karl said. Placidly he went on munching, but his eyes were alert, unsmiling.

" I'll find her."

" She won't see you."

" She will. I know her better than you do."

Karl shrugged impatiently. " Because you've made love to a

woman doesn't imply you know her. I tell you she won't see you."

"How do you know?"

"She told me so." With unexpected gentleness Karl waved to a chair. "Better sit down before you fall down."

Felix stood motionless as if he hadn't heard. "Why—why did she go?" he asked, his voice starting to crack with the approaching sob.

"Because she loves you. She couldn't bear watching the crumbling of her dream." He took another bite, chewed for a moment. "What're you going to do, Felix?" he asked softly. "Go home?"

Felix did not reply. Suddenly he felt very tired. Two tears rolled down his cheeks. "I think I'll go to Paris and see Chopin for a while. Then I'll go home . . ." Yes, soon, in a few weeks, he would be able to face his father, his family, Nina . . . But not now, not now. . . .

Chapter 3

FOR THE few months there had been a new legal counsel at the Mendelssohn Bank. His name, written in flowery cursive on the door of his office, was Felix Mendelssohn. His salary was not large, but since the work he produced in exchange was much smaller, he considered himself adequately paid. He had carefully chosen his office at the end of a long carpetless corridor, at the greatest possible distance from his father's. It contained a tall bookcase filled with leather-bound law books, a flat desk littered with legal documents and a single window that opened on a vast expanse of sky. There Felix spent his days feeding the birds that alighted on the window sill, reading poetry, taking long siestas, writing reams of music and, now and then, reminiscing of things past.

To-day, for no particular reason, he was thinking about the three months he had spent in Paris before returning home. Memories drifted back as he sat at his desk in his shirtsleeves, nibbling his quill, gazing at the bright summer sky. Little scenes like brief animated vignettes . . . Sounds, colours, faces . . . Some were still clear, others already blurred by the erasing hand of Time. He recalled his arrival on that dismal October afternoon, so well in harmony with his mood of aimlessness and desolation. The narrow bustling streets noisy with the clatter of hoofs, the cracking of whips and the buzzing mist of French rattled everywhere at vertiginous speed. The sidewalk cafés deserted under their dripping awnings. The creaking sound of the rickety stairs as he climbed the five flights to Chopin's garret-studio, 27 rue Poissonnière. From the second floor he could already hear the pounding and crashing of the keyboard. Frederic was playing one of his polonaises . . . How that man could play the piano!

At last the top floor, damp and ice-cold, immediately under the roof. Below the bell-pull a card: " Frederic Chopin. *Professeur de piano* " . . . A knock. The music stopping in mid bar. The door apprehensively pushed ajar. The sliver of a face, a questioning eye. Then suddenly the joyous cry of recognition. *" Mon cher Felix, quel plaisir!"* . . . The door flung wide. And there he stood grinning, blinking from excitement, bundled in his thick travelling coat, a green woollen scarf around his neck, his long thin nose jutting out from his pale face like a shark's fin out of water. " You must forgive me, I thought it was the landlord . . ."

Instantly they were old friends again. Indeed better friends than before, for now both were poor. In ten minutes they had exchanged histories. Maria . . . The summer idyll. The castle, the cottage. Her sudden heartbreaking flight . . . It was good to talk about her, scratch the itchy spot of pain. What else but talk remains to the deserted lover? . . . " You understand, Frederic, it wasn't just an *amourette*. We loved each other passionately . . . madly . . ." Frederic was patient, tactful. He understood. " *Oui, oui, je comprends . . .*" With each nod his blond hair would swing across his face. " You'll see, it will pass in time . . . It was an excellent idea to come here . . . We'll starve together . . ." He pointed to the dilapidated divan. " This will be your bed. I'll do the *cuisine*—that is whenever there is any *cuisine* to be done. You will attend to the house cleaning, appease the landlord when he comes for the rent . . ."

And so it was arranged. Bohemia . . . Real, unadorned Bohemia. Not at all the amusing romantic thing it was supposed to be. Frederic hated it. He had a few pupils—pimply youngsters from the district's shopkeepers or sou-pinching bourgeois. One franc and fifty centimes an hour. He returned from these lessons white-lipped and discouraged. " They say money corrupts; let me tell you poverty degrades. It breaks your spirit, takes away your dignity and in the end kills you. It killed Mozart, it killed Schubert . . ." Then he would go to the piano, play for an hour or two. He would relax. Gradually his prankish gaiety, half French, half Polish, would return. He would improvise rollicking polkas, mimic his friend Liszt at the keyboard, spring suddenly to his feet. " Well, *mon ami*, let's see what we'll have for supper to-night." He would disappear into the kitchen, return with two bars of chocolate. " Wonderful food, chocolate . . . Extremely nutritious . . ." And between coughing spells he would explain, " Contains milk, sugar, cocoa. All the basic foods for perfect health . . ."

Felix tilted his chair against the wall, knotted his hands behind his head and gazed smilingly at the tall bookcase with its neat rows of law books. Felix Mendelssohn, *Advokat* . . . On Tiergartenstrasse and Unter den Linden important men of business gravely raised their tall hats to him and just as gravely he raised his tall hat to them . . . If only Frederic could see him walking through the bank's corridor, some legal sheet in hand, with that absorbed, unseeing look of people who carry weighty matters in their heads . . . To think that nine months ago he was dining on a chocolate bar and living in a Paris garret . . .

Again time receded and he was back in rue Poissonnière. It was mid afternoon and he was alone, stretched out on the rib-breaking sofa watching the rivulets of rain slide down the big sash at the end of the room. If he raised himself a few inches he could see the frieze of glistening slate roofs, the forest of chimneys, even the flowerpots on the mansards' window sills. At night with the lights in the windows it made a pretty picture, but now it was all grey. Grey, like the sky, the rain, the walls, life, the future. Everything . . . A knock on the door. Damn, that landlord again. The same excuses: " You see, *Monsieur le propriétaire*, we're expecting money next week . . . Yes, next week. Absolutely . . . You can positively depend on it . . ." He shouted "*Entrez*" and the door opened. It wasn't the landlord, it was a lady. My God, a pupil! . . . Beautiful, young and obviously very wealthy . . . That emerald was as big as Maria's . . . A leap from the sofa. "Your servant, Madame . . . Won't you please sit down, Madame? . . . My friend, *le professeur*, will be here in a moment . . ."

She was a little out of breath as she sat down on the couch, Frederic's bed. " I am not looking for your friend, *le professeur*," she began, giving him a swift but all-seeing glance. " I am looking for you and I might as well tell you you gave me a devil of a time to find you. I'm Betty Rothschild. Would you mind telling me what on earth you're doing here?"

And all the time her eyes were smiling at him, not flirtatiously but amusedly. As if she were some ninety-year-old grandmother scolding her simpleton of a grandchild . . . And she wasn't any older than Fanny . . .* " I love it here," he replied challengingly. " I intend to stay here a long time. I suppose my father sent you——"

" Not exactly—although he's getting a little worried about you. So long as you were in England we could keep track of you——"

He looked at her aghast. " You mean you knew where I was?"

" My cousin Nathan knew every move you made and reported regularly to your father on your whereabouts——" Her lovely eyes were downright laughing at him; it was very humiliating.

" And so Father knows everything," he said with a hopeless shrug.

She nodded. " But don't worry." There was a new gentleness in her voice. " He loves you very much and he is a very intelligent man. He understands that a young man is entitled to at least one escapade. But he misses you and would like you to come home. He's getting old, you know . . ."

Suddenly all the defiance was out of him. He didn't really want to stay in this dreary Paris. He longed to be back with his family again, hear his father's grumbling, come into his mother's sitting-room and kiss her hand, see Fanny and Rebecka again . . . " I miss him too, I miss them all," he murmured. " I've been trying to get hold of myself——"

* Betty Rothschild was four years older than Felix. She died in 1886.

"I know," she said softly. "You've been hurt. Everyone is at one time or other."

Before he knew it he was talking to her as if she were his sister Fanny, his closest confidante and friend. He told her about Maria, but now he was calm, sensible. "I see now we weren't suited to each other . . . It was just a physical attraction, nothing else . . . She is a gipsy, a wanderer. I want a home, stability . . . Some day I'll meet the right girl for me and I'll be the right man for her and we'll be happy . . ."

Because she nodded and approved and no longer laughed at him, he even burned his bridges behind him and told her how he was supposed to strike a friendship with her, win her sympathy so that she would influence her husband in the matter of the Prussian loan . . . "It was my father's idea," he chuckled. "I was supposed to be very smooth, very clever . . . I think I'll never make a good diplomat . . ."

She gave a short laugh and rose to go. "On the contrary. You've won my sympathy and friendship. Come and see me before you leave. Sixteen rue Saint Dominique . . ." At the door she turned round, held out her hand. "And if you are in trouble and need help, let me know."

Her perfume remained in the room long after she was gone.

He went back to his sofa. How wonderful to know Father had forgiven him and was waiting for his return . . . Yes, the Maria adventure was over. It had been an escapade, nothing more. He was cured of his infatuation. He held himself firmly in hand. He had learned his lesson. Already he was living in anticipation of the scene of the Prodigal Son's homecoming. Falling into his father's arms . . . kissing his mother's hand . . . hugging Fanny, Rebecka . . . A handshake for Paul, for good old Gustav a jovial greeting. . . .

Why must Life blow on our good intentions as on a castle of cards? Why must it perversely show us how weak and self-deceiving we are? . . . But the gods must have their little chuckle at the poor humans, and that's why Chopin ran across Franz Liszt in the street that same afternoon. It could have happened two days or a week later, but no, it had to happen that same afternoon. And of course Liszt was with a pretty girl and in high spirits. When he wasn't in church beating his breast and confessing his sins he always was with a pretty girl and in high spirits . . . And naturally they stopped at a café, and who was there but Berlioz, angry at the world and in great need of diversion and what could be nicer than a little party in Frederic's studio that evening? . . . Of course. Everyone would bring whatever he could and tell his friends. . . .

If there is anything that travels faster than bad news it is the news of a party. By eight o'clock all the seats were occupied and some of the guests were sitting on the floor. By nine they were sitting in each other's laps. Everyone was talking and no one was listening, the reason being that the women were French and couldn't possibly remain silent and the men were nearly all intelligent, talented artists with many interesting things to say. A roomful of egos each clamouring for attention. By ten o'clock the air was thick with smoke and bright remarks. In the dim haze of candlelight faces floated in a bituminous Rembrandtesque chiaroscuro. Balzac was there, fondling his drooping moustache, telling about his creditors. Berlioz was waving his spindly arms, shaking his mop of flaming hair. " *Les salauds!* They'll play my music when I'm dead . . ." In a corner Niemcewicz and Mickiewicz were addressing a group of Polish exiles, speaking in ardent whispers about their beloved country. Poles never spoke of anything but Poland, especially those who lived far from it. Heine was there venting his bitterness in barbed aphorisms. Delacroix was talking painting to a poet who was talking poetry to him. For a while Chopin played, ending with the Polonaise in A flat, whereupon Mickiewicz rushed to him, tears streaming down his beard, and crushed him in his powerful arms. Liszt, who couldn't resist either a woman or a keyboard, gave a short impromptu concert, and you could have sworn there were four pianos in the room. Then the conversations were resumed, brighter and louder than ever. Suddenly, out of nowhere, someone said, " Didn't you know La Salla's been engaged at the Opera? . . . *Mais oui, mon cher!* . . . She's singing Lucia the week before Noël . . ."

Now the room was whirling, like a slow carousel. There was no one about but Maria with her clear eyes and parted lips. And the only sound was the pounding of his heart . . .

Felix unknotted his hands from behind his head, set the chair back on its four legs. He rose from his desk and walked to the window. For a moment he watched a sparrow careening joyously in the air, a darting atom of happiness dancing some ritual cosmic dance in the blueness of the summer sky. Did sparrows fall in love? . . . Did they forget their good resolutions, did they make fools of themselves as he had done that night . . .?

Everybody was gone. The room was silent. Chopin was snuffing out the candles.

" Frederic, what do you think of me as a pianist?"

" You could be one of the best if you wanted. Why do you ask?"

" If I worked hard do you think we could give a two-piano concert together?"

Chopin glanced over his shoulder. " I didn't know you wanted to be a concert pianist. You never mentioned it."

"Composing is tedious." How easily the lie rolled on his tongue. "I think I'd like the excitement of a pianist's life. Travelling, the applause . . ."

"Where would we find the money for a concert? It costs a fortune. The hire of the hall, printing the invitations, a hundred other things."

"I'll find it somehow."

He did. The trunkful of London clothes went. His father's gold watch made its way to the Mont de Piété, the municipal loan office. A desperate letter to Karl, full of sanctimonious lies, brought back fifty pounds. Another grand piano was installed in the room opposite Chopin's Pleyel and the rehearsals began.

They decided the programme would be composed of their own compositions. Felix contributed his two-piano concerto, a specially written two-piano transcription of his Octet and the *Midsummer* Overture. Frederic's polonaises, Scherzo in B flat and Revolutionary Etude made up the balance.

Work, work all the time. When Frederic was out on his lessons, Felix practised. Scales, arpeggios, chromatics. Faster, faster, faster . . . When Frederic returned it was time to start rehearsing again. He was indisputably the better pianist and in his gentle way he would correct Felix's playing. "That trill should be a trifle lighter . . . Now you see that chromatic should run like this . . . Let's try it again . . ."

That Sunday they had been at it all day. It was getting dark and they were tired. They looked at each other, smiling wearily across their instruments. Their profiles stood out in sharp silhouettes against the sunset, one of those dramatic winter sunsets of gold-hemmed purple clouds and great smears of salmon red. "Another two weeks and you'll play like Franz," said Chopin. "We'll be ready."

He then told him he had reserved the afternoon of December 14th, a small concert hall in the rue des Saints Pères. The invitations were already at the printer's. They were delivered a few days later and now, when they were not rehearsing, they addressed and sealed envelopes. The air reeked with the smell of sealing wax. "We needn't send any to our friends," said Frederic. "They know about the concert and they'll be there. Only the critics, the professors at the Conservatoire and of course society . . ." They sent five hundred invitations. "Since the hall sits only two hundred, we should have a full house," he said.

Well, it wasn't. Not even half, not even a tenth full . . . It was a disaster. Not a single critic, not a publisher, not a society lady. No one but their friends. They were there, the frayed-sleeved bohemians in loud waistcoats and patched redingotes, their girls in their home-made bonnets, their rabbit-trimmed capes. And naturally the Poles. They were there, lugubrious behind their beards, as if attending Kosciusko's funeral.

As for himself, he wanted to crawl into a corner and gently die. He had hoped so much from this concert. Maria would hear about it. Perhaps she was in town already and would surreptitiously attend, as she had attended his two London concerts. She would see he was a great pianist and they could live together. They would travel together, perform in the same cities . . . Oh, so many dreams he had spun in his mind. And now *this* . . .!

And suddenly he knew. By one of those sudden, fulgurant flashes of intuition he knew why only those who had received no invitation had come. " Frederic, have you one of our cards of invitation?" And there it was in black and white. " Look, look, Frederic! . . . ' Messieurs Frederic Chopin and Felix Mendelssohn beg the honour of your presence at a joint recital of their compositions to be held January Fourteenth . . .' January! . . . You, miserable piano-player . . ." Incredulously Chopin was staring at the card. His lips were trembling, he was about to collapse and Liszt was holding him up by the elbow. *" Bohze Moy . . . Bohze Moy . . .!"* He kept repeating in Polish. He wanted to go straight to the Seine and drown himself.

"That wouldn't solve anything. Wait . . .!" The thought was forming in his mind. It was mad, but it was a chance. One in a thousand. "Take my place," he said to Liszt. "And listen to me. You two keep on playing, you understand, keep on playing until I come back . . . Just don't go away. Stay here and play until I come back . . ." Already he was racing through the wings into the street. Thank God a landau was passing by, its roof white with snow. " Rue Saint Dominique and please hurry . . .!"

Speed is a relative value. To a man in a hurry a comet would seem slow. That fiacre seemed rooted to the ground. "Hurry, for Heaven's sake!" At last there it was, the Rothschild mansion. The butler was unused to dishevelled, frantic visitors. " Yes, *Madame la baronne* is in, but——" A door opened. "What is it? Oh, it's you . . .!" It took a little time to explain things because he was too excited to be concise or even coherent. But she understood. " Rue des Saints Pères, did you say?" Already she was pulling the bell rope, summoning her majordomo. " I want everyone in this house—everyone, do you hear—to go out at once to the following addresses. Every carriage must be used . . ." He left her dictating names and addresses.

Then there was the race back to the concert hall. Like a fool he had let his fiacre go. Oh, well, it didn't matter, he could run almost as fast. And he did run through the slushy snow, bumping against people, flinging excuses over his shoulder. People turned to look at this hatless perspiring young man running in evening clothes . . . And then he saw *it*, and he stopped dead in his tracks. It was one of the hundreds of yellow posters announcing Maria's début and it was crossed by two strips of black with the word 'Cancelled' printed in red. The next one he saw was similarly crossed, and so was the next and the next. He spied an old man pasting those strips of paper and walked to him. " She's sailed for America, that's what they told me . . . Changed her mind at the last minute. Just like a woman . . ."

He said, " *Merci*," and walked away. Strange he could stand up, feel the snowflakes gently kissing his face. He was not in pain. Just numb. " She isn't coming." The words kept repeating themselves in his mind. He would never see her again. That was all. He would never see her again . . . He was not angry, he was not sad. He was tired. Something had died within him. Perhaps it was his youth. He wanted only one thing—to go home. This time he meant it.

He resumed his walk towards the concert hall. There was no need to hurry any more. He did not know the district well and lost himself in the maze of crooked alleys and winding side streets. Night was approaching—a night without stars, without beauty. Only a darker greyness through which danced snowflakes. As he neared the hall a strange sight met his eyes. An endless cordon of carriage lamps glowed through the snowy mist. Liveried coachmen sat patiently on their seats. He found the stage door, made his way through the wings. Facing each other, bent over their keyboards Liszt and Chopin were coming to the end of the Revolutionary Etude. It was thrilling to watch them. Liszt was his usual phenomenal self, but Chopin was the greater of the two, playing for his beloved and vanquished Poland, the little house in Zelazowa he would never see again, the happy days he had left behind.

He walked to the edge of the stage and peered out into the hall. It was full and somehow he was not surprised. His own defeat required some sort of compensation. Well, there it was. This tumult of applause that was greeting the end of the concert, that was it. Just as he had hoped. A moment ago it would have meant so much, now it meant nothing . . . Strange how empty the world could become just because one person wasn't there . . . Oh, well, the whole foolish venture hadn't been in vain. Success was at last coming to Frederic. He was standing, one hand on the piano, smiling his shy smile, brushing back his long hair, acknowledging the ovation while Liszt with one of those unexpected gestures of modesty that were a facet of his charm, stood behind and joined in the applause. No, it hadn't been in vain. To-morrow Frederic would be the darling of the Paris salons. He would move to some elegant *rez-de-chaussée* and teach piano to adoring countesses. They would drain some of his genius away but they would give him the fragrance of their expensive perfumes, the birdlike twitter of their patrician babble, the glitter of mundane life which was necessary to him. He would be happy, as happy as a fundamentally unhappy man could be. He was on his way to a new life.

He, too, was on his way—home. To 3, Leipzigerstrasse, his waiting family, his beloved Germany. He didn't belong to his charming, heartbreaking Paris. He was neither bohemian nor salon puppet. He wanted a home and music—the kind that is born from silence. And perhaps some day, if Life gave him a second chance—Love. . . .

With the clatter of applause in his ears he turned around, went back to the street and trudged away through the falling snow.

And now it was all over . . . It didn't hurt any more. London, Paris, the concert, Carrington Castle, the cottage by the brook, Half Moon Street, Buckingham Palace, the great pains, the great joys—sometimes he wondered if they had ever been real. Perhaps it was all a dream or something he had read. The memories themselves had begun to fade. For instance, he couldn't remember the exact colour of Maria's eyes or the precise pitch of her voice. Not that he would ever forget her entirely. He wouldn't do that. Why? Because—well, because she had taught him so much about himself he didn't even suspect, because she had given him a glimpse of what love could be, and also because complete oblivion is the ultimate cruelty and he never could bring himself to be cruel to her. No, he would never forget her entirely, but already she had withdrawn to that weedy and isolated spot in the mind which was the cemetery of memories, those secret, trivial and tragic memories we carry all our lives and never talk about.

It was all over and he was happy. Not deliriously, idiotically as he had been last summer. But happy, as it is permitted to be. Life frowned on great happiness as it did on genius, murder, all extremes. But it tolerated a modicum of unobtrusive contentment. And that's what he had and he asked for nothing more. One of these days Nina and he would make up their minds to get married and they would be happy. Again, it is permitted to be happy. One of these days some orchestra conductor—in Munich or Dresden or Hamburg or perhaps even in Berlin—and that of course would be best—would obligingly resign or die and he would be offered his post. Then his existence would be settled, straight and unexciting, like the lines of a stave.

Meanwhile he was *Advokat* at the bank, specialising in financial matters, doing very little work, dreaming—not dreaming exactly, for there was nothing to dream about—and writing a heap of music. He was living at home and loving it. He was beginning not only to love but to appreciate his wonderful family, and strangely his father most of all . . . A fine old gentleman, Father, behind all his rumbling and grumbling. A keen mind and a lot of emotion, but hidden deep, very deep like the bank's reserves in the underground vaults.

Yes, he was happy. The cafés, the evenings in billiard rooms and smoky rathskellers, the strutting promenades on Unter den Linden with other rich young blades, the shabby affairs with charming and inept women—they no longer intrigued him. Somehow he had outgrown all that. He didn't miss them; he didn't miss anything or anyone—not even Maria. He asked nothing, wanted nothing. Not even love. Especially not love. Love was a very tiring experience. It made your blood rush or freeze, it kept you awake, it made your heart swell like a balloon, it scraped your nerves and it always ended in pain and disappointment, the taste of ashes in your mouth and a throbbing headache. Love was like those fruits that tasted sweet at the first mouthful and sour at the last. No, he didn't want love. He was content as he was. He slept well, he had his music. He was happy in a bland, vapid sort of way. And that was all right with him . . .

He stood at the window gazing at the flying sparrow, the pale summer sky almost white with sunshine. Even Berlin was quiet at this hour. How about a little siesta? . . . Already he was eyeing the old leather arm-chair when he caught the unfamiliar sound of footsteps along the uncarpeted corridor. His father was coming, heralding his approach with much clearing of the throat and tactful coughing.

" Sit down, Jakob, sit down," said Abraham Mendelssohn shuffling into the office and waving his son back to his chair from which he had sprung with haste and the appropriate expression of surprise. " I'm pleased to see you hard at work. How do you like being at the bank?"

" I love it, Father." So far so good . . . What could he have in mind?

" The work isn't too hard, I hope. Salary satisfactory . . .?"

" Most satisfactory, Father."

The banker scanned his son's face, leaned back into the chair and knotted his hands over his paunch, which meant he was about to come to the object of his visit. " Remember this business of the Prussian Treasury Loan?" He accepted Felix's nod as an answer and proceeded. " It's almost settled, but I still need a few more details from the Rothschild Bank."

"Father, if you're going to send me on another of your shady missions—"

Abraham let out a small chuckle. "Nothing of the sort. This time it is not a question of influencing any lady, although your method in Paris—whatever it was—proved most successful. You will deal with Herr Amschel Rothschild, and this is what I'd like you to do."

Patiently Felix listened to his father's instructions. "When do you wish me to leave for Frankfurt, Father?" he asked in due time.

"As soon as you've made your arrangements," said the banker, preparing to rise, "taken your leave from Nina and finished the piece of music you're writing at the moment."

Felix began a gesture of protest but gave it up in mid air. "Would the day after to-morrow be satisfactory, Father?"

"Entirely satisfactory," said Abraham Mendelssohn shuffling away. "And I suggest you take Gustav with you."

Dear Father, he wasn't taking any chance this time . . . Did he fear another Maria in Frankfurt? "I'll be delighted," he said, holding the door open. "The whole business should take only a few days. I should be back in less than two weeks."

"You should. Let's hope you are."

The morning after his arrival in Frankfurt, Felix presented himself at the Rothschild bank.

"Well, how do you like our little town?" asked Amschel Rothschild, as Felix let himself down into a tufted green arm-chair. He spoke in a gentle, faintly wheezing voice, as if he were somewhat out of breath. His greying blond hair and side whiskers, the white cashmere tie which he wore loose around his high collar, the languid elegance of his slender hands gave him a strangely romantic look. In different surroundings he might have been mistaken for a poet. "Rather provincial, I imagine," he went on, answering his own question, "after the bustle of Berlin."

Felix assured him he found Frankfurt full of delightful quaintness. "Of course I've seen very little of it and this is only my first impression. But even the shops have a certain old-fashioned charm. The ladies seem to pay scant attention to current fashions."

"You mean our women are rather dowdy," said the banker with a smile, "and frankly they are. It's their particular form of vanity. They pride themselves on being ladylike and unfrivolous and succeed in becoming extraordinarily dull. But they are accomplished housewives. In our richest families the girls are trained to do the marketing and supervise every detail of housekeeping." The smile deepened in thin lines of quiet amusement. "The truth is that

Frankfurters are ashamed of their wealth and make amends for it
by not enjoying it."

There was some further leisurely exchange of generalities on the
subject of Frankfurt, its people, its monuments, its traditions and
overwhelming tediousness. While this went on, Felix felt he was
being scrutinised and measured by the romantic-looking banker.
Thus by easy stages the conversation reached the business matter
that was the object of this meeting. Amschel Rothschild's features
settled into a courteous but inscrutable expression as Felix explained
the details of his mission. Like all good bankers, Rothschild had a
talent for listening. He did so while looking out of the window or
gazing musingly at his desk, but Felix could almost see the delicate
machinery of his shrewd mind at work.

"I think I understand your father's proposition," Rothschild
said at last. "Let me think about it a few days and I'll give you my
answer."

"I shan't conceal that I am anxious to report to my father at
your earliest convenience."

"I understand. You are in a hurry to get away from this town."
The banker permitted himself a small chuckle. "If I were your age
I'd probably feel as you do. I am sorry, however, for we do have
a few attractive young ladies and they would have been delighted to
have a chance at such an eligible bachelor as yourself." Felix made
a deprecatory gesture. "But duty comes first and since you must
return to Berlin I shall give you my answer as soon as possible.
Probably the day after to-morrow. Meanwhile "—he rose to his feet
and Felix did the same—" won't you have supper with us, my wife
and me—to-morrow night? Two of my brothers, Salomon from
Vienna and Charles from Naples, happen to be here and I know
they will enjoy meeting you."

It sounded rather dull, but Felix declared he would be delighted
and with a courteous bow took his leave from the banker.

Back in the street, Felix found himself with nothing to do and all
the time in the world to do it. It was an odd feeling this having nothing to do, no one to see, no place to go. To kill time he ambled
through Zeil, Frankfurt's main street, peering into shop windows at
the pathetic displays of old-maidish bonnets and antiquated finery.
Never had he felt so much a foreigner as in this German town. Not
even in Paris, not even in London. People spoke a strange patois
he barely understood. Even money was different; Frankfurt was a
Free City and had a monetary system of its own. He was aware
people were looking at him. Well, let them look. They probably
were shocked by his pearl-grey frock-coat, his blue silk neckcloth
and his gold-nobbed cane. Perhaps he should be dressed in black

like everybody else. To the devil with them. If they enjoyed dressing like undertakers it was their affair . . .

He idled along the quays and watched the loading and unloading of river barges. He scooped up a few pebbles and leaning on a parapet dropped them one by one in the Main. No pleasure is eternal and even this exciting diversion finally palled on him. He found himself shambling through the Fahrthor district, purposely losing himself in the web of ancient and narrow streets. Now and then he came across some quiet little square, sun-freckled and deserted. Public benches on which no one sat stood under gently rustling trees. Behind the tracery of foliage grave and handsome residences showed their neo-classic façades. My God, what a town! What did people do all day long in Frankfurt? Didn't they ever go out, give any parties, have any fun—any fun at all?

Once again he found himself on the Zeil. In Frankfurt you always ended on the Zeil . . . His attention was caught by a delicate Dresden porcelain in an antique shop. Nina would like that . . . He entered the shop which was empty, and smelled faintly of musk and old age. He gazed about at the old clocks, the seventeenth century fashion dolls still bearing the mark of a great Paris dressmaker, the ancient beer steins standing in orderly rows on dusty shelves. Well, wasn't anyone going to wait on him . . .!

He turned around and looked out at the street as a young lady, escorted by a middle-aged, fierce-looking maid carrying a wicker basket on her arm, drifted across the window. She paused an instant to glance at the display. He caught a glimpse of her face. It was the most beautiful face he had ever seen.

Already she was walking away, crossing the street in a rustle of her black-hooped skirt. He rushed to the door, just as an elderly lady, as antique and fragile as her dolls, emerged from the green curtain at the rear of the shop.

"Excuse me, Madame," he cried over his shoulder. "I'll be back."

Now he was crossing the street, making his way through the carriages, keeping his eyes on the girl. She was talking animatedly to her escort, he could see the motion of her lips. How lovely she was! Her profile was faultless. She couldn't be more than eighteen or nineteen. Yet girls did marry early. What if she had a husband, some dull, stout Frankfurt merchant? . . . The thought pierced him with the burning sharpness of a needle plunging into his flesh.

At this precise instant she entered a cheese shop and vanished from sight.

He waited in the street, not daring to follow her into the shop. He noticed he was breathing hard and his hand was clenched over the gold knob of his cane. "What's the matter with me?" he asked himself, half aloud. He didn't know, he only knew he must not lose this girl. Cautiously he inched towards the entrance of the shop, peering into the dim, strongly scented interior. He could not see her. Panic overcame him. What if there was another exit, what if she had walked out without his seeing her? He rushed into the shop.

Thank God she was there, inspecting the various pieces of cheese, daintily poking their crust. She was talking to the cheesemonger. No, this one was a little too new . . . This one seemed a bit rancid . . . How clever, how conscientious she was! . . . He had never suspected there was so much to buying a hunk of cheese. Imagine her buying cheese for *him* . . .! The thought sent a shudder of sheer rapture through him. The tradesman was respectful. "Yes, fräulein, you're right, this one's a bit soft . . . Yes, Fräulein, this is the best . . ." God be blessed, the man called her *Fräulein*. She wasn't married . . .

At last the *Fräulein* appeared satisfied. She watched the cheesemonger weigh the piece of cheese in the shiny brass balance. She leaned forward over the counter as he wrote the amount in his ledger. How prudent, how wise she was! . . . There was a real housewife, nobody would take advantage of her . . .

Then with a gracious smile she walked away, her maid behind her.

"What'll it be?"

Felix heard the words. The man was looking at him, his knife still in his hand. "This one," he said, pointing at random at a round cake of Dutch cheese.

"How much do you want?"

Felix stared at him. How would he know, he had never bought a pound of cheese in his life. "Three pounds," he said.

The man leaned behind the counter to fetch the cheese. Already the girl was at the street corner. Now was the time to bolt . . .

He heard the cheesemonger's voice behind him, got a flash of his knife at the end of his hairy arm, but already he was out of the shop.

The young girl and her escort turned into a side street, then another and finally entered Goethe Platz, one of those quiet shady squares that were one of Frankfurt's features. It reminded him of Berkeley Square—a provincial and bourgeois Berkeley Square. From a distance he watched them disappear into one of the severe and elegant mansions that lined the place on all sides. As he neared the door, he noticed a small bronze plate under the bell. On it was written "Jeanrenaud."

It sounded French and unloosened a thousand absurd fancies in his mind. She must be the granddaughter of one of those French emigrés who had found refuge in Frankfurt during the Revolution.

A window opened above his head on the second floor and once again he had a glimpse of her. She had removed her bonnet and he saw that she was a blonde. For an instant she stood motionless in the framework of the window, then she withdrew into the mysteriousness of the room.

It didn't occur to him that he cut a rather ludicrous figure standing there, gaping at an open window. For nothing in the world would he have walked away. He spied a public bench facing the house and went to sit down on it. A few instants later the sound of piano-playing came down to him. She was a musician! . . . Instantly his feverish mind presented him with a swarm of attractive and fanciful vignettes. She was a musician! . . . Wasn't this a sign that she was meant for him? . . . They would grow old together, spending several hours at the keyboard every day, playing four-hand transcriptions of all master works, exploring side by side the enchanted realm of music.

While these visions drifted through his mind, his ears became increasingly aware of repeated mistakes, incorrect pedalling, faulty reading. Poor Mozart, the things she was doing to his minuet! . . . Cruel indeed was the composer's lot. His music was unappreciated while he lived and mangled after his death by endless generations of stumbling adolescents . . . Down from the window came the music. Wincing with each false note he watched his dream of four-hand playing crumble. Regretfully he had to admit that this exquisite creature was a much better cheese buyer than a pianist.

Curiously he derived a genuine pleasure from this observation. With the disarming incoherence of a mind now diseased with love he at once turned this liability into an asset. Her deficiency became her finest achievement. He was glad, yes, glad she was not a musician! Who wanted an artistic wife? What could be more intolerable than two artists in one family. Maria had been an artist, and look at the shambles she made of their romance . . . No more artistic women for him. A sweet, loving housewife, that's what he wanted. An artist needed a housekeeper, not a competitor.

With a final jarring chord the minuet came to an abrupt end. The interruption was both a relief and a torment to him. Now that she was no longer at the piano he did not know where she might be. Well, at least they were near each other, breathing the same Frankfurt air, enjoying the same pleasant temperature. Although she was unaware of his existence, this created some small bond between them. They were contemporaries. More, they were neighbours. That was almost being friends already, wasn't it . . .?

To pass the time, for naturally he wouldn't think of leaving, he began studying the front of the house. It was elegant and austere with an indefinable ecclesiastical air about it. He was trying to

imagine the inner arrangement when he became aware of a man
standing at his side. A glance told him it was a policeman.

"Been watching you for a while," the policeman said, "and it's
clear you're a stranger in this town. You've been sitting on this
here bench for a mighty long time."

"Frankfurt's a Free City, I've heard. Is there any law against
sitting on public benches?"

The policeman fondled his luxuriant moustache while pondering
the next question. "Why are you looking at this house?"

"Because it stands in front of me."

The answer nettled the policeman, whose face turned a deep
magenta hue. The blue veins of his bulbous nose stood out like
rivers on a map. "Here in Frankfurt we don't like people who peer
into other people's houses. You'd better move on."

"I'll stay here as long as I please." This was the wrong thing to
say and Felix realised it at once. "This is the nicest little square in
the whole town," he added hastily. "And do you know what I
like best about it?"

The policeman, who was about to put the whistle to his lips and
call the watch, remained motionless and perplexed.

"The way it is being policed," Felix went on. "In this town
you feel safe, you know you're being protected. In Berlin, where I
come from, our police aren't any good." This struck a sympathetic
chord in the policeman's heart. His face returned to its normal
beefy red. "In Berlin a man could sit all day on a public bench
and nobody would come and tell him to move on."

"Well, you see this is a high-class district. Only rich people
live here."

"You can see that. This house, for instance," Felix pointed to
the Jeanrenaud home. "You see that only very fine people would
live in a house like this."

"That's not a house," chuckled the policeman. "That's a
church."

"A church?"

"Yes. Some kind of French Protestant church. It's been here a
long time. They preach in French, they sing in French, they even
pray in French. There's a nice chapel and up there," he waved to
the second-floor windows, "is the pastor's apartment."

"How interesting! A young lady just went in——"

"Blonde with a pretty face and a fat woman with a basket?
That's Fräulein Cécile and her cook Catherine. Known her since
she was a baby. She lives there with her mother. A real lady. A
bit stiff-necked maybe."

"And her father, of course?"

"No. Her father's dead. Died many years ago when he was a

young man. Just to give you an idea what a fine man he was, in this town where people don't go to funerals, more than three hundred people went to the cemetery when he died. And not just people from his own church either. Even Catholics, even Lutherans . . .!"

Felix no longer listened. Suddenly all the ebullience, the foolishness had gone out of him. He, Jakob Ludwig Felix Mendelssohn, had fallen head over heels in love with the daughter of a Protestant pastor, of all people . . .!

Great wealth is as difficult to conceal as poverty, yet the Rothschild house managed to convey an impression of merely modest affluence. Felix was startled by this simplicity, which he compared inwardly with the luxuriousness of his own home, and found it difficult to believe that Europe's richest banker chose to live in the manner and surroundings of a moderately prosperous merchant.

Eva Rothschild guessed his surprise. " You see, Herr Mendelssohn," she remarked during dinner, " Amschel and I are small-town people. We've lived in Frankfurt all our lives." She was a grey-haired, motherly-looking woman of small beauty and great charm. She attracted confidence and Felix had liked her at first sight.

"We have no children and our tastes are simple. We have no desire to impress anyone." With a teasing side glance at her brothers-in-law, she added, "We leave that to Salomon and Charles."

Salomon Rothschild, who lived in Vienna, let out a chortle of protest. "Because I have a wretched carriage and a box at the opera you'd think I was living like a prince! . . . Why I am not even allowed to own a home." He turned to Felix in quest of sympathy. "Would you believe that I'm obliged to transact business from an inn!"

"It's true that you occupy the whole inn," said Amschel with a chuckle.

"And it is a very large inn," added Charles with a sly grin.

With amused astonishment Felix watched this boyish bantering among the three brothers, each one a colossus in the field of international finance. A moment ago they had talked about the mercury mines they owned in Spain, the railroads they were financing in Austria and Belgium, the enormous financial transactions they and their two other brothers in Paris and London were negotiating with various European treasuries. Charles Rothschild mentioned the large loan he had just concluded for the Pope.* " His Holiness has graciously received me in private audience and conferred upon me the Grand Cordon of I don't remember which order," he announced.

* Pope Gregory XVI needed funds for the defence of the Papal territories.

"Watch out," laughed Salomon. "His Holiness will convert you and then he'll pay us in Indulgences."

At the head of the table Amschel was leaning back on his chair, a grin on his handsome face. "I expect you to be made Count of the Holy See any day," he told his brother Charles. "You'd look very fetching in silk pourpoint and doublet attending Mass in Saint Peter's."

Charles smiled broadly in his black beard. "You're jealous. Already His Holiness gave me his hand to kiss instead of his foot, as is customary. I regard this as a mark of distinct favour."

Salomon gave out a quiet chuckle. "I spend most of my life bowing to princes who owe me money. You know, Amschel," he went on, turning to his elder brother, "sometimes I think Father started us in a very strange business."

They talked with the unguarded intimacy of total confidence. For once they could relax and enjoy themselves in these familiar surroundings of their childhood. This was their home. They had grown up in this ancient and gabled ghetto house. Here their father had read to them from the old Hebrew Bible and warned his five sons to remain united in order to be strong. "Behold how fine and sweet it is for brothers to live in good accord . . . To them the Almighty gives His blessings . . ."*

Felix sensed the three brothers had accepted him into their inner circle because they looked upon him as one of them, a member of their long-suffering minority, the grandson of the great Moses Mendelssohn. Their trust disturbed him. What would they say if they knew he'd fallen in love with a gentile?

"Yes," said Amschel, slowly running his hand across his forehead, "it is a strange business, this lending money to kings and princes." He looked at Felix across the table. "Perhaps you may not know that our father founded our bank by selling old and rare coins to His Highness Wilhelm of Hesse. This prince had become one of the wealthiest in Europe by the simple expedient of selling his soldiers to King George III—those famous Hessian regiments who so valorously lost the American colonies for England. But if he thus unpopulated his state he did his best to repopulate it in another manner. At his death he admitted the paternity of seventy-seven children."

"Amschel!" rapped Eva Rothschild severely but with a twinkle in her eyes. "You shouldn't say such things."

"But it's true," insisted the banker with the vehemence of a schoolboy. "Everybody knows it. Anyway," he proceeded, "His Highness was so pleased with our father's services that he recom-

* Psalm 133.

mended him to the King of Denmark. Since then we've been bankers to practically every crowned head in Europe."

"Don't make it sound so tragic," laughed his brother Charles. "We have not done too badly."

"True," admitted Amschel with a rueful smile. "Just the same I would've liked to become a doctor and James told me once he would've liked to be a farmer. On his estate near Paris he spends every minute he can snatch from his office planting, ploughing, pruning . . . But of course, as Jews, these professions are forbidden to us."

For a while they discussed with a sort of patient and shrugging resignation the never-ending difficulties and handicaps Jews had to overcome to earn a livelihood in Germany.

"Christians are strange people," remarked Salomon. "They complain we overrun the banking business and it is the only one they haven't closed to us."

"Aren't you feeling well, Herr Mendelssohn?" Eva Rothschild broke in, looking at Felix with a solicitous frown. "You seem preoccupied and haven't said a word."

"Don't you see he's bored?" chortled her husband. "He thinks Frankfurt is a cemetery and cannot wait to get out of it."

"On the contrary," blurted Felix with unexpected vivacity, "I think Frankfurt is an extremely colourful and interesting city."

"What a change since yesterday!" exclaimed the eldest Rothschild.

"It has magnificent monuments and a great deal of charm."

"I appreciate these compliments, but Frankfurt is a dull town and we all know it. I understand perfectly your anxiety to return to Berlin. You may leave in the morning. Tell your father we are in complete accord."

Felix's heart sank. Leave Frankfurt, leave Cécile . . . Never! "I'd feel I had failed in my mission if I didn't bring back a complete and detailed agreement," he declared with unnecessary emphasis. He felt the brothers' glances focused upon him. He sensed that with their long experience of insincere protestations the three bankers did not believe him. "I must bring him a complete written agreement," he went on with a forcefulness that confirmed their doubts, "even if it entails my staying here longer, *much* longer than I planned."

"Your sense of duty is very commendable," observed Salomon with an imperceptible irony in his voice.

"Admirable indeed," stressed Amschel. "Somehow I'd formed the idea you were marking time, so to speak, working in your father's bank until you found an opportunity for a musical career." The edge of amusement was unmistakable in his tone. "If you wish,

I could delay the drawing up a detailed agreement a few months
to give you ample time to admire this colourful and interesting city
of ours."

"Now you stop it, Amschel," snapped Eva Rothschild. "And
you, too," she added with a sharp glance at her brothers-in-law.
"Can't you see this young man is worried to death about something. He is alone in this town, away from his family and you're
making fun of him. Shame on you." She leaned forward and
looked at Felix with motherly concern. "Do you want to tell us
what's worrying you, Felix?" she said with great gentleness. "You
can speak in confidence. You are among friends."

"I'm in love with Cécile Jeanrenaud."

The words fell of themselves from his lips. He had to speak,
declare his love. The tenderness in Eva Rothschild's voice had
broken his reticence. She was right, he was among friends. "Somehow," he said somewhat defiantly and for no particular reason,
merely because the thought presented itself, "I'll make her love me
and marry me."

A silence fell around the table. The three men averted their eyes,
even Eva was staring at the tablecloth. He knew what they were
thinking. Moses Mendelssohn's grandson wanted to marry a gentile.
His children wouldn't be full-blooded members of their race. A
great Jewish family was coming to an end, seeping away into the
encroaching sands of Christianity.

"Cécile Jeanrenaud," muttered Amschel under his breath, as if
gathering his thoughts. "She's the granddaughter of Cornelius
Souchay," he said to Salomon in an aside. Then turning back to
Felix he added, "Herr Cornelius Souchay was one of the most
important merchants of this town with warehouses in England,
Italy and even Russia. He did a little business with our father before he opened his own bank. Did you know that?"

Felix shook his head. "I didn't. I know absolutely nothing
about her except that her father was the pastor of some French
church on Goethe Platz and she lives there with her mother. I
haven't even spoken to her. I only saw her in the street yesterday
and since then I have done nothing but sit in front of her house
and look at her window in the hope of catching another glimpse of
her."

As he spoke he realised how juvenile and ludicrous his declarations must sound to those hardened businessmen who were watching
him. Yet they were not laughing or even smiling. Their worldly
experience had taught them that love was the only power as strong
as money. Sometimes even stronger. You didn't joke about it.
"How do you know you love her?" asked Eva Rothschild. "After
all you haven't even met her."

"I know it sounds foolish," Felix admitted. "I can't explain it even to myself."

"Of course she is extremely pretty," ventured Eva Rothschild.

"Yes, but it's something else," said Felix as though speaking to himself. "It is . . . I don't quite know how to put it . . . it is as if I couldn't help myself." He looked straight into her eyes. "Believe me, Madame, I've tried to reason this out. I've told myself it was ridiculous. I've thought of what my family would say, of what her family would say, what Nina would say——"

"Nina?"

"Nina Wetzel. We've known each other all our lives and we're practically engaged. I know it will hurt my father and mother deeply and I love them. As for my grandmother, she'll probably never speak to me again."

"I can't believe that," protested Eva Rothschild.

"You don't know her!" cried Felix hotly. "She disowned her own son, my mother's brother, because he became a Christian. Since then she has never spoken to him or let him set foot in her house."

An embarrassed silence greeted these words. On his chair Amschel was shaking his head and softly clucking his tongue. "Sometimes I think men invented religions so they would have a reason to hate and kill one another," he said with a sigh. "More blood has been shed in the name of God than for any other cause. The moment the question of religion intervenes people seem to lose their common sense. Yet all religions teach exactly the same things. They all tell you to be kind, tolerant, fair . . ." The sentence finished in a hopeless shrug.

"Your uncle lives in Rome, doesn't he?" asked Charles Rothschild. "I know him. He owns a magnificent villa which is called 'La Casa Batholdy.' He is a great patron of the arts."

Felix paused an instant, then he said quietly, "I'm going to marry Cécile Jeanrenaud, if she will have me." He ran his eyes around the table pleading for approval. "Is this wrong?"

The men did not reply, but Eva Rothschild spoke without hesitation. "No, it isn't wrong," she said in ringing, almost defiant tones. "And I, for one, am going to do everything I can to help you."

Amschel turned to look at his wife with the air of a man who has learned to forgive women's emotional impulsiveness. "Before we see what we can do to help our young friend, he may perhaps like to know something about his future family."

"I would," said Felix. "Very much."

"Well," began the banker, fondling his sidewhiskers, "the Souchays de la Duboissière are, I believe, Calvanists or Waldensians,

and like many other noble families they moved to Frankfurt in the
seventeenth century at the time of the persecutions of the
Protestants in France. They are one of our most respected local
families. As I told you, Cornelius Souchay, Cécile's grandfather,
was a very wealthy businessman. His son Theodore is a banker as
well as one of the town's senators. His daughter Wilhelmine, your
future mother-in-law, fell in love when she was sixteen with Auguste
Jeanrenaud, a young Swiss pastor who had been appointed to the
French Reformed Church at Frankfurt. Her father didn't like it
very much. After all, she was beautiful and an heiress and, Jeanrenaud was a poor cleric. So he packed her off to Italy for two
years, hoping she would get over her infatuation. But she didn't
and when she returned the two young people were married. Incidentally this Jeanrenaud turned out to be a remarkable man and
an excellent pastor, but he died four or five years after his marriage.
Cécile was two years old when he died. She must be about nineteen
or twenty now."

"And a wonder she hasn't married yet!" exclaimed Eva Rothschild.

"Perhaps she was waiting for me," risked Felix with a hesitant
smile, his first that evening.

"Perhaps," echoed the banker's wife. "But be prepared for a
fight. Half the young men in town are in love with her, which
is easy to understand—rich and beautiful as she is."

"All I ask is a chance to meet her."

"We'll see what we can do," Amschel said with a prudent smile.
"Meanwhile go back to your bench and be miserable to your heart's
content."

With its gold-framed paintings and fringed velvet portières,
Senator Souchay's huge drawing-room was a masterpiece of oppressive and opulent provincialism, but to-night in the glow of the
candelabra, the swirling of hooped skirts and the waltzing strains
from the six-piece orchestra behind a screen of greenery, it
managed to look both festive and elegant. The large carpet had
been removed to permit the young people from the town's best
families to indulge in an innocent and well-behaved capering under
their parents' watchful eyes. At the end of the room a buffet had
been set, heaped with delicacies. Along the walls, Frankfurt matrons
in expensive and dowdy finery sat in forbidding rows, stiff-backed
and sharp-eyed, choking in their corsets and fanning themselves.

"You dance beautifully, Fräulein Jeanrenaud," whispered Felix,
drawing Cécile closer to him as they whirled about the room.

"Thank you, Herr Mendelssohn. You are an excellent cavalier,
but I think you're holding me a little too tight."

Hastily he relaxed his grip. " Please forgive me."

" I don't mind, but *Maman* is watching us. This is not Berlin, Herr Mendelssohn."

" How do you know I come from Berlin? We've just been introduced."

" I know a great deal about you, Herr Mendelssohn. Careful . . . You're squeezing me again."

Once more he released the pressure of his hand against her back. " I am terribly sorry. I hope you won't think I'm being forward."

" I won't tell you what I'm thinking, Herr Mendelssohn."

" Why won't you, Fräulein Jeanrenaud?"

" Because I don't know you well enough, Herr Mendelssohn."

She did not turn her calm blue eyes from his gaze. For an instant he stared at her, oblivious of his surroundings, the dancing couples about them. She was even more beautiful than he had imagined—and she wasn't impressed by him, his expert dancing, his elegant Berlin clothes. In fact, she seemed to be making fun of him. Yes, she was . . . He could feel it. There was a suspicion of a smile playing on her lips, as if she held back some gleeful secret. It was infuriating.

The sound of her voice brought him out of his thoughts. " Herr Mendelssohn, you're squeezing me again. I can feel your fingers digging into my back. Are you trying to crush me?"

" I assure you, Fräulein——"

" You seem perturbed about something. Won't you tell me what it is?"

" You're right," he hissed, leaning close to her ear, " I am perturbed, I am extremely perturbed. I am despondent, furious, happy, in Heaven and in Hell. I have been since I came to this God-forsaken town. I am ready to explode. But, of course, I don't know you well enough to tell you my troubles."

" *Touchée!*" she exclaimed. For the first time she laughed. It was the loveliest sound he had ever heard. It made her smooth throat tremble and brought gleams into her eyes. " When we know each other better," she said, " we'll tell each other what we think of each other, won't we?"

" I hope it'll be soon, for I may have to return to Berlin any day now."

" I know. You work in your father's bank, but you're really a musician, a famous composer. You even gave concerts in London."

It was gratifying to see that she knew about him, but her tone was light, faintly amused when it should have been humble and admiring. " You don't sound very impressed," he said.

" I am." There it was again, that mocking, impudent little grin . . . " I too am a musician, I play the piano. Perhaps I'll have

the pleasure of playing for you some day. I know you will enjoy
it . . ."

The music stopped and she disentangled herself. Her cheeks
were flushed. With the back of her hand she brushed a curl off
her temple.

"May I have the honour of the next dance?" he asked.

Demurely she opened the *carnet de bal* dangling at her wrist. "I
am sorry, I've promised it to Heinrich."

A gush of jealousy swept through him. He wanted to snatch
her *carnet de bal*, fling it away. How did she dare to promise dances
to those small-town yokels? Didn't she know he'd been waiting
three days on that confounded bench for the joy of holding her in
his arms?

"The next one then?" he asked. The pleading note in his voice
infuriated him. He was begging, that's what he was doing, begging
this provincial little coquette for a dance . . . "Unless you've
already promised it to someone else, of course," he added, looking at
her with undisguised malevolence.

"As a matter of fact, I have," she said, glancing at her booklet.
"But I could give you the one after that." She looked at him with
exasperating blandness. "Would you like me to reserve it for you?"

He felt his hands clench into fists. Yes, confound it, yes! . . .
And all the other dances, all of them, do you hear? . . . And you're
lucky there are so many people around and your dear *Maman* is
watching us or I'd take you in my arms and——

"Would you?" she repeated, offering him the limpid blueness
of her eyes.

"Nothing would give me greater pleasure."

Dutifully she wrote his name down. "Now let's go to the
buffet," she said. "I'm dying of thirst."

They sipped champagne, conscious of glances and whispered
comments about them among the fan-waving matrons. To give
themselves a countenance they talked of unimportant things, trying
to look unconcerned and well at ease.

"How do you like Frankfurt, Herr Mendelssohn?"

"It depends, Fräulein Jeanrenaud. Sometimes I like it very much
and sometimes I wish it would gently collapse and vanish from the
face of the earth."

She laughed. "You are a man of deep feelings." Before he
could say anything she went on, raising the glass to her lips. "Have
you visited our beautiful cathedral? Do you know it takes sixteen
men to ring its main bell?"

"This is most interesting. But I haven't visited the cathedral.
As a matter of fact I've seen practically nothing of the town."

"What've you been doing then?"

"Sitting on a park bench and——"

The music started again, and a handsome young man with fuzzy side whiskers materialised at her side.

"Our dance, Cécile," he said, slipping his arm around her waist.

Resentfully Felix watched her melt into Heinrich's arms and glide away. He gulped with jealousy and remained motionless and awkward, glass in hand, following her with his eyes about the room.

He heard a voice at his side. "What, you are not dancing!" It was Senator Souchay. "Come and let me introduce you to some of our charming *Fräuleins*."

And so Felix danced the next two dances with buxom freckle-faced girls whose names he did not remember. Once again he was asked how he liked Frankfurt and he dutifully replied he liked it very much. He extolled the beauty of its monuments, its lovely streets, its elegant shops, all the while searching for Cécile among the whirling couples and feeling miserable each time he caught a glimpse of her babbling and laughing in someone else's arms.

"You seemed to enjoy yourself enormously," he remarked dryly as they were dancing together again.

"I did. I love to dance and we have so few opportunities in Frankfurt."

"You certainly make the most of them."

She gave him that look of teasing innocence that infuriated him. "Shouldn't I?"

"Of course, but I resent all these young men who take your time."

"I'd be very unhappy if no one asked me to dance."

"What I mean is that I wish we could sit somewhere and talk. I have so many things I want to tell you."

"Please don't look so strangely at me, Herr Mendelssohn. Everyone's watching us."

"I don't care. When could I see you?"

"Perhaps you could call at our house before your departure." She gave him a lidded glance that sent the blood racing through his veins. "But of course you don't know where I live."

"Could I come to-morrow?"

His eagerness made her smile. "I'm afraid to-morrow is a little too soon," she said. "This is Frankfurt, Herr Mendelssohn. People wouldn't approve of your calling before Thursday."

"Thursday!" The word came in a wail of protest. "But that's three days, Fräulein Jeanrenaud."

"I know it, Herr Mendelssohn."

"What if I'm being called back? Important business is awaiting me in Berlin. I——" He felt she wasn't impressed; he wasn't even sure she believed him. "Please let me come Wednesday," he entreated "Please."

A new softness, almost tenderness, came to her eyes. "All right," she nodded. "Eight, Goethe Platz, Wednesday afternoon."

The dance came to an end.

"In case you have trouble finding the house," she said, slipping away from him, "remember there's a public bench just in front of it . . ."

He walked back to his hotel that night in a confused state of mind and not too pleased with himself. He had made several strategic mistakes. Instead of being cool and charming he had betrayed his longing and behaved like a jealous husband. Now brilliant sallies, amusing repartee came to his mind. Why did wit always come too late? Oh, to the devil with it. . . .!

His room was dark except for the pale lucence from the bright summer night. Absently he unwound his cravat, removed his coat. Leaning on the window sill he gazed at the star-sequined sky. Wisps of dance music still drifted through his mind. He could almost feel Cécile's swaying body, see her blue eyes, embedded like two pure sapphires in the pure oval of her face, the gleaming whiteness of her teeth through the oblong arch of her parted lips. He loved her, and that's all there was to it. Now that he had found her he couldn't imagine living without her. Oh, yes, there would be obstacles and problems. They were different, as different as could be. He was an artist, moody, extravagant, hypersensitive; she was a little Frankfurt bourgeoise, conventional, thrifty and very beautiful. Would they get along, would they understand each other? Who could tell? But he loved her, and now all he had to do was to make her fall in love with him. . . .

Sharply at three o'clock on Wednesday afternoon he rang the bell of the Jeanrenaud residence. For the last half hour he had paced the street, glancing at his watch every few minutes. As he pulled the bell handle he gave a friendly glance at the bench where he had spent so many watchful and lonely hours. He was making progress, he was going in . . .

The door was opened by the same fierce-looking woman who escorted Cécile on her errands. She looked every bit as forbidding as before with a new gleam of suspiciousness thrown in. Yes, the ladies were at home and would he please wait for them in the parlour.

Meekly he followed through the carpeted hallway and was duly ushered into the empty drawing-room. It bore a startling likeness to that of Senator Souchay. Same family portraits, same tufted furniture, same intense and affluent provincialism. He had just lowered himself into a green plush arm-chair when another door opened and Frau Jeanrenaud rustled in in a murmur of black taffeta, a smile on her thin aristocratic face. Obviously she had been a very beautiful woman. Her manner was courteous and ladylike in the extreme, with a faint undertone of watchful reserve.

"Indeed, it was gracious of you to call on us, Herr Mendelssohn," she began, holding out her hand to him. "Unfortunately my daughter is not here, she's been called away unexpectedly." Felix felt his gullet tighten and his heart capsize in his chest. "But I expect her to be back before long."

While speaking she had taken her place on a plush and mahogany settee and Felix had resumed his seat. The conversation opened on a tempo of allegretto by a series of effusive questions on Herr Mendelssohn's reactions to Frankfurt's architectural beauties. Like a well-trained jumper going through its hurdles he passed this preliminary test with flying colours. Frankfurt was about the most gorgeous city in Europe, no less. Then there was the lively interlude on the question of refreshments. Would Herr Mendelssohn like tea or would he prefer something more robust? A glass of their wonderful Rhine wine perhaps? Or even a liqueur? . . . This last was thrown as a bait to ascertain whether Herr Mendelssohn was a drinker of alcoholic beverages and therefore a potential drunkard.

With skill he eluded the trap, declared his preference for a glass —a small one, of course—of that wonderful Rhineland wine. This brought a flush of patriotic pride to Frau Jeanrenaud's cheeks. "One of my lifelong regrets is that Cécile wasn't born in Frankfurt," she sighed. "Through sorrowful circumstances she was born in France. Lyons, to be exact."

There followed a brief account of the short-lived Jeanrenaud marriage, ending in a futile trip to France in search of a milder climate. "Cécile was only two years old when her father died and since then I've tried to be for her both a father and a mother."

This called for some comment and Felix remarked that indeed she had been most successful.

"I've endeavoured to make a lady out of her," continued the pastor's widow. "There are so few ladies in the world to-day!"

"How right you are, Frau Jeanrenaud," Felix agreed with just the right tone of compunction. "It is one of the most alarming signs of our times."

He went on to ask her what in her opinion were a lady's most important attributes and qualities. A lady, Frau Jeanrenaud declared, was a paragon of all domestic, social, moral and feminine virtues. At all times she conducted herself in a blameless manner, attended to her religious and social obligations, provided a well-managed home for her husband, brought up his children and created around him an atmosphere of orderliness and serene contentment.

The conversation was losing itself in generalities when Cécile came in and again Felix felt a spasm of pleasure at the sight of her beauty. She apologised for being late and after removing her dainty straw bonnet sat down with them, nibbling one of the biscuits that had been brought in. Soon Frau Jeanrenaud recalled an urgent appointment and announced that she reluctantly must tear herself away.

"I hope we may have again the pleasure of your company before your departure," she said, and Felix interpreted her words as a sign that he had been weighed, examined and found acceptable as a suitor. "What have you been doing these last two days?" asked Cécile, taking another biscuit. "Following any more young ladies about?"

He gasped. "What do you mean?"

"You weren't behind us yesterday when I went to the market with Catherine and I missed you. I thought you might have decided to follow someone else."

He considered her, speechless from astonishment. "You mean you knew I was following you?" he said at last.

"Of course."

"It might have been someone else. How did you know it was I?"

She laughed. "Even before you arrived every girl in town knew about you. After all, it's not every day that a handsome and rich bachelor from the big city comes to Frankfurt. When I saw a young man I had never seen before, in foreign-looking clothes and twirling his cane, I knew it was you."

"And you didn't even give me a glance," he said reproachfully.

"On the contrary. I gave you many glances but you were too busy being clever and spying on us."

"I object to the spying, but we'll ignore it. What, may I ask, was your opinion of me?"

"That you looked very much as I expected. A handsome, rather supercilious, rather spoiled young man with a roving eye and too much money."

"Thank you," he said dryly. "At least you are frank."

"Aren't I?" She gave him a bewitching smile. "I am also an excellent cook."

"A most excellent achievement," he said with what he hoped was scathing irony.

"*Maman* taught me that the way to a man's heart is through his stomach."

"Madame your mother is a fount of wisdom." He would have

liked to take her in his arms, cut short this bantering with a kiss.
" Why do you call her *Maman?*"

" Because I spoke French as a child. As a matter of fact I am
something of a linguistic *bouillabaisse*. My father was Swiss, Mother
is German and I was born in France. My godmother and my first
governess were English and my godfather Italian. So you see," she
added with a twinkle of her magnificent eyes, " I'll be able to
talk back to you in several languages."

Her words opened a window in her heart. To talk back to
someone you must see that someone, must you not? . . . It meant
that she intended seeing him again. It was still too early for tenderness and serious talk, but all this was a step towards intimacy. They
were far from the talk about Frankfurt and its beautiful Cathedral.
" And so, that's all you thought of me," he said. " A supercilious
young man."

" Rather supercilious," she shaded. " Later when I saw you
sitting on that hard bench——"

" Do you mean you saw me?" he asked, utterly deflated.

" Of course. I was watching you from behind the curtains of
my bedroom. It's at the end of the apartment and you never thought
of looking at it."

There was no end to women's cunning and duplicity, even
innocent young Frankfurt maidens. " And what did you think
then?"

" I thought you were a very patient and determined young man.
At times I felt sorry for you, especially that afternoon when it rained
and you got drenched to the bone. I wanted to come down and
give you an umbrella."

" Very thoughtful of you. Why didn't you?"

" It wouldn't have been proper. Remember this is Frankfurt.
But I did entertain you with my piano playing."

The recollection of the mangled Mozart minuet made him
wince. " You should be glad the way to a man's heart isn't through
his ears or you'd end up as a spinster."

" I can see that you despise me," she said with well-simulated
despair. " You'll probably never want to see me again."

" Perhaps I could give you a few lessons while I'm being detained
in Frankfurt and you could give me a sample or two of this wonderful cooking of yours?"

She hesitated. " I'll have to ask *Maman,*" she said. But already
he could read assent in her eyes.

And so it became known in Frankfurt that the handsome and
wealthy young man from Berlin frequented the Jeanrenauds under
the pretext of giving piano lessons to Cécile. This bit of deceit
deceived no one. Disappointed mothers of marriageable daughters

remarked among themselves that some girls would stop at nothing to catch a husband.

Meanwhile a sort of pattern established itself between Felix and his pupil. He arrived promptly at two o'clock and was ushered by Catherine into the presence of the Jeanrenaud ladies. There was an exchange of talk about the weather, the temperature and Cécile's progress. Then Frau Jeanrenaud would excuse herself and sometimes she would actually go out. Felix would hear the ancient brougham as it squeaked away from the house. Most of the time she merely withdrew to her room to knit or write those endless gossipy letters that were the fashion in those days.

In the drawing-room the piano lesson would begin, with Catherine erupting into the room whenever the piano stopped.

"You see," Cécile explained, "she's been with me since I was born and she feels she must watch over me."

"I have an old valet, Gustav, who is a little like that."

"Piano lessons are especially suspect because two years ago a perfectly brought-up young lady, a friend of mine, ran away with her piano teacher."

A few days later she remarked, "Does your father know you're giving piano lessons instead of attending to his business?"

"Herr Rothschild has written to him explaining I must stay in Frankfurt for a while, but even if he hadn't I couldn't go home now."

She glanced at him over her shoulder. "Why?"

"Because I can't bear the thought of going away from you." The words fell in the silence of the room like pebbles in a pool.

She remained calm, her eyes unblinking. "I don't want you ever to go away from me," she murmured.

Suddenly they were in each other's arms.

"Then you do love me, don't you?" he asked in a whisper.

"I didn't at first. I thought you were just having fun with a silly small-town girl. But when I saw you sitting on that bench hour after hour I began to like you. Then the day it started to rain and you didn't go away——" They were speaking lips to lips, gazing into each other's eyes. "That day I fell in love with you."

"That was almost three weeks ago, why didn't you say anything?"

"I wanted to be sure."

"And now?"

"Now I am sure. I'll love you, Felix, to the end of my life."

Chapter 4

FELIX PUSHED away the page of music he was writing, rested his quill in the inkwell and leaned back in his chair. He was knotting his hands behind his head, a familiar gesture of his, when the thought struck him that although he had been married three months, only now did he really *feel* married.

Marriage was, among many other things, a state of mind. He hadn't felt married during their honeymoon—let alone during the wedding ceremony in Frankfurt's French church, when he had looked at Cécile as though she were a perfect stranger. He hadn't even felt married during those first few months in Düsseldorf.

Now all of a sudden he did.

It was a complex, elusive feeling, yet very real. For instance, he enjoyed the quiet of the house on this Sunday afternoon. It was only a rented house and rather commonplace, although it had a nice view of the Rhine. Cécile had chosen it after a great deal of hesitation, for it had to be neither too grand nor too humble, just the right kind of a house for the young Herr Direktor of the Düsseldorf Orchestra. He, of course, wanted to take the first house that had been shown to them, an enormous over-ornamented mansion that had belonged to a former burgomaster, and of course it would have been all wrong, a gesture of ostentation . . . He liked the arrangement of this study with his pianoforte in a corner, the portrait of his father over the mantelpiece and the bright flowery curtains Cécile had chosen, sewn and hung herself. He enjoyed knowing that Catherine and Gustav were somewhere, probably in the kitchen or the pantry arguing like cat and dog about the infinite superiority, both social and financial, of their respective master and mistress. But most of all he loved knowing that Cécile was upstairs in their bedroom, hunched at a little mahogany secretary, writing one of her interminable letters to her dear *Maman*. It made him happy just to know that she was close at hand, that he could call her and he would instantly hear her answering voice. He enjoyed the prospect of dining alone with her to-night, a simple, well-prepared, well-served meal; and they would chat and look at each other across the candlelit table and she would be well groomed, ladylike and beautiful, and he would be proud she was his wife.

That's what it was to *feel* married. You discovered you enjoyed a lot of little things you didn't even know existed. It was a quiet joyousness that stayed with you all day, pervaded your whole life.

114

A feeling of stability, security. An assurance that you had reached the harbour, found the solution, the only solution to the problem of living.

It transformed your thinking. The things you'd done before appeared suddenly incongruous, absurd—the acts of some younger and silly brother you didn't quite approve of . . . For instance, it was hard to believe that less than a year ago he had followed her into a cheese shop, sat for hours on a public (and very hard) bench, gazed at her window, dreaming dazzling and incoherent dreams. Why, a child would have had more sense! . . . But then falling in love was some sort of mental collapse, an innocent wonderful madness. You became an idiot—a harmless, irresponsible, star-gazing, window-gazing idiot.

In retrospect, the whole Frankfurt episode had a glow of un-reality, a flavour of operetta. The ball at Senator Souchay's—" You dance beautifully, Fräulein Jeanrenaud." "Thank you, Herr Mendelssohn "—the first stiff visits in the Jeanrenaud parlour, the sham piano lessons, with Catherine popping up each time the piano stopped, the careful badinage, the ritual gestures of a provincial courtship. And later, back to Berlin, the difficult moment when he had to face Nina. Fortunately luck was with him. Immediately he had sensed something was wrong. Nina, usually so gay and carefree, was uneasy, averting her eyes, making conversation. And suddenly she was in his arms, sobbing like a child, stammering, "Felix, I can't marry you, I've fallen in love with someone else!" and he, the master hypocrite comforting her, trying to look heartbroken, asking her to tell him all about it. And poor Nina, nibbling her handkerchief, shedding real tears, describing how she had met Arthur Riemann, a young architect, and lost her heart. "Will you ever forgive me, Felix?" Of course he would, didn't he want her to be happy? And of course he had overplayed the part of the jilted but magnanimous lover and she had begun to resent his generosity and stoicism, and in two minutes she had shattered his posturing, pried his secret and soon they were laughing and crying on each other's shoulders, like the two love-sick idiots they were.

Father had been splendid. Sad, of course, but understanding and superlatively intelligent about the whole thing. He had instantly grasped the difficulties arising from the difference of religions. " It's going to take a little time, Jakob. You must be patient. It's going to require finesse and savoir-faire, breaking the news to your mother and your grandmother." Father loved to use French and sometimes Italian words to show he wasn't just an ignorant money-making banker. "Better let me handle it." Naturally he was right. Even with his finesse and savoir-faire it had taken time and patience. Mother was adamant at first. Her objections were social as well as religious. " My son marrying a pastor's daughter . . .!" In her mouth the " pastor's daughter " sounded abysmally plebian, the lowest step in the social order, somewhere between a sexton and a gravedigger. But Father was ready. He had gathered enough information about the Jeanrenauds and the Souchays to fill a book. Patiently he had explained that while Jeanrenaud was a poor though distinguished clergyman, his wife, Cécile's mother, was a descendant of a noble French family and one of Frankfurt's heiresses. " I shouldn't be surprised if the Souchays were richer than we are," he had declared. Which of course wasn't true but had produced some effect, for money impressed everyone—even rich people.

Having at last obtained the grudging approval of everyone in the family he had at once journeyed to Frankfurt, travelling in his customary style—that is, with his doctor, two secretaries, a coachful of cooks and servants and for the occasion a trunkful of expensive presents. In Frankfurt he had with proper formality acquainted himself with Senator Souchay, head of the Souchay clan and like him a banker. It was inevitable that they should like each other on sight, which they did, and after that it all was very easy. Father had been introduced to Frau Jeanrenaud and her daughter and proceeded to charm them both with his compliments and his excellent French, all the while making inner observations and reaching definite conclusions. The ladies—especially the pastor's widow—having done the same and the interview having proved mutually favourable, the two bankers had then begun negotiations on the matter of dowry, future inheritances and various clauses of the marriage contract. Both being intelligent, fair and wealthy, they had reached rapid and complete agreement. Whereupon a formal request for Fräulein Cécile Sophie Charlotte Jeanrenaud's hand was addressed and granted amidst much rejoicing, culminating in a formal dinner and the distribution of presents. Father had returned after making an unexpected detour to Düsseldorf, bringing joyous tidings and glowing reports about his son's future in-laws.

Three weeks later the Jeanrenaud ladies, duly escorted by the Senator, the indispensable Catherine and a small retinue of servants had arrived at 3, Leipzigerstrasse, in two mud-splattered berlins. And then the miracle had taken place—everybody had fallen in love with everybody. Mother had instantly taken to Cécile's *Maman*. Two days later they were calling each other by their first names, knitting together and exchanging reminiscences about their children. Cécile had conquered Fanny and Rebecka with her smile. Senator Souchay had proven a demon at chess and beaten Father twice in succession, thus arousing much grumbling and sputtering, but cementing an already solid friendship. Even Grandmother Salomon, looking like a disapproving spectre in her powdered hair and blazing diamonds, had finally succumbed to the concerted blandishments of the Jeanrenauds, Souchays and Mendelssohns. Suddenly her sharp, still handsome eyes had clouded with tears, her stern face had contorted in a spasm of emotion. She had drawn Cécile to her bosom, kissed her brow and lovingly caressed her blonde hair. It was a thrilling moment. Whereupon Fanny, quick as a flash, had thrown herself at her grandmother's feet begging her to forgive poor Uncle George in Rome. To everyone's stupefaction grandmother had announced that, Christian or not, her son was still her son and she wanted to kiss him before she died. Thus the visit ended in an orgy of sentimental effusion, a small-scale preview of the millennium with everybody weeping, falling into one another's arms and kissing to his heart's content.

To crown it all, sometime in July, a letter had arrived from Düsseldorf. An official-looking letter profusely sealed in red wax and signed with a flowery paraph by the Town's President, Doktor Worringen. It began by a formal declaration that the Honourable Members of the Honourable Town Council of Düsseldorf, having met in special session, were sending their warmest greetings to Herr Felix Mendelssohn, residing at 3, Leipzigerstrasse, in the city of Berlin. It proceeded to state that, whereas the present Herr Direktor of the Düsseldorf Orchestra, after many years of dutiful and glorious services, had elected to submit his resignation, said resignation to become effective on the first day of the forthcoming month of October, the Honourable Members of the Town Council having considered Herr Mendelssohn's exceptional musical capacities were offering said Herr Mendelssohn the post of Herr Direktor of the Düsseldorf Orchestra, together with all privileges, honoraria, bonuses and special attributes attached to said post: To wit, a fixed salary of four hundred thalers per annum, three cords of burning wood and one cord of kindling, two barrels of ordinary Rhine wine and one barrel of choice Rhine wine, the official title of Town Kapellmeister as well as Direktor of Musical Activities. . . .

"What, no fire, no light!" Cécile's voice shattered his musings like a stone crashing through a pane of glass. "What are you doing in this dark room?"

"Saving money." This was said in a tone of long-suffering plaintiveness, as a rebuke to her constant charges of extravagance. "After all, candles are very expensive, and a poor four-hundred-thaler-a-year Kapellmeister——"

With wifely concern she was clucking her tongue about to pull the bell cord when he called after her, "Leave that bell alone and come here. Here, on my knees," he said, pulling her down. "Now let me look at you."

Slowly he ran his eyes over her lovely face. "Only twenty years old," he sighed despondently, "and already the signs of advanced decrepitude are visible——" Furiously she fought to free herself and he had to grip her two wrists. "But we're now chained in the iron bonds of Holy Matrimony"—a brave sigh—"and I'll make the best of it."

"Listen to him!" she protested, struggling ineffectually. "I should've let you sit on that bench! *Maman* was right. You never know the sort of man you've married until after the honeymoon."

"Your *Maman* has a gift for the obvious. Now as your lord and master I command you to give me a kiss."

"After what you've said? . . . Never!"

"Am I to understand you refuse to kiss your husband? Do you know I could have you put in jail for conjugal insubordination?"

She made a face at him and placed a peck on the tip of his nose.

"Do you call this a kiss, Frau Mendelssohn? I have a good mind to send you back to your village."

"Frankfurt's not a village," she flung hotly. "It's a beautiful town. Much more beautiful than Düsseldorf or Berlin." How lovely she looked when she argued. Her eyes flashed, her delicate nostrils flared, her young bosom throbbed in the blue bodice of her dress. "And the people there are much nicer."

"Perhaps, but they don't know how to kiss."

He drew her to him, gently lifted her face, pressed his lips against her lips. He felt her mouth soft and moist, her body turn limp. He held her in his arms a long time.

"This is better," he announced with clinical detachment. "But you need much practice. I prescribe a daily lesson."

Of such nonsense happiness is made. To the joyous in heart everything is excuse for happiness.

"Besides," she said in a fresh outburst of vexation, "everything here is more expensive than in Frankfurt. Do you know how much they wanted to upholster a chair? Four thalers!"

"The robbers!" he exclaimed with sweeping indignation.

"But I argued with them and they took off twelve pfennigs."

"Isn't this wonderful . . .!" A faint undertone of genuine reproof crept into his voice. "But, after all, we aren't exactly poor. Aren't you a little bit ashamed, just a little bit, to haggle with tradesmen over twelve pfennigs?"

Her reply was unhesitant. "Merchants don't respect you if you don't haggle a bit. That's what *Maman* said."

"Did your mother ever stop talking?"

"Now you are impertinent. But when we were engaged you used to tell her what a wonderful education she'd given me."

"She has. But, my little Cilette, I am not a poor man. You

know that. You yourself are a very wealthy lady, in case you don't know it . . . Why those ridiculous economics of pfennigs?"

She stared at him as if he had spoken an obscene word. " But, Felix it's a sin to squander money."

" But not pfennigs. Come on, darling, let's be reasonable about this thing."

He felt her flinch from him slightly. " Little brooks make big rivers," she said. Her childhood had been haunted with proverbs, homely sayings and righteous platitudes. To her they were God's commands and her refuge in time of stress. " If a housewife doesn't watch pfennigs, soon she won't watch thalers. She will be a bad housewife and before long a bad wife and God will withdraw His blessing from her home."

He remained silent an instant, struck by the intense seriousness of her tone. She really did believe that if you didn't watch pfennigs you wound up a dissolute wife . . . For the first time he sensed a fundamental difference between them. To him luxury was necessary, more precisely the subdued elegance that only wealth could provide. Money was to be enjoyed, not flaunted or ostentatiously displayed, but certainly not buried in iron safes. To her, luxury meant extravagance and extravagance meant sin. He felt that she must have disapproved of his sumptuous Berlin home. One day she had said, " God doesn't reside in palaces." Another one of those pious sayings that had been sown into her childish mind. Yes, God frowned upon extravagance—even pfennig extravagance. He was on the side of the meek, the modest, the thrifty . . .

" Anyway," he said, pushing his thoughts aside, " why do you have this chair upholstered? We won't be here next year, I hope. You don't think I want to be the conductor of a provincial orchestra all my life, do you? My old music teacher Zelter has written me he's pushing my cause with the board of trustees of the Singakademie. I may get his place when he resigns next year. And after that there's nothing else but the Berlin Philharmonic. How would you like to be the wife of the conductor of the Berlin Orchestra?"

She did not join in his excitement. " I'd like better to have a house of our own and live a happy life in a quiet little town."

" But Cilette, you can be just as happy in a big city!" he exclaimed. " Don't you see, darling, that I'd die if I had to spend the rest of my life in one of those provincial towns."

He felt that the discussion was becoming too serious and intense. With an effort he resumed the bantering tone of a moment ago. " You may not know it, my dear Frau Mendelssohn, but you've married a first-class man, and a first-class man belongs in a first-class position in a first-class city . . . Now let's have a little light in this place."

The dinner was, as usual, simple but excellent.

"One thing can be said for Frankfurt housewives," he remarked teasingly. "They feed their men well."

The compliment brought a spark of pleasure to her eyes. In the golden gleam of candlelight her beauty seemed to grow. It became iridescent and flowerlike. Indeed she was a joy to behold. Again he was struck by the thought that but for the grace of God she could easily have become an illustrious courtesan. What mysterious alchemy of Nature had combined such dramatic beauty with such purity of soul. A thrifty blameless housewife with the face of an adventuress. . . .

They talked of various things. She told him the innocuous and unexciting gossip she had heard in sewing circles—the wife of the first councilman had had a quarrel with her dressmaker; the wife of the tax collector had burst the laces of her stays when she had found herself seated *below* the town treasurer's wife—for in the few weeks since they arrived in Düsseldorf she had already become a part of the city's social and charitable organisations. While he was still regarded as a foreigner from Berlin, she had been instantly welcomed by the local ladies as one of their own. They loved everything about her. Even her slight Frankfurt accent endeared her to them. Of course, her family background—people had heard of the Souchays in Düsseldorf—and her wealth, which for being carefully concealed was none the less well known, had done the rest.

He regarded her popularity with detached amusement, pleased that she could easily make friends and would not be lonely during the long hours he spent composing or rehearsing the orchestra.

"If you don't watch out they're going to elect you president of the sewing circle one of these days," he remarked with a chuckle.

"Me? . . . Gracious, no! I'm too young." Her modesty was genuine and disarming. "In a few years perhaps."

He wanted to say that in a few years they wouldn't be in Düsseldorf but in Berlin. He checked himself. "You'll be the prettiest president they've ever had."

She thanked him with a narrowing of her blue eyes as they rose from the table. They passed into the study for their after-dinner coffee. Both preferred it to the drawing-room, which was too big and formal. Cécile had worked hard to make it intimate and restful, and she had succeeded. There they spent their evenings enjoying its peacefulness, the crackling of the logs in the fireplace.

They sipped their coffee in silence, savouring the tenderness of the moment. Relaxed, he leaned back on his chair. This was happiness, this was married life as he dreamed of it . . . A fine dinner with a beautiful wife, gaiety, tranquillity. And now coffee before a cheerful fire . . .

As he gazed at the flames his mind wandered into the past, the recent past of his strange wedding night. They had left Frankfurt late in the afternoon with a blustery August rain beating against the coach windows as it jostled and squeaked and rocked over the ruts of the country lane to the "charming and secluded" inn someone had selected for them. Cécile cuddled sleepily against his chest, exhausted by the strain of the day, the religious ceremony in French, the interminable allocution also in French—why were pastors of all faiths such confounded and pompous chatterboxes? —the enormous afternoon reception. They had dined in their room, low-ceilinged with hewn smoky beams and a small window at the back, before a huge fire. The wine and champagne had kindled a semblance of gaiety, a semblance of amorousness. They had laughed—the champagne had made her giggle—kissed and made love in a daze of fatigue and apprehension . . . People shouldn't make love on their wedding night—at least they shouldn't be taught they must make love . . .

They had gone to Paris on their honeymoon. It had been a delight to watch her gasp in wonder, feel her little hand clench his arm at the sight of the Louvre, Notre Dame, the cafés, the dazzling shops. He had insisted on buying her a complete wardrobe, and in a week she had become a bewitching Parisian. Then had begun the whirl of festivities. Dinner here, dinner there. Everyone wanted to meet "*la belle* Madame Mendelssohn." The Rothschilds, James and Betty, had given a magnificent *soirée* in her honour. Naturally Chopin had been on hand since they had arrived. He was still dazzled by his success as Paris's fashionable piano teacher. "*Mon cher* Felix, do you know how much I get for a lesson? Twenty francs . . .!" Publishers had begun to buy his compositions. He had rented an elegant apartment on Chaussée d'Antin, acquired a carriage and a valet—a Pole naturally—a dandy's wardrobe and four dozen pairs of white gloves. Of course he wanted to introduce Cécile into that world of cosmopolitan aristocracy in which he moved. And so it came to pass that one evening they all had gone to a *soirée dansante* given by Princess Potocka—and there was Maria . . .

A blow is a blow, and there's little difference between shocks— whether of pain or pleasure. He had spied her at once, gowned in a cloud of white tulle and surrounded, of course, by a pack of pant-ing males. He knew she'd seen him, but fortunately dancing was in progress and he had been able to lead Cécile away. Two hours later as he was going to the buffet to fetch her a glass of champagne he had felt a hand on his sleeve. Maria had been waiting for him, concealed behind a velvet portière. How pale her face was. Her eyes had grown enormous. " Now you have the beautiful wife and maybe you forget me, no?" she breathed in his ear. " But I still love you." Then before he knew it, with a motion of reptilian grace her mouth was covering his in a kiss that was like a gulp of some enchanted and burning brew. And she was gone. . . .

" Darling, what're you thinking about?" Again Cécile's voice jerked him out of his thoughts. " Your coffee's getting cold."

" I was thinking of the wonderful time we had in Switzerland, after we left Paris." Of such small lies married life was made. " Remember the little village with its toy chalets and our inn that looked like a cuckoo clock? And the river where I used to go fishing?"

" And never caught anything," she added with a twinkle.

" That's because the fish were looking at you instead of nibbling at my bait and getting caught, as they're supposed to."

" Let's go back there this summer for our holiday," she suggested impulsively.

" I'd love to. There's something unique about Switzerland. It's a universe in miniature. You feel you are in another world—a world of beauty and peace." He rested his cup on the small side-table. " I think I'll have some cognac."

She looked at him curiously but rose to pull the bell rope. Gustav appeared and returned a moment later with an assortment of brandy bottles on a silver tray.

Felix took an appreciative sip after warming the glass in his cupped hands. " I know you're thinking I am on my way to Hell," he grinned, catching her covert and anxious glance.

" Not at all," she said testily, going on with her knitting.

" But you do," he insisted. " I can read it on your face. Already you see yourself as the wife of a drunkard and you're going to be brave about it." He chuckled softly. " My little pastor's daughter."

" Liquor is the tool of Satan," she said. " And there's nothing wrong about being a pastor's daughter."

" On the contrary. But it gives you such exalted standards of virtue that no man can possibly live up to them." His grin deepened. " Do you know why I'm having this infernal thimbleful of cognac? Because to-day is our third-month wedding anniversary."

" So you *did* remember!" she cried. " Oh, darling!" She tossed her knitting aside and came to sit next to him on the sofa. She was almost crying from joy. " I thought you'd forgotten."

" As usual you were misjudging me." From his vest pocket he drew a small jeweller's box. " Not only did I not forget but I brought you a little trinket. Of course it was much too expensive and I had to haggle a lot to get it at my price——"

" Now you're making fun of me," she cried, snatching the box from his hand. Of course he was making fun of her, but this was his way, and she didn't care. He had remembered, he hadn't grown tired of her as husbands often did after the honeymoon . . . " Oh, Felix!" she gasped, staring at the diamond-studded cameo brooch. " You shouldn't have done it!"

" Think so? . . . I think you're right. It was much too expensive and on second thoughts, I'd better take it back." He pretended to reach for it, but she grasped it fiercely and pressed it to her bosom. " Now I know you married me only for my money! Oh, well . . ."

" I love it, I love it, I love it!" she cried, clasping the brooch on her bodice. " And I love you," she cried, flinging her arms around his neck. " I think you're the most wonderful, the most handsome, the most——"

She was kissing him on the cheeks, the ears, the corners of his mouth—avid little kisses that sent ripples of pleasure through him. While talking she was mussing his hair, cuddling herself deeper to him, playing a game that was both sensuous and innocent. Gradually the contact of her young body stirred, then inflamed his flesh. Now it was he who was kissing her on the nape of the neck, the pink shell of her ears, her smooth warm throat while she let out little cooing gasps of protest and delight. His muscles hardened, his blood ran hot in his veins. Suddenly he lifted her in his arms, carried her protesting and laughing up to their bedroom.

" That'll teach you to arouse the beast in men," he said, plumping her down on the bed.

They were happy that night. Happier than they'd ever been. She gave herself with an acquiescence, an abandon he hadn't found in her until now. For the first time her sensuality matched his own, for once there was no reserve in her caresses. Later, as she lay at his side, she still whispered words of love. " I love you, I . . . love . . ." Mumbled litany that dissolved before it reached his ears. At last she fell asleep, her face buried in his shoulder.

Once again, in the stillness of the night, his thoughts wandered. Yes, now he really *felt* married . . . He knew at long last that this beautiful and modest pastor's daughter, this thrifty housewife of his was capable of passion. She was his completely and forever. He wanted her at his side for the rest of his life. He no longer regretted anything—anything—from the past. He wanted only to make her happy, bring gleams of pleasure to her blue eyes . . . She was his wife and he was her husband. They were one, body and soul. Oh, yes, before them stood Life with its problems, its disconcerting trivialities, its secret disappointments, but they did love each other and their love would endure. Together they would make the journey through the alleys of Time, hand in hand, their hearts beating in unison . . .

Winter closed in, bringing its snows, its icy winds, but Cécile was ready. She had been taught how to deal with it, keep it where it belonged—outside. By now every double window had been checked, every rattling shutter secured, every chimney scraped and swept by sooty-faced little boys. There were buckets of salted butter and cooking fat in the kitchen, provisions in the larder. The cords of wood promised by the town council had been carefully stacked in the cellar. Now let it snow, let it freeze, let the wind howl and rage all it wanted, the Mendelssohns were snug in their little house overlooking the Rhine.

Even when they ventured outside—Cécile to her marketing or sewing circles, Felix to his rehearsals—the Mendelssohns knew how to keep winter at a distance. She had seen to that also. Nice woollen underwear for him and quilted waistcoats that protected the chest and heavy woollen gloves that kept the hands warm. The very best and, unfortunately, the most expensive . . . But *Maman* had taught that warm clothing was cheaper than doctors and there was no haggling about such things.

If only Felix would understand the difference between the things that were important and the things that weren't . . . But he didn't. To him money was to be spent. And he certainly could spend it, sometimes on the most foolish things! . . . A month ago he had arrived home preciously carrying a tiny package. " Look Cilette, look what I've bought!" He was as excited as a child on Christmas morning . . . " Isn't she beautiful! . . . Can you believe she is more than two thousand years old! Look at those breasts, the curve of that hip! . . . Of course she has no head and only one arm but it doesn't matter . . ." Naturally she didn't want to hurt his feelings, but she could have cried from spite. A knick-knack, that's what it was. An old disgusting little marble statue of a naked woman, the kind they have in museums. That's what he was so excited about! He couldn't stop looking at her, caressing her. " I'll put her on my desk, so I can look at her when I work. And you know, Cilette, the dealer didn't want to sell her to me, he said he was reserving her for the museum's annual purchase. But I put a quick stop to that!" He certainly had—with four hundred! four hundred thalers—his year's salary.

Thank Heaven, she'd kept herself in check, remembering that a good wife must indulge her husband—at first. She'd even said it looked fine when he put the statue on his desk. But a few days later when he was in a good mood—for there were days when he brooded, his head lost in his music or something—she had cuddled to him and told him how the ladies of the sewing circle were meeting at the house the next day and what would they say if they saw a naked woman on his desk? Sure enough, he'd burst into a long tirade about "those stupid narrow-minded provincials" and how glad he would be to get away from Düsseldorf. She had let him rant on and on, all he wanted. Finally he had said quietly, "You don't like her much, do you?" And he had put the statue in a closet. And he hadn't put it back on his desk. Which proved that *Maman* was right when she said that though it took patience and tact, a good wife could always make her husband see his mistakes.

That winter Felix applied himself to his duties as Direktor of the Düsseldorf Orchestra. It was not a very good orchestra. Düsseldorf had exalted artistic pretensions, but the musical budget was small. The musicians could not devote their full time to the practice of their instruments. They kept shops, played in taverns. Some were employees in some other municipal service; others exploited farms in the suburbs. They arrived at rehearsals with their violins or their clarinets under their coats when it rained, under their arms when it didn't. But they were good people. They were proud of him and did their best.

He too, did his best. Because he liked them and also because he knew that this Düsseldorf post was the first rung of the ladder. Important cities, especially Berlin, were watching him. Occasionally they sent scouts who reported on his merits. And so he did the best with what he had. At rehearsals he was patient, did not shout or rave or indulge in sarcastic remarks. To the flutist—or the tuba player or the cellist—who had played the wrong note, he would say, "See if the copyist hasn't made a mistake. This *F* should be sharp." And the flutist was grateful. During recesses he had coffee sent in and he would tell little anecdotes about the great masters. How Handel used to conduct opera sitting at the clavichord, then rush on the stage to sing the part of a missing singer, then hurry back to the pit and become a conductor once again. How Haydn would go down on his knees and pray for inspiration, how Mozart had written *Don Giovanni* in two weeks and Casanova, the old reprobate, had helped him with the libretto; how Beethoven used to play the violin in the Bonn Orchestra . . . Then he would rap his baton and the rehearsal would be resumed.

He did something during those long winter months. He learned the intricacies of provincial life. In this Cécile proved of invaluable help. This twenty-year-old housewife had an unerring social instinct. And one needed it to guide oneself through the maze of small-town social hierarchy. Düsseldorf counted only twenty-eight thousand inhabitants, but it had more razor-edged class distinctions than India and more mundane prejudices than London.

"But Cilette," he would wail, "do we have to invite Worringen and his wife to dinner? They're such bores."

"He is Town President," she would reply with an almost imperceptible tightening of lips. "And she's been very kind to me at the sewing circle."

And so they would have the Worringens to dinner and perhaps von Schadow, the direktor of the Fine Arts Academy, and Judge Immermann. The Mayor would orate about Düsseldorf civic problems. Von Schadow, who was very pious, would explain that a painting should be "a sermon on canvas," and Immermann, who besides being a judge was a scholar and a poet, would rave about Sophocles. "Such a remarkable man, this Sophocles!" he would cackle in his high-pitched voice. "He was a priest as well as a general, a man of great charm and wit, a gourmet, a sensualist. Something of a musician too. At sixteen he conducted a chorus in a paean on the victory of Salamis." Immermann's great love was the theatre, he burned with a passion to present his translations of Greek tragedies. Doggedly he harassed the town council with tracts and pamphlets on the creation of a classical theatre and the prodigious benefits Düsseldorf would derive from it.

Those dinners were Cécile's masterpieces. She would enchant Worringen with her fervid attention as he told her about the sewage problem. Von Schadow she would conquer with a smile and Immermann with a compliment. "How wonderful it must be to read Greek and Latin!" she would coo, fluttering her long eyelashes in awe-struck admiration. Felix would smile and say little, remembering the sumptuous dinners at 3, Leipzigerstrasse, graced by the presence of the intellectual and artistic élite of Europe. Once again he would promise himself an escape from the stifling, deadening atmosphere of small town life. No, he didn't belong in Düsseldorf. He had captured London, he had played for the Queen of England, he had been welcomed in the homes of duchesses and international bankers. His place was in Berlin, London, Paris, St. Petersburg, even New York, perhaps. This was where he belonged and, by God, this was where he would be.

He had tried to make Cécile see the differences between great capitals and pretentious little towns. He had made fun of Düsseldorf's cultural aspirations, laughed at von Schadow's sanctimonious verbiage and Immermann's Greek delusions. With surprise he had discovered she resented his levity.

"They're fine people and you shouldn't laugh at them," she said one day, her eyes sharp and reproachful.

" Of course they're fine people, but don't you see they aren't really first-class? Yes, they have some talent but nothing more. They've settled here because instinctively they feel that this is where they belong. In Berlin or London they wouldn't count. Here they can play the oracles. Don't you see, darling, they're second-rate."

" No, I don't." Her voice was cold, almost cutting. " Herr von Schadow is a famous artist. His paintings hang in many museums. And Herr Immermann is a great scholar. And a judge."

He looked at her as if she were a stranger. There was no use. She didn't understand and never would. She really liked those people, was impressed by them. She wouldn't recognise the difference between a van Schadow and a Delacroix, an Immermann and a Goethe .. " You're right, Cilette. They're fine people and I shouldn't make fun of them. Now tell me what you've been doing to-day."

Spring arrived and brought Felix a bitter disappointment. His candidacy to the conductorship of the Singakademie had run afoul of a great deal of intrigue and opposition. In a long and doleful letter his music teacher Zelter explained why his efforts had been of no avail. The trustees had felt that Felix was too young to head such an important and venerable institution. And there was the question of religion. The Singakademie was a Christian institution, devoted mostly to sacred music, and the trustees, while admitting his musical superiority, had deemed it unwise to choose as conductor a man of another faith. A certain Rungenhagen had been appointed.

The news shattered Felix. In one stroke his hopes to move to Berlin crumpled to the ground. He fell into a mood of brooding despondency. " They admit I am a better musician, but because I am young and a Jew they give the post to someone else," he commented angrily. During this troubled period Cécile was all patience and understanding. Knowing she had never been in sympathy with his Berlin ambitions, he could only admire the selflessness of her devotion.

" You are a wonderful woman," he told her one day, taking her into his arms. " I don't know why you ever married me. I am moody, selfish, vain. Perhaps I am not such a first-rate musician as I thought. I am just another Immermann or von Schadow."

" Don't say such things," she retorted hotly. " You are a great musician and they'll soon recognise their mistake. Why, you are a wonderful conductor. And composer, too. Every bit as good as Beethoven or Mozart."

He smiled, touched by the enormity of her compliment. Of course she was only trying to soothe his feelings, salve his bruised ego. She knew nothing about music. Beethoven, Mozart meant little to her. She was doing her wifely duty, standing by her husband, her poor, unhappy, unappreciated husband. " My wonderful Cilette," he murmured, kissing her blonde hair, " my loyal little wife! . . . Let's forget about the whole silly business. After all, I still have my position here. I have the most beautiful, most adorable wife in the world. We are in good health, we have a nice little home, we love each other, and in three weeks we'll be in Switzerland. What more could a man want?"

As soon as they could, they hurried to Switzerland and returned to their toy village over Lake Thunn. Nothing had changed. The inn still looked like a cuckoo clock and the innkeeper welcomed them back with genuine effusiveness. They took long walks through sun-shafted forests, hand in hand, happier than they had ever been, even on their honeymoon. He went trout fishing in a clear mountain stream and once stumbled headlong into the water. They lazed in green meadows and lay side by side on the grass, gazing at the snowy peaks frozen in stormy splendour, listening to the distant chiming of cow bells.

Not once did he mention Berlin. Instead he told her about his Düsseldorf projects for the next winter. " I think now I'll perform some of my works. You can't imagine the pleasure of conducting your own compositions, even if the orchestra isn't very good . . . And then Immermann said the town council has finally approved his plan for a theatre. We may even be able to collaborate on an opera I've always wanted to write. It would be based on Shakespeare's *Tempest*. He might give me a good libretto. You see, darling, a good libretto isn't easy to write . . ."

" I am sure Herr Immermann will write a beautiful libretto." She was happy, sensing he was becoming reconciled to provincial life. Great cities frightened her, they were full of beautiful, unscrupulous women . . .

" We may even be able to produce two or three operas during the winter season. He would attend to all business matters, I would supervise the artistic side, train the choruses, direct the orchestra. Imagine directing *Don Giovanni*, for instance, in Düsseldorf!"

" It'd be wonderful!" She did not care for opera, but she wanted to share his enthusiasm. A good wife must show interest in her husband's work. " But I hope you'll be content with directing the opera and stay away from those opera actresses."

He gave her a swift glance. Had she heard something about Maria? . . . " Why, I wouldn't even look at another woman. I am now an old and sedate married man."

" You aren't old and I don't know how sedate you are," she rejoined with a smile.

This flurry of jealousy delighted him. It proved that she loved him. Real love is always jealous. " You have nothing to fear."

On his return to Düsseldorf, Felix mentioned to Immermann his lifelong dream to write an opera based on Shakespeare's *The Tempest*. At once the judge offered his services as librettist. " Although a Greek scholar by preference, I am a great admirer of the Bard. Ah, Shakespeare! The magnificence of his language, the grandeur of his metaphors . . .

Felix found himself deluged with reams of German poetry, most of it bad. With dismay he realised he had started an avalanche. Cautiously he ventured some amendments, suggested some slight changes. He came in contact with that most inflammable of all explosives—a poet's vanity. The would-be librettist turned pale, then angry, then abusive. What did musicians know about poetry? . . . It required miracles of rhetoric on Felix's part to avert an open break. He took refuge in lame and insincere excuses. The libretto was a masterpiece, a gem of timeless poetry, but his duties as conductor of the Düsseldorf Orchestra left him no time to compose. Immermann who, though a poet, was not a fool, pretended to believe these explanations, but a coolness developed between them. The semblance of friendship was precariously maintained. The poet still came now and then to dinner, but there was no longer any talk of Shakespeare.

Anyway, another project was soon engaging their attention. The town council had finally seen the advantages, importance and urgent necessity of an operatic season in Düsseldorf. Immermann could barely control his excitement. " Naturally," he assured Felix, " you'll be in full charge of the musical part. No interference of any kind . . . You'll have free rein, *carte blanche* as they say in French. I'll merely attend to business details. Together we'll make this town into another Berlin."

To Felix such words had an insinuating persuasiveness. Here was the chance to show those dullards of the Singakademie the kind of man he was, the kind of man they had snubbed. As a first production he selected his beloved *Don Giovanni* and launched into rehearsals with all his energy. At dinner time he told Cécile of his hopes and she listened with a patient smile of encouragement on her lips. Perhaps this was the thing that would bind him to Düsseldorf, cure him of his restlessness. Men forged their own chains. . . .

The production of an opera is at best a complex and trying enterprise. Felix discovered it could become a superhuman chore and a speedy short cut to insanity. Imprudently he agreed to hire the singers and started negotiations with various ones in Berlin, Dresden, Stuttgart and other towns. He experienced the trials and

B.D. E

tribulations of theatrical managers. Tenors, he found, entertained the most inflated opinion of their worth. They were demanding, supercilious, jealous and unreliable. Always on the look-out for some slight to their dignity, some affront to their artistic honour. Women singers were, if possible, worse. They possessed all the faults of their male colleagues and several of their own. They stormed or they wept or they sulked. Any correction of their singing became a personal insult.

He came home tired, dispirited, damning prima donnas, Immermann, the town council, cursing himself for falling into that operatic trap. "I was a fool to get involved in this small-town carnival," he would sigh.

Every day the confusion increased. At the theatre tempers were growing short. Overworked, his nerves taut, Felix sometimes lost patience. Blindingly he saw now the unsoundness of this provincial operatic venture. You didn't improvise excellence, didn't conjure up co-operation. Immermann, as poor an administrator as he had been a librettist, had become the victim of megalomania. He fancied himself as an organiser, gave thundering orders which he countermanded the next day. An atmosphere of panic descended upon the theatre. Felix realised he was heading into disaster, but it was too late to withdraw.

Suddenly Immermann announced that the price of the seats would be doubled. Great Art, he declared, was not for the penurious; only the well-to-do could afford the exquisite privileges of Kultur. The repercussion of these remarks was felt on the opening night. The theatre was packed to the rafters, but the public was in an ugly mood. The first cat-calls were heard during the first scene, growing more numerous and insistent as the opera progressed. Soon the tumult became uncontrollable, the singing on the stage merely adding to the pandemonium in the audience. The curtain was lowered. Felix disappeared into the wings, where he found Immermann livid, dishevelled, helplessly clenching his fists, giving absurd orders, threatening the singers, wavering on the verge of madness. At the sight of Felix he sprang at him, blamed him for the debacle. In stammering, incoherent abuse he heaped upon him his pent-up resentment. He was no musician, no conductor, nothing. " Nothing but a Jew!" he spat with venomous fury.

Felix blanched and turned away.

Next day he quietly informed the town council that for personal reasons he would relinquish his post at the end of the current season, immediately after the Rhine Festival, only two months away. The Festival was the great musical event of the year. It would be his farewell and he wanted it to be a vindication and a triumph.

It was.

The weather was perfect. For more than a week in advance people began to arrive in Düsseldorf from neighbouring towns. They drove in carriolets, hayricks and char-à-bancs. Entire families came on foot: the men in their best Sunday clothes, their beavers on the backs of their heads, field flowers in their lapels, the women dressed in brightly-coloured skirts and fetching bonnets, holding children by the hand. All year they had been waiting for this. Cheerfully they accepted every discomfort, slept six to a room in the overflowing inns. In the morning the men shaved informally by the fountain on the Grand Platz, exchanged jokes in their mushy patois while their wives pulled sausages and *Würste* out of wicker baskets.

Three days before the Festival, Abraham Mendelssohn arrived, escorted by his usual travelling retinue. " I came to see you, Jakob," he declared with a happy chuckle, " and decide whether or not I was right to let you get out of the banking business."

To Felix, his father's presence was the final incentive to surpass himself. In his honour he performed Handel's *Israel in Egypt*, and when he turned to take his bow he saw him, clapping his hands while tears fell from his filmy eyes.

" I am proud of you, Jakob," the banker said a few days later when they were alone in the study. " I'll go away happy." There was a tender solemnity in his voice. " Until now I've been known as the son of my father, now I'll be known as the father of my son."

For the first time Felix noticed how much his father had aged. He was almost blind, his gestures had lost their vivacity, his voice its querulousness. With a pang he realised that he might not have much longer to live. " I'll try to make up for all the trouble I've given you and repay you for all you've done for me." With an effort at gaiety he went on, " Don't think I don't know who got me this post."

The banker cleared his throat embarrassedly. " Well, you see, Jakob, while I was in Frankfurt arranging the formalities of your wedding, I learned that the conductor of the Düsseldorf Orchestra was about to resign and——"

" And you dashed here and convinced him that no one could possibly fill his post as well as your own son . . ." Suddenly he leaned towards his father and took his hands. " I'll never thank you enough for what you've done for me."

" You can by doing at least one great and good deed in your life."

" I'll try Meanwhile, thanks to you I am the happiest man in the world. I have a wonderful wife and a new career is opening before me. This morning I received a letter from the trustees of the Singakademie. They have reconsidered and want me to meet them before the end of the summer to discuss my appointment as direktor."

"A great honour indeed for one so young. Have you spoken about it to Cécile?"

Felix hesitated. "Not yet, Father. Somehow she feels we'd be happier if we lived in a small town. I'll speak to her when we are on our holiday. She'll understand."

The old man was silent a moment, then he said, "Women have strange intuitions sometimes. It was your mother who suggested our moving from Hamburg to Berlin. You will never regret following Cécile's advice. A good wife is the greatest fortune that can befall a man, even if at times he doesn't think so."

Immediately after Abraham Mendelssohn's departure Cécile began packing and closing the house. With heavy heart she took down the curtains she had so joyously hung two years before. One by one pictures, knick-knacks, gold-framed daguerreotypes left their places and found their way into gaping trunks. Even the "disgusting" statue of the naked woman came out of the closet, digging its little scratch of regret. Yes, thev'd been happy in this prim little house overlooking the Rhine. They'd known many peaceful and tender moments. Above all they'd begun knowing each other. And now they were leaving. Leaving like gipsies, for they didn't know where. Felix had resigned. At the time he had been too hurt and too angry for her to try changing his mind. After the triumph of the Festival the town council and the trustees had pleaded with him to remain He had declined. Oh, he could be stubborn! . . . That was another thing she had learned about him. He listened to her, usually followed her suggestions, but if he made up his mind, the Holy Ghost couldn't make him sway from his decision. Meanwhile he didn't have any position, not even the serious prospect of one, and he didn't seem to care. Some university had written offering him the chair of music, he had tossed the letter in the fire. "A professor! . . . Can you imagine me turning into a professor!" And he had launched into a pantomime—it had made her laugh despite her disappointment—of a pompous bespectacled music teacher addressing his class . . . Where would they go after their holiday in Switzerland? . . . Berlin, probably. He was keen on it, and where else could they go? Certainly not Frankfurt, "the village" as he called it . . . Oh, well, God would watch over them and guide their steps. . . .

Felix accompanied her on her round of farewell calls. He was courteous as always, said the right things, kept a vapid smile on his face, but she knew he was bored and anxious to leave. At last the day of departure arrived. Gustav and Catherine were to remain in the house and wait for instructions. Felix was gay as a robin as the stagecoach jostled away from Düsseldorf.

"God, I'm glad it's over!" he said with a sigh of relief. "If anyone mentions music to me I'll shoot him. For two months I want to do nothing but eat, sleep——"

"Go fishing."

"Not even that. I just want to lie on the grass and doze with my head in your lap."

The day came, three weeks later, when he did precisely that. Around them the meadow spread like a green carpet. Her straw hat lay on the grass like an enormous daisy. Near them a river rippled by, dashed into foam by glistening rocks. It was mid afternoon and in the cloudless sky the sun hung high and still.

"Do you realise you've been lying more than an hour with your head in my lap?" she said.

He went on munching a blade of grass. "Man was created to lie on his back," he declared sententiously after a while. "A glance at human anatomy should convince you of that. If God had intended man to stand up, He would have given him the shape of a pyramid." He squinted at her bent-down face. "You would have made a very attractive pyramid."

Smilingly she shook her head, like a mother forgiving her child's nonsense. "You'll never grow up."

"Men grow up and become wiser and more handsome with the years. Instead women grow first in height, then in width and rapidly turn into objects of repulsion. Such is the law of the Universe." He relapsed into silence, the blade of grass working between his smiling lips.

She leaned down and kissed the tip of his nose. "You can say the silliest things, but I love you." She was happy because the tenseness of the last Düsseldorf weeks had left and he had regained his gaiety, his teasing gaiety that was the expression of inner contentment. At first she had been puzzled, almost distressed, by this juvenile banter. Married men were supposed to be grave, taciturn, always thinking about serious things. Now she understood it was a reflex of relief, the instinctive relaxation of a high-strung, oversensitive nature. "Don't you want to look at your post? It came this morning."

"Throw it away," he said with a dismissing gesture of the hand. Then without transition he went on, "The Swiss are the most intelligent people in the world. With different nationalities, different religions and different cultures crowded on a territory as large as one of my father's handkerchiefs, they've managed to live in peace with themselves and their neighbours." He gazed at her as though absorbed in some weighty thought. "As a matter of fact, I realise now that the main reason why I let you snare me into marrying you was that your father was a Swiss."

Playfully she mussed his hair. "Snare you, did you say?"

"Certainly. You were then an eighteen-year-old spinster and getting desperate for a husband. The moment you saw me you guessed I was the fount of wisdom, the pink of courtesy, with the courage of the lion, the magnanimity of the elephant——"

"Are you or aren't you going to read your post?" she cut in.

"All right," he grumbled, sitting up. "Let's look at the confounded stuff."

From the flower-filled basket she pulled a sheaf of letters and held it out to him. He thumbed through the pack of mail, casually tossing envelopes into her lap. Abruptly his hand froze.

"What's this?" he muttered to himself.

His face stiffened into a mask of frowning concentration as he broke the wax seals.

"What is it, darling?" she asked when he finished reading the letter.

"It's from the board of trustees of the Gewandhaus Orchestra in Leipzig. They're offering me the post of conductor. They say the King himself suggested my name."

"The King. What King?"

"Friedrich Augustus the Second, darling," he said, controlling his impatience. "He is the King of Saxony. Leipzig is in Saxony," he added unnecessarily.

"I know that, but why should he——"

"Because I met him in England when I played for the Queen," he explained with strained calm. "He was with Prince Albert." He made a gesture of annoyance. "But this is neither here nor there. I won't accept it."

"Why?" Her blue eyes were large with anxiety. "You don't have any other engagement."

He looked at her. The discussion he had dreaded couldn't be avoided any longer. "Well, I—I almost have."

Awkwardly he told her about the offer from the Berlin Singakademie he had received in Düsseldorf, tried to explain why he had failed to mention it until now. "It was at the time of the Festival, we were all under a strain. I didn't feel we could discuss it quietly."

He knew she was hurt by his deceit, but she listened in silence, her eyes fastened on his lips. With growing nervousness he stressed the advantages of the Berlin post. "Think of it, Cilette. I have my family there. We could live with them or have a home of our own, a really beautiful house. We could entertain interesting people."

It was the wrong thing to say and he felt it at once. She did not want a " really beautiful house," she did not want to entertain interesting people . . . "And then the salary is much larger," he added, hoping to arouse her parsimony. " Almost double." He saw she was not impressed. " For heaven's sake, why are you against our going to Berlin?" he almost cried.

"I didn't say I am against it."

" But you are. I can see it on your face. Why? It's a beautiful city, you'd love it there."

"I am sure I would, but I wish you'd accept the Leipzig post instead." She spoke quietly, with the exasperating meekness of a stubborn and unreasonable child.

" But why?" he repeated, raising his voice. "You must have a reason."

" I don't know why," she said with the same infuriating gentleness. " I just have a feeling you should go there."

" A feeling!" This time he shouted the words. He would have welcomed a quarrel, a spirited exchange of arguments. But she was not fighting back, she was merely stating she had a " feeling " he should accept the Leipzig post. " Don't you see, Leipzig is just another little town?" he said, grasping her hands. "Another Düsseldorf. Only a little bigger and with a better orchestra. It's not even the capital of Saxony. The King and the court are in Dresden. The opera house is in Dresden. All Leipzig has is a university, a concert hall in the Drapers' Guild building, the Gewandhaus as they call it. We'll have the same kind of life we've had in Düsseldorf. The same kind of friends. Pompous Herr Professors, fat brewers and wealthy merchants. Is that what you want? . . . Do you want me to be a small-town conductor all my life? Two or three years in Leipzig, two or three years in Stuttgart, or Cologne or Frankfurt or Danzig or Munich, when I could have Berlin? . . . Don't you realise that as conductor of the Singakademie I'll be in line for the same post with the Berlin Philharmonic as soon as it becomes vacant? I'll be the first musician in Germany! I——" He stopped wearily. "You don't understand, you just don't."

She leaned closer to him and her voice grew tender with pleading. " I'll go with you to Berlin, my darling, if that's what you want."

" I don't want it if I have to drag you there," he said sulkily.

" I am sorry, I really am. And please don't think I'm being selfish about this. I swear I am not thinking of my personal preferences, but I have a strange feeling . . . I can't explain it. Like a presentiment. As if God wanted us to go to Leipzig . . ."

There was no reasoning with women. They didn't advance arguments, didn't care about logic. They talked about feelings, presentiments, God . . . You couldn't argue against that . . . Father had said follow her advice. Perhaps it was one of those intuitions women were supposed to have? . . . And then she was his wife. He wanted to make her happy . . . "All right," he said with a smile of surrender. "We'll try Leipzig for a year or two."

Like a distant echo a church bell tinkled far away, in the valley below.

BOOK TWO

Love Has Many Names

Chapter 5

On THAT festive afternoon in April, His Majesty Friedrich Augustus, looking very handsome in a gold and scarlet field marshal's uniform, was standing on a baldaquined dais upon the stage of the Gewandhaus Hall and telling Leipzigers how right they were to be proud of their fine Music Conservatorium and its founder-direktor, Doktor Mendelssohn. "Where, in the whole of Germany—nay, in the whole of Europe—can one find another such brilliant institution of musical learning? . . . Although but two years old, its fame has already spread beyond the horizon to distant America . . ."

These words sent a ripple of civic jubilation through the audience. At last Leipzig had something Dresden did not have. Dresden might have the King, the court, the embassies, the opera house, the cafés and elegant shops, but did it have a Music Conservatorium? No! But Leipzig had, and since it already possessed the Gewandhaus Orchestra, also under Doktor Mendelssohn's direction and admittedly the first symphony orchestra in Germany, and there was talk of an opera season next year, then culturally speaking, where would Dresden be? Nowhere. Who would regard Dresden as an artistic and intellectual centre? Nobody. It would be just a shallow, frothy town of pleasure where people thought of nothing but fun and frolic, while Leipzigers would revel in the austere but refined delights of Kultur.

His Majesty turned to Felix, who was sitting at his right at one of the two tables flanking the royal dais. "When some years ago, I suggested his name to the trustees of the Gewandhaus Orchestra, he was then a young man of exceptional promise. To-day he stands as the most famous musician in Europe. Time and again larger cities have tried to lure this extraordinary man away, but——"

Wearily Felix ran his slender hand over his eyes. How many years? The devil of a long time! It seemed only a few months ago that he was lying on the grass of that Swiss meadow and Cécile was telling about that strange " feeling " of hers, that they should go to

137

Leipzig. How swiftly time had flown, even if the days had been slow to pass. . . .

Well, they had come to Leipzig and Cécile's intuition had proved right. Everything had turned out well. For a year or so after their arrival he still had longed for Berlin and the life of great cities. He had fretted, talked about moving away from this " Düsseldorf-on-the-Pleiss," as he called it. Then the children had started to arrive, and before he knew it, it was too late. He had regretted it at the time; now he no longer did. He would spend and end his life in Leipzig and that was all right. After all, wasn't he happy here? Didn't he have everything he could want? Of course . . . A lovely and faithful wife who was also a perfect mother, a diligent *Hausfrau* . . . Five beautiful children—three boys and two girls, all blond like their mother, the last, Lili, only a month or so old . . . A nice house in Lungerstein Garden, just off the Promenade, in the most exclusive residential district . . . More money than they could ever need . . . What more could a man want. . . .?

Now the King was addressing the audience, praising their love of music, tossing compliments to the city officials. His Lordship the Mayor, the councilmen, the trustees of the Gewandhaus Orchestra. " If to-day Leipzig is known as Athens-on-the-Pleiss, the art capital of Saxony, a city of harmony and progress, it is due to the untiring efforts, the vision and selfless devotion of those true champions of the arts——"

Felix repressed a smile. How well he knew them, these champions of the arts! . . . Unscrupulous merchants, arrogant drapers and brewers, hard to their employees, tricky among themselves. They had dined at his house and he at theirs. They came to his concerts as they listened to Pastor Hagen's Sunday sermons when they would much prefer to be playing cards or telling scabrous stories over a stein of beer; but they came because in Leipzig it was fashionable to be an art patron and to go to church, a proof of gentility, and it was the duty of the better classes to display a semblance of Christian virtues and an appreciation of the arts.

With Christoph Muller, the Mayor, Felix had struck up something like a friendship. He had grown to like the red-haired, loud-mouthed politician, who was less hypocritical than the others and capable of an occasional disinterested good deed. With all of the others he performed the ritual gestures prescribed by small-town etiquette and maintained cordial, if not warm relations. He was respected, even well liked, though not half as popular as Cécile, who had become a real Leipziger and whom everybody liked. He sometimes forgot to laugh at their jokes, he didn't always hide his boredom at their account of their latest business trip to Dresden and what thrilling adventure had happened to them while they were

in that city of rampant vice. After all these years in Leipzig he was
still " the foreigner from Berlin."

And I suppose I'll always be, he thought, forcing himself back to
reality. The King was reaching the end of his address. In tones of
pontifical unction he was urging his beloved subjects to continue
their generous and heartfelt support of the Gewandhaus Orchestra
and the Music Conservatorium, which, under Doktor Mendelssohn's
inspired leadership, was spreading the fame of their glorious city to
the far ends of the world.

The anniversary ceremony was over.

" Wasn't it wonderful, Felix!" cried Cécile as they were driving
home. " I was so proud of you. I wanted to cry. Did you hear what
His Majesty said?"

" About what?"

" About you." She gave him a sharp glance. " Weren't you
listening?"

" Of course, but I don't remember his saying anything special.
I thought it was the same flowery address he'd delivered last year
and the year before, full of lofty generalities about harmony and
progress and compliments to everyone."

She frowned. This kind of talk almost smacked of *lèse-majesté*.
One owed complete admiration to a King as well as complete
obedience. " I thought His Majesty spoke beautifully," she said, a
shade of defiance in her voice. " He said the Conservatorium was
your monument and he looked upon you as the First Citizen of his
Kingdom." A note of impatience pierced in her tone. " Didn't you
hear?"

" I am sorry. I must have been thinking of something else."
He felt the impact of reproach in her eyes.

" What were you thinking about?"

" How fast time flies. I hadn't realised we've been here so long."

A shadow of anxiety mingled with annoyance brushed across
her face. " Still thinking about Berlin? . . . Aren't you happy here?"

" Of course, darling," he said, taking her hand. There was no
use trying to explain to her that one could be unhappy without
any tangible cause for unhappiness. It was one of those things that
had grown between them, this inability to sense each other's moods.
" As happy as anyone can be." Then, to change the subject,
" Incidentally, I wish the King wouldn't pay me such high-flown
compliments. I am not a citizen of Saxony—neither the first nor
the last. I still am a devoted subject of His Majesty Wilhelm
the Fourth of Prussia. It's that sort of compliment that can bring a
lot of trouble and arouse jealousy."

" I thought it was wonderful."

" You did," he said, smiling at her naïveté, " but others may not.

After all, the Conservatorium is merely a music school. True, I am direktor and teach composition, but I don't run it all by myself. If the Conservatorium is a monument to me, it is also to those who help me keep it on its feet. Before you know it, someone will say I drafted the King's address and wrote those compliments myself."

"Don't be silly. Nobody would think such a thing."

Gently he patted her hand. "There's no limit to what people will believe."

The carriage had stopped in front of their house and Gustav held the door open. In addition to being Felix's valet, he had become—Cécile feeling that a full-time coachman would be ostentatious—the family's coachman.

"The more absurd it is," said Felix, ducking out of the carriage, "the more easily they believe it."

"By the way," remarked Cécile as they were entering the house, "we must have Amelia Dossenbach and her husband to dinner sometime. I know you think she is a shrew and he a bore, but he is chancellor of the university and we owe it to them."

Felix stifled a sigh, but he wanted to make amends for his absent-mindedness during the King's address and said as cheerfully as he could, "By all means. That is an excellent idea."

They did not speak while crossing the entrance hall, on their way to their upstairs bedroom. Then abruptly he said, "If the weather's nice to-morrow do you think we could drive to Schmidt's farm in the afternoon?" He felt she was displeased and tried to arouse her sympathy. "The poor man's been asking me for so long. It'd make him and his wife terribly happy if we came—even for a short while."

"We'll see," she said evasively. Hermann Schmidt, a stocky old man with a crown of fuzzy white hair around his bald pate, was the flutist and the dean of the Gewandhaus Orchestra. His wife had been a cook, it seemed. The most ordinary sort of people. Yet Felix could call the chancellor of the university a bore and be friendly with people like the Schmidts. At times she just didn't understand him, didn't understand him at all . . . "Mathilda Schwalbach told me she might come, but you can go alone, if you want."

The first thing Felix noticed when he awoke the following morning was that Cécile was not at his side. She could slip out of bed without waking him, dress without making noise. Obviously she had gone to church, taking Karl and Marie with her. That's why the house was so quiet . . . The second thing was that it was raining. Well, that took care of the Schmidts. It was better that way. He wouldn't have to show up at the farm alone with some improbable excuse—he wasn't clever about inventing plausible excuses—as to why Frau Mendelssohn had found it impossible to come and was sending her regrets.

Oddly he had looked forward to driving to the country, spending a few hours with the Schmidts. They were warm and friendly. Real people . . . Now with the junket to the farm off the day stretched before him dull and empty, with the Dossenbachs for dinner as a fitting climax. Oh, well, it couldn't be helped, and what couldn't be helped should be endured. He smiled. Pretty soon he'd be quoting proverbs and almanac aphorisms, as Cécile did. . . .

Suddenly, for no reason, Maria's face floated before his eyes. He recognised the tilt of her head, the flowing line of her throat, the slow parting of her lips before the kiss. He could hear her voice that could be furry with tenderness or strident with anger, her peculiar syntax, her liquid Venetian accent that slurred the consonants. " Now you have the beautiful wife and maybe you forget me, no? But I still love you . . ." These had been the last words she had spoken to him. Since then he had now and then read her name in the *Zeitschrift*, the music magazine, along with accounts of triumphant engagements in Vienna or Paris or St. Petersburg. Once or twice he had heard echoes of some spectacular romance. Twice her engagement had been announced. Dear Maria, where was she now? . . . Who was her current lover? . . . Did she still remember the madcap days of Carrington Castle? . . . He closed his lids to shut out her image. But she wouldn't vanish, and in a secret shudder of rapture he still could feel the caress of her trailing hands and the hot moistness of her kisses.

He pulled the bell rope by the bed and informed a frowning Catherine—Gustav having driven the mistress and the children to church—that he wished to have breakfast in bed, a Byzantine indulgence of which both the mistress and Catherine disapproved. He was well aware of the fact, but a faint inflection of command in his tone restrained the old servant from making any comment. Instinct coupled with experience had taught her the value of caution. The master was generous and easy-going most of the time, but on occasions he could take the breath out of her with a single withering glance.

Breakfast over, he rustled open the *Spenersche Zeitung* and read the exultant account of His Majesty's participation in the ceremony of the Conservatorium's anniversary. The article was sprinkled with complimentary references to himself and this cheered him up somewhat. He got up, dressed leisurely and went down to his study.

It was as large a room as his Düsseldorf study had been, but severe of aspect and plunged into permanent dimness. Because of its position in a recess on the western side of the house it caught little sunshine but the melancholy glow of sunset and this only for a short period of the year. Its best feature was the window which opened on a public park and the rear of Saint Thomas's School and Saint Thomas's Church. Its spire hung like a motionless arrow between the swooping velvet curtains. It could have been a dreary room, and it was due to Cécile's grim determination and decorating flair that it had become a comfortable and pleasant room. It was beyond her powers to make it a joyous one.

It looked almost gloomy in the greyness of that rainy morning, and Felix stood a moment near the fireplace warming his pale hands at the flames before sitting down at his desk. An unfinished page of orchestral music lay upon it, and his eyes travelled slowly over the neatly quilled staves. As he read on, the chillness of discouragement descended upon him like a cold damp cloak. What had happened to him? What had become of the winged iridescence of the *Midsummer* Overture? The colourful descriptiveness of *The Hebrides*, the lyricism of the Italian Symphony? Why couldn't he write another Octet, another Sonata in E major?

He leaned his elbows on the desk, took his head between his hands. How long was it since he had felt the quickening heart-beat the gushing rapture of inspiration? Two years. Since the Violin Concerto . . . And before that, he didn't remember. Three, four years—maybe more . . . Many times he had felt the wonderful old excitement, the growing exaltation that used to reach a climax in a burst of relieving flow of music, but now the stirring and churning of his mind turned to pain, changed into those blinding racking migraines that made his brain throb and swell in his skull and his eyeballs burst in their sockets. Some purulent abscess, some malignant tumour, had implanted itself in the flesh of his mind, forced itself into the womb of musical thoughts. It had become a part of him, like his hand. He could feel it, he had felt it for a long time but had tried to ignore it. With nimble self-deceit he had explained his recurrent headaches as evidences of fatigue or overwork. In sombre defiance he had selected larger and larger tasks, as if the size of the canvas would bring a secret reassurance of his powers. Massive oratorios, huge chorales, enormous billows of sound which somehow never took flight. With each succeeding opus he had known the growing terror of sterility, and success—for, ironically, success clung to him—had merely barbed the stab of failure.

Yet he had acknowledged the acclaim, bowed with smiling modesty to the applause and stifled his qualms. But he could no longer. Perhaps it was the rain, perhaps the greyness of his room, perhaps himself . . . Suddenly he couldn't pretend any longer. He knew that some stealthy and deadly disease dwelt in his brain, and he was ill, desperately ill, and would never get well.

A recoil of animal fear contracted his muscles, choked the breath in his throat. His hands turned clammy and he felt rivulets of cold sweat in the small of his back. He, Felix Mendelssohn, was very ill, he was going to die and no one but he knew it. It was his secret. A secret that would never leave him, like the murderer's secret which goes wherever he goes. His secret was death already inside him, slowly destroying him. The thought was too new, too shattering to comprehend. Oh, yes, he had thought about death, as everyone did. Something vague, remote. Inescapable, of course, but somehow improbable. A distant eventuality softened by the slow decline of old age, the gradual acquiescence of the weakening body and finally the tranquil resignation made still easier by spiritual comforts and heavenly promises . . . But not at thirty-seven! . . . Not in the spring of life, in the flush of success and the enveloping warmth of domestic happiness . . .

Feverishly his mind careened into the future. How long did he still have? . . . How long would it take death to finish its work? Two years . . . three years? Perhaps many years. After all, he had youth on his side, and youth meant strength. He was sane. Thin and nervous, but sane. Never been sick in his life. His father had died at sixty, his grandfather at fifty-seven—both in their sleep, as everyone should die . . . His mother was still hale and hearty at seventy-one . . . Why should he die at thirty-seven? . . . Besides there were doctors. Some fine ones here in Leipzig. Medicine was making tremendous strides . . . And then perhaps . . . perhaps he was imagining things. He wasn't ill at all. Headaches? . . . Everyone had headaches.

Now he was trembling from excitement, mumbling his arguments, frantically trying to uproot the thought of death that had just embedded itself in his mind. There was nothing wrong with him. He felt fine, had never felt better . . .

He was startled by the rap of a knock on the door. Catherine appeared, filling the doorway. " His Lordship the Mayor's here, Master Felix."

She was now in the habit of calling him Master Felix, as Gustav did, to stress her standing in the house, infinitely superior to that of the parlourmaid and the children's nurse Elga, who had been with the family only a few years and called him Herr Doktor. " He'd like to know if you're home."

" Of course, I am at home," he exclaimed, springing to his feet. " Let His Lordship in."

He just had time to run his handkerchief across his forehead and was reaching the door as Christoph Muller entered, beaming, already chuckling and holding out his fat hand.

"Well, how's Saxony's First Citizen?" the burgomaster chided, crossing to his usual chair across the desk.

Felix gave a nervous laugh. "And how's His Lordship the Oberbürgermeister of Leipzig?"

Muller's chuckle lasted until he lowered himself into an over-stuffed chair opposite Felix's desk. "I hope I don't disturb you from your creative labours," he said with feigned concern.

"God, no. My creative labours can be very tedious sometimes."

"I just couldn't stomach another of the Reverend Hagen's sermons. Not after yesterday's oratorical orgy. So I asked my beloved wife to present my regrets to our dear pastor and tell him I was sick in bed." He grinned at his own deception.

"You couldn't have chosen a better time," said Felix with un-usual effusiveness. "What will you have? Sherry or port, or perhaps a little schnapps?" He read the Mayor's preference in his eyes. "I think I'll join you and have one, too."

A moment later they were discoursing in convivial leisure of the previous day's affair at the Conservatorium. "I thought it went off rather well," remarked the Mayor, taking a sip of schnapps. "The speeches were too long, but they always are. I like making speeches but I hate listening to them."

"I wish there were some way to dispense with those flowery harangues that mean nothing and bore everybody. Incidentally, I wish His Majesty hadn't made that 'First Citizen' remark. If the King of Prussia ever hears of it, I'll be in a fine mess."

"I wouldn't worry. I don't think anyone saw anything in it but a well-deserved tribute. Except perhaps Kruger." His tone lowered as he looked down at the glass in his hand. "He is such a treacherous and jealous scoundrel. Dangerous too . . ." There was a pause. His eyes rested speculatively on his drink. "Do you know, Felix," he said, "sometimes I wonder if the man isn't mad. I mean it."

"Mad!" Felix knew Muller's deep antipathy for his first council-man, but he had never heard him question his sanity. "I don't like him very much either, but I wouldn't call him mad."

The Mayor's expression did not change. "You don't know him as well as I do."

"That's true," agreed Felix, raising his glass to his lips. "I only see him at the meetings of the board of trustees."

"That's it. I see him almost every day and I tell you there's something wrong with him. I don't mean he is a ranting lunatic foaming at the mouth, but I've seen a strange look come into his eyes sometimes. Believe me, this man is capable of doing something crazy. It wouldn't matter, but as you know he is very wealthy, he is part owner of the newspaper and he is burning inside with the

obsession of running this town. He is a fanatic. Did you know he
was the only member of the board who voted against your appointment as conductor even after His Majesty had suggested your
name?"

"No, I didn't," said Felix with a shock. "Of course I heard
rumours he is an anti-Semite."

"He is anti-everybody. Once he tried to have the council close
a hospital operated by Catholic nuns. Another time he wanted us
to pass an ordinance forbidding all churches to ring bells on Sunday
except Saint Thomas." Absenuy he twisted the stem of his glass
between his fingers. "Watch out for him, Felix."

"Every creed has its fanatics. I have known a few Jewish
fanatics in my life, and I believe they are just as bad as any other.
My own grandmother refused to see her own son for more than
ten years because he had changed his faith."

"Yes, but she was only hurting herself. Kruger will try to hurt
you or me if he ever has a chance and he'll use every means, fair
or foul. That's the thing I hate most about him. He'll try to ferret
something out of your private life and use it against you. I know
he'd use the fact I'm keeping Olga if he dared. But we've been in
this town for three centuries—one of my great-great-great-great-
great-grandfathers was burgomaster at the time of Luther—and he's
watching himself." For the first time a gleam of amusement came
into his small and crafty eyes. "And he knows I'm watching him."

The conversation died, but the silence that ensued was unstrained
and comfortable. For a moment the two men followed their own
thoughts. Casually the Mayor leaned forward to pick up the
decanter on the desk, refilled his glass and resumed his musings.

"It's an unpleasant sensation," remarked Felix, "this feeling that
someone's trying to do you harm."

"You get used to it," said Christoph Muller with a shrug. "It's
the price you pay for being on top."

"But surely Kruger doesn't want to conduct the Gewandhaus
Orchestra."

"No, but you're a superior man." With his hand he cut short
Felix's gesture of protest. "I don't mean to pay you a compliment,
but to explain to you how he thinks. You are a superior man, a
famous musician, now the First Citizen of the Kingdom of Saxony
—and a non-Christian, as he says. All this rankles. I tell you the
man's mad."

His broad chest rose and fell in a long wheezy sigh. "That's
the trouble with these small towns. Not enough doing. Minds grow
stagnant and fester. Take this Olga business, for instance. In
Berlin nobody would pay attention, but here people talk about it

because they haven't anything else to do. All right, I have a mistress and I go to see her once or twice a week. I keep her here because it's more convenient than going to Dresden and having a fling with some Altstadt whore, as all the councilmen and the trustees do. It doesn't mean I don't love my wife. Elsa is a fine woman, a wonderful mother, and I'm devoted to her. But you wouldn't exactly call her a beauty, would you? And in a flannel nightgown and a night bonnet, let me tell you she's even less alluring."

The last words ended in a chuckling cough. Felix, beholding the vision of the double-chinned mayoress in a flannel nightgown and cap, had to pinch himself to keep a straight face. " And so I got myself a beautiful girl. She's quiet, discreet, kindhearted and gives me no trouble at all."

On an impulse of confidence he asked, " Do you know how I met her?"

" Somewhere out of town, I heard. I didn't pay any attention."

" I was in Wiesbaden taking the waters and she was singing in one of those third-rate theatrical companies that tour the resorts and are always on the brink of bankruptcy. This one was just about to fold up and she leaped at the prospect of three meals a day and a house to herself. That's how it started. She came here with another girl of the same company; I don't know what became of her, but Olga's been here ever since. She isn't doing any harm to anyone and I intend to keep her here whatever they may say behind my back."

This seemed to end the matter of Olga Becker, and neither of them spoke for a moment. Felix refilled his glass. Christoph Muller lit a thin brown and ill-smelling cigarillo. " How are things at the Conservatorium?" he asked, watching the curling smoke through half-shut eyes. " Have you found a substitute for Schumann?"

" Not yet. Moscheles and I have been dividing his class so the students wouldn't suffer, but I'll be glad when the school closes next month for the summer."

" Strange this running away to Russia like this in the middle of a term."

" His wife had concert commitments there and he felt he should accompany her. I think he was right, don't you?"

" Perhaps," said the Mayor noncommittally. " The poor fellow had so much trouble marrying he probably couldn't bear letting her out of his sight."

" They make a wonderful couple. Both are remarkable artists. Robert in my opinion is one of the greatest composers alive to-day, even if his work doesn't receive the recognition it deserves. As for Clara, I've often played piano with her and I really think she is as great a pianist as Franz Liszt."

"Old Wieck, her father, must've thought so too," remarked Muller, lifting his glass to his mouth, "for he certainly hated giving her up and letting her marry that moody, silent and day-dreaming Schumann fellow. And poor besides."

"Robert isn't poor," Felix protested.

Christoph Muller made a condescending gesture. "Well, not penniless perhaps, but you'd hardly call him well off . . . Ach! . . . What an imbroglio that was! It kept Leipzig talking for months. Exactly like the libretto of an operetta . . . The crotchety old piano teacher with a pretty daughter who is also a child prodigy, already making more money with her concerts than he did with his lessons. Enter the blond, handsome and melancholy Schumann, her father's student. The two youngsters fall in love. The father falls into a rage, kicks the young man out, grabs Clara by the neck and takes her away. Curtain. Torn apart, the lovers continue to pine for each other and manage to correspond surreptitiously. Alas, the father intercepts one of the love letters. Thunder and damnation! . . . More tantrums, more maledictions. Again he grabs his daughter and takes her away. Farther away. But love must triumph in the end, and with the courage of despair the two lovers decide to take the matter to Court. They sign a petition—it must have taken pluck on Clara's part to sign a petition against her father—asking the judge to force Wieck to give his consent. The judge reads the petition, melts into tears, lectures the old cuss and orders him to let his daughter marry the boy she loves or go to jail. Snarling, gnashing his teeth, the old man consents. The two young people rush into each other's arms and the curtain falls."

"Other people's love affairs always do sound ridiculous, don't they?" remarked Felix. "The more dramatic they are, the more hilarious they seem."

Muller nodded pleasantly. "Love and the pursuit of love are fundamentally comical themes, whatever poets may write to the contrary."

"Sometimes I wonder whether life itself isn't just a huge and witless farce." The words seemed to have spoken themselves and it surprised him to hear them. He caught Muller's sharp questioning glance and went on hastily in a light conversational tone. "Before we begin indulging in aphorisms about love and life, you asked me if I'd found someone to take over Schumann's composition class at the Conservatorium. There's a man I've been planning to contact, but I don't know too much about him except that he has talent. His name is Wagner."

"You don't mean Richard Wagner, the police clerk's son, do you?" exclaimed the Mayor.

" I didn't know his father was a police clerk."

" Stay away from him!" broke in Muller. " I told you I knew everyone in this town and I do know Richard Wagner. He was born in the Bruhl district and at one time he was a charity student at Saint Thomas's School. Just after he was born his father died, and his mother remarried almost immediately an actor named Geyer. There were nine or ten children in that family and Richard was the youngest. They were all involved in one capacity or another with the theatre. His sister Rosalie and his brother Carl sang here for a while. He himself has been in on several theatrical ventures, and not too successfully, I understand. I think he even married an actress. Watch your step, Felix. He is the kind of man who is always in trouble and brings trouble to everyone around him. For one thing he has an impossible disposition."

" So had Beethoven," smiled Felix. " I know very little about Herr Wagner. Several years ago, when I'd just become conductor of the Gewandhaus Orchestra, he brought me a symphony of his. I read it and found it a very immature work. I refused it. He was a very young man then, no more than twenty-one or -two.* But three years ago we both contributed a composition on the occasion of the unveiling of Friedrich Augustus' statue and——"

" I know all about it," interrupted the Mayor, eager to display his familiarity with musical matters. " And you know what he wrote about it, don't you? That his own 'simple and heartfelt composition entirely eclipsed Mendelssohn's complex artificialities'."

" I know," said Felix. " And the strange part of it is that he was right. Somehow the unveiling of a statue, even a king's statue, failed to inspire me." Slowly he took a sip from his glass. " You're probably right about Herr Wagner; he may be a rather difficult man, but——"

" Another thing," interrupted Muller. " He dabbles in politics and is going to find himself in jail one of these days."

" I don't care what his political convictions are. Or his religion, or his tastes in clothes or cooking. He may be a Mohammedan and eat snails, as the French do. The point is that we're looking for a composition teacher and he knows composition. I've read some of his latest works, the score of his opera, *Rienzi*, for instance, and while I do not personally like his kind of music I do recognise his talent. Besides, he lives now in Dresden and might like to return to his home town, especially "—he paused hesitantly—" especially if he had the prospect of succeeding me as conductor of the Gewandhaus Orchestra."

* In later years Wagner himself concurred with Mendelssohn in his judgment of this work and dismissed it as " an old-fashioned *ouverage de jeunesse*." The original manuscript of this symphony is lost. Parts of it (but not in Wagner's handwriting) were found in an old trunk discovered in 1872 in Dresden.

"Are you thinking of resigning?" Muller was watching him with intense concern.

For a while Felix gazed at his glass in front of him. "Yes," he said at last. "In a year or two. The Conservatorium won't need me then. One should step down and make place for younger people." With a deprecatory smile he prevented the question Muller was about to formulate. "I know I am only thirty-seven but somehow I feel tired. I often have painful headaches and I'd like to retire and go away. Perhaps to Italy, some little sunny town."

Muller's florid face had lost its jovial grin. For a while he did not speak. "You know, Felix," he said at last, "I've often wondered why you've remained so long in this town."

"Frankly, I don't quite know myself. I've often asked myself this question. Cécile was very keen on my coming here. She had a feeling I must come here, you know, one of those mysterious intuitions women have sometimes."

"I know. Elsa has them all the time and they invariably prove wrong." He gulped down his drink and rested the long-stemmed glass on the small table at his side. "And now what are your plans? Going to England this year?"

"Next month," Felix nodded. "I used to look forward to these trips to England but somehow this year I don't feel up to it. I wouldn't go if arrangements hadn't already been made, although I adore England and my best friend lives in London."

"Do I know him?"

"I don't think so." He caught himself. "No, I think you did meet him at the dinner we gave for him three years ago when he came to visit us. The typical *bon vivant*. Rather fat, witty, extremely intelligent and efficient under his apparent nonchalance. He is First Councillor at the Hanover Legation. We've been friends since we were students together."

Muller pulled out a watch and frowningly held it in his hand as if it were some unpleasant insect. "I must be going," he said, "or I'll meet everybody on their way back from church and the Reverend Hagen will immediately be informed that instead of being sick in bed I came to pay you a call. That's the trouble with these damn' little towns. You can't belch without everybody knowing about it."

With a grumble he struggled to his feet and started towards the door. "It's too bad you and I cannot really be friends," he remarked, shaking his head. "I like you and admire you, but in my position you can't afford friendship. Once I had a friend, one of my councilmen. We'd known each other all our lives, we'd gone to the same schools. We were like brothers. Then one day we quarrelled over some stupid question of politics. We've never spoken since."

He let out a sigh and shrugged. "Well—*c'est la vie,* as the French say."

He was already out of the door and had put his beaver hat on when he turned around. "If I were you I'd go to see Dr. Hurbach. You don't look well."

Without waiting for an answer he waved his pudgy hand and went out.

From the door Felix watched his bulky top-hatted silhouette disappear into the carriage. He caught a last glimpse of Muller's round flushed face already in motion. He felt sorry to see the Mayor go, and curiously alone. They were not friends really but merely felt in some obscure way each other's loneliness. For a moment he had escaped his thoughts and now they were swarming back, each to its cell, ready to resume possession of his brain. Muller had said he didn't look well. Could fear and loneliness show, could you read the fear of death in a man's eyes?

As he was crossing the entrance hall on his way back to his study he stopped in front of an oval mirror in a mahogany frame. Making sure no one was around he quickly studied his face. Yes, he was pale, but then he'd always been. Except that now the skin had an unhealthy waxy tinge. His temples were hollow and the ridges of his forehead showed. Strange, he hadn't realised how grey his hair had turned in the last few years. It meant nothing, some people went grey very young. It was rather attractive . . .

Cécile returned from church shortly before lunch and when she entered the room he knew she'd already been told about his having breakfast in bed and the Mayor's visit.

"What did you two talk about?" she asked at lunch with that instinctive suspicion of women for men's conversations in which they had no part.

He was about to say they had exchanged dirty stories, just to shock her and watch her indignation. "Nothing special," he said. "He was bored, I think, and dropped in for a little chat."

"And a few schnapps. I noticed the bottle and the two glasses."

He looked at her swiftly with a beginning of anger. "Any objections?"

"None whatever." Her lips had tightened, exactly as her mother's did when displeased. "I merely think people shouldn't drink in the morning. It spoils the appetite. You see, you ate almost nothing."

He felt like a rebuked child. If only she were unreasonable or raised her voice like so many wives. But she didn't and she was always right. It was the way she spoke, the look in her eyes. Her schoolmistress look, as he called it. And each time it widened a little more the gap between them.

After lunch they repaired to the study as they usually did on Sunday afternoons. For a while he pretended to work. Outside the rain had stopped but the sky had not cleared. He rose from his desk, chose a book from the glassed cabinet and came to read by the window. She went on with her knitting. Now and then he glanced at her over the pages. Again her loveliness struck him. It always did, he couldn't get used to it. Now, in her middle twenties, she was more beautiful even than at the time of their marriage. Her face had the perfection of classical statuary. Also its remoteness, its calm inhumanity. Once at a reception she had been told by the King she was the most beautiful woman in his kingdom. She had glanced at him with surprise and forgotten the compliment. Often he had spied the glint of desire in men's eyes when they looked at her. She didn't even notice them. She was without coquetry as she was without intellectual or spiritual anxiety. Virtue was as natural to her as the gold sheen in her hair. Then why wasn't he happy? Why had the chasm between them grown so wide, when had they started moving away from each other so that now, living side by side, dining together each day, sharing the same bed, they had become strangers?

It had begun shortly after moving to Leipzig. She had gone to Frankfurt because of her mother's illness, staying away two months. On her return she was changed. Oh, so little that at first he almost hadn't noticed it. Not that she'd stopped loving him, no, nothing like that. She merely had stopped being in love with him. The joyous bantering, the amorousness of the Düsseldorf days had vanished. She no longer cuddled to him, no longer sat on his knees after dinner. She had been pregnant at the time, and her pregnancy had brought a long pause in their sexual relationship. After the child's birth they hadn't recaptured the fervour of the first two years. She had remained aloof and ladylike, even in her pretty embroidered nightshirt. A new maidenhood had closed around her. The irresponsible and now sinful outbursts of animality had quietly subsided, giving way to the joys of parenthood, the calm pleasures of domesticity. The rules of Christian wifely behaviour instilled by her mother had strangled her budding sensuality. Her capacity for passion had withered, frozen into demure ladyhood. If she still submitted to his advances it was with an air of dutiful compliance that discouraged his desire. He had made no scene, uttered no reproach, and controlled his pain and his anger. If he had torn her pretty nightshirt and forced himself on her, perhaps all would have been saved. But he hadn't. Wounded in his pride, unsatisfied in his desire, he had concluded she was tiring of him and had withdrawn into himself. Since then he had tried to renounce happiness and be content with her kisses on the cheek and the caresses of his children.

"I guess Mathilda won't be coming after all," Cécile said, breaking the silence. She rested her knitting in her lap. "We didn't have a definite engagement anyway. You shouldn't be trying to read, darling. It's getting dark."

She pulled the bell cord and Gustav appeared, white haired and white-gloved. He lit the candles, stirred up the fire and went out. The study seemed more friendly now, more intimate.

"You look tired," she said when they were alone. "Is everything all right at the Conservatorium and with the orchestra?"

"Yes. Why?"

Slowly she scanned his face, frowning with concern. "I don't know. You've been very quiet all day."

"Have I?"

"Is something worrying you? You didn't eat anything at lunch." Her anxiety made her voice urgent. "You feel all right, don't you, darling?"

It wasn't a question but a request for reassurance. His heart leaped in his chest. She did love him after all. For one mad minute he fought the impulse to rush to her, bury his face in her bosom, tell her about his headaches, his fears, the gnawing knowledge that he was sick, very sick, and would soon die. "Of course I feel all right. Just a little tired, that's all." He glanced at the window, where in the candlelight the rain made little rivulets of gold. "And this beastly weather doesn't help much."

A thought struck him unexpectedly. "Darling, did you ever figure out why you wanted so much for us to come to Leipzig?"

She looked at him with surprise. "It seemed like the right thing at the time. And it was, wasn't it?"

"Of course," he said hastily. No, he wasn't going to ask her to move to Berlin . . . "But you said you had a ' feeling '—I remember you used that word—as if God wanted us to come here."

"It's true. At the time I felt as if a hand tugged at my sleeve and a voice spoke inside me."

He was silent a moment.

"I'm going to tell you a big secret," he said, almost in the bantering tone of old. "In the beginning I used to think God wanted us to come here so that I'd find the rest of that Bach score. You know, the manuscript in the red leather folder. . . . After all, Johann Sebastian Bach lived in this town most of his life, and I thought I might run across the rest of the manuscript. For months, whenever I had a moment to myself, I used to browse through old book stores and libraries. I even went to Saint Thomas's Church— Bach used to be a choirmaster there—and asked permission to search their archives. The man I spoke to thought I was mad. He'd never heard of Johann Sebastian Bach and he told me they didn't even have any musical archives."

"Really?" She listened politely but he knew she was not interested. "What a shame."

His flurry of excitement kept him going a few seconds longer, but now there was an undertone of deflated irony in his voice. "Already I could see myself discovering the manuscript and performing it at a Gewandhaus concert. Just like that first performance of Schubert's Unfinished Symphony I gave a few years ago, remember?"

She nodded but he saw she did not remember. To her, Schubert's Unfinished Symphony had been just another bulk of music paper lying on his desk a few weeks and performed at some regular Gewandhaus concert.

"Never mind." Brusquely he got up. "I think I'll go to say good night to the children," he said, walking away.

Later that evening, just before blowing out the candle, she said, "I wish you didn't have to go to England."

"So do I, but I won't stay long and the change will do me good. You know how much I love England."

Her cheek hugged the pillow but her eyes moved slowly over his face. "You *are* all right, aren't you?" she asked once again.

"I told you, I feel fine. Just a little tired."

"You've been working too hard, that's what's the matter with you. You'll be all right after a good holiday." She leaned forward and kissed his cheek. "Good night, darling," she said, turning around to blow out the candle.

She didn't understand. A holiday would solve everything. That's what holidays were for . . . "Good night, darling."

Now all was darkness. She had settled on one side and was probably asleep already. How wonderful to be calm, have no anguish, no tormenting secret . . .

Finally he too fell asleep and dreamed that a rat was nibbling at his brain. He awoke with a start. She stirred and made a little sound, almost a word, but did not awake.

He remained silent, stiff in the shroud of his cold sweat, his eyes wide open, listening to the thumping of his heart, like a toll in the night.

As usual, his friend Karl was waiting for him at Charing Cross, looking very dashing in a pale blue frock-coat, a grin of welcome on his fat pink face. He hadn't changed, Felix thought with a twinge of envy the moment he saw him, the years seemed to glide on that smooth baby's skin of his like water on the back of a duck.

"How do you do it, you old roué!" he exclaimed as the carriage left the station and entered the bustle of the London streets. "With the life you lead you should look like a crumpling ruin, if there were any justice. Instead you look like this morning's rose. You are a living ode to the virtues of vice."

"True," admitted the diplomat with rueful modesty. "I do feel well. Virtue doesn't agree with everyone and it doesn't with me. I tried it once. I stopped drinking brandy. I went to bed early, I avoided women, I even paid my debts. In two months I was the jaundiced shadow of myself. However," he went on, settling back on the leather seat, "I owe my present excellent condition entirely to my own persevering efforts. Last November I caught a slight cold and made the mistake of calling a doctor. Since then his solicitude has been a constant threat to my health. I manage to feel well only by doing the opposite of what he suggests. After all, it is asking too much of a doctor to make you well when his living depends on your being ill, don't you think?"

Felix smiled at him with pensive tenderness. It was good to be in London again, a London in springtime attire of pearl-grey skies and chartreuse foliage. It was good to be driving back to old Bury Street with this debonair and faithful friend. Lucky Karl. He'd always known how to play the tricky game of Life. He had retained his enthusiasms while losing his illusions, ensconced himself into the business of living as into a comfortable arm-chair, squeezing a few chuckles, a drop or two of wisdom and happiness from each passing day.

"I shan't ask you what you've been doing," Karl remarked after raising his grey topper to an elderly lady in a shiny victoria. "Your life in Leipzig sounds so noble, so virtuous and boring that I couldn't bear listening to an account of it."

They were rolling through the pastoral elegance of St. James's Park. Horsemen and carriages flashed by in brief rumbles of trotting hoofs. The trees still had the convalescent look of early spring. Now and then young men and women, perilously high on their velocipedes, brought to Felix memories of Maria and his own foolish youth.

"As for myself," Karl went on when Felix failed to protest, "this winter has been memorable. I've known the unusual experience of being loved for spite, I might say. The lady chose me as her lover for the sole purpose of making her husband jealous. Women contrive such tortuous stratagems occasionally. For three months I enjoyed this delicious creature, wondering all the time when her husband would become aware he was being cuckolded and shoot me like a dog.

"Obviously he didn't," said Felix with a grin.

"We did everything. Kissed in public, made rendezvous in stage whispers, arranged to be caught in compromising *tête-à-tête* behind portières. All in vain. The poor chap had such faith in his wife's virtue he could not entertain the slightest doubt about her. In the end we had to give up. At my suggestion she has now returned to the man she loves."

The carriage was entering Bury Street. Peering out of the window, Felix recognised the charming brick house where he had spent so many happy hours.

"Even the flowerpots are blooming," he said softly. "It has not changed."

"But the landlord has," rejoined Karl, preparing to climb down. "I had so much trouble with him about the rent that in the end I decided it was simpler to buy the house." With a grumble he squeezed his corpulent self through the door and alighted in front of the entrance steps.

The following three weeks brought Felix such a whirl of engagements, both musical and mundane, that he saw little of his friend and had no time for his own gloomy thoughts. He performed his oratorio *Elijah* in Exeter Hall and once again knew the heady rapture of triumph. Another ovation awaited him in Manchester and a few days later in Birmingham. Back in London he found himself the most coveted lion of the season. Soon the pressure of social details became so great that he turned over to Karl the task of selecting the dinners and receptions he would honour with his presence.

"Trust me," declared his friend with finality. "I shall be firm. Nothing lower than embassies and duchesses. If you start being seen with marchionesses and lowly countesses you might as well enjoy yourself and go where you like. Nothing doing. I shall make a snob out of you yet."

By a fortuitous coincidence Jenny Lind happened to be in London at the time and Felix resumed his warm friendship with the great Swedish singer. As proof of his admiration, he even acted as her accompanist at one of her concerts, where she sang one of Chopin's mazurkas with the incredible cadenza especially written for her. Together they shared the applause of a delirious audience. "I'll never forget what you've done for me," she said to him as they were taking their last curtain call. "Perhaps some day I may be able to do something for you."

Again he was received in private audience at Buckingham Palace and again he entertained the Queen and Prince Consort with his piano-playing. On his return from the Palace he remarked to Karl that the Marchioness of Dorsythe was not among the ladies-in-waiting. "What happened to her?" he asked.

Karl stared at him open-mouthed. "Don't you know?"

"No, I don't. Remember, I live in Leipzig, not London."

"Well, she's committed the unforgivable, placed herself beyond the pale and rocked London as it had never rocked since Guy Fawkes tried to blow up the Parliament. She got married."

"A lot of people get married. That's not so terrible."

"But to whom? That, as Shakespeare said, is the question. For your information the beautiful, aristocratic, inaccessible Marchioness married her groom. Yes, the liveried menial who followed her on her morning rides. One day, five years after he had been in her service, she happened to glance at him for the first time and her Plantagenet blood froze in her veins. The bounder, I must admit, was handsome, a regular Apollo, but his conduct was unspeakable. For months the Marchioness tried to get him into her bed, but the blackguard declined, saying he wouldn't submit to Her Lady-ship's caresses unless she married him. Finally she couldn't stand it any longer and she did. Which proves you can get a woman to do anything if you deny her long enough something she wants."

"Where are they now?"

"At her Italian villa, somewhere near Rapallo. Although the mere whisper of her name is tantamount to treason, I've heard they're deliriously happy—though married."

"By the way," said Felix with a grin, "since we're talking marriage, how about you getting married?"

"Married?" wailed the diplomat with a look of injured innocence. "How could I possibly fall in love with a woman stupid enough to want to marry me? Once, two years ago, one of those well-meaning pests who are forever meddling in your love life insisted I should get married. She arranged the encounter. Like George IV I nearly collapsed with a mixture of brandy and horror when I beheld the lady I was expected to marry." A look of reminiscent terror lingered on his merry face, as he pulled his snuff box out of his vest pocket. "I know that Man is the only animal who does willingly what he dislikes to do but I must draw the line somewhere."

He was leaning against the angle of a walnut cabinet full of rare faïence. With his finger he snapped open the lid of the snuff box and looked straight at Felix standing a few feet from him, propped against the window sill. "What's wrong, Felix?" He said it quietly, but his eyes did not move and there was no smile on his face. "Everything's all right between you and Cécile?"

Felix averted his eyes as if caught in a lie. For a while he looked down at his watch chain, which he coiled and uncoiled absently around his finger. "Nothing's perfect," he said at last. Then: "She is a wonderful girl."

He did not speak for a minute, feeling Karl's eyes on him, waiting and watching. "I am not an easy man to live with, you know," he said, still playing with the thin gold chain. "We had a lot of adjustments to make. There always are in a marriage. You learn not to expect the impossible and try to be content with what you have." Brusquely he lifted his face and looked at his friend. "Cécile is a wonderful girl," he repeated with a sort of restrained vehemence. "No man ever had a better wife."

"All right," said Karl. "We'll let it go. But the question still stands. What's wrong, Felix? Don't tell me there's nothing wrong, for I won't believe you."

Again Felix lowered his eyes. Words formed in his mouth, pressed against his teeth. He wanted to tell his friend that during the Jenny Lind concert he had been racked with pain and the throbbing in his head had made him want to scream and run off the stage. He wanted to tell him of his secret visit to a famous doctor on Harley Street and the cold, helpless, almost angry look in the man's eyes. "I could tell you a lot of nonsense, Herr Mendelssohn, and prescribe some pills but I won't. I fear you're right and some organic disease is the cause of your headaches. But I don't know what it is and nobody else does either. Some day we shall know what goes on in our skull; to-day we don't. It'll be three guineas, sir." What'd be the use of saying those things? Why call for help when help can't be given? "I am a little tired, I suppose," he said. "But there is nothing wrong with me that a good holiday won't cure."

Karl snapped the lid shut and slipped the snuff box into his pocket. He walked to Felix and put his arm around his shoulder. He did not speak, yet Felix sensed that somehow his friend had guessed, for there were tears in his bulging eyes.

It was raining the day Felix left London. At Dover the wind blew a gale and the Channel crossing sent the passengers down to the privacy of their cabins. The *Attwood* became a moaning ship tossing drunkenly on white-combed waves. After his nautical ordeal Felix was glad to feel once again the comfort of solid ground under his feet, and for several minutes walking was a heavenly delight. The coach journey through the well-tended Normandy farms restored his spirits. He reached Paris on the following evening, and although he was several hours behind time, Chopin was still waiting at the depot.

"*Bohze Moy!*" he exclaimed when at last he spied his friend climbing down from the stage. "I thought you'd never arrive."

They drove to Place d'Orleans, where Chopin now lived. His valet had prepared a light supper and they dined in the small yellow-walled dining-room, neither of them eating with much appetite, talking shop in a desultory way as a screen to their thoughts. Felix was shocked by his friend's appearance and alarmed by his frequent fits of coughing. Chopin's voice, never strong, had become a mere whisper that barely carried across the rather large round table. He, too, is deathly ill, Felix thought with a pang.

At dessert the valet brought a large pot of steaming chocolate which he set at his master's elbow.

"You see, *mon ami*, I still drink chocolate." Chopin smiled, catching Felix's amused glance. "I like it unsweetened and have it made especially for me in Bordeaux. Another of my unjustified extravagances."

Idly they discussed new compositions by fellow musicians, compared publishers, exchanged harmless gossip about common friends.

"Meyerbeer's new opera——" said Chopin. He broke into a fit of coughing, quickly pulled a handkerchief from his sleeve and pressed it against his mouth. "Excuse me, *mon cher* Felix," he proceeded with a wan smile, "my lungs and I are parting company. As I was saying, Meyerbeer's new opera is the rage. Some people are born with the secret of success." He raised his cup, took a short sip and let out a feeble chuckle. "I am not one of them."

"You seem to be doing very well," said Felix, glancing about.

"An illusion. If I stopped giving lessons for a week, I couldn't pay my rent . . ." He shrugged and went on, "By the way, have you heard about our friend Liszt's latest liaison—with Princess Karolyn zu Sayn-Wittgenstein?" Again the little chuckle. "That man has a passion for princesses."

"Each one to his taste," said Felix with a smile. "Princesses aren't worse than any other women and their undergarments are sometimes better."

Frederic Chopin gazed down at his cup for an instant. "Franz is a strange man," he remarked pensively. "A snob and a saint, a mountebank and a mystic—in flashes, a genius. Do you know the two-piano duet he wrote on one of your themes?"

"No," said Felix, surprised. "He never sent it to me."

"It hasn't been published, but I have the manuscript here. If you want we'll play it to-morrow."

They went to their rooms shortly after dinner. For a long time Felix heard his friend's racking cough through the thin partition. Poor Frederic, alone and ill, away from his family, his beloved Poland . . . Poor Frederic . . . poor Felix . . . poor everybody . . . Life was a melancholy fugue on the theme of disenchantment . . . Was it worth it for God to create the world? . . . A quiet sadness fell over him as he closed his eyes and at last glided into sleep.

He awoke tired and depressed. "I'd planned to stay in Paris a few days," he announced at breakfast, " but I think I'll leave to-morrow. I am anxious to join my wife in Frankfurt and go with her to Switzerland for our holiday."

" I understand," said Chopin quietly. " You need one, you look tired."

" Somehow I don't feel like going to the opera or visiting my publishers or seeing friends. Not even my dear Madame de Rothschild. By the way, how is she?"

" Wonderful, as always. She's been very kind to me and sent me many pupils. She's had me to dinner a thousand times here and at her Château de Ferrière." A smile narrowed his lids. " I've dedicated one of my ballades to her.* It's my way of returning social obligations."

His voice trailed off and Felix sensed that he wanted to say something. " If I can do anything for you in Germany, my dear Frederic," he began to ease his friend's embarrassment, " please depend on me."

" Well—well, if you could arrange a concert for me with the Gewandhaus I'd appreciate it greatly. I know I am a drawing-room pianist but I'd do my best." His manner became nervous, almost feverish. " It's not only a question of money; it would give me a reason to get away from Paris, see new faces and try to forget."

" Madame Sand?"

" Yes. We're cracking up . . . Our affair is at an end. We both know it."

Cautiously Felix inquired. " How long have you and Madame Sand——"

Chopin did not give him time to finish and Felix noticed he was trembling. " Seven years . . . Almost like being married, isn't it? It was Liszt who introduced us. I had seen George before, but oddly she did not attract me at all. Her mannerisms, her books, her eccentricities—wearing men's clothes and smoking and all that . . . everything about her repelled me. Then, one day——"

And suddenly he was talking, talking as if the words fell of their own accord from his lips. He told Felix about George Sand, the complex, brilliant and powerful woman who had dominated his life and captured his heart with her mixture of sensuality and motherliness. In searching and lucid sentences he analysed the greatness, the foibles, the contradictions of this novelist who could be courtesan and bourgeoise, thinker and nurse, artist and house-keeper. He described their summers together at Nohant, her country home. Their tranquil afternoons in the garden—he, musing or dozing on a chaise longue; she, bending over some humble womanly task. Their candlelit evenings in the salon with its tall French doors

* Fourth Ballade in F minor. Opus 52.

opening upon the balustraded terrace—he, improvising softly at the piano; she, at her desk, writing, tirelessly, endlessly writing.

He told about their famous journey to Majorca which had started like a picnic and ended like a funeral march. His cell in the abandoned Valdemosa Monastery full of sombre, brown-robed ghosts. The chapel still smelling of prayer and mustiness and cold incense. The savage beating of winter rains on the leaking tile roof, the shutters slamming in the howling wind, the doors creaking in the night. And then, poorer in health and in money, the dismal return to Paris—she, to her pen; he, to his life of mundane pretence. Oh, yes, he was Monsieur Chopin, the fashionable piano teacher whose lessons cost a golden louis, the drawing-room virtuoso who sat at the keyboard and performed at his hostess's purring command. Petted, pampered yet not quite accepted socially by a clique of cosmopolitan, capricious and neurotic countesses on whom his living depended. The endless drives in yellow gloves and hired cabriolet to his pupils' mansions. The drudgery of lessons to shallow but wealthy *femmes du monde* who looked upon him with patrician hauteur underneath their gushing and cooing. And now and then to salvage his tottering finances, to pay a pressing doctor's or tailor's bill, a semi-private recital at twenty francs the ticket in the salon of some kind-hearted countess or Polish princess.

But George was there, loving and motherly. His friend, his mistress, his companion in the days of discouragement, urging him to compose, finish that mazurka, correct those publisher's proofs. She too worked hard for her bread and that of her two children, piling up novel upon novel, dashing off essays, articles, plays—anything to make ends meet. She was the stronger of the two and she infused him with her strength. At her example he, the dreamer, the improvisor, chained himself at his desk, found time to compose after a tiring day of lessons. He even tried to haggle with publishers, fighting for a decent price for the labour of his sleepless nights. But of course he never won, for they could wait and he couldn't. And so he let go the Nocturne in C minor for three hundred francs, the Polonaise in F sharp minor for four hundred. The landlord, the doctor, the monthly hire of the cabriolet were paid. He was safe for another month.

And so seven years had passed, precarious but warmed by a woman's love. Then one day the first misunderstanding had occurred, quickly patched, apparently forgotten. But soon there was another one. Then another, then another. Discussions degenerated into quarrels. In the heat of anger, unexpected reproaches, old grievances, rose like slime in a churning pond. Now the disputes were no longer patched but dwindled from exhaustion, smouldering in acrid resentment. Their hearts could no longer forgive words shouted in anger. Pride intervened, distilling its venom. Now the lovers found themselves apart, each nursing his wounds, the corpse of their love stretched between them.

Felix let him speak on, straining his ear to catch the rapid whispered French, knowing that he was finding in talk some measure of relief. Reticent people had sudden outbursts of confidence as placid people fell into sudden angers.

" Be patient, Frederic. It'll pass," he said, when Chopin was silent at last. " You're still young, you——"

He could not continue. Why speak empty words? Young? Frederic wasn't young any more than he was, for age was not measured by the years you had lived but by the years you *still* had to live . . . Frederic's time was short, like his own. There was nothing to say. Nothing.

Gently, as Karl had done, he placed his arm around Chopin's shoulders and said nothing.

The next morning he left Paris, promising to do his best to arrange a Leipzig concert. " I'll speak to the board of trustees," he said, as the coach started moving. " I am confident they will agree."

By the end of the week he reached Frankfurt, where Cécile and his children were awaiting him. Together they journeyed to their Swiss village. There they spent two months of tranquil idleness. By mid September they all were back in Leipzig and he was conducting the Gewandhaus weekly concerts and teaching composition at the Conservatorium.

" Tell me. Hans, how many natural keys are there in music?"

Hans Bluth sprang to his feet. " Two, Herr Direktor. C major and A minor. Any other is a transposition of one of them."

" Good. Now pay attention, for this is a little more difficult. How do you recognise the major key from the minor?"

His eyes ran over the rows of young rapt faces. It was nice to see those youngsters so attentive, so anxious to learn. Perhaps one of them would amount to something . . . Of course they were terribly impressed by the fact that the Herr Direktor was their professor, even though they were only beginners and his regular students were all advanced, with two years of harmony, counterpoint and the rudiments of fugue. Of course, they didn't know that the reason for this special honour was simply that Schumann's successor hadn't yet been found. . .

Through the veil of his thoughts he could hear the piping adolescent's voice rattling off the answer. " The major key is known by its major third, Herr Direktor. The minor key by its minor third."

" Very good, Hans. Sit down, my boy." Again his eyes swept over the class. Would any one of those boys ever write anything

B.D.   F worthwhile, earn fame and some money, or would they all vanish into obscurity, eke out a precarious living as tavern and beer-garden players, hungry piano or violin teachers, cursing the years they had spent at the Leipzig Conservatorium, *his* Conservatorium? . . . Had he the right to lure those innocents into a profession that promised nothing but heartbreak and poverty? "Wilhelm."

A bright-eyed tousle-haired boy fairly squeaked from excitement as he jumped to his feet. "Yes, Herr Direktor?"

"Wilhelm, can you tell me what is a major third?"

"Yes, Herr Direktor," sputtered the future Beethoven, almost too excited to speak. "When from the tonic to the note above there are four semitones, the third is major and the key is called major key."

"That was very fine, Wilhelm. Of course you understand that those four semitones mean five keys on the pianoforte. For instance, the four semitones of, say, the major third of C, are C, C sharp, D, D sharp and E. You understand that, don't you?" The boy nodded eagerly, too eagerly to be altogether sincere. With beating heart he was waiting for the next question. "Now tell me what is a minor third?"

Again the boyish treble squeaked through the classroom. "When from the tonic to the third note——"

Smiling, Felix ran his hand over his eyes. Once he had been like this, replying to Zelter's questions with the same childish trepidation. Now, thirty years later, he was listening to the same parrotlike answer. It was nice, rather touching—and also rather ridiculous. Downright idiotic, if you stopped to think of it. Here he was, Felix Mendelssohn, at the summit of his career, decorated with the Pour le Merite Cross, the highest German order, and what was he doing? He was teaching musical catechism to a roomful of provincial youngsters. And why? Because years ago in a Swiss meadow his wife had had a "feeling" they should move to Leipzig! . . . Was this the glorious achievement behind Cécile's mystic impulse, her God-inspired "feeling," or just his reward for being a patient and obliging husband, indulging his wife's taste for small towns and small-town living?

"That's right, Wilhelm. Three semitones." He heard himself speak the words as though someone nearby were uttering them. "The major third is four semitones and the minor third only three semitones. Now let's see if you can answer a *really* difficult question." He saw the boy stiffen with expectation. "Are there still just two keys, even if you have one, two, three, four or a million sharps and flats at the signature? Take your time."

"Yes, Herr Direktor, only two, because——"

He looked ahead, unseeing, the smile of encouragement frozen

on his lips, anger stirring confusedly within him. He had lost
so that Cécile could have the life she liked, attend sewing circles,
haggle over trifles with shopkeepers and go shopping with dowdy
ladies in quaint and musty stores. Hadn't he any rights? After all
he still was young—you couldn't call thirty-seven old, could you?
He was rich, famous and in good health. Yes, in perfect health.
His headaches had vanished. Well, almost . . . He hadn't had
a single one during his two months in Switzerland. They had merely
been caused by overwork. Nothing else. Overwork and the stifling
drudgery of his life in this small town. Well, he was going to change
all that, he was going to speak to Cécile. And this time . . .

"Very good, Wilhelm," he said as the school bell rang in the
corridor. "Now for the next lesson you will study——"

A moment later he was in his office, his handsome directorial
office with the impressive bronze-encrusted desk and Friedrich
Augustus' portrait over the mantel, pacing the thick green carpet,
his hands clasped behind his back. By now his anger had changed
to a feeling of outrage and personal injustice. Why should he be
made a victim? What reason was there for him to stay in this
town? The children? They could be brought up as well in Berlin
as here, couldn't they? His mother would enjoy seeing her grandchildren now and then . . . Well, then—Cécile's preference for small
towns? Surely some sewing circle and ladies' benevolent society
could be found for her to patronise, and some virtuous *Hausfraus*
with whom to drink tea and go on shopping expeditions. Well, he
was going to speak to her, tell her plainly his wishes and lay down
the law . . .

"Come in," he flung petulantly over his shoulder in reply to a
knock on the door.

Hermann Schmidt burst into the room as if butted in by a goat.
He was a square little man with baby cheeks, foamy white side
whiskers and two impish eyebrows that curled up over his blue eyes
like misplaced little moustaches. He was fretful, timid and for no
reason whatever in a perpetual hurry. He also was, in Felix's
opinion, a superb flute player and an excellent all-around musician.
His devotion to Felix was fierce and absolute, mingled with a subtle
feeling of proprietorship. He had formed the conviction that the
young Herr Direktor acted frequently on his suggestions and that
therefore, as a man old enough to be his father, he owed him the
benefit of his experience. Without any official title or remuneration
other than his regular musician's salary, he had attached himself to
Felix, discharging innumerable little chores, winning his affection
and confidence and asking nothing but to serve and love him.

Before he could say anything, Felix turned on him. "Do you
know any reason, any reason at all why I should stay in this silly

town?" he barked at him, sending Hermann's eyebrows high in his
forehead. "Would you kindly tell me what on earth I am doing
here, working myself to death, teaching, rehearsing and conducting
concerts when I could be enjoying myself?"

"Because that's what you're supposed to do, Herr Direktor,"
said Schmidt, taken aback by this unexpected outburst.

"That's it!" snorted Felix, glaring at the old man as if he were
a personal enemy of long standing. "You've been with me for years
but did you ever say anything? No! ... Did you ever tell me, 'Herr
Direktor, why do you stay in this stupid town?' No! . . . On the
contrary you're partly responsible for my being here, for you came
to Düsseldorf to spy on me when I was giving the Rhine Festival
and reported to the trustees I was just the man for Leipzig."

"But, Herr Direktor——"

"No explanations and no apologies. Next year at this date
there will be a new Gewandhaus conductor and new Conservatorium director, and I shall be living the life of a gentleman
of leisure." He noticed the wad of letters in Schmidt's hand.
"Leave it on the desk. I'll look at it to-morrow."

"Anything else?"

"Nothing," said Felix, sitting down at his desk. "Make sure all
the instruments' parts for the next concert are on hand for to-
morrow's rehearsal." He was about to dismiss the old man with a
wave but turned around instead. "Please don't say anything—not
even to your wife—about what I just told you."

"You can count on me, Herr Direktor."

"I know that," said Felix, with an affectionate smile. For a
moment he considered his unofficial secretary with visible fondness.
"You're a good man, Hermann. I don't know what I'd do if I
didn't have you."

It was for such compliments that Schmidt lived. A look of
undiluted adoration came into his eyes. "You know I'd do anything
for you, don't you, Herr Direktor?"

Felix nodded. Then, with sudden and feigned abruptness, "Well,
then get yourself out of here or your wife will skin you alive. I'd go
too, except that Frau Mendelssohn told me she'd come and pick
me up. But you know how women are. Never on time."

On this man-to-man note the interview came to an end and
Hermann Schmidt whisked out of the room.

Like a dark stain dusk was creeping through the office. Already
Friedrich Augustus' scarlet uniform had turned into a blurry purple
over the fireplace. The green carpet had turned black. In the
windows curtains of shadows already hung. Another day gone,
he thought. Another laborious uneventful tedious day. In London
Karl must be dressing to go to dinner at some Mayfair house. In

Paris, Vienna, Berlin the streets must be humming with lit carriages and the lights of cafés. And he was here, alone in a silent and darkening office waiting for his wife to take him to a home-cooked dinner and a long quiet evening in the study.

He heard the door open and whirled around. Cécile was entering the room, looking lovely in her beribboned bonnet and short fur-lined cape, for already the autumn evenings were growing cold. She leaned down and kissed his brow.

"Forgive me, darling," she said, a little out of breath. "I went shopping with Elsa and she couldn't make up her mind."

"And how is Her Ladyship?" he asked, rising.

Irony was lost on her. "The money some women spend on their clothes is simply sinful," she exclaimed.

"Especially when the results are so distressing," he remarked, stepping aside to let her go out.

This time she caught the barb of his remark and her tone bristled with reproof. "I think it's very ill-mannered to speak like that about Elsa." She was fiercely loyal to her friends and her devotion struck Felix as touching and faintly ridiculous. "She's a wonderful woman."

"Of course she is. A pity her qualities cannot improve her looks." He saw she was getting angry and to pacify her he took her arm. "You little goose, don't you see I'm joking?"

"I don't like that kind of joke," she said through tight lips.

"I love Elsa. I think she's a fine woman and I'm glad you two are such good friends." For an instant he thought of broaching the subject of moving away from Leipzig, but he judged the moment inopportune. He would speak to her after dinner in the study. Quietly but firmly . . . "Now tell me what you've been doing."

Excitedly she told him about her tour of the town's various dress shops with the Mayor's wife. She had a quick, observing mind, spiked her comments with deft and sometimes humorous asides, and it always came to him as a surprise that she could be an entertaining conversationalist. Occasionally, when excited, she would lapse into French or into the Frankfurt patois of her child-hood. This afternoon she was in high spirits, still flushed with the excitement of the afternoon's expedition, and she prattled happily as they ambled through the long corridors of the Gewandhaus building, describing the commotion aroused by their entrance, Elsa standing in her stays and pantlets before the full-length mirror of the *salons d'essayage*, the sales ladies' insincere cries of ravishment each time Her Ladyship tried on a new dress.

"But she couldn't make up her mind," she said as they were reaching the entrance, "and so we finally drove to Dorbeck's, on Markt Platz."

They paused on the outer landing, stretching almost the entire length of the building at the top of a flight of broad marble stairs. Below, Gustav, his profile silhouetted against the yellow glow of the carriage lantern, was standing on the kerb, about to shut the door.

"You should see those new Paris fashions!" she babbled on as they went down the stairs. "Skirts are twice as wide as last year."

Still talking, she bent down and with a rustle of taffeta slipped in to the carriage. "And the *canezous, mon Dieu!*" . . . she exclaimed, sitting in the corner and smoothing her skirt around her knees.

"Good evening, Gustav." With one foot in the door Felix turned to his old valet. "You must be tired with all this driving around. Let's go home."

"No, no!" cried Cécile, leaning forward. "Stop first at Koehler's."

"Very good, Madame," said Gustav, closing the door behind Felix.

"It's on our way home," she explained as Felix took his place at her side. "You don't mind, do you, darling? It won't take a minute."

"Of course not," he smiled. "Now what on earth is a *canezou?*"

During the short drive to the butcher shop he learned that a *canezou* was a blouse. Of course there were all sorts of *canezous*, just as there were all sorts of *berthes* and *jockeis*.

"I declare." she observed indignantly, "those Paris couturiers change the fashions just so you have to buy a new wardrobe each year."

"That's what couturiers live on, Cilette," he murmured soothingly, trying to calm her aroused thriftiness. "Why didn't you buy a dress or two while you were there?"

"I should say not."

He smiled to himself, glad she could not see his amusement in the dimness of the carriage.

"But I got a few ideas," she went on with sly cunning. "Tomorrow I go and see Frau Hoffmann, my dressmaker, and . . ."

She was still chatting away about those "ridiculous Paris fashions" when the carriage came to a halt in front of Martin Koehler's shop.

"I'll just be a minute," she said as he helped her out of the brougham.

"I might just as well go in with you." He pushed back the door and followed her. "You might start haggling about with the poor man and I'll be sitting there for an hour."

In the effulgent glow of tallow candles the shop looked like some nightmarish medieval slaughterhouse. Meat was lying about everywhere in obscene disarray and profusion. Behind the counter wide-open carcasses of beef and legs of lamb hung from hooks. Hams and strings of sausages dangled from a huge beam black with grime and age. On a blood-stained plate a pig's head rested, naked and glassy-eyed, faintly smiling in death. The choking smell of dead flesh caught Felix unaware and almost sent him reeling back into the street. Cécile, however, appeared unconcerned and so did the three housewives who moved about the room like shadowy, discriminating buzzards oking, sniffling, poking tranquil fingers into pulpy hulks of raw meat before making their choice.

Martin Koehler himself, sweating, grinning, his bare and hairy arms protruding from his blood-spattered apron, was engaged in a technical discussion with a stubborn hatchet-faced woman who argued with him through the slit of her mouth without moving her lips. At last she nodded in assent and the butcher snatched the piece of meat, weighed it under the woman's watchful eye and, after a glance at the counter, flung it on the chopping table.

"What's she doing upstairs?" he growled, his face turning a shade of darker magenta with righteous annoyance. Turning around, he opened a door at his back, craned his thick neck and let out a blast of invectives at his invisible spouse.

"Be quick with that paper, will you?" he shouted, his words booming through the living quarters upstairs. "There's people waiting in here."

A woman's voice came trickling down from the loft together with the thumping of descending footsteps. Returning to the hatchet-faced customer, he pasted his professional smile back on his lips and explained they had run out of wrapping paper but that stupid wife of his was bringing down another stack from stock lying in the attic

Presently Frau Koehler, half concealed behind the heap of paper in her arms, kicked open the door and made her way to the counter, where she dumped her load with a sigh of relief. Felix, abandoned by Cécile, who was inspecting a thick slice of steak, watched the butcher's wife bend down and puff her cheeks to blow the layer of dust lying on top of the stack.

"Ach! This time we've got music!" she beamed, wiping the sweat from her brow with the back of her hand.

Gruffly her husband shoved her aside, his hand already lifted to slam down the hatchet-faced woman's piece of meat. It was then that Felix's eyes happened to brush over the first page. His blood turned cold and his heart stood still, for there, written in ancient and yellowed cursive, he had read the words: "The Passion of Our Lord, According to Saint Matthew, by Johann Sebastian Bach."

Chapter 6

" It is my pleasure to inform the board that we may be able to secure Monsieur Frederic Chopin as our first recitalist of the winter's season." Felix ran his eyes along the table at the trustees' complacent faces, drowsily smiling at him in the after-lunch digestive torpor. " As you are well aware, Monsieur Chopin is not only an outstanding pianist, but also a composer of exceptional talent. His appearance with the Gewandhaus Orchestra will mark another step——"

The board of trustees of the Gewandhaus Orchestra was regarded as Leipzig's most exclusive club. Its eleven members were selected from among the most wealthy and socially prominent businessmen who coveted appointments to it as a mark of distinction and fought for the privilege of sharing in the discharge of its unexacting duties. Under the Mayor's benevolent chairmanship, the meetings assumed the aspect of a good-humoured discussion among old friends. He stressed the informality of the proceedings by dispensing with most of the parliamentary rules, allowing smoking and even the serving of liquor.

" Of course." nodded His Lordship, rolling his cigar in his mouth. " By all means let's have Monsieur Chopin." Personally he did not care. He longed for the meeting to come to an end. A mood of somnolent amorousness was stealing over him. He wanted to go and see Olga, remove his high collar that cut into his jowls, lie down on her bed and caress her firm, smooth flesh. " We leave it to you to reach a satisfactory agreement," he said to Felix. " What date would you suggest?"

" Early December, Your Lordship."

" Fine," agreed the Mayor with the compliance of complete indifference. He seized his gavel and perfunctorily glanced at the trustees. " All in accord?"

Heads nodded in casual assent, and he was about to lower his gavel when Wilhelm Kruger raised his spidery hand in a timid yet demanding gesture.

" I do not wish to abuse the board's patience," said the First Councilman with an apologetic clearing of throat, " but there's a matter I think we should discuss before giving our approval to Monsieur Chopin's concert."

The trustees looked at him with a mixture of boredom and uneasy curiosity. Christoph Muller waited, gavel in hand, a squint

168

of irritation in his small agile eyes. Now what did he want, that one? Was he going to stir up trouble here as he did on the city council? " Please be brief," he snapped.

" We all agree that persons in public life, whatever their field, should give an example of blameless conduct, don't we?" Kruger began, looking away from the Mayor and addressing himself to the other trustees.

Abruptly the atmosphere in the room had changed. The board's members had caught the allusion to the Mayor's mistress and were now sitting straight in their brocaded chairs, sensing the approach of a clash.

" If the spectacle of moral turpitude is given by those in high places," Gruger went on, sucking his upper lip as though he inhaled rather than exhaled the words, " how can we expect obedience and respect from the lower classes?"

The Mayor felt a flush of anger rise to his face in a wave of prickly heat. His hand closed in a tight fist around the gavel's handle. Dirty, sanctimonious blackguard. If only he weren't so powerful and didn't know so much . . . " We do appreciate the inspiring value of these remarks," he broke in with a dangerous smile, " but the board would appreciate it if the Honourable Trustee would confine his observations to the matter at hand, namely, Monsieur Chopin's concert."

Kruger swallowed the rebuke and nodded with sly meekness. " I'm coming to it, Your Lordship. For several years Monsieur Chopin has given the revolting spectacle of his affair with a woman novelist who calls herself George Sand. Now, as the trustees of a public institution we have a moral responsibility to the people of this city and I, for one, question the moral fitness of this artist to appear in our Gewandhaus Hall."

" You—what?" Felix's words exploded in the ensuing silence with the impact of a pistol shot and the trustees stiffened.

" I am not addressing you, Herr Direktor," Kruger flung over his shoulder.

" But I am addressing you, Herr Kruger."

The councilman swung around, his pale eyes slit with anger. " This is a matter for the board to decide." His words seemed to slam a door in Felix's face.

" This is a matter for anyone to decide. Monsieur Chopin is my friend and I won't have him insulted in my presence."

Muller had taken the cigar from his mouth and was leaning forward, ready to intervene, his eyes swivelling nimbly from Felix to Kruger, computing their respective chances. Kruger, he knew from experience, was a swift and dangerous debater. Felix, on the other hand, was an unknown quantity. In his relations with the board he had always shown himself courageous and reticent, inclined to keep out of arguments. But now his lips were clamped tight and there was a glint of determination in his eyes.

"This is not a musical matter," said Kruger, turning to the Mayor, "and I request a ruling from the Chair barring the Direktor from this discussion."

Muller leaped at the chance to repay him for his remarks of a moment ago about moral turpitude in high places. "The issue being one of policy affecting the future appearance of artists in Gewandhaus Hall, the Chair rules that the Herr Direktor may be heard."

With clenched jaws Kruger accepted the denial of his request. Felix ignored him and turned to the trustees, like a lawyer addressing a jury. "The question of morality in art is an old one. At all times some misguided fools tried to make art an adjunct of virtue and to take down paintings of nude women from the walls of museums and glue fig leaves on antique statuary. But the issue before us to-day is an even more ridiculous one, it is that of the artist's morality in relation to his work. If we were absurd enough to entertain the suggestion advanced by Herr Kruger, museums would close, orchestras would disband and books would no longer be read. Raphael's madonnas were posed by his mistress. Filippo Lippi was a defrocked monk who had married a wayward nun. Michelangelo and Leonardo da Vinci have been accused of sexual abnormality and Titian was suspected of incestuous relations with his daughter Lavinia. Handel, Mozart, Beethoven, all gave the 'revolting spectacle' of their affairs with women of all types, classes and descriptions. Should we stop playing *The Messiah, Don Giovanni* or the Ninth Symphony? Should we stop reading *Faust* because Goethe lived in almost permanent concubinage with one woman after another? And what about Plato, Villon, Voltaire, Boccaccio and Byron and a hundred others of the greatest writers, thinkers and philosophers? Some artists have been saints and some have been rogues. Some have been heroes and some cowards. It doesn't in the least affect their artistic stature. If we were stupid enough to bar Monsieur Chopin from Gewandhaus Hall on moral grounds, perhaps we should probe into the morals of the orchestra players—and my own? And what about that of the audience?"

Kruger's face had turned a greyish white, almost the colour of his eyes, and for an instant his face was a pallid mask of anger. "Artists love to ridicule virtue," he broke in, "but the fact remains that we shouldn't condone scandal by our applause and give money to a man whose life is an affront to all moral principles. In Paris they may overlook such things, but in Leipzig we have higher standards of conduct."

"No doubt," said Felix with amused sarcasm, "Herr Kruger has made a comparative study of the degrees of virtue among the cities, but unfortunately our higher standards of conduct do not give concerts and Monsieur Chopin does."

A faint ripple of laughter spread among the trustees. Beneath his impassive countenance, the Mayor smiled inwardly.

"I take it you approve of Monsieur Chopin's conduct," said Kruger icily.

"I neither do nor don't I merely pointed out that his private life is irrelevant. He is a great pianist and that is and should be enough."

"I'd like to say that for a man who's been called Saxony's First Citizen your moral standards are very pliable."

"You may say whatever you wish."

"Will you deny Chopin and George Sand are lovers?" said Kruger pressing his advantage.

"I neither deny nor admit it. I simply don't know. Perhaps you'll tell us how *you* know they are lovers. Do you possess some secret information on the matter?"

Kruger shrugged. "This is ridiculous. Everyone knows it."

"Well, I don't," said Felix with a great show of innocence. "Monsieur Chopin lives in Paris, 10 Place d'Orleans. Madame Sand spends most of the year at her country home, the Château de Nohant. True he has been her guest there, but so have Balzac, Liszt, Berlioz, Delacroix and most of the great artists of our time. Are they also her lovers? Do you happen to have some bedroom information on the subject and does your information include keyhole spying?"

He knew he was going too far, but he couldn't take the sarcasm out of his voice. He felt he was making a mortal enemy, but the sight of this treacherous old man smearing his friend's name sent him into a passion of fury. Already he felt the throbbing in his temples that announced the coming of a headache. For an instant he longed to resign, profit from this incident to move away from Leipzig. The vision of Chopin asking him to arrange a concert faded, and another flashed through his mind. He couldn't resign, he needed his orchestra to perform the Passion . . . "I think this discussion has already lasted too long," he said, tiredly passing his hand over his aching brow. "A man's private life is his own. All freedoms are worthless without the freedom of privacy. I hope the board will agree with me. Whatever its decision I shall abide by it."

The Mayor gave a circling glance. "I am sure I express the board's opinion in thanking both our distinguished Herr Direktor and the Honourable Trustee for their exchange of views." He was speaking in his political tone of voice, smoothing feelings, bringing peace like a benevolent umpire between excited and foolish contestants. " It is from such discussions that progress is made."

He felt around him the trustees' approving nods and relieved smiles. He knew and understood them well, these selfish and cautious burghers who played at being art patrons. They wanted peace. They didn't care whether Chopin played or not, whether he had a mistress or not. They didn't want trouble. An open rift between the Mayor and his First Councilman might degenerate into a local feud and they might be forced into taking sides, declaring their loyalties. They had no loyalties but to themselves. . . .

" However, since negotiations have been opened "—nothing had been said about that and Felix looked up sharply at him, but Muller pretended not to see and went on in his resonant and unctuous voice—" we hope that Monsieur Chopin will redeem by his artistry the doubts that may be entertained about his private life, and once again our beloved Leipzig, our Athens-on-the-Pleiss will be the scene of another memorable artistic event. For more than a century the Gerwandhaus Hall——"

Felix did not listen any longer. He felt tired, curiously dispirited. His head throbbed painfully. He had made a mortal enemy and a powerful one, but no new friends. He was still the foreigner from Berlin. Muller, he saw it clearly, would never be his friend. He couldn't afford being anyone's friend. He was too vulnerable, he had to watch out for himself. . . .

The Mayor ended his oration in his usual flowery style. Then abruptly he brought down his gavel on the table and declared the session ended.

The trustees pushed back their chairs and hurriedly started to leave. Herr Kruger was among the first to depart, followed shortly afterwards by the Mayor. With half-hearted waves at Felix the other trustees straggled out. Alone, Felix leaned his head against the palm of his hand. Why hadn't he let someone else tackle Kruger? . . . Meanwhile he had weakened his position just at the time when he needed the board's support to perform the Passion . . . It would not be easy to convince them, get them to allocate the necessary funds for the chorus, the soloists, the additional orchestra rehearsals. . . .

He felt despondent and alone. If only Cécile understood, if only she were at his side, if only she could understand that he must perform the Passion, that this was the true reason for his coming to Leipzig. But she couldn't. Strangely she, who had felt the mysterious impulse to come to Leipzig couldn't understand that a bundle of old paper could give a meaning to a life. He had played for her some fragments of the Passion, tried to make her feel the magnificence of this gigantic work. He had read in her eyes her bewilderment. How could a man get so exercised over some old Church music? ... Poor Cilette! He was asking too much of her. Only great loves were blind enough to create blind faith. ...

He shrugged wearily and began gathering his papers as the door opened. An usher handed him a note and withdrew without a word. He unfolded the paper and the five-word message leaped to his eyes: YOU WILL PAY FOR THIS.

It was written in clumsy capitals and there was no signature, but he knew from whom it came.

"Did you tell the board about the Passion?" Cécile asked at dinner that evening.

He shook his head. "Didn't have a chance." He wished she wouldn't speak, wouldn't ask questions about the meeting. "Did you take Karl to the barber?" he inquired to change the subject.

He saw that she hadn't. "Why didn't you? You know he hates those long curls. It makes him look like a girl."

"He is still so young."

"He is old enough to look like a boy."

"All right," she nodded, stifling a sigh. "If that's what you want."

"That's what he wants. He told me himself."

She lowered her eyes in a gesture of wifely obedience. After a silence she said with an effort, "I'm sorry about the Passion. I know how anxious you are to have it performed."

He looked across the table at her with rueful tenderness. Poor Cilette. Still trying to be the perfect wife, making her husband talk about his work ... "I'm sorry, too. We don't have too much time if we're going to perform it this spring, as I'd like to. Instead we wasted a lot of time discussing the morals of artists ... By the way, I picked a nice row with Kruger."

His light tone did not deceive her. "A row?" Her brow creased with anxiety. "About what?"

"Chopin. Kruger thought he was morally unfit to appear in the hall. He got me so angry that I blew up and really told him what I thought of him. I never liked him anyway. Did you know he was the only trustee who voted against my appointment as conductor?"

"Really?" But already she was asking the question paramount in her mind. "How did it end?"

"He survived, if that's what's worrying you," he replied, his disappointment cloaked in irony.

"I don't mean that," she said with impatience. "How did it end?"

"In the usual flow of meaningless, hypocritical oratory. Muller was at his best. This man is a born Pontius Pilatus. He delivered a lovely homily. You know, ' Now come on, children, we may have our little differences but we all love our dear old Leipzig, don't we?' That type of speech." He almost mentioned Kruger's after-meeting message, but something held him back.

" I wish you hadn't antagonised him," she said with doleful censure. "He's such an important man."

He knew her remark was objective and well meant, yet it infuriated him. He yearned for comforting words, declarations of approval, and he was getting criticism . . . In a flash of bitter humour he conjured the image of home-returning David reprimanded for hurting Goliath. " Perhaps I should go and apologise?" he suggested with mock contrition. " Do you think he might forgive me, if I went down on my knees?"

Her eyes turned cold. " You don't have to be sarcastic," she said through tight lips, " I merely remarked I was sorry you'd antagonised him, that's all."

" Which does credit to your kind heart."

She lowered her lids and her face closed in a mask of hurt remoteness. They did not speak any more after that. They avoided each other's eyes and nibbled at their food. Dinner over, they rose and in strained silence passed into the study.

Usually he sipped his demi-tasse, occasionally poured himself a small glass of schnapps or French cognac and afterwards worked at his desk for a few hours. But to-night he lingered idly in his chair, stretching his legs to the fire, twisting the stem of his brandy glass between his fingers.

" Aren't you going to work to-night?" she asked, threading her needle.

" No. Don't feel like it."

Silence fell between them. In the fireplace a log broke with a geyser of sparks. He leaned down, poked with the tongs into the salmon flesh of the logs. Then, taking a little fire broom, he carefully swept up the ashes. This done, he returned to his brandy.

" If you aren't going to work, why don't you go to sleep?" she said without looking at him. " You look tired."

" I'm all right." He took a sip and again lost himself in the contemplation of his twirling glass. " Do you know that if you look at yourself in the hollow of a spoon, your reflection is upside down?" he said unexpectedly.

" No, I didn't." She barely moved her lips. In the glow of the fire her pure oval face reminded him of Lippi's blonde Madonnas. After a pause she said, " Again you ate almost nothing to-night."

" I wasn't hungry and my argument with Kruger gave me a headache."

" Perhaps you should go and see the doctor."

" Perhaps I will one of these days." Her concern touched him. She did love him ... He rested his glass on the small round table at his side and turned to her. " I'm sorry darling, for what I said at the dinner table."

She went on with her sewing. " It's all right."

" No, it isn't. You were asking perfectly proper questions and I was rude and offensive." Oh, if she'd only look at him, come and sit on his knees as in the old Düsseldorf days! ... " Darling."

" Yes?"

" Darling "—now his voice was urgent and pleading—" after I've performed the Passion let's get away from this town."

" What do you mean?" Her blue eyes rested on him in troubled inquiry. " Away from Leipzig?"

" Yes." In one flowing motion he was sitting at her side on the sofa, his face close to hers. " Yes, darling," he said, excitement rising in his voice. " Let's get away from here. I've been meaning to tell you a long time. I knew you were opposed to it, but now it's all right. I know now why we came to Leipzig. You were right, it really was God Who was sending us here. He wanted me to perform the Passion, bring back to life this magnificent work. All right, I'll perform it and then we'll be free, we can go away."

She blinked uncomprehendingly. " But—but where, Felix?"

" Anywhere. We could take a villa in Rome for instance. Not Rome proper, but on the hills. My uncle had one. You can't imagine how beautiful it is there. Sunsets have a beauty they don't have anywhere else. The whole sky rent apart in veils of different colours. Or if you preferred, we could rent a *palazzo* in Venice. Have you ever seen the Rialto in moonlight?"

" No. What about the children?"

" We'd take them with us," he said sweepingly. " They have wonderful schools in Italy."

" Do you mean "—her astonishment was turning to annoyance —" we'd live in Italy—the rest of our lives?"

" Of course not." His gesture seemed to brush Italy aside. " We could travel. How'd you like to go to America? They've been begging me to come to New York and to conduct my work. I know, I know ... you think there's nothing but Redskins there, but you're wrong. New York's a big city of fifty thousand souls." His excitement faltered under her disapproving stare. " Or London? Or St. Petersburg? Wouldn't you like to see Russia? The churches with their onion-shaped domes, the troikas, the peasants in their fur bonnets ..."

His words hung in mid air, pleading for a response, an echo of encouragement. She knew she should say something, give him some word of hope. But what could one say to such nonsense!

. . . The things that went on in his brain! He seemed content with
his life and suddenly he burst out with some foolishness about a
villa in Italy or New York. At times she felt she didn't know him
at all . . . " That'd be very nice," she said, at a loss for anything else
to say. " I'm sure it would be very interesting. We must talk
more about it."

She scanned his pale gaunt face, tense with longing, and her eyes
softened   " You're tired. You work too hard at that Conservatorium.   Haven't you found someone yet to take Herr
Schumann's place?"

" We've had a few applications, but nobody really good. There's
a man in Dresden I'd like to contact. I may go there for two
or three days during the Christmas holidays."

She was gathering her sewing, putting it back into her basket.
" Why don't you?"

He jerked himself up. " You're right. I may do that. Let's go
to bed."

During the following days he did not mention Italy or New
York any more. Instead he berated himself for his ridiculous outburst of confidence and once again, for the hundredth time, he
promised himself to steer away from dreams and confine his conversation to the factual account of the day's happenings. Would
he ever learn to check his impulses, resist those sudden urges to take
her into his confidence. Imagine coming to her—to her, of all
people!—with this addle-brained proposition of a villa in Rome, a
palazzo in Venice? And this silly talk about New York and Petersburg? Why not suggest taking to the road in a gipsy waggon and
sleeping under the stars? . . . She must have thought him mad and,
frankly, you couldn't blame her . . . When would he understand
that she didn't understand, that he couldn't expect her to follow
his unpredictable, unreasoning moods?

There were things she simply didn't comprehend—and that's all
there was to it. Music, for instance. How many times had he tried
to explain to her the pellucid perfection of a Mozart phrase. " *Lá ci
darem*," for instance, those few exquisite bars in which lived the
fragrant and foolish soul of the eighteenth century. Poetry was
also a closed book to her. One day, gazing at her perfect features,
he had murmured Byron's lines, " The light of love, the purity of
grace, The wing, the music breathing from her face." She had
giggled, saying she'd never heard such nonsense . . . Each time,
after one of such incidents, he'd swear he'd never open his foolish,
romantic heart again. And yet he still went on. Which merely
proved that some people never grew up. They merely grew old—
and he was one of them.

Anyway, there was no time for confidences. His days were

crowded with his heavy schedule of teaching at the Conservatorium, orchestra rehearsals and bi-weekly concerts in Gewandhaus Hall. In addition, there was now this gigantic score of the Passion, which had landed in his life, like a spent meteor. He studied it each evening after dinner and every day his admiration increased. This was indeed a cathedral of sounds, the work of a genius of almost frightening stature. Next to it even Handel's colossal *Messiah* shrank in size. But also, every day the realisation of its difficulties forced itself more imperiously. It would take the combined efforts and talents of a great many people to achieve a fine performance. Also a great deal of money . . . And the board of trustees had a repugnance to spending money. They would be even more reluctant to doing so on some forgotten work by an obscure Saint Thomas choirmaster. He would have to be very persuasive. And this time he would have to be patient and not lose his temper and not get into any argument.

He was being patient that afternoon as he explained to the trustees how he had come across the manuscript and how important it was that it be performed. " In my opinion, gentlemen, this is a work of sublime beauty, unique in the sum total of existing music, and the world will ever be grateful to you for making its recovery and performance possible."

His words fell in a complete and uneasy silence. None of the trustees stirred on his chair. He might have been addressing a row of wax figures. They sat, their hands crossed over their paunches, various shades of surprise on their faces, looking at him, and he at them, as in a living tableau. They didn't know what to make of his story and not having yet spoken about it, they hadn't yet formulated any thought about it.

" It's all very strange," said one of the members at last. " Very strange, indeed. All those years in the attic of a butcher shop, eh?" He raised his hand and began rubbing his chin, as though in great mental labour. " Very strange."

" Yes. It is strange. But strange things do happen. During the Revolution the Blue Diamond of the French Crown was found in a gutter of the Champs-Elysées and later was sold in London for one shilling."

Another trustee spoke. " Have you any idea how the manuscript got there—in the attic, I mean?"

" I asked Frau Koehler about that. She remembered playing in the attic as a child with her grandfather one day, and he had told her about an old woman who lived in a garret on Hainstrasse. She used to come to his shop and he'd give her bones and scraps of meat now and then. He had become quite fond of her and one day, not seeing her for some time, he'd gone to visit her and found her dying.

She had pointed to the manuscript on the table by her bed and asked him, as a last favour, to store it in his attic."

Again there was a long stretch of silence broken only by the first trustee, who kept muttering, " Strange, very strange indeed . . ." Kruger had not spoken a word during the entire meeting, but Felix had felt the dart of his eyes upon him.

Finally the Mayor took the cigar out of his mouth and let out a long plume of smoke. " Well," he declared in the tone of a judge summing up a puzzling case. " it's an interesting story, but personally I haven't yet made up my mind about it."

" I am ready to furnish whatever explanations might be required," said Felix, trying to control his impatience. " I should like to emphasise that a decision should be taken now, so that the preliminary task of copying the manuscript could begin at once. Time is pressing, if we want to perform this work in the spring."

The Mayor raised his hand. " We appreciate your enthusiasm, Herr Direktor, but the board cannot be expected to act hastily in such a matter. You've asked us to allocate special funds for the performance of this work. Have you any idea how much it will cost?"

" A great deal, I am afraid, Your Lordship."

" And our budget is closed for the year," remarked a trustee.

Felix turned to him, keeping his voice calm and his manner courteous. " I realise that. But let me assure you this is decidedly a most exceptional occurrence. And time is of the essence."

The trustees resumed their pondering attitudes, enjoying the sense of power of their position. It was pleasant indeed to hold the young and celebrated Herr Doktor in anxious suspense, keep him waiting for their collective wisdom to crystallise into a final verdict. One of the rare privileges of seniority was to command youth.

This time it was Felix who broke the silence.

" Considerable savings could be made if Pastor Hagen would lend us the four choirs of Saint Thomas's School. This would give us more than one hundred well-trained voices. There are also several choral societies in this city and the surrounding towns. No doubt they could be induced to join in the rehearsals. There would only remain the matter of soloists, which shouldn't prove too difficult or costly. Naturally, I shall volunteer my services for the training of the choirs and the necessary additional orchestra rehearsals."

" Well," said the Mayor, and his tone implied he had at last reached a decision, " the first step is to obtain Pastor Hagen's co-operation. I suggest you approach His Reverence and try to enlist his support. You'll then be in a position to draw a detailed estimate of cost. Meanwhile, we'll all do some thinking and I'm confident we'll reach a decision at our next week's meeting."

As he spoke the last words he pounded his gavel, and the meeting was over.

"How did it go?" asked Cécile when Felix came home that evening.

He shrugged. "Nothing's been decided. I pleaded with them to hurry, but Muller said they needed more time to make up their minds."

"Any more fights?"

"God, no! I kissed everyone's boots. You would've been very proud of me. Kruger didn't open his mouth, but if looks could kill, I'd be dead."

She noticed he looked pale and nervous. During dinner he said abruptly, "How about going to the theatre to-night? I don't know what they're playing, but it might do us good."

The play was a five-act melodrama called *The Two Cousins*. It was gory, maudlin and very bad. The heroine was alternately in tears or in danger. When she was not defending her honour from one cousin, she was offering it to the other who, for some reason, would have no part of it. Hence the tears. It all wound up in a rash of rapid murders in the last five minutes of the play with the villainous cousin staggering drunkenly all over the stage, a dagger in his chest, writhing in horrible convulsions and finally breathing his last foul breath in a last imprecation. During the intervals Felix and Cécile promenaded through the crowded brightly-lit lobby, eating oranges from Spain and discussing the play. Felix spied the Mayor and two of the trustees engaged in earnest conversation. He tipped his top hat to them and after a slight hesitation they tipped their hats to him.

On the way back home Cécile remarked it had been a poorly spent evening.

"I'm afraid you're right," he said. "Forgive me for suggesting it."

That night he could not fall asleep. For a long while he lay in bed, staring at the darkness, his hands locked under his head. Suddenly Cécile turned on her side and faced him.

"What are you thinking about?" she asked softly.

"The Passion," he said, without moving.

"It's worrying you, isn't it?"

"Yes. It's going to give me trouble, I can feel it."

"Couldn't you wait until next year to perform it?"

"I don't know where I'll be next year and I couldn't live with myself if I didn't perform it."

"Is it really so important?"

" Yes, Cécile."

" You already have so much work to do."

" This is more important than anything else I have to do."

" Why? Why is it so important?"

" Because if I don't do it, nobody ever will."

Pastor Hagen was by common consent the most powerful man in Leipzig. Yet this pious and solitary man took little part in the life of the city, and his Sunday sermons, full of Biblical imagery and resonant unction, constituted almost his sole contact with his congregation. He lived in the parsonage at the back of the church, a retiring, sheltered life, spending most of his time reading the scriptures and the voluminous writings of Martin Luther in the quiet of his study, a large dim room with coloured panes of glass in the windows and three huge cabinets filled with leather-bound volumes.

Solitude, however, breeds complexity, and a lifetime of theological studies had given this mild-spoken cleric a mystical and obstinate state of mind. Having overcome the tormenting doubts of his youth he had now, in his old age, reached the stage of untroubled certitude. God had become to him an august yet intimate acquaintance in Whose Name he felt entitled to speak, whether to praise or condemn. Like many men of deep virtue, fierce convictions and limited intelligence, Pastor Hagen had slowly become a fanatic.

That afternoon he bent over his desk engrossed in the composition of his sermon, the weekly cannon ball of wrathful oratory he had fired every Sunday for the last eighteen years at the forces of Satan. Once again this meek and naturally kind man rounded his thundering periods, reading them softly to himself to judge of their effect. working himself into a lather of righteous indignation at the spectacle of Leipzig's incorrigible sinfulness. Of this sinfulness he personally saw very little, preferring the sheltered peace of his study to the vain agitation of mundane life. He was, however, thoroughly informed about it by the whispered accounts of his manservant, Gottlieb. who was also the church's sexton and knew most of the town gossip. Whatever rumours might escape Gottlieb, Friedricka, the pastor's cook, was sure to know. Between the two they kept him thoroughly informed of his flock's transgressions as well as all strange and suspicious happenings. In this fashion the recluse churchman astonished his congregation by the breadth and variety of his information and acquired inexhaustible material for his Sunday sermons.

Whenever Pastor Hagen was not branding the immorality of his parishioners, he was hurling his anathemas at the world at large, this wretched world that refused to become Lutheran. To those

who questioned the mercy of the God Who chastiseth the trans-
gressor as a matter of course and the just as an experiment, and who
resented this depressing habit and apparent contradiction in One
Who insisted on being called the God of Love, Pastor Hagen had
a simple answer. Things would go on like this until the world had
become Lutheran. How could the Almighty experience any other
feeling but that of a permanent and consuming rage when the earth
continued to be infested with millions of Catholics, Mohammedans,
Jews, Brahmins, Buddhists, Calvinists, Baptists and other Satan-
inspired religions three hundred years after the coming of Martin
Luther? Until the day the population of this miscreant planet saw
the light, mended its ways and adhered to the Lutheran dogma,
God would continue to punish the just and the unjust alike with terrible impartiality.

The pastor was reading to himself a paragraph of the next day's
sermon when he was interrupted by a knock on the door. Gottlieb,
white-haired and ghostlike on his felt soles, oozed in and in
whispers informed him that Herr Doktor Mendelssohn was waiting
outside.

A minute later Felix was ushered into the study.

"This is indeed a pleasant surprise!" the pastor exclaimed with
that peculiar brand of beaming geniality churchmen and politicians
reserve for people whose convictions do not coincide with their
own. "I hope you and the lovely Frau Mendelssohn are enjoying
the best of health," he went on, waving him to a dark red chair
across the desk.

While sitting down and resting his top hat on his knees Felix
assured him that the Mendelssohns were enjoying perfect health.

"And the children?"

They were fine, and it was most kind of His Reverence to remember them. Felix then expressed his gratitude for His Reverence's
graciousness in receiving him at this late hour of the afternoon without a previous appointment.

"But I shall take as little as possible of Your Reverence's
precious time," he said, hoping that the interview's preliminary
amenities were at an end.

He was about to come to the object of his visit but the pastor
wouldn't hear of it. Would the Herr Doktor enjoy a cup of
camomile tea or some other fortifying brew? The Herr Doktor
declined with thanks, and the churchman reiterated the pleasure that
this unexpected visit was giving him. "As you see," he said with a
glance at the half-written page on his desk, "I'm preparing to-
morrow's sermon and even as humble a toiler in the Lord's
vineyard as myself is entitled to a few moments of wholesome
diversion."

Whereupon he began telling Felix about Leipzig's crumbling morals. Among the rich as well as the poor. Taverns and rathskellers were full. Money was being squandered on liquor that could be used on charitable crowds. The theatre, always a place of perdition, was attracting crowds. Everywhere the signs of spiritual decadence could be seen. Never in the whole history of Leipzig had there been such a wave of corruption.

Felix listened with polite attention, nodding occasionally and remarking to himself that the priest, rabbi or pastor would never live who didn't regard his generation as the worst in history. Apparently humanity had made no progress at all since Jeremiah's days. He wished that the pastor would cut short his laments. He had felt a vague, unexplainable apprehension of this interview and postponed it for several days. Now he was anxious to state his business, get the pastor's reaction and be off.

But, with the unexpected loquacity of recluses, Pastor Hagen was warming up to his subject. Of course, one of the main reasons of Leipzig's moral debacle was the example of flagrant immorality that came from the better classes.

"Vice rears its ugly head in the highest places," he declared, raising a solemn finger towards the ceiling. "Yes," he repeated, "the highest places."

That's for Muller and his mistress, Felix thought, while keeping his face a perfect blank and waiting for the cleric's oratory to exhaust itself.

It did and rather abruptly, which took Felix by surprise.

"I could go on like this forever," said the pastor a moment later, "but surely you must be anxious to come to the object of your visit." As he spoke his expression changed from indignation to guarded watchfulness.

"It's a simple matter," began Felix with a cautious smile. "Two weeks ago I came across an old manuscript——"

"I've heard about it. In Martin Koehler's shop, wasn't it?"

Felix controlled his surprise and proceeded. "One of the things that makes this score of special interest to Your Reverence is that it was written more than a hundred years ago by a choirmaster of your own Saint Thomas's School." The pastor's face remained expressionless. "It would be of invaluable help if Your Reverence would permit the four Saint Thomas choirs to participate in the performance of this remarkable work. Naturally, a reasonable fee would be paid."

Pastor Hagen joined the tips of his fingers before his lips and closed his eyes. For an instant he seemed to be lost in prayer.

"What is the title of this composition?" he asked, still holding his eyes shut.

"The Passion of Our Lord, According to Saint Matthew."

"And I take it you're planning to conduct this performance yourself?"

Felix blinked with astonishment. "Of course."

"And where would the performance take place?"

Felix was beginning to feel the tightening of his muscles. "At the Gerwandhaus Hall, Your Reverence. Although the most suitable place for it would be Saint Thomas's Church itself, for which the work was written."

Abruptly the pastor opened his eyes. A vein in his forehead swelled. "Don't you see the impropriety for a man of another faith to conduct a performance of sacred music in a Lutheran church?"

This time Felix stared openly at the man across the desk. "But surely Your Reverence can see that it isn't a matter of religion, but of music."

"Sacred music."

"There are only two kinds of music—good and bad."

"There are two kinds of music—sacred and profane. Sacred music is a province of the Church and I do not think it fit for a non-Christian to mingle in matters of the Church. This composition is a musical version of the New Testament "—his voice had risen to pulpit volume—" and the New Testament belongs to the Christians."

"If the New Testament belongs to Christians, then surely the Old belongs to us." He was conscious of a buzzing in his ears. His heartbeats seemed to cover the sound of his words. "How do you dare then to sing our David's Psalms? How do——"

"Sir, how dare you?" thundered the pastor.

Felix sprang to his feet and walked to the desk. He was trembling with anger and his face had turned an ashen grey. "And our Miriam, who graces thousands of Christian churches, was she ever baptised? And what right had Michelangelo to carve a statue of our Moses? And why does it stand in a Christian church?"

He stopped, looked fixedly at the pastor, who was too agitated to speak. "You fool!" he said slowly. "You poor, bigoted, misguided fool!"

Whirling around, he stalked out of the room and almost collided with Gottlieb, who had been listening at the door.

When he arrived home a short time later, Cécile glanced at him and thought he had been taken ill.

"You look like a ghost. What's the matter?"

Still shaking from anger he told her about his visit to the pastor and its disastrous end.

"You . . ." She looked at him aghast, almost incredulously. "You called His Reverence a fool?"

"Yes, I did." His voice was cold but his eyes pleaded for understanding, if not approval. "But don't you think I had a good reason?"

She stood before him, her mouth half-opened, the tips of her fingers touching her lower lip. For an instant she looked at him in silence as though she had never seen him before. Then the words came out in a breathless rush. "How could you? How could you do such a thing?"

"And how did he dare speak to me as he did?"

She was not listening. "How could you insult Pastor Hagen?"

Anger was clenching his hands into fists. She didn't understand, didn't want to understand. . . . "If anyone has been insulted it is I, don't you think? I should expect my wife to understand that!"

"It's you who are a fool." She spoke in cold fury, and each word struck him like a stone. "Yes, a fool! Only a fool would insult Pastor Hagen I hope you're happy. You now have two enemies in this town, Herr Kruger and His Reverence. They'll never forgive you"

"I don't expect them to," he flung back with brutal irony. "Christians seldom do."

For an instant she glared at him, her lips trembling, unable to speak. Suddenly, like an overstrained string her tenseness snapped. Tears gushed out of her eyes, and she started to sob noisily, unrestrainedly. "I don't know what's come over you," she said, speaking in a choked stammer. "Since that music has entered this house you've been acting as if you were out of your mind. Do you want to ruin us, is that it?" She lifted her tear-drenched face to him. "Is that what you want to do? Ruin us all? Do you want us to be banished from this town?"

He looked down on her lovely face, now ugly with grief. His fists unclenched. Anger left him, leaving only an immense weariness that slackened his muscles and sagged his shoulders. She didn't understand, she never would . . . Only great love would make her understand. . . .

"Please leave me alone, Cécile," he said calmly, running his hands over his eyes. He walked to the window. "Please leave me alone," he repeated, gazing out into the approaching night.

They spoke no more about it that evening. They tried to act naturally and with an effort talked of indifferent things. But now resentment hung between them like the smoke lingering after an explosion. Silence had acquired a new density, a new texture of bitterness. Their long-concealed misunderstanding had finally come out in the open, taken shape and form and sound. They were afraid. An expectancy of disaster chilled their hearts. They lowered their

voices and avoided each other's eyes, as if, in the house, someone lay
mortally ill.

Strangely, he fell asleep the moment his cheek touched the
pillow, after brushing a cold good night kiss on her cold unrespon-
sive lips. When he awoke he was not surprised to see that she
had gone Somehow he had expected it. Then he remembered it
was Sunday. She had gone to church, taking the children with her.

Of course it was Sunday. The pastor had been writing his
sermon, remember? . . . And the humble toiler in the Lord's
vineyard had welcomed his visit as a nice little break in the day's
work . . . Suddenly he recalled his visit with startling clarity. He
tried to recapture his mood of anger, but somehow the memory
had lost its fangs. If Pastor Hagen felt that the New Testament
belonged exclusively to Christians, that was all right. Why, by all
means, he was welcome to it. The Old, too, for that matter . . .
How inept to start an argument over David's Psalms and Michelangelo's Moses! If the dear cleric didn't wish to lend his choirs,
well, that too was all right . . . And if he didn't like the idea of a
non-Christian conducting a performance of sacred music, well,
every man was entitled to his opinion and there was nothing anyone
could do about it. As a matter of fact the whole business was
becoming ridiculous. Cécile was right, this music was beginning
to take much too much place in his life. He had done all he
could—and more for this poor Johann Sebastian Bach. He had
approached the board, approached the pastor. Nobody seemed
interested in his music, and he couldn't very well force it upon them,
could he? After all, he couldn't endanger his position, antagonise
everyone in the town because someone one hundred years ago had
written a beautiful oratorio. He had no wish to be a martyr. No,
thank you . . .

The saddest part of the whole incident was Cécile's attitude.
She had proved she was more concerned with other people's
opinions than with his own feelings. She was one of those people
who manifested their love by telling you how wrong you were. Like
those " friends " who insisted on being " frank " with you and then
proceeded to tell you the most unpleasant things on the grounds
they were your friends and must be frank at all costs . . . Yes,
she was the kind who thought you must apologise to anyone who
happened to stamp on your feet. Perhaps that was the Christian
spirit, the " other cheek " doctrine. Well, he didn't like it, didn't like
it a bit. It wasn't very intelligent—and it hurt. Especially when it
was *your* cheek that was being turned . . . She hadn't said so but
she probably expected him to go to the pastor and apologise. Well,
she could wait . . .

"And to hell with the whole thing!" he grumbled aloud, violently turning around and jerking the bell rope.

He gazed out of the window. Well, at least it wasn't raining. In fact, it looked like a lovely day, one of those golden October days that arrived unexpectedly amidst the greyness of autumn and reminded you of summer like a warm and cheerful message from a long-departed friend.

The door opened. To his surprise it was Gustav who entered.

"You didn't drive the mistress to church this morning?"

"No, Master Felix. The mistress said she'd walk."

It was the tone of gloom in which these words were spoken that alerted Felix. "What's wrong?" he said sharply.

"Nothing, Master Felix."

"Stop pretending dumb, will you?" He was startled by the violence of his own voice. "Something's wrong. What is it? Has Catherine been giving you trouble?"

"No, Master Felix. No more than could be expected from any female." The words ended in a long-suffering shrug.

"Well, then what is it?" Felix rasped impatiently. "Are you ill?"

The old servant shook his head and lowered his voice. "There's trouble, Master Felix. People are talking."

"How do you know?"

"When I entered the milk shop this morning, everybody stopped talking."

"Then you can't know what they're talking about."

"I heard whispers behind my back."

"What do they say? For God's sake go on."

"They say you insulted His Reverence."

"Insulted him!" Felix laughed. "Why, it was he who——" He checked himself. What was the use? You couldn't stop people from talking and best of all they loved to talk about things they didn't know—politics and people's private lives. "You've known me long enough to know I wouldn't insult anyone, let alone His Reverence," he said lamely, groping for reassurance. Instead, he got a right-or-wrong-you're-my-master look of obtuse devotion that infuriated him. "Anyway, I don't give a damn what they say," he snapped. "Bring me my breakfast."

"Very well, Master Felix."

"And have my horse ready in an hour," he called after him. "Also tell the mistress when she returns from church not to expect me at dinner to-night."

He found he had no appetite, set the breakfast tray aside on the coverlet and got up. He dressed hurriedly in his riding clothes and walked to the nursery. Marie, his daughter, was sitting on the floor talking absorbedly to her doll Mina. For an instant he watched her scolding the small porcelain doll, pressing her to eat her dinner. He felt his throat tighten and a moistness come over his eyes. Suddenly, Marie turned her blonde head and spied her father standing in the doorway. Snatching up her doll by the arm she ran into his arms.

At once they were deep in conversation, the subject being Mina's misbehaviour and refusal to eat her dinner.

" But, darling," he remonstrated, " it's too early for dinner. Did she have her breakfast?"

" Of course, she had her breakfast," replied Marie hotly. Did Daddy think she was starving Mina? " But that was a long time ago."

" How long?"

It turned out to be five minutes and again he marvelled at children's tranquil disregard of time. He tried to argue that Mina couldn't possibly be hungry, but Marie looked at him oddly, somewhat patronisingly, as if he weren't making much sense and she knew better than he what was good for her child. Abruptly her attention was caught by her reflection in Felix's riding boots. Her wonder knew no bounds and there was no end of questions.

He went away with a feeling of enchantment, as if he had stepped into a gossamer world of never-ending excitement and innocence. He still felt the imprint of her soft cool lips on his cheeks and the tinkling of her laughter rang in his ears. Was there in all nature a lovelier sound than a child's laughter?

Rapidly he rode through town, crossed the Grimma Gate, usually bustling with the traffic of country carts bringing produce from the surrounding villages and soon found himself out of the city. At a crossroad he turned and took the road to Reidnitz where Hermann Schmidt's farm was located.

The ground was still soggy from the week's rains and the dull clop of hoofbeats lulled his drifting thoughts. A light mist had risen and veiled the orange October sun. Thatched-roofed farms appeared now and then behind a tracery of autumnal foliage. Occasionally a rusty leaf fell to the ground of its own accord, from sheer weariness.

It was good to be out of Leipzig, away from gossiping tongues. At times trees were better company than men, they taught you the value of silence. People talked too much and created that miasma of words that hung over cities like a putrid fog. It was good to breathe again the clean country air, rich with the crowing of roosters, the chirping of birds and the scent of field flowers.

He turned into a grassy lane that forked out of the road, and soon Schmidt's farm came into view. It was a large establishment in a state of considerable and picturesque disrepair, consisting of a main low-roofed building which contained ample living quarters, and several barns, sheds, stables and other buildings of various descriptions. The farm had at one time been part of a vast baronial estate, and Felix vaguely recalled Schmidt's telling him how his father, a canny peasant, had come into possession of it through some dexterous and questionable piece of legal chicanery. Schmidt derived no profit whatever from the farm, but he nursed the hope of finishing his days there with his wife Gertrude, whom he adored and with whom he quarrelled all the time.

Felix's entrance into the courtyard was signalled by fierce barking and the cackling of excited hens that scattered in all directions. A door opened in the main building and Gertrude's moon face appeared in the doorway.

" Herr Direktor!" she cried, clapping her hands, as if gazing on some unearthly vision. " Hermann, come quick! The Herr Direktor's here."

Grasping her voluminous skirts with her two hands, she ran towards Felix, followed an instant later by her husband, slipping on his coat, obviously aroused from a peaceful slumber. From one of the barns a red-headed youth who, Felix learned, was one of Schmidt's many cousins, came rushing and led the horse away.

Amidst excited questioning Felix made his way across the courtyard into the house.

" Why didn't you tell us you were coming, Herr Direktor?" Gertrude complained. " We would've been expecting you."

This, he understood, was to justify her husband's informal attire and her own wooden shoes. " It was such a lovely day, I decided to come on the spur of the moment."

" Of course, you're staying for dinner, aren't you?" she asked as they entered the house.

An enormous room with a hooded chimney at one end and a gigantic kitchen stove at the other occupied most of the ground floor of the building. It was paved with red tiles and its white-washed walls were decorated with a profusion of brass kitchen utensils. Chequered curtains hung at the small recessed windows. A wooden staircase led to the living quarters on the first floor.

" It's a little big for just the two of us," explained Schmidt, taking his place at the fireside, " but at least my wife and I don't run into each other. In the old days when the farm was part of the baron's estate the farmhands and the harvest workers had dinner in here. My father told me they had up to a hundred people in this room."

" Any time you feel like coming, you just come." Gertrude's voice came floating from her end of the room, the kitchen end,

as if from another planet. "That is, if you don't mind eating plain
country food."

"And you can stay as long as you want," elaborated Schmidt,
every inch the lord of the manor. "And you can bring as many
people as you like." he added as an afterthought. "Plenty of rooms
upstairs." His tone implied that Felix could bring a vast retinue if
he chose.

Under the buoyant kindness of these simple people Felix felt
himself relaxing. His nerves grew quiet. For a while, sipping his
beer from an old faïence mug, he talked with Hermann of unimportant things. A mile away Frau Schmidt was preparing dinner,
humming to herself. There were long friendly silences. Now and
then a dead leaf fell across the window. The trees stood in black
silhouette against the sunset. Leipzig, the rumours, the malicious
gossip seemed very far away. . . .

"I am glad I came here," said Felix after a long pause.

The old flautist took a sip of beer, slowly wiped the foam from
his lips with the back of his hand and gazed for a while at the fire.
Then, without moving his head, he said quietly, "There are
moments when you can't stand looking at the human race another
minute. Even the few people you like. That's why I come here on
Sundays."

"You're lucky to have this place."

This simple statement Hermann mulled at length and in silence.
Finally he seemed to make up his mind about it. "A man should
have a place where he can be by himself once in a while," he
declared somewhat sententiously.

Obviously he looked upon his wife as a part of himself or a
piece of furniture encroaching in no way on his solitude, but Felix
understood what he meant and didn't labour the point.

In this fashion the hours passed until it was time to sit down at
the table and enjoy Gertrude's dinner. To his surprise Felix displayed a splendid appetite, which endeared him to her and brought
smiles of gratification to her florid and watchful face.

As she was refilling Felix's plate she turned to her husband,
"Ach, you see, Hermann, the Herr Direktor likes my cooking."
Pride made her eyes gleam. In the light of the two tallow candles
on the table she looked like some benevolent and motherly Ger-
mania. She turned abruptly, the plate still in mid air. "Why don't
you sleep here to-night, Herr Direktor? In the city the night air is
full of fevers and vapours, but here "—her lips puckered into a silent
kiss—" it is like perfume and it helps the digestion. You'll sleep
like a baby."

At once he was tempted and seduced by the idea. He longed
for a night by himself, away from Cécile's tight lips and resentful

gaze. " I'd love to, but Frau Mendelssohn is expecting me," he
said, feeling he should register some feeble protest. " I'm afraid
she might worry."

Gertrude's ample bosom rose in a snort of tolerant derision.
This was no problem, this was the simplest thing in the world.
Another of Hermann's cousins—there appeared to be a number of
them living scattered all over the farm—was going to town in a little
while. He would be honoured to ride the Herr Direktor's horse back
to Leipzig and reassure the lady. In the morning the Herr Direktor
would ride to town with the Schmidts in their char-à-banc. " That
is, if you don't mind driving with us."

He didn't in the least, but wouldn't it be an imposition on his
gracious hosts? . . . Schmidt's fluttering eyebrows bobbed up in
protest. As for Gertrude, she merely shrugged and didn't bother
to discuss such nonsense. " You'll see you'll sleep well," she said
and let it go at that.

Dinner over, she busied herself with the dishes while the two
men resumed their places at the fireside. A pleasant digestive
torpor fell over them. Schmidt was smoking a curved long-stemmed
pipe, Felix was staring at the embers, his boots on the andirons.
Gertrude climbed the wooden staircase and was away for a moment.
When she returned she announced that everything was in readiness
upstairs. Then, dismissing Felix's renewed thanks, she asked to be
excused and, candle in hand, disappeared once again into the fastness of the house.

There was another pause, then suddenly Felix found himself
telling the old flute player about his visit to the pastor. " I know
I shouldn't have called him a fool, but he made me so angry I lost
control of myself."

Schmidt looked worried and thumbed the tobacco down the
bowl of his pipe. " Bad business," he said at last, his eyebrows
joined in a frown of concern. He shook his head for a long time in
thoughtful dismay. " That means trouble, Herr Direktor."

" I'm afraid so. Do you think—do you think if I went and
apologised——?"

Hermann shook his head, this time in flat disapproval. " Don't
do it, Herr Direktor, don't do it."

" Why?"

" First, he wouldn't receive you. Second, he wouldn't forgive
you. Third, it wouldn't stop people from talking." He smoked
in silence for a moment, then took his pipe from his mouth and
looked at Felix. " Forgive me, Herr Direktor, but this music "
—he hesitated and his curled eyebrows crept anxiously up his
forehead—" is it worth all this trouble?"

This time it was Felix who was slow to reply. " I don't know any more . . . I think it is. In fact I am sure it is . . . but it seems to have brought me nothing but trouble. Even Frau Mendelssohn thinks I'm being ridiculous about it." Brusquely he turned to Hermann. His face tensed with sudden passion. " But let me tell you one thing, Hermann." His voice had become oddly intimate and solemn. " I am not being ridiculous. This Passion is the greatest music ever written. I've studied the score, every note of it, and I know what I'm talking about." Quietly he repeated, pausing after each word, " It is the greatest music ever written." A bitter smile parted his lips. " And nobody wants to listen to it!"

Hermann watched him slam his open hand on his knee. " You really do feel about it, don't you?"

Felix shrugged. " I don't know how I feel any more." And suddenly he was speaking loud, almost shouting, his gaunt handsome face tense with defiance. " I only know that somehow this music must be heard. If they don't want me to perform it—all right. I'll step aside. But I know that if I don't perform it myself nobody will. It was the same with Schubert's Unfinished Symphony, remember? Who wanted to listen to an unfinished composition? They all had some reason why it shouldn't be performed, but, God, I did get it performed."

He paused and the expression of perplexity returned to his eyes. " Of course, that was a symphony and all I needed was an orchestra. This time I need more than that. I need singers. A lot of them. Men and women. At least four hundred . . . I need soloists. I need an organ—and the Gewandhaus Hall doesn't have one. That's why this music should be given in Saint Thomas's Church. They have a splendid organ there and it's the only place big enough to absorb this volume of sound . . . And then, of course, I need an orchestra. I tell you, Hermann, this is a colossal work. It's all humanity singing the death of Christ!"

He stopped with the abruptness of people not given to long speeches. The exaltation went out of his eyes. His shoulders sagged and he let out a muffled snort. " And I can't even get the Saint Thomas's choir! All I've accomplished is making an enemy of the pastor. The whole thing becomes more impossible than ever. I am sure the board will refuse to allocate the necessary funds. My friend Herr Kruger will see to that. They're all afraid of him on the board. Even Muller . . . They'll say the budget is closed. They'll say the cost would be exorbitant. They'll say ' Where can we get the singers!' And they'll be right—I don't know where I can get four hundred trained voices in Leipzig. And so "—a sigh of anger hissed through his lips—" the most magnificent music ever written will never be heard!"

He gazed at Hermann with a hopeless shake of the head. " I just don't know what to do. I've tried. but somehow everything I do goes wrong." Exaltation, this time mingled with helpless fury, returned to his face. " If only Cécile were with me! If only she were standing by my side. I'd find some way out. I'd bring singers from Berlin, if necessary. I'd get this Passion in a Catholic church, in a Calvinist church, in a synagogue . . . Anywhere where there is an organ . . . And if I couldn't do it in Leipzig, I'd go to Dresden, I'd go to Düsseldorf, I'd go to London, by God! . . . But somehow I'd get this music heard."

His vehemence collapsed. " But she isn't by my side!" he said with a detached shrug. " She isn't even in sympathy with me. She only thinks of our social standing, of the enemies I may make. I can't blame her. She doesn't understand. She can't see why a bundle of music can be more important than social recognition and the friendship of Elsa Muller or the wife of some councilman . . . And perhaps she's right."

Unseeingly he gazed at the fire, his brown eyes speckled with the golden reflections from the flames. " I don't know," he said, talking as to himself. " Perhaps she's right and I'm being ridiculous about this whole affair . . . Perhaps I should dump that score in a drawer and forget it . . ."

Then in a sudden rush his anger burst out again. " But I won't!" His fist pounded his knee. " I'll be damned if I let that music die again. I don't care if I antagonise everybody in town but I'm going to perform it. Don't ask me how, but I'm going to. I've got to!"

From the depth of his being the words came out in a broken whisper. " I wouldn't die in peace if I didn't."

He straightened up in his chair and blinked as if awakening from a trance. A smile flashed slowly in his face and his eyes softened. " I think I'll have that glass of schnapps after all."

Like a wound-up toy Hermann dashed to the liquor cabinet and returned at the full speed of his short legs, holding a bottle and a glass in his hand.

" Would you like to hear some of this music?" he asked with studied casualness, while filling the glass with an elegant wing-like uplifting of elbow. Seeing the astonishment on Felix's face, he went on with the air of a magician asking a handkerchief from the audience. " If you let me have a section of the score, I'll have our members sing it for you."

" What members?" asked Felix, taking the glass from Hermann's hand.

" The members of our society."

" What society?"

The flautist regained his seat and took comfort in a generous swig of beer. "The Cecilia Vocal Society," he explained from behind his foam-wiping hand. "That's what it's called. We chose that name because Saint Cecilia is the patron saint of musicians. I am the president." He said it as though he were acknowledging a sin.

"You—you are president of a choral society and you never told me anything about it?"

"Well, you see, Herr Direktor, it isn't much of a society and I was afraid you'd make fun of me. Nothing but amateurs—and some with voices that frogs would be ashamed of. But we have fun just the same, and singing is one of the few pleasures we can afford. It costs nothing."

"Neither does love-making," said Felix wryly, "that's why the poor have so many children. How many members have you?"

"About seventy. In summer we have less because some find employment in beer gardens."

"And who conducts them?"

Hermann had dreaded this question. He lowered his bald head and blushed to the roots of his white foamy fringe of hair. "I do."

"You?"

"Yes, Herr Direktor." Hermann kept his pink pate down as if taking a bow. "I don't have a baton like you, I beat time with my flute." Cautiously he lifted his jovial face. "You see, I am the only professional musician in the whole lot."

"You don't have to apologise. I think it's wonderful. And where do you hold rehearsals?"

"In Frank Tanzen's shed. He's a wheelwright and his shop is near the Grimma Gate. He is one of our members. Perhaps——" He hesitated, "Perhaps you'd like to come some evening and hear us sing It'd be a great honour."

"I'd like to very much."

A little taken aback by Felix's ready acceptance, Hermann felt that some additional warning was necessary. "As I say, they're only working people and they sing just for fun. We don't ask questions at the Cecilia. So long as you love music, that's enough. So we get all sorts of people. Some of the women—well, you know what I mean . . . But they all love to sing, and if you let me copy some little part of the Passion, I'll have them sing it for you. It won't be anything like the Dresden opera, but it'll be something."

Felix thanked him and promised to let him have one of the choruses. "Just let me know when you're ready," he said, draining his glass and rising from his chair, "and I'll come."

Still talking about his beloved Cecilia, Schmidt escorted Felix to his room. He insisted on lending him one of his woollen nightshirts, assured himself that Gertrude hadn't forgotten to slip a hot brick into the bed. Then with many admonitions and good wishes he took his leave and disappeared down the corridor, holding the pewter candlestick in his hand, his elongated shadow trailing after him.

The house in Lungerstein Gardens seemed cold, almost hostile, after the warm hospitality of the Schmidt farm. Cécile said little, but her pressed lips and uneasy glances betrayed her anxiety and discontent. An awkward attempt on his part to justify his conduct merely brought out a curt reply. "I'd rather not speak about it." Gustav cast worried glances at him and seemed full of secret and alarming information. Catherine kept to herself, but her censure wafted from the kitchen mingled with the smell of cabbage. Even Elga, the nurse, and the parlourmaid shared in the silent condemnation and moved about the house like figures of tragedy. Felix felt angry and alone, a stranger in his own house. He spent much time with his children. Their laughter and the pressure of their little arms around his neck would bring a suspicious moistness to his eyes and he would explain he had caught a cold and sneeze profusely to prove it.

Outside the air itself seemed to have changed. In the streets people averted their eyes to avoid returning his salute. The doorman at the Conservatorium now gave him a skittish grin instead of his previous effusive greeting. From Schmidt he learned that Pastor Hagen had delivered an eloquent sermon full of allusions to "the arrogant fools who, under pretext of art, dared to meddle in God's affairs."

"Perhaps I should deliver a lecture on the sanctimonious fools who, in the name of God, meddle in matters of art." His remark was intended as a joke, but there was no mirth in his voice.

Before long the flautist reported news more alarming still. "*Mein Gott*, Herr Direktor, do you know what they say? They say you threatened His Reverence with your cane. Some say you struck him."

Felix listened with helpless consternation. "Is there anything I can do?"

The old musician shook his horseshoe of snowy hair. "No, Herr Direktor," he said sadly. Timidly he placed his hand on Felix's sleeve. "In the mood they're in now anything you'd say or do would be twisted and turned against you."

His blue eyes had the gentleness of a faithful dog. "Be patient. It all will pass in the end. Just say nothing."

And so Felix went about his business and said nothing. He found relief in work. The long rehearsals with the Gewandhaus Orchestra did not seem long any more. Even his teaching at the

Conservatorium became a welcome diversion, a brief escape from the surrounding hostility. Despite the rumours about him, his students looked at him with the same worshipful gleam in their eyes. They worked harder to please him, assure him of their unfaltering loyalty.

The evenings at home were the most trying part of the day. Dinners had become strained encounters in which formal courtesy had replaced tenderness. Cécile spoke about the weather, the children. He orated—he who hated long political speeches—over France's political unrest. " I shouldn't be surprised if they have another revolution one of these days, and this time, you'll see, it will spread to our country." They talked in stilted sentences, each doing his share to fill the silence, each trying to maintain a semblance of naturalness as though nothing had changed. Occasionally their gazes collided across the table and their mutual grievances clashed during a brief painful silence. Then quickly they resumed their forlorn pretence, feeling themselves drifting farther and farther apart, yet unable or unwilling to bridge the widening abyss between them.

After dinner she excused herself and under some pretext repaired to her room, while he sat in his study by the fire, sipping cognac, wrestling with his thoughts. He reviewed his conduct, searched his conscience for some shortcoming or dereliction that might explain their growing estrangement. But there was no simple explanation. He had been a good husband, tried his best. She had been an excellent wife, almost a perfect one. If their marriage was to-day tottering on the brink of collapse it was due to nothing but differences of temperament that only a great love could have overcome. And she wasn't capable of great love. No, that wasn't true . . . She wasn't capable of a mad, lyrical and passionate love, and he had no right to expect it from her. The heart also had its genius, she merely had its talent. She was not a *grande amoureuse*, as the French said, she was a perfect *Hausfrau*.

In this matter of the Passion, for instance, he had no right to ask her to renounce her social standing, incur the ostracism of her friends to join him in some ridiculous and probably unsuccessful crusade over a bundle of yellowed music paper. On the other hand, this music had come into his hands and he couldn't, he had no right, to let it disappear again. And there it was in a nutshell. A dilemma, very simple and unbreakable. How would it all end? He didn't know. He knew only that their love was very sick and that neither knew how to make it well. . . .

His inner turmoil had one clear result. His headaches became more frequent. One day, driven by intolerable pain, he went to see Dr. Hurbach, who received him in his office, which was also his library—an impressive, overfurnished room, dusty and dim and heavily draped, with a fine piano in the corner, and a sickly potted palm over the mantelpiece. Dr. Hurbach was a professor of medicine at the Leipzig University. He had a great reputation, which he enhanced by a stern appearance and a thoughtful way he had of fondling his side whiskers.

He listened to Felix with the air of a man who knows all about his patient's complaint but condescendingly allows him to relieve his anxiety in harmless but unnecessary explanations.

"My dear Herr Direktor," he declared at last with an indulgent smile, "there is nothing remarkable or alarming about your headaches."

These, he explained, were due to a combination of organic factors which themselves were caused by a combination of physiological disturbances, mostly of a digestive order, all very common and very well known to him.

A protracted pause ensued during which the professor absently fingered his luxuriant side whiskers. Then with a wheezing sigh, he went on, "Rest, my dear Herr Direktor, much rest. Regular bodily habits and above all the complete avoidance of worry. You must stop worrying. As soon as something worries you, just dismiss it without further ado. The same goes for any undue emotion and excitement."

Having outlined this infallible treatment, he then scribbled a prescription. "Take those pills four times a day," he said, handing the prescription to Felix, "and you'll be as good as new."

He pocketed the ten thalers and the consultation came to an end. Felix went to the pharmacist's and had the prescripion filled. Secretly he swallowed the pills as prescribed and went on suffering from headaches as before.

The day before the meeting of the board of trustees Felix received the visit of an extraordinarily thin, stoop-shouldered man of quiet manners.

"My name is Jakob Meyer Howlitz," the visitor began when the usher had withdrawn and shut the door. He stood, hat in hand, in the middle of the room with that unequivocal respectful characteristic of people very sure of themselves. "I am a banker by profession."

In response to Felix's inviting gesture he sat down, knotted his bony slender hands over the handle of his ebony cane and seemed to gather his thoughts. He was dressed with the studied unobtrusiveness of expensive tailoring in a grey double-breasted frock-coat. His silken hair had gleams of burnished silver and hung down the sides of his long sharp-angled face. There was about him an air of unhurried purposefulness and coiled strength that reminded Felix of his father.

"Although I have not attempted to establish social relations with you and Frau Mendelssohn, I had the privilege of knowing your father, with whom I maintained excellent business relations." As he spoke he kept his deep brown eyes on Felix, observing him with so impassive a face that the words seemed to fall out of a mask. "For years I've attended your Gewandhaus concerts and watched with attention your efforts and accomplishments for the cause of music in this town. My interest stems primarily from the fact that I love music passionately. I play the violin, and as a youth I entertained the reckless ambition of becoming a second Paganini. My father, after listening to me, persuaded me to become a banker instead."

He paused, blinked his hooded eyes and took a long breath. "I've come on an unpleasant errand," he proceeded in his unhurried but strangely compelling manner. "One of which I do not approve, but which was thrust upon me by the members of Leipzig's Jewish community. In their name I beg you to desist from any further attempt to perform Johann Sebastian Bach's *Passion*."

A flush of anger swept through Felix. Nervously he tapped the ivory letter-opener on his desk. "You seem to be extraordinarily well informed of my plans," he said coldly.

"The town speaks of nothing else."

"And why, may I ask, should the Jewish community of Leipzig presume to dictate to me what music I should or should not perform?"

"Those who have sent me do not wish to dictate to you in any way. They merely want to avoid trouble."

"Trouble? Why should the performance of a piece of music affect them?"

"Because, due to a set of unfortunate circumstances, it has become a political and religious issue, and could easily turn into a political and religious conflict. In his Sunday sermon, Pastor Hagen made clear that he would regard your presentation of this sacred Christian music as an offensive gesture and an unwarranted interference in religious matters. And also because of Herr Kruger's personal enmity towards you."

Felix frowned irascibly at the visitor. "What has Herr Kruger to do with it?"

The banker's face remained expressionless but a light of warning came into his eyes. "Herr Kruger has been waiting for an opportunity to arouse anti-Semitism in this town and you may provide him with just such an opportunity."

" How do you know all this?" asked Felix.

The shadow of a smile drifted across the banker's lips. " When you are weak you must keep your ears and eyes open. We cannot afford not to be watchful. Herr Kruger is our enemy. Has been for a long time. It is our interest as well as our duty to watch him."

For the first time an undertone of emotion crept into his voice. " It has taken us a long time to obtain tolerable living conditions in this town. We are content. We keep to ourselves, pay our taxes, mind our business and do not mingle into the gentile social life. We want peace, Herr Mendelssohn. We've earned it and would like to keep it. It would indeed be a cruel irony if one of our race, the grandson of Moses Mendelssohn, was the cause of new strife and persecution."

" I appreciate your remarks," said Felix, " but this question of the Passion has been twisted and confused beyond all recognition. Everyone wants to inject into it new and obscure and irrelevant meanings. Let me state it clearly once and for all so that you may report my point of view to the persons who sent you here. Some magnificent and forgotten old music has come into my hands, and I feel it should be performed. That's all. Whether Johann Sebastian Bach was a Lutheran choirmaster or a Mohammedan camel driver has no bearing whatever. Equally irrelevant is my personal religious conviction or that of the singers and musicians called to perform this work."

He stopped as if waiting for a word of approval or at least some comment from Herr Howlitz, but the banker remained silent and Felix went on, " I, as a man born in the Jewish faith, have as much right to perform this music as a Catholic to gaze upon the Teheran Mosque or a Calvinist to admire Chartres Cathedral or an atheist to surrender to the splendour of a Brahmin temple. Beauty transcends religion. It is the only field on which all humanity meets in concord and brotherliness. On the grimy pages of this bundle of old paper lies the greatest music ever written by man. It rightfully belongs to the world's musical patrimony. It is my duty to try to make it heard, for I know that, once brought to life, it will be heard as long as there is music on this earth."

Laboriously, with the help of his cane, Herr Howlitz struggled to his feet. " I shall report your words, Herr Mendelssohn."

Felix lingered an instant in his chair, then got up. " I regret to disappoint your friends and I hope they will understand my reasons." Then, with sudden sympathy for this reserved gentleman who reminded him of his father, he said, " I know you will."

The banker took a few steps towards his desk. He looked directly into Felix's eyes as a smile came to his face. " Your father would have been proud of you, Herr Mendelssohn."

With old-fashioned courtliness he bowed, pronounced the ritual, "Your servant, sir," and shuffled out of the room.

Felix could not sleep that night. For hours he lay motionless like a disembodied yet alert spirit in the total darkness of the bedroom, aware of his own physical reality only by the beat of his heart and the soft pumping of his lungs. Cécile, he knew, was sleeping at his side, for he could feel the faint warmth that emanated from her body. And it was raining, for a gentle dripping sound came from a spot in the darkness where he knew the window to be. Downstairs, in the entrance hall, the grandfather clock chimed three. Cautiously he slipped out of bed, stretched out an invisible hand towards an invisible bathrobe, wrapped that portion of breathing darkness that was he into the invisible yet tangible darkness of enfolding silk and, a formless shadow moving in shadowy stillness, he crept out of the room and went to his study.

Logs still glowed pink in the fireplace. He lit a candle and the room awoke to an amber-hued vacillation of reality. He filled himself a glass of cognac and sat down by the fire. Then, like a man opening a dyke, he let the gurgling turbulence of his pent-up inner conflict burst out into the field of his consciousness.

All right, he would go over the whole damned business once again for the last time . . . He would reach a decision and that would be the end of it. One thing was sure, it couldn't go on like this. All right, the Passion was magnificent music and it should be performed. Well, he had tried it, hadn't he? He had done all he could, hadn't he? . . . Was it his fault if the pastor was a bigoted fool? If the trustees were clods of beer-sodden fat, incapable of any vision, any generosity? Was it his fault Kruger was a half-crazy fanatic who dreamed of ruling Leipzig? If Muller was a shifty politician without honour or principles? Well, what could he do if they'd all banded together against him and determined to stop him —each one for his private reasons—from performing the Passion. What? . . . Import four hundred singers from Berlin? Hire a full orchestra? And what about the organ? And where would he give the performance? In the street? . . . It was absurd.

And now there was this Howlitz man with his story about the Leipzig Jews. They would also turn against him. For God's sake, wasn't there anyone on *his* side? Anyone who understood anything? . . . No, there wasn't. Not even his wife. Not even his servants. What was he supposed to do? Challenge everybody? Was he the only one right and everybody wrong? . . . Was he to be crushed and run out of town on account of that old oratorio? . . . Behold Felix Mendelssohn, the Don Quixote of Music! The knight of lost causes! He didn't charge against windmills, he merely fought entire cities single-handed!

Well, he'd had enough of this nonsense! Someone else would present the Passion if he wanted, but not he . . . He'd had enough, he washed his hands of the whole thing. He was through.

"Through! . . . Through! . . . Through! . . ." he repeated aloud, his voice echoing weirdly in the stillness of the room.

With one sweeping gesture he gulped down his drink and went on staring at the dying fire. The cognac tasted sour in his mouth. He felt curiously empty, spent. The image of his father arose in his mind and angrily he pushed it aside. No foolish remorse, no sickening sentimentality. He was through with the Passion and that was all. He never wanted to perform it or even hear about it. Cécile would be happy. Poor Cilette, she was entitled to some happiness after the rough time he'd given her with his obsession about that ridiculous affair. He would make up for it. Buy her some fine piece of jewellery. She would forgive him. Perhaps she would understand him better now, see how much he needed her, how much he loved her. The happy Düsseldorf days would return. As for the others—the pastor, the trustees, the Mayor, Howlitz—they would relent when they learned he was renouncing his absurd project. They'd all be friends again. Everything would be fine, everybody happy.

He refilled his glass, drained it again in one gulp, tossing his head back. He winced, got up and walked to his working table. The score of the Passion stood on it, the imprint of bloody meat still visible on the first page. He lifted the heavy bundle of paper, tossed it into a drawer of his music cabinet and with his slippered foot kicked the drawer shut.

"Well, that's that!" he muttered with a low chuckle.

He walked to the window and stood there gazing out. The rain had ceased. Across the public park Saint Thomas's School stood, huge and square, with its rows of small windows. In the stillness of the house the clock struck four. Over the roofs a mauve greyness had come into the sky, announcing the coming of dawn.

Dawn—the hour of treason . . .

He stood at the window, white-faced and afraid, as if he expected to hear the distant crowing of a rooster. . . .

The chairman rapped his gavel on the table and announced the meeting open.

"As you know," he began in a brisk businesslike tone, "we are here to discuss our distinguished Herr Direktor's suggestion that a certain work of ancient music, recently discovered, be performed this season. However, before we enter into the discussion of the merits of this proposition, I feel that, as chairman of the board, it is my duty to——"

Felix scarcely heard the Mayor's words. His eyes felt hot and gritty from lack of sleep. He hadn't eaten anything and the taste of cognac still soured his mouth. He felt tired, discouraged and angry . . . Why must people always make speeches over a corpse . . .?

Through drooping lids he studied the eleven men at the table. Kruger had come well armed and fingered a sheaf of notes, ready to spring into action, already savouring his revenge. The others sat stiffly in their highbacked chairs, assuming judicial attitudes. He knew they had talked the matter over among themselves and agreed to deny his request, but collective cowardice has a passion for legality, and they wanted to go through the comedy of a debate. And so they gazed stonily ahead, avoided one another's eyes and did their best to impersonate the grave and impartial judges they were not.

" And now," concluded the Mayor, " I shall give the floor to the Honourable Trustee, Herr Kruger, who will tell us his views on the question."

Kruger cleared his throat, but already Felix was speaking. " It won't be necessary, Your Lordship," he said in a flat, tired voice. " I've reached the conclusion that a performance of the Passion would impose an intolerable financial burden on the board——"

" It is not a question of money," cut in Kruger, clenching his useless notes. " We have plenty of money."

" But no singers."

For an instant the blades of their gazes clashed in silent duel. With a faint shrug Felix turned away and addressed the other trustees. " Therefore I withdraw my request that this work be performed and apologise to the board for wasting their valuable time."

Slowly his eyes travelled around the table and he saw their faces sag with disappointment. They had felt so well prepared—each with his argument, his devastating sally. So strong—eleven against one. And now there would be no debate, no chance to turn down this proposition.

His heart pounded in his chest, but he felt a strange exultation of relief—the relief of finality. He had spoken, the deed was done. He would not perform the Passion. Johann Sebastian Bach could resume his sleep of oblivion . . .

The sound of his own voice startled him. " I hereby tender my resignation as conductor of the Gewandhaus Orchestra and director of the Conservatorium, as from the end of the current season, May the fifteenth."

He hadn't meant to say that. It had come out of itself, like a breath. What would Cécile say? . . . Well, she would say what she liked. He didn't care. Didn't care about anything . . . With rueful detachment he surveyed the effect of his announcement. Disappointment had changed to stupor. Some of the trustees gaped at him, some stared, some blinked incredulously, shaking their heads.

" You mean you're resigning?" said Muller. His apoplectic face was flushed scarlet.

Felix nodded. " At the end of this season, Your Lordship. You may start looking for my successor."

They were speechless. Leipzig without Mendelssohn! Why, it was inconceivable . . . It was he who had made the city famous, envied by every other German town. And now he was going . . .

" If it's a question of salary," ventured one trustee.

" Yes," chimed in another, " if you've received a more attractive offer I am sure that the board——"

Felix stopped him with a gesture of his hand. " It isn't a question of money."

" Then what is it?" asked Muller almost aggressively.

" Let's say that I am tired," said Felix, getting up. " And now, if you'll excuse me, I'd like to return to my office. I have work to do."

He gave a nod and went out of the room. A moment later he entered his office, walked directly to the small round table by the fireplace and filled himself a glass of port. He drank, then sat down at his desk, holding his throbbing head between his hands.

Then, for no reason, quietly—he wept.

He had not wept in so many years that he didn't know why he was weeping now. The last time he had felt that slow rising of tears was that day in Paris when he stood in his evening clothes and ankle-deep in snow before the yellow poster announcing that Maria's opera engagement had been cancelled. There were a few moments like that in the span of a life. When everything in you collapsed and you couldn't go on any farther and all you wanted was sleep, sleep at any cost, even if you were never to wake again.

He remembered reading somewhere that a full-grown man was entitled to weep as many times as Jesus had stumbled under His Cross on His Way to Golgotha. Three times . . . And indeed in every man's life there were at least three times when you stumbled under the cross of living and you were ashamed and tired and afraid —afraid of the present, more afraid of the future—and you felt alone and bruised and lost and you longed for your mother, like a child. These were the times when you forgot you were a full-grown man, fearless, tearless and heartless, and you hid somewhere and wept.

That was why he had rushed out of the board room. He had felt that strange inner liquefaction, as if his bones were turning to jelly, that he had felt that day in Paris before the poster. Suddenly he couldn't endure the sight of these people. He couldn't endure staying in the same room after telling them he was abandoning the performance of the Passion. It made him feel like one of them. Not that he was any better . . . He wasn't. He should have gone down fighting. He should have shouted, pounded his fist on the table, fired every argument he had—for he, too, had arguments— and threatened to resign if they didn't let him perform the Passion. That would have scared them. He should have threatened to go to Dresden and speak to the King. He should have told them he would write to every newspaper in the country and start a press campaign against them. There were a thousand things he could have done. After all he had prestige, power, money.

Instead he had done nothing. He had conceded defeat without a fight, like a coward. He had strangled his conscience for their benefit and now he would have to live without it, spend the rest of his life with the memory of his betrayal, and each time the image of his father came to his mind he would wince and push it away. Poor Father, who had died thinking his son was a great man. An honourable man. " You can repay what I've done for you by doing at least one great and good deed in your life." That's what he had said in Düsseldorf during the Rhine Festival, shortly before dying. And his son had repaid him by being a coward and turning his back on his one chance to do a really great and good deed. Think of it, he, a Jew, could have given Christians their greatest music. What a magnificent gesture, what a lesson of tolerance and artistic brotherhood it could have been! But no, he hadn't made the gesture, hadn't given the lesson. He had surrendered like a poltroon, meekly, cravenly—without a fight, without a word.

Why? Why had he done such a thing? Because—because he was tired of gossip, incomprehension, misunderstanding and plain stupidity. Because he didn't want to engage in a polemic with the pastor and the whole Lutheran Church, because he didn't want to bring new trouble to the Jews of Leipzig, because he didn't want to start an open war with the trustees, the Mayor and Kruger. But above all he didn't want to drag Cécile into a fight with which she had no sympathy, didn't want her to lose her precious friends. That was the real reason. He couldn't brave the storm alone, face the fight without Cécile. He couldn't endure her tight lips, her nagging silences, her long-suffering glances. He was in pain, his headaches were growing worse, he didn't have very long to live. He wanted peace, at least peace at home. And he had bought it—at the price of his conscience. That was all.

He heard a sound of rushing footsteps in the corridor. Swiftly he snatched his quill from the elaborate brass inkstand and pretended to be writing a letter when there was a knock on the door and the Mayor walked in.

Without a word he plumped himself down on a chair, waiting for his panting to abate. "I am sorry," he began at last with unexpected gentleness. "I know how much this music means to you and how much it must have cost you to give it up. I wish I could have helped you, but I couldn't. Not after your row with the pastor——"

"There was no row, as you say."

"All right," said Muller with a shrug. "Call it a difference of opinion if you prefer. The point is that my hands are tied, understand? I can hold my own against Kruger, but I can't have both him and the pastor against me."

"I understand," nodded Felix wearily. "Anyway, it's all over now. Let's not speak any more about it."

"What I came to tell you is that after you went out, we discussed the matter of your resignation and the board has decided not to accept it."

"Not accept it?" snapped Felix. "I don't care whether they accept it or not, I——"

"Now, now, don't get excited." The Mayor sketched a placating gesture. "Of course we can't hold you if you want to go. But I suggested that no mention of your resignation be inserted in the minutes of the meetings, so that you may have a chance to reconsider your decision. Sometimes we say things in the heat of an argument that we may regret the next day."

"My mind is quite made up."

Muller let out a sigh of resignation. "Well, if it is, you can always resign a month or two before the end of the season. And if you decide to change your mind you can do it without losing face. Very important to save face in a small town." He paused an instant and considered Felix thoughtfully. "You don't look well," he said quietly. "This business has got your nerves in tatters. I'm used to gossip and arguments and people whispering behind your back, but you aren't. Why don't you take two weeks off and go to Dresden?"

"Dresden? What for?"

"Look up the fellow Wagner for your Conservatorium. Investigate the opera situation. Anything . . . You know how we've been screaming for the last twenty years for an opera season in Leipzig—well, go and see what our chances are, if any, of having one . . ." Again the gentleness crept into his voice. "Believe me, Felix, it will do you good. Give you a chance to relax and change your train of thought."

"Perhaps you're right," said Felix, half convinced. "I could take Cécile with me."

"If you want to." Muller's face showed that he didn't think much of the idea. "If you do, you'll be the first Leipziger who's gone to Dresden with his wife. But of course you happen to have a beautiful one. Anyway it would be a good thing all around. It'd get you back on your feet and it'd give people here time to forget. Thank God, people do forget . . . On your return everything would be as it was before this confounded Passion affair."

With a groan he hoisted himself up out of the chair.

"I'll think about it," said Felix, rising. "Thank you, Christoph."

The Mayor faced him for an instant. A hesitant wistfulness softened his small crafty eyes. "A pity we can't be real friends," he muttered under his breath with a slight shaking of his head.

Brusquely he turned around and lumbered out of the room.

After the Mayor's departure Felix stood at the window, idly gazing at the billowing grey clouds hanging low over the roofs. It was going to rain again. Another forlorn drizzly evening. And tomorrow it would be the same. And the day after that. Oh, the joylessness of these Saxony autumns, these sodden skies, these everlasting dripping eaves . . . At this moment in Sorrento the lemon groves were dozing in the sunset. The sky exhausted itself in a last frenzy of splendour. Glistening blue waves hurled themselves at the rocks with passionate amorousness, crushing themselves in splashing bursts of pink foam. In Rapallo the little pizza lay quiet and time stood still. Some old woman sat on the threshold of her *casa*, watching the sun go down, a dog asleep at her feet. Somewhere someone was singing. In Italy people were always singing. The poorest, the most miserable. From some kindly God they had received the gift of song and laughter. But here, in Leipzig, there was no song and no sun. And another dreary day was ebbing to an end in muted sobs of rain.

Suddenly he was aware of a presence in the room. Turning around he saw Hermann Schmidt standing a few feet away.

"I knocked twice," said the flute player, "but you didn't hear me. I just wanted to know if you needed anything before I go home."

"No. Thank you, Hermann."

"How—how did it go at the meeting?"

"Splendidly." A brittle bitterness crept into his voice. "We were all in perfect accord that the Passion should not be performed."

Schmidt's bushy eyebrows bobbed up in startled dismay. "You didn't fight for it?"

"My dear Hermann, there is no sense in starting a fight that's already lost, is there? One has to be reasonable in this world."

The strained smile turned into a grating chuckle. "Compromise, compromise and always compromise. This, my friend, is the secret of success. Of course, you may end up by cutting your throat one morning, but that's beside the point." He walked to the small table and filled a glass. "A drink?"

"No. Thank you, Herr Direktor," said the flute player, watching him closely. "I think I'll be going home now."

"By the way," Felix called after him, "I think I'll take two weeks off and go to Dresden. The board wants me to see if I could arrange an opera season for Leipzig next year."

"It'll do you good, Herr Direktor, to get away for a while." He spoke coldly, like a doctor. "You need a change and you'll enjoy yourself there. I understand they're having that great Italian singer, Maria——" He groped for the name. "Maria Salla, that's it. Never heard her myself but they say she's wonderful."

In the dimness of the room he did not see Felix's face turn white.

Cécile looked up from the letter she was writing to her mother. "You came early, didn't you?" It was not a reproach, merely a statement uttered without pleasure. Dutifully she offered her cheek, and he leaned down to kiss it. "Is it still raining?"

"Yes, my pet, it's still raining," he said, sitting down on the ottoman near her desk. "Don't you know it is always raining in Leipzig?"

How little it took to change a mood. A few words, an intonation, a gesture . . . On the way home he had hoped she would be tender. Not tender, perhaps, but affectionate. The way she'd given him her cheek to kiss had been enough to destroy that hope, as a pin prick bursts a balloon. And now he was getting angry and despite himself irony pierced through his voice. "And how's dear *Maman?* Well, I hope."

"Very well. You'd better go and change your clothes. The Dossenbachs are coming to dinner."

"They are?"

She frowned with annoyance. "I told you. Don't you remember?"

"I don't. It doesn't matter anyway."

"You never listen when I tell you anything."

"I do, but I don't quite memorise every word you say." He could feel the tension growing between them. Perhaps she, too, was coming to the end of her patience? "I shall try to do so in the future."

He said it while getting up with a feigned meekness that disconcerted her sharp glance. She wasn't intuitive and occasionally he amused himself by arousing her suspicions and then lulling them with a bland smile, an innocent look. " By the way," he said, walking to the door, " you'll be glad to learn that I've given up my notion of performing the Passion."

She had returned to her letter and she quickly glanced over her shoulder. " I am glad you came to your senses."

His jaws clenched and he felt the hair rise at the back of his neck, but he said nothing and went out, softly closing the door behind him.

The Dossenbachs arrived on time. Hosts and guests promptly repaired to the drawing-room, where the customary amenities and exclamations of delight at seeing each other after an interruption of several days were exchanged in the artificial, faintly breathless pitch of excitement that was regarded as the proper accent of mundane conversation. Felix sipped schnapps and took little part in these well-simulated effusions. He didn't need to, for Siegfried Dossenbach was always in search of an audience and to-night he was at his most verbose, wheeziest best.

" Yes. my dear Herr Direktor, I feel well, thank you," he declared as he lowered his bulk on the plush sofa, " but as you know, I am a student of political trends and I'd feel much better if we were not living in such grave and momentous times." He let out a hissing ominous sigh and went on, addressing himself to Felix, since the two ladies were already engaged in a twittering discussion of their own. " Times that are fraught with perils of all sorts. Times that require on the part of our leaders a commanding grasp of history as well as a subtle understanding of the economic factors and conflicting ideologies that are moving to a clash behind the European scene."

These two requirements, his tone implied, nobody possessed but himself. Foreign policy was his province, a subject in which he recognised no superiors, and to be frank, no equals either. His self-esteem was colossal and so genuine that he had succeeded in imparting to many people the opinion he entertained of his merits. The King, it was rumoured, regarded him as a potential foreign minister.

" To-day Saxony stands at the crossroads of history," he rumbled on, proving he had a flair for political platitudes. " But, alas, at this tragic hour when irresistible forces are about to collide, when stormy clouds darken the political horizon, where are we?"

" Yes," echoed Felix, between two sips. " Where are we?"

He was not listening but maintained that expression of rapt attention so easy to assume and so encouraging to the speaker. Occasionally he nodded in assent or let out a grunt of approval, knowing from experience that nothing more was expected of him. He liked Dossenbach. He had long ago discovered that behind the impressive Roman-senator mask was cleverly concealed a shallow, confused mind as well as a timorous nature. This man, who seemed to be perpetually posing for his bust and haranguing the entire forum, lived in dread of his wife Amelia. In the course of a long and adroit career he had made every compromise that was required of him while mouthing declarations of principles. Gifted with a superb memory he had loaded his brain with so many of other people's thoughts that there was no more room in it for any of his own. His conscience had died many years ago from chronic disappointment. Not a bad man really, just weak and vain. He lived penuriously beneath the prestige of his position, harassed by his shrew of a wife and a brood of unattractive children, haunted by ambition and terror of criticism. His lot was not a happy one.

" I'll tell you where we stand," he flung with a tribune's gesture. " Nowhere! That's where we stand. Our foreign office in Dresden is a disgrace."

How much of a disgrace he was still explaining when Gustav announced that dinner was ready and they trooped into the dining-room.

After a few unsuccessful attempts at including the ladies in his audience, the chancellor concentrated on his single listener. Felix picked at his food, drank glass after glass of Moselle and thought about Maria. Since Schmidt's innocent revelation he had tried to avoid thinking about her but with each new glass of wine he found it increasingly difficult. By the time the third course had been served he'd given up the struggle. Lovingly his mind journeyed back to Carrington Castle, the Surrey inn with climbing roses peeping into the room, the thatch-roofed cottage by the brook. Long-forgotten images drifted by in slow procession. The way she would sleep with her face against his chest. Her caressing hands. To think she was in Dresden, only a few hours away . . . What if he burst unannounced upon her? . . . Of course, he wouldn't. He wouldn't even try to see her. Surely she'd forgotten their foolish escapade. No doubt she'd had many other romances. Deeper and more adult, certainly more rewarding. She probably was in love with some handsome youth at this very moment. She would laugh at her Herr Direktor, pity his grey hair and hollow cheeks. Better spare her the sight of what years had done to him and let her keep the memory of the presentable young man he'd once been. . . .

" But do they understand this in Dresden? No! . . . Do they understand the most elementary rules of international statesmanship?" By now Dossenbach was sailing on the high seas of oratory, waving his fork, talking with his mouth full, asking questions and supplying himself with the answers.

Felix felt that such fervour deserved more than a nod. The poor man was panting for a word of encouragement, a bone of flattery.

"Your mastery of politics simply astounds me," he said, as the professor paused for breath. Because he was beginning to feel the headyness of the wine and felt in a hilarious mood, he added, "Tell me how do you find time to delve into such weighty matters?"

Dossenbach needed no more. Like a terrier plunging after a ball, he launched into the description of his laborious nights.

Felix let his eyes wander around the table. The wine was doing its work. His ears hummed. The table wavered and the flames at the tips of the candles waved in a windless storm. Cécile's exquisite profile trembled like a reflection in a rippling pool. His gaze rested on Amelia. Poor woman, it must be heartbreaking to spend a lifetime with that hatchet face of hers; that spotty bilious complexion that no unguent could improve, no powder disguise; those grey lifeless curls that hung over her ears like clusters of suet candles. She was so unattractive that she was entitled to be difficult. Spectacular misfortunes gave you the right to make other people miserable.

Slowly the dining-room was beginning to whirl. All of a sudden, with the brutality of a rock crashing through a window, a thought exploded in his mind. He must get away from Leipzig. If he didn't break loose now he'd never pull himself out of this quagmire of bourgeois futility. He must leave this bigoted, venomous town. This overfurnished, carpeted, curtained prison he called home. This pretty woman who had ceased to love him and endured his presence in the name of Christian charity and because of her marital vows. How stupid of him not to see it sooner! She was tired of him, had been for many years. With a sigh of relief she would welcome his departure, the prospect of a separation.

His gaze went back to the chancellor. This time with acute distaste. Dossenbach was still talking, rolling the words on his tongue. "Should His Majesty ever deign to place me in a post of high responsibility, I shall stand on my principles. For what is a man without his principles? . . . Come what may, I shall do my duty."

Angrily Felix echoed the words in his mind. His hand shook as he refilled his glass. Old fool! Listen to him after a lifetime of compromise and shady deals . . . Abruptly, almost unknowingly, he cut the professor short and began to speak.

"Of course, you'll do your duty. You'll do it until it proves inconvenient or unwise or merely unprofitable."

He caught Cécile's frightened glance, Amelia's narrowing look, the open-mouthed stupefaction on the chancellor's face. But nothing could stop him now. The room was a vortex of faces and candle-light. Under his feet the floor swayed like the deck of a ship. A wave of black despairing gaiety was surging through him, escaping in fits of mirthless guffaws.

"You see, my poor Dossenbach, you are no more a man of principles, a man of duty, than I am. You'll betray your conscience at the first chance, as I have betrayed mine. So stop prattling about duty and things that don't belong to us, and let's have another drink."

He raised his glass but the chancellor never joined him in that drink. Already he was on his feet, sputtering, purple with rage, tossing his crumpled napkin on the table, while his wife was fleeing the room as if it were on fire, with Cécile at her heels pleading incoherently, tears running down her cheeks.

But there were no tears in her eyes when she returned to the dining-room a moment later.

"How could you?" she said with ominous slowness. "How could you?" she repeated, standing across the table like a trembling statue.

"Could I what?" He drained his glass, clucked his tongue. "Excellent wine! . . . I told the truth, didn't I?"

"You're drunk." She spat the word at him.

"What if I am? But not from wine. From too many years of loneliness and disappointment." He slammed his fist on the table. "Now sit down," he roared. "Sit down and listen to me."

But her anger was equal to his own. In her bloodless face her eyes did not blink. "I won't! I won't listen to you. I've listened to you too long already."

He sprang to his feet. "Oh, you have, have you?"

"Yes . . . yes . . . and I won't any more!"

After that they no longer answered each other but shouted at the same time across the table, hurling their pent-up grievances in a mêlée of words, screaming to make themselves heard, like brawling plebeian newlyweds. They fought as only people who have loved can fight, without coherence or sportsmanship, aiming their verbal blows with the deadly accuracy of long familiarity, no longer trying to convince but only to hurt. She had endured his moods, his mockery, his extravagance. She had been a good wife, given him a good home, good children.

"But you're destroying everything!" she shrieked. "Everything!"

"And you, you're destroying me!" he shouted back.

A good wife? Hahaha, that was a good one! . . . A good wife didn't merely run a home and give dinners, she gave her husband companionship, tenderness, love.

"Yes, love!" he bellowed. "But you don't even understand the meaning of the word."

"How can you say that?" she flung back. "I've loved you with all my heart."

"But you don't any more. Is that it? Say it, for God's sake, say you don't love me."

She stared at him, shaking her head. "I don't know any more," she murmured.

For a tremulous instant he wanted to lift her in his arms, carry her upstairs as in the happy Düsseldorf days. But years of misunderstanding held him back. "There's nothing more to say." His voice was cold, his eyes hard. "We don't understand each other and never will. Go back to your dear wonderful *Maman*. She'll be delighted to have you back and will tell you what a brute I am and how glad you are to be rid of me."

"So this is the end?"

He was about to say yes but the word wouldn't pass his lips. "Time will tell," he said in a toneless voice. "I'm going to Dresden for a few weeks. Then we'll see. But I'll never come back to this town. I've resigned anyway."

The news stunned her. "You—what?"

"This afternoon. When I gave up the Passion. There's no more reason for my staying here. I was planning to leave at the end of the season, but I'll write to the board from Dresden and make it effective immediately, as soon as I have accomplished my mission. I owe them that."

She remained silent for several seconds. "You want to go, is that it?" she asked coldly. "You're tired of me?"

"I am not tired of you." His tone matched her own. "I am tired of our being strangers in the same house."

All of a sudden her body shuddered in a spasm of anger. "Well, go then! Go . . .!"

The last word swirled with her, as she ran out of the dining-room. He heard her footsteps racing up the stairs, the slamming of a door. Then all was silence.

Quietly he walked to the study and stood at the window for a moment. It was raining. It always was raining in Leipzig . . . Well, it was over. It didn't take long to break a life—two lives . . . He was alone now. Only Karl remained. Dear old Karl in London. He would understand . . .

He sat down at his desk, took his quill and began to write:

"My dear friend:

"For two years I was as happy as a man can be, but for a long time now I've been miserable . . ."*

* This letter, one of the most moving Mendelssohn ever wrote, leaves no doubt he could have become a great writer, had he not chosen to be a musician.

Chapter 7

IN THE pallid afternoon sunshine Dresden had the frail baroque charm of the porcelain knick-knacks for which it was famous. Upon his arrival Felix drove to his hotel on Theater Platz and was welcomed by the manager, who insisted on calling him "Your Excellency" and conducting him personally to his suite. It was on the second floor, at the end of a long, red-carpeted corridor, and consisted of a large high-ceilinged bedroom, a spacious *cabinet de toilette* decorated with fresco medallions of coy and buxom nudes, and a sitting-room which had on one side a fine view of the Elbe River and the Augustus Bridge and on the other the Zwinger and its formal garden.

"This is the finest suite in the hotel," declared the manager. "How long does Your Excellency expect to stay?"

"Only a few days," said Felix, absently glancing about the bedroom's red-damasked walls. "Three or four, I'd say."

During the train journey from Leipzig he had made up his mind about Maria. He wouldn't try to see her. Nothing, he had decided, could be gained from such an encounter. On this point he was very definite. The past was past and better left alone . . . He would dispatch his business as speedily as possible, send his report to the board, along with his resignation, and leave for Berlin.

"At most a week," he added, as his luggage was being brought in.

The manager withdrew and shortly afterwards the hotel valet appeared and began to unpack while Felix repaired into the frescoed bathroom and scrubbed coal grime from his face, neck and ears. An hour later, dressed in fresh linen and neatly pressed business suit, he called on the direktor of the Dresden opera, whose office was located in the nearby opera house.

Herr von Wierling received him at once and with genuine cordiality. "And so Leipzig wants its little opera season," he chuckled after Felix told him of the board's operatic aspirations. He was a handsome grey-haired man with lines of mischievous gaiety fanning out from his eyes. "I've often marvelled at the strange and fatal attraction opera seems to have for laymen and musicians alike."

He got up, filled two glasses with sherry and, handing one to Felix, returned to his desk. "It's all the more remarkable since everything about opera is absurd. To start with, composers have an unerring flair for choosing the most inept libretti. For instance, do you know anything more idiotic than the libretto of *Fidelio?* When I recall that Beethoven wrote four overtures for this master-piece of nonsense I lose all respect for him. He wasn't a very intelligent man, really. Few geniuses are."

He took a sip from his glass, leaned back on his chair and went on. "And do you know of anything more ridiculous than the sight of those warriors in helmets and mailshirts bellowing their love or hate or disappointment or remorse or whatever happens to be ailing them at the time? As for the production of operas, it is one of the most thankless and diabolical of human endeavours. There's something about opera that prompts everyone connected with it to commit mayhem or suicide."

Felix agreed. "Once in Düsseldorf I got involved in a produc-tion of *Don Giovanni.* It was a nightmare I'll never forget. I did my best to discourage the trustees, but they won't rest till they have their opera season."

"They will when they're called on to make up the deficits. For, while everything about opera is unpredictable, the financial outcome is mathematically certain. It always loses money. The more brilliant the season, the larger the deficit. We're now enjoying an excep-tionally brilliant one. It is ruining us." He was the kind of man who said serious things lightly, with the result that people thought him a fool when he was merely a cynic. "Strange, isn't it?"

"It does sound like a paradox," admitted Felix. "But nothing about opera seems to be controlled by ordinary rules."

"Let me give you an example. As you know, Maria Salla is at present honouring our opera house with her artistry. A rare, and I may add, ruinous honour. Each one of her performances is a financial as well as an artistic triumph but her salary is so staggering that if her engagement lasted another three months we'd be bank-rupt." He leaned forward to reach his glass. "Do you happen to know her?"

With an evasive gesture Felix replied he had once met Miss Salla many years ago in London. "I went to one of her performances at Covent Garden and I must say she does have a magnificent voice."

"It is finer than ever. Frankly I think she is as great as Jenny Lind. Would you like to hear her to-night? She's singing *Lucia.* I could let you have my box. There isn't a single available seat in the house."

Felix declined the gracious offer with profuse thanks. "Un-fortunately I already have an engagement for this evening. I'm afraid I shan't have the pleasure of hearing her again, for I am anxious to leave town as soon as you can give me the information required by the board."

" If they are determined to go ahead, I'll be delighted to help
them all I can," the direktor said in the tone of a chemist selling
poison to a would-be suicide. " However, it may take a few days."

Felix drained his glass and got up. " I'll be greatly obliged if
you can expedite this matter."

Herr von Wierling rose and escorted him to the door. " I'll do
my best. Although I must say you are the first Leipziger I've
ever seen so eager to go home. Come back in three or four days
and I'll have something for you."

He opened the door and bowed courteously. " Your servant."

" Your servant," said Felix, returning the bow.

A few minutes later he found himself back on Theater Platz.
Dusk had come. Dresden's elegant shops glowed with the flicker
of candelabra and oil lamps. On the sides of the main entrance of
the opera house two bronze torches made festive patches of yellow
light, announcing the evening performance. It was still early, but
already expectant excitement was in the air. The old building seemed
to be awaiting the commotion of carriages, the footmen leaping
down from their boxes to open the doors, the ladies in glittering
jewels and rustling skirts climbing the wide stairs on the arms
of attentive gentlemen in frilled shirts and silk-lapelled coats—all
the brilliant agitation of a gala performance opera. At the gate
of the popular-priced seats a queue had formed. The Dresden poor
were waiting to see Maria, and for no reason he experienced a strange
feeling of pride. These were the real opera lovers—they knew
great singing. They paid for their seats with their hard-earned
savings and waited patiently in the evening chill. Did they know
she was one of them, that once, barefooted and hungry, she had
sold flowers at the corner of San Marco? When the performance
was over and she took her curtain calls, she would blow them a kiss
and the men would return to their dingy lodgings, dreaming of
her, hearing her golden voice in their sleep. He, too, had heard it
many years ago. In a flash he remembered her warbling happily
while scrubbing the floor of their little Surrey cottage. Their love
nest, as they used to call it. Their love nest—where their love
had died.

Nervously he walked away. After a few steps he was struck by
the thought he had nowhere to go and nothing to do. The whole
evening—his first evening of freedom—gaped before him, empty.
In the past he had sometimes longed for an evening of complete
freedom, a breathing spell from his crowded schedule. Well, his
wish had come true. But to-night freedom had a bitter taste. Yes,
he was free—free like the vagabond, like the ship that has lost its
way and sails aimlessly through the empty sea.

For an instant he considered calling on the Schumanns. Robert and Clara were old friends. They would be glad to see him, would surely invite him to dinner. It would be nice being in a home again, sitting by a fire. But they would ask questions about Cécile, about the children. He didn't feel like talking about them. He had all he could do not to think about them. . . .

For a long time he loitered along Seidnitzerstrasse, stopping in front of shop windows and gazing at the displays. Unexpectedly he found himself before a restaurant. He entered, sat down at a corner table at the end of the room. Leisurely he ordered dinner, studying the menu with care, discussing the various dishes with the waiter.

" Now send me the wine steward," he said.

With the wine steward he engaged in a long and learned debate over vintages, argued about bouquets, discoursed at length on the respective merits of French and German wines. For a long time he hesitated between a rare old Vouvray and a fine Saint Emilion. He scarcely touched his food but between courses he indulged in bits of flippant conversation with the waiter, an old man with patient and knowing eyes. The waiter answered readily. He had seen many like him. Lonely men who chatted with waiters to beguile their loneliness. Usually they were grateful and tipped well.

He drank a good deal and found it helped a little. A pleasant dizziness stole over him. He felt light and faintly hilarious. He took a long draught and grinned to himself. Yes, wine helped a lot. He didn't feel lonely at all. Dresden was a wonderful city. After dinner he would go to some theatre. Something like the Friedrich Theater, where Anna Skrumpnagel used to sing. Yes, that was the thing to do. And who could tell, there were many pretty girls in Dresden. One of them should be willing—for a few thalers of course —to help him celebrate his first night of freedom . . .

The trouble with wine was that it relaxed your self-control. It loosened all sorts of ideas in your mind, ideas you didn't care to entertain. Cécile, for instance. Now if there was one person in the world he didn't want to think about it was Cécile. But that's what wine did. It forced ideas into your brain and you just couldn't avoid them. Like that watercolour Cécile had hung in the bedroom. A snowcapped mountain reflecting itself in a lake. Couldn't escape the damn' thing. Always there in front of you . . .

Cécile . . . It was just about that time the Dossenbachs had left and Cécile was returning to the dining-room. The way she had said, " How could you?" Practically spat the words in his face. And later, when they were shouting at each other, she had held her own very well. She had spirit, Cécile. Afraid of nothing. There was strength in her. And passion. But it had all been squeezed out by her confounded *Maman*, who insisted on making a perfect lady out of her. But last night she was no lady, she was trembling with rage and so damn' beautiful he wanted to grab her and kiss her until she had no breath left to speak.

The waiter took his plate away, returned a minute later with the coffee tray. Expertly he filled the small porcelain cup.

" Will that be all, sir?"

" Bring me a cognac. Who ever heard of drinking coffee without cognac?"

" Very well, sir."

He was back a moment later. Felix watched him pour the amber-hued liquor.

" Tell me, waiter, are you married?"

" Yes, sir. Twenty-seven years."

" Tremendous problem, marriage, don't you think?" He was beginning to slur his words. " Tremendously difficult."

" You're right, sir. But it's still better than trying to live alone."

Felix dismissed him with an impatient wave of the hand.

This waiter was an ass. Didn't know what he was talking about. Living alone was no problem at all. If you had money it was a never-ending delight. No responsibility, no wife nagging you with her eyes. Breakfast in bed. And plenty of women . . He would show Cécile how much fun he could have all by himself. She would be sorry she had lost—and entirely by her fault—the best husband in the world. He'd show her . . .

Meanwhile the poor girl was on her way to Frankfurt with Catherine and the children. They'd taken the coach, for naturally she was afraid of the train. Most women were like that. Enemies of progress. Thought locomotives were an invention of the devil . . . She could have been home by now. Instead she must be in some inn. The children must already be tucked in bed asleep. Perhaps they had asked questions about him. Why wasn't Papa with them, when would he come back . . . ?

He felt a sob rise to his throat, gulped down his cognac and called for the cheque. He paid, tossed an extravagant tip to the waiter and went out into the street.

The night had turned cold and he shivered in his cape. He thought of returning to his hotel, but he knew he wouldn't sleep. For a while he shambled aimlessly through the narrow ill-lighted streets of the Altstadt. Twice he was approached by lone women who tried to take his arm. Gently he freed himself, gave them a thaler and walked away. He felt tired but his mind wouldn't slow down. The exultation of a moment ago was leaving him. He was sobering up. Suddenly the realisation that Maria was in Dresden, only a few hundred yards from him, struck with such devastating intensity that he stopped in the middle of a deserted street, listening to the pounding of his heart. She was here. He could see her. Not talk to her, of course. Just see her. He'd probably never see her again in his life. Surely there was no harm in glancing at her. After all, they'd been lovers . . .

Already he was tormented with the thought that it might be too late, that she might have left the theatre. Almost running, he went back to the Theater Platz. The performance was over, but people were still coming out of the theatre. The last carriages were rumbling away. She couldn't have left yet. Cautiously he walked around the building. People were waiting in a short alley leading to the stage entrance. He joined them, keeping himself in the background.

The door remained shut for a long time. Then, abruptly it opened—and he saw her.

She was dressed all in white—some frothy material he could not identify. For an instant she stood in the lighted doorway, literally glittering with diamonds, like some Asiatic idol. She turned her head impatiently, as if waiting for someone, and sure enough a man appeared. Tall, blond, in a white silk-lined cape. She took his arm and started crossing the alley, smiling, nodding, waving to her admirers as was expected of her.

She passed only a few feet away from him and he saw her face distinctly. She hadn't changed. She still wore her hair parted in the middle and knotted in a low chignon on her neck. He heard her voice as she spoke a few words to her escort and he caught a glimpse of her clear eyes. With pounding heart he watched her disappear into a closed carriage. Once more her white-gloved hand waved through the window. Then she was gone. Silently the crowd dissolved and scattered into the night. A moment later, an old man came out of the stage entrance, lowered the lantern, and blew it out. The alley sunk into blackness. Slowly he walked away.

He wandered at random through the deserted town. He felt cold and bitter. Now he was sorry he had seen her. He berated himself. Of course she had a lover. What did he expect? He told himself he didn't care and found a mournful relief in reviling her in his mind. She was nothing but a slut who happened to have a beautiful voice. That's all. She was incapable of love. She was greedy. She had no taste. Those diamonds! . . Just like her to deck herself like a Christmas tree . . . It was typical of her, this vulgar display of opulence. Like those *cocottes* wrapped in sable, mink and ermine who carried their shame on their shoulders.

He heard a clock strike three somewhere and found himself on the Augustus Bridge. For a while he leaned on the balustrade and gazed down at the black rumbling waters. Only then did he notice it had started to rain. A thin stealthy rain that splashed softly on the crown of his top-hat and slid down his cape. He straightened up and recognised his hotel. Hurriedly he finished crossing the bridge and at last reached the hotel. The night clerk came rushing to let him in.

"Good evening, Your Excellency," said the man with a bow.

"Good evening."

With heavy steps he started climbing the stairs. On the second-floor landing he turned into the long red-carpeted corridor. As he was approaching his suite he noticed a slit of yellow light under the door. He quickened his steps and entered.

Maria was in the room.

They did not speak, didn't even smile. Blindly they rushed at each other, and there was nothing but the hunger of their lips, the clenching of their fingers, the gasps of their mingling breaths.

Time receded from them. Once again he was young, his hair black, his face unlined, and once again their love was new and the air was fragrant with the scent of climbing roses, and foliage rustled in the sun and they were back in that little out-of-the-way inn, back in the cool green thickets where they had loved and lain side by side through the golden radiance of that long-vanished English summer.

That night, in the candle-lit silence of that Dresden hotel room, the madness of youthful desire was upon them once more until the greyness of dawn frosted the window and sleep threw its blanket of oblivion over them.

Next afternoon he dazedly peered through slitted lids and found himself looking straight into her eyes. She was lying on her side, watching him, her head against her folded arm. For a fraction of a second he did not recognise her and she caught the blink of unrecognition.

"You think what woman I am, no?" she murmured with a smile. "Already you forget."

He was too drowsy to reply. His lids closed again, but his lips moved in a silent request for a kiss. She slid closer to him and he felt the softness of her mouth on his.

After a while, he mumbled without opening his eyes, "How long have you been awake?"

"I watch you sleep a long time. You don't look good."

"I know that. I am an old man now. Did you notice my grey hair?"

Their lips touched as they spoke and their words came out in almost inaudible whispers.

"Your hair I like very much. But your face I don't like."

A sleepy grin etched little lines at the corners of his eyes. "I don't like it either, but it's the only one I've got."

"You are thin like a fish. I give you the medicine, *si?*"

"Give me a kiss instead."

Her lips covered his in a lingering, drowsily sensuous kiss. "I wish we stay like this always," she purred. "Never get up."

He was awake now behind his closed lids and he sensed that she dreaded to leave the safety of sleep, the haven of their unquestioning sensuality.

"How long you remain in this city?" she asked, her fear piercing through her voice.

"A week. Perhaps more."

"A week!" She sprang up, open-mouthed, eyes wide with joy. "*Una settimana!*" she gasped. She crossed herself, joined her hands in fervent prayer. "*Grazie, Madonna, grazie per il miracolo!*"

"What are you sputtering about?" he asked, sitting up and propping himself against the pillows.

She flung her arms around his neck, pelted his face with jubilant little pecks. "I say thanks to the Virgin because you stay here a week," she explained between kisses. "Yesterday, when I hear you are in the city, I have the fear you stay only one day and to-day you go back to the wife and the little *bambini.*"

Her words ended in another flurry of caresses. "For many years I pray the Madonna to make the miracle so you come back for a week and now she makes the miracle."

He was watching her, moved by the sight of her happiness. She was laughing, muttering incoherently in Italian, gazing at him with unbelieving rapture. No, she hadn't changed . . . Passionate and excitable as ever. She still mangled English and expected miracles from her little coloured plaster statue of the Virgin. She prayed and sinned with the same fervour. Now her eyes, her clear hazel eyes, were dancing with joy. Her cup was running over because the Madonna had made a miracle and arranged for them to spend a week together. Nothing in the world would convince her that the Virgin had nothing to do with it. What a hodge-podge of devotion, superstition and paganism in that little Venetian head . . .

For an instant he was on the verge of telling her he could stay as long as he wanted and was not going back to his wife and the little *bambini,* but something held him back. Let her believe what she wanted. She was here, she was in his arms, she still loved him. Nothing else mattered.

"Stop mumbling in Italian, will you, and tell me if you still love me," he asked with the assurance of a man who already knows the answer.

She pressed herself against him in a gesture of obedient amorousness. " You ask me because you like to hear, but in your heart you know I always love you, no?"

" Even when you ran away from me? Remember that day at the cottage?"

" Yes, even that day," she said, with tender seriousness. " I know you don't understand but I run away because I love you so much and we have quarrels all the time and I see I am no good for you, *si*. So I write your friend Karl and I explain everything to him and he says yes and I run away. But all the way to London I cry until my eyes have tears no more. I try everything. I tell myself I am stupid and in a week I forget. But I do not, not in a week, not in a year. I pray the Madonna. 'Please make me forget,' I ask. But I cannot. All the time, even when I got to America, I think of the little cottage with the straw on the roof, I think of the big castle and the time you fall from the velocipede and you look so ridiculous——"

" I didn't look ridiculous," he protested. " I was mad—and hurt."

" To me you looked very ridiculous," she insisted with tender obstinacy. " But I love you all the same."

He watched her through squinting eyes, wondering whether or not she was lying. Her very lack of emphasis carried an irresistible impact of truthfulness. She wasn't trying to convince him, she was merely reminiscing aloud.

Oddly, her humble confession of love aroused his jealousy. In a flash he remembered her coming out of the theatre in the frothy white dress—the dress which now lay torn and crumpled on the floor —nodding, smiling, waving at her admirers, traipsing through the alley on the arm of her lover. " You weren't thinking of me last night," he said with a snort.

She looked uncomprehendingly, but he went on, his anger gathering momentum. " Yes, last night when you came out of the theatre with that stupid-looking young man."

He spoke like a prosecutor who has cleverly trapped a lying witness, but she didn't look contrite or discomfited, merely surprised.

" You were at the opera last night, *carino*?" She was staring at him with joyous expectation. " You like my singing, no?"

" No, I wasn't at the opera but I saw you come out. And let me tell you that you looked ridiculous with all those diamonds."

" You don't like?" she asked with a look of a heartbroken child.

" No, I don't. And where did you get them?" He knew he was hurting her, but he felt a perverse relief at venting his feelings, like the mother who slaps her child who has just escaped an accident. " Did you have your lover rob a jewellery store for you?"

She didn't flare back or argue or even protest. She bent her head and lowered her lids. With stupefaction he saw two diamond-like tears squeeze out of her lashes and roll down her cheeks.

" Many men give me the diamonds," she murmured.

His anger vanished. " Forgive me, darling," he pleaded, drawing her to him. " I have no right to——"

She didn't let him finish. Gently she pressed her fingertips on his lips. " You have the right to say anything and do anything," she said with the submission of total love. " I feel the shame because I know many men, but only you I love. I swear on the Madonna."

Then he knew she was telling the truth. It seemed incredible that a love could live so long on two months of memories, but apparently some women never forgot.

" Last night when I hear you are in this town, I tell the blond man I don't see him again," she said.

Before he could speak she bent down and their lips joined in a kiss. Once again passion swept over them, healing the bruises created by words and memories, bringing them peace and the understanding of fulfilment.

Now they were lying side by side, still unable to talk because of the pounding of their hearts. Suddenly he laughed.

" Why you laugh?" she asked, herself smiling.

" Because we are two nitwits. We've been quarrelling over diamonds. I've already made you cry and you've told me I looked ridiculous on that confounded velocipede——"

" Not on the velocipede," she protested. " Only when you fall."

" All right. Only when I fell down . . . But I still don't know how on earth you happened to be in my room last night. But first, where do you live?"

Over the hem of the blanket her eyes gleamed with impish gaiety. A delicate forefinger came to view pointing to the ceiling. " Upstairs."

" Upstairs? You mean you are in this hotel?"

His look of dumbfounded astonishment brought forth a tinkling of laughter. " Perhaps you think only you in this hotel, no? Many other people in this hotel. When I come the manager says, ' Miss Salla, I give you the best apartment.' "

" The scoundrel, that's what he told me about mine."

Now they were both laughing. Impulsively they kissed. Without passion, without feeling even, as they would have taken a sip from a glass, simply because in a certain mood of love, kissing is the natural thing to do.

" Mine's same as yours," she went on. " Same furniture, same paintings in bathroom. Only change is colour on the walls—yellow instead of red." She pondered an instant and concluded, " I think mine's nicer."

" Well, we got that straightened out. Now how did you sneak into my room?"

That was more complicated and it took Maria much time and many digressions to go into the details of the operation. She had learned of Felix's arrival from the chambermaid. There followed a description of the maid—her age, appearance, working habits and all-round personality. "When she come to pull the curtains and turn down the bed yesterday afternoon she say a very handsome and important musical man arrives from Leipzig and I ask if this important man comes with the wife and she says no, nobody with him." At once her plan had been made. Simple and effective. She had bribed the maid into giving her the key to his room. After the theatre she had let herself in and waited.

" And many hours I wait," she complained. " Why you come home so late?"

" I was walking all over town, trying to tire myself out so I could sleep."

She accepted this explanation without comment. " While I wait, I look everywhere. In the bathroom, the wardrobe, even the pockets of all your suits," she revealed with complacent serenity.

He smiled tenderly. " You have the makings of a perfect pick-pocket."

Somehow everything seemed crystal-clear. The past had been explored and dismissed. The years of separation had vanished, never had been. A feeling of irresistible contentment lulled their minds. They looked at each other, their faces very close, finding nothing to say, smiling for no reason. Of course, there still remained the future the decision about what they were going to do with that miraculous week of sinful happiness the Madonna had especially arranged for them. But that could wait. Besides, they were starving.

" Let's have some food," he declared, reaching for the bell rope by the bed.

With catlike swiftness she caught his hand. " *Maledetto! Cosa fai?*"

Was he crazy? Had he lost the brain? What would his wife say if she learned he not only had had a woman in his bed on his first night in Dresden, but they had breakfasted together in the middle of the afternoon and, also in bed. He tried to argue that Leipzig was many miles away and Cécile wasn't likely to learn at what time he had breakfasted or where or with whom. His remonstrances produced no results. She was adamant. The poor *signora's* ignorance must be protected.

Languidly he agreed, wondering at the peculiarities of her ethics which condoned her spending the night with a woman's husband but condemned her having breakfast in bed with him. And so to appease her qualms he consented to engage in a bit of complicated deception. She would sneak back to her suite by the service stairs. This done, she would order a substantial breakfast-lunch-dinner for herself and Romola to be served in her apartment. Yes, Romola was still with her. And getting worse every year. At this point she would knock on the floor which happened to be his ceiling and he would make his way upstairs, also by the service stairs, and eat Romola's portion of the meal. In this way Cécile would never know of her husband's infidelity, the lovers would be fed, the hotel manager would never suspect the romance in progress beneath his roof and everybody would be happy.

"What about Romola?" he inquired. "Is she supposed to starve to death?"

Romola was no problem. She would go out of the hotel and fend for herself. Anyway, she had discovered a little Italian restaurant where they had the most wonderful *past' asciutta.*

He couldn't think of any other objection and declared himself satisfied. She gave him a last hurried kiss and leaped out of bed.

The strongest deterrent to many illicit love affairs is the difficulty of keeping them secret. Between two well-known people this difficulty becomes well-nigh insurmountable. Maria undertook the almost impossible task of hiding her relationship with Felix from the entire world and tackled the problem with all the resources of her contriving mind.

In this undertaking she wasn't governed by preoccupation with her own reputation, for which she hadn't the faintest concern, but solely with that of Felix. The challenge, as she saw it, consisted in spending together every possible moment they could steal from their respective obligations but in such a furtive and clever way that no one in the city of Dresden might entertain the faintest suspicion about their having an affair so that, the week over, Felix would be able to regain Leipzig and the bosom of his family, mantled in unimpeachable, though spurious, innocence.

Repeatedly he was on the point of telling her the truth, but his instinct warned him of the danger of such a disclosure. Maria was living in a paradise of her own making and he couldn't bring himself to disenchant her. She was living a melodrama in which love and duplicity went hand in hand. Her romantic nature couldn't conceive of a more exciting situation. Not only had the Madonna made a *miracolo*, a miracle to bring them together, but she had left her the responsibility to make sure that no one would ever know anything about it. Especially Cécile. This was Maria's haunting anguish. If Cécile never learned of her husband's infidelity, then she wouldn't be hurt, wouldn't make any reproaches to Felix. Everything would be fine. The only ones to know would be Romola, who didn't count, and the Madonna, who counted a lot but was surpassingly merciful, understanding—and her accomplice anyway. But if Cécile ever learned, then *mamma mia!* . . . Then it was a catastrophe. She might get it into her head to leave Felix. Some women did such stupid things . . . Felix would be disconsolate, the Madonna would disclaim all authorship of the miracle, and she, Maria, would find herself in the heinous position of a home-wrecker, let alone in the state of *peccato mortale,* of mortal sin.

Thus the gamble presented itself to Maria. She was aware of its fearful risks. At all costs she must protect Felix's home, safeguard his reputation and keep in the Madonna's good graces while sinning rapturously with the man she loved. In short, it wasn't the deed that mattered, but only being caught.

Therefore, as she explained that afternoon as they were devouring the meal she had ordered, they must be prudent. *Prudentissimi . . .* Nobody must ever see them together.

" Do you mean we can't ever go out of this hotel," he protested, his mouth full.

" Yes. We go out, but nobody sees us."

" How are you going to manage that?"

" You see," she smiled mysteriously, " I arrange everything."

He shrugged. Darling Maria, let her " arrange " to her heart's content. It made her happy. Her eyes were soft with love. He didn't ask for more. When the time came he would tell her the truth. But not now . . . not now. . . .

Henceforth their lives became an intricate game of subterfuges. It was dusk when they ventured outside and always in a closed carriage. He would leave the hotel alone, meet the carriage at some pre-arranged place. The door would open and swiftly he would duck inside. Then, leaning far back in their seats and holding hands under the wool blanket, they would drive towards the outskirts of the Alstadt or far along the quays, past the last bridge, where the city tapered into isolated farms.

It was the third day, as they were entering the lovely Vogelwiese Woods and the hush of twilight was broken only by the clip-clop of hoofbeats, that he made his first mistake.

" I love you very much," he said, gently taking her hand.

She pulled her hand away. " You must not say such a thing, *carino.*" Her voice was sad and afraid

" And why not?"

" Because you have the good wife and the little *bambini.*"

" Can't I say I love you because I'm married?"

" No. It's a *peccato*."

" A sin?"

" Yes. A great sin. If you say such thing God punishes you."

He looked at her, slowly shaking his head. " Don't you think that in a world rent with hatred God would forgive a little love?" He saw she did not understand and he went on teasingly, " At least may I say I have a genuine sympathy for you, or is this forbidden too?" Her eyes softened in assent. " And may I have your hand back?"

She smiled and gave him her hand. He held it, studied it, pretended to read the lines of her palm.

" I see a dark-haired man," he began in the oracular tone of a fortune-teller. " No, not dark. A grey-haired man. Now let me see . . ." He kissed a fingertip. " He isn't much to look at, but he has a heart of gold." He kissed another fingertip. " He is very fond of animals and of a certain opera singer . . ."

And so it went. It was a long time since he had indulged in that sort of bantering nonsense, but to-day he felt young and foolish. Soon he had her laughing, and the sound of her laughing rippled through his mind. He made a note of its pitch so that he would remember its exact tonality. The laughter of children, the laughter of the woman you loved. The two loveliest sounds in the world. . . .

She insisted on reading his palm. " I see a dark-haired young woman . . ." She kissed his fingertip. " Now let me see . . . She is very much in love. Oh, so much in love! . . . It's terrible to be so much in love, but she cannot help herself, for she is a very stupid woman. . . ."

As they were returning to the city he felt suddenly the softness of her lips on his ear.

" I love you," she said in a whisper.

He turned around, smiling. " So. I can't say I love you but it's all right for you to say you love me?"

She nodded, and he understood what she meant. She hadn't pronounced any marriage vows, her heart was as free. His wasn't. Again he wanted to tell her about Cécile and the breaking up of his home, and again he kept silent. The week would soon be over. Only four days remained.

Next afternoon she had to attend a rehearsal. Her absence oppressed him with an intolerable feeling of loneliness. Unwanted memories which the presence of Maria kept in abeyance returned to harass him the moment she was gone. With a stab he thought of his children and longed for the sight of their tousled heads and the sound of their laughter. He thought of Cécile. He recalled their last quarrel but surprisingly discovered he couldn't recapture his anger. To churn up some sort of resentment he imagined her in the sedate drawing-room of the Frankfurt house, telling her grievances to her mother. Conveniently he forgot he had suggested that she go to Frankfurt and interpreted her sojourn there as proof of her intention to get rid of him.

To escape the fabrications of his mind and kill time he called on Herr von Wierling, who greeted him at the door of his office. " I have your information," he began with an expansive smile. " In fact, I've had it since yesterday for you'd told me how anxious you were to return to Leipzig, and I was expecting your visit."

While talking he was filling the two sherry glasses and Felix was glad his back was turned to him. With as much naturalness as he could command he explained that an unforseen circumstance had caused a change in his plans. " I may even be forced to stay two or three weeks," he said, trying to sound quite put out by the delay.

" Good," the direktor said cheerfully, handing him one of the glasses. " You'll then be able to hear Signorina Salla. I know you've heard her already, but she is ten times better than she was. Her talent is reaching full maturity and she is simply phenomenal." He sat down at his desk and took a sip from his glass. " Her performance in *Lucia* the other day was beyond description."

" She is truly a great artist," agreed Felix. " Now about the information you've so kindly procured for the board of trustees——"

But the direktor wasn't listening. " You should've seen her in the Mad Scene of the third act. . . . It's a great bravura piece and I've heard about all the great sopranos in it, and I say she was the greatest."

" Coming from you this is high praise indeed. Now," he went on, clearing his throat, " to come back to the various documents you've so graciously gathered——"

The direktor broke in again, this time in tones of the deepest apprehension. " But I feel she is up to something, and I've been living in fear and trembling these last days. I haven't been able to find out what she is up to but I know there's something brewing. Do you know what she's done?"

There was nothing for Felix to do but to lift his eyes from the glass and blandly shake his head. " No. I haven't the faintest idea."

" She's given Otto his walking papers."

Noticing the look of perplexity on Felix's face, the direktor hastened to explain. " In order to understand why I lie awake at night you must first know she was having an affair with Otto von Friedler, the son of our minister of finance. A blond young man, handsome and extremely wealthy. Everybody knew about it and I for one approved heartily. You'll learn "—his tone became confidential, almost that of a colleague—" that love is the greatest single disturbing factor in opera production. Whether present or absent, it makes no difference. If a diva is in love, she is restless, temperamental and difficult. If she is not in love she is restless, temperamental and difficult. The only happy medium is when she gets involved in some slight love affair with someone she likes but doesn't really love."

He paused to take a bracing draught from his glass and proceeded. "This was precisely the case. She obviously didn't care a pfennig for von Friedler, but the affair kept her quiet. Her mind was on her work. She was a delight, everyone at the opera house adored her. When she went out to dinners or receptions in her honour she was graciousness itself. Naturally she was escorted everywhere by Otto and they made a splendid-looking couple. The King himself gave an intimate, very exclusive soirée for her and fell under her spell. Everything was fine and I was a happy man. Then all of a sudden, guess what happens?"

To heighten the suspense he slammed his open hand on the desk. "She tosses Otto overboard, refuses all invitations, locks herself in her hotel suite and becomes unapproachable. Now what do you think this means? Has she found another lover? Has she given up men. or could she be planning to enter a convent?"

The direktor's last supposition almost broke Felix's self-control. He felt the prickling of laughter in his throat, but he choked it down and with a desperate effort maintained an expression of polite bewilderment. "Like you, I am at a loss to explain her conduct. Have you thought she might be tired and wishes to rest?" he offered lamely. "The life of a diva is a strenuous one. Now about the information you so generously——"

"She isn't tired!" exclaimed von Wierling hotly. "She isn't tired at all. You don't know those Italian women, they are indestructible. At the soirée His Majesty gave in her honour she danced until dawn. Personally, I think she's found a new lover and for some strange reason she doesn't want anyone to know." A glint of craftiness came into his eyes. "But I'm having her watched and I'll soon find out what I want to know."

"I hope you do," said Felix, rising. "Once again, on behalf of the board of trustees let me thank you——"

Plainly the direktor couldn't abide the thought of the Leipzig trustees, for he made a gesture of impatient acknowledgment and pursued his train of thought. "A person as well known as she is cannot possibly have an affair without being found out. Secrecy is the most difficult thing to achieve when you are famous. As a matter of fact, it is impossible."

He got up and with genuine friendliness took Felix's arm. "Let me know what day you'd like to come to the theatre and I'll arrange it."

Felix promised he would do so and with a courtly bow took his leave.

That evening, when she returned from the rehearsal, Maria looked depressed.

"What is it, darling?" Felix asked, drawing her into his arms.

"I think in three days you go and I never see you again."

"Perhaps I can stay longer," he ventured cautiously. "I haven't quite finished my business here."

She didn't believe him and shook her head. "No, *carino*. You forget the business and go back to the good wife and the *bambini*."

"I could easily arrange to stay another week. Cécile wouldn't mind at all. On the contrary, she'd probably be glad to have me out of the house for a few days."

She went on, shaking her head. "No, *carino*." She spoke like a condemned man who refuses a reprieve. "The Madonna, she keeps her word. She makes the special *miracolo* so we can stay together one week only. In my prayers I always ask for only one week. Now the week is almost finished and you must go."

He knew no argument would change her mind. "And you, darling," he murmured, kissing her hair, "where will you go?"

She shrugged. "When you go it matters not where I go." She paused and then added in an almost inaudible whisper, "Soon perhaps I die."

He tried to cheer her up, told her about his visit to von Wierling, carefully omitting the direktor's suspicions. "He says you are the greatest singer he's ever heard. You have the most brilliant career open before you."

She scarcely listened. Her eyes went on gazing ahead unseeingly. Apparently for some women nothing mattered but love . . .

"You'll see, sweetheart, everything will be all right," he said to break the silence.

She paid no attention and pressed herself closer to him. "Hold me tight," she said in a small frightened voice.

That night she flung herself into passion with a desperate frenzy, as though she hoped to die from it.

The last three days of the week were for Maria a slow but unrelenting torment. She couldn't bear to be away from him even for a moment. Each passing hour became another step towards some inner gallows.

On the evening of the third day she sang at the opera house but returned to the hotel immediately after the performance still in her stage make-up.

"You are early," he said softly as she entered his room.

"I come quick so I can be with you."

She sat down on the edge of the bed and leaned down over him to run her fingers through his hair, looking at him as if to reassure herself he hadn't gone yet. They did not speak for a while. The approach of their separation had brought a new sort of silence between them, resigned yet exasperated, humming with the whirl of their thoughts.

With gentle amusement he scanned her heavily painted face with its daubs of vivid red on the cheeks and the charcoal lines rimming the eyes.

" I know," she said with a pale smile. " I take it off now."

She was about to straighten up but he held her back. " Don't go yet. Do you realise I've never seen you with your make-up on?"

" I look ugly."

" You do not. You never could look ugly. Not to me."

His words trailed off in a lingering smile. He felt her eyes resting on him unblinkingly with caressing anguish and knew that in her mind a clock was ticking away. To divert her thoughts he asked, " How many curtain calls to-night?"

It was one of their private little jokes. A few days ago, when it seemed that the week would never end, she had boasted of taking twelve curtain calls after her performance as Norina in *Don Pasquale*. Teasingly he had informed her that Jenny Lind had on one special occasion taken fourteen. This remark had started off an explosion of professional jealousy, culminating in a dramatic boast that some day she would beat the record of the famous Swedish soprano.

But there was no explosiveness in her to-night. She shook her head and said, " No curtain calls to-night."

Haltingly she told him she had fled the theatre as soon as the curtain had come down.

" So I can be with you because soon you go away."

He couldn't endure the sound of her voice or the sight of her pain-stricken eyes. He turned his head aside, and they did not speak for a long time. And again that night, passion brought them a reprieve from their thoughts and the mercifulness of sleep.

The following day they took their last drive to their Vogelwiese Woods in a closed carriage, their fingers entwined under the lap robe. It was a raw, fitful November day of sporadic, squally downpours and gusts of whirling wind that scooped the dead leaves from the ground and sent them careening in the air like floundering russet-winged butterflies.

And then it was Monday, the last day. It rained all day, and they didn't go out. Sometimes in the afternoon Romola furtively brought them something to eat. Evening came, and he lit the candle on the nightstand. The muffled patter of rain seeped through the drawn window drapes. The room was very still and dim, except for the splash of soft yellow light on the upper part of the bed.

They were looking at each other in silence, their heads on the same pillow. He saw two tears overflow the rims of her eyes. She did not bother to wipe them off. One dripped on the pillow, the other rolled slantingly across her cheek.

"To-morrow at this hour you have the dinner with the good wife," she said quietly.

The time had come to tell her.

"I don't have a wife any more, Maria," he said in a whisper just loud enough for her to hear. "She's left me. I don't have to go."

She knew he was lying, but the lie was too sweet to resist. For a moment she stared at him in an ecstasy of relief mingled with unspeakable fear. A change came over her face, a change he was to remember until he died. Her features seemed to alter before his eyes. Her lips started to tremble. All he could think was that the early Christians who recanted their faith at the sight of the pyre and obediently spat upon the Cross must have looked like that.

"You tell the truth, *si?*" she asked tremulously.

He sensed she had already surrendered to temptation but needed his help to finish silencing her qualms. He promptly gave it to her. "She told me to go." He caught her glint of gratitude which already was an acknowledgment of their complicity. "In fact she shouted it at me."

"Why she does that?"

"Because she didn't love me any more."

They talked in whispers, like two malefactors who give themselves excuses which neither of them believes.

"Maybe it is you that leave her, *si?*"

His reply came swift and smooth. "She was tired of me, she didn't want me any more."

This was enough. If Cécile didn't want him any more, then it was all right for them to love, wasn't it. . . .?

Chapter 8

AND SO the lovers were not separated, but their relationship changed. They knew they were living a lie, and a lie can fester a love. Laughter went out first. Then a certain reverence they had previously felt towards each other. He, for her impish honesty, her extravagant generosity, her sincere, if bizarre pity; she, for his social and intellectual superiority. They lost that. In its place an uneasy equality established itself—the equality of accomplices.

Now that she no longer respected him, she quickly shed the little niceties of speech and behaviour she had always maintained in his presence. She openly resumed her smoking. She didn't smoke in defiance of conventions, like George Sand, but sensuously, because she liked the bite of tobacco, the prickling of smoke streaming down her nostrils. It shocked him to see her idling about the room in a crumpled lounge robe, a brown cigarillo dangling from her lips. Gently he remonstrated that smoking might endanger her voice. She shrugged and said she didn't care. Her speech, always picturesque, lapsed with increasing frequency into vulgarity. She would address Romola with familiar coarseness or the good-humoured ribaldry of people for whom obscenities have long lost both their sting and their offensiveness. He discovered a new Maria, a creature of slovenliness and Byzantine apathy.

Even her face underwent a change. Its vivaciousnes, its tremulous tenderness vanished. All of a sudden she looked tired and worn. He couldn't believe she was exactly the same age as Cécile. There was about her a satiety of disenchantment, a sagging lassitude. She had lived too much and too soon, known too many men, worked too hard. At times she reminded him of a bud withered before coming to bloom.

Oddly she still refused to go out with him.

"What difference does it make now?" he demanded irascibly. "We're going to live together, aren't we?"

She nodded uncertainly.

"Then why don't you want to be seen with me? Are you by any chance concerned over my reputation—or yours?"

She didn't resent the offensive implication, but still she wouldn't give in. In Paris, she promised, they would go out together. "But not here," she said with finality.

He sensed that in some obscure way she was still protecting his prestige, and even more that of Cécile. He argued that Cécile didn't love him, didn't care what he did. But this time the lie had no effect.

"Maybe," she said with a stubborn shake of her head. "But she is your wife just the same, no? The mamma of the *bambini, si?*"

He tried another way. What was the use of this ridiculous secrecy? Several people in the hotel had found out about their liaison. Twice the manager had seen him sneaking into her room.

"And the maids, the waiters, the valet, don't you think they know what's going on?" he scoffed.

Maybe, she replied with a shrug. But hotel managers, waiters and chambermaids didn't count. They wouldn't talk. It was to their interest to be discreet. A scandal was as injurious to a first-class hotel as a suicide.

Finally he gave in. "Have it your way," he said wearily.

Since much of her time was taken by fittings and rehearsals, he spent most of his days alone. He attempted to arrange some sort of life for himself at the hotel and found it extremely difficult. With surprise he discovered how much a creature of habits he had become. Used to Gustav's unobtrusive efficiency, he was baffled and defeated by trivialities. It irked him to dress without the help of a valet, yet he recoiled from the services of the hotel man. Trifles irritated him. If he misplaced his cuff links or his shoe horn, he threw his suite into confusion looking for them. Once, when a button of his frock-coat came off, the incident assumed the proportions of a minor tragedy. At such times he recalled with longing the smooth orderliness of his home. Yes, Cécile was a good *Hausfrau* . . . She had many faults but you had to admit she was a good housewife. She knew how to run a house . . .

One day, prompted by some inner urge of self-deceit, he decided to turn the sitting-room into a study. He would, he told himself, write music while waiting for Maria. Work would make time pass and keep him away from his thoughts. He purchased several reams of music paper, an assortment of quills, an inkwell and a sand box. Eagerly he sat down at his desk, quill in hand. But his eyes sought the portrait of his father on the wall, his beloved pianoforte, the friendly presence of familiar objects. The little round table by the fire, the knick-knacks they had brought back from Switzerland, an old engraving showing his grandfather Moses having dinner with Frederick the Second. Even, to his annoyance, Cécile's stiff water colours of snow-capped mountains and glassy lakes . . . He missed the steeple of Saint Thomas's Church in the window, the chirping of sparrows that came in the spring to alight on the ledge, the peals of children's laughter drifting down from the nursery. The memory of the Passion, lying in a drawer of his music cabinet, returned to him with unexpected impact. Impatiently he tossed away his quill, snatched his top hat and went out.

Sometimes, out of sheer boredom, he would walk upstairs and chat a moment with Romola. At the sight of him the old woman's face would light up as if touched by sunshine. She would rush to him, grab his hand and kiss it, calling him "Your Illustrious Lordship." She felt towards him a profound respect and had formed the notion that he was an indolent and rich aristocrat, a *gran signore* whose shoes neither she nor Maria, for that matter, was worthy to shine. She would always brew some dark aromatic concoction and while watching him sip it, would tell him about Maria's childhood, the appalling squalor of her surroundings and the drunken prowess of Vittorio, her gondolier father.

"You understand. Your Illustrious Lordship, Vittorio, he was a man with a fire in his belly. If he can't have a bottle of wine to put out this fire then he turns into a ferocious animal. But if he has the bottle of wine then he is happy, he makes love and he sings with such loudness that you can hear him from the Rialto to the Riva degli Schiavoni. So, with much sadness the mother of Maria, the poor woman, she goes with many men so that Vittorio can buy the bottle of wine. This I reveal to you with much shame, for she is a cousin of mine and I swear on the Madonna della Salute it's the truth."

Here she would dab her eyes with a corner of her apron while raising her free hand in a perfunctory oath. "So you see, Your Illustrious Lordship, the poor Maria she is a *disgraziata,* born under the Bad Star, the star with the Evil Eye."

He would listen, concealing his misgivings, and once again he would wonder at the whim of the Providence that had endowed this poor flower girl with great beauty and embedded in her throat, like a diamond in a lump of red clay, the gem of her glorious voice. . . .

Cut off from her professional life and with no work of his own, Felix had no choice but to kill time the hard way, by doing nothing. He learned the difficult and melancholy art of loafing. He sat for hours in cafés reading newspapers that did not interest him. He became an expert window shopper and ambled through public buildings and parks and churches and art galleries. He spent several afternoons in the Royal Museum, his footsteps echoing through the empty rooms. Leisurely he inspected the collection of paintings by Cranach, the banker-artist who refused to honour Luther's draft because he didn't approve of his extravagant charity. He smiled at the flat faces and bulging bellies of his medieval temptresses, reflecting how changeable were the standards of feminine beauty and how plain were the courtesans who had once fired the blood of kings. Dutifully he stood before Raphael's Sistine

Madonna, trying to understand why this vapid canvas was considered the finest painting in the world.

He became the forlorn pedestrian who shambles along the quays and discovers the pungent melancholy of aimlessness and how tiring walking can be. He meandered through ancient cobbled streets, tramping a second time with each footstep. And when his thoughts grew too heavy or confused and his heart swelled with regrets of the past and fear of the future, he would lean on the parapet of the Augustus Bridge and watch the flat-bottomed barges glide below on the Elbe, and vanish into the arched dimness of the nearest bridge, only to reappear in a light the moment later, leaving behind their shallow, ephemeral wake.

One afternoon he called on the Schumanns.

A tired-looking maid opened the door. While bundling up her hair, she informed him that Frau Schumann was out of town. As for Herr Schumann, she didn't know whether or not he was in, which of course meant that he was. Felix handed her his card and waited in a small musty ante-room.

A moment later Robert Schumann came in; he looked like a man waking up from a trance, unshaven, dishevelled, his eyes bloodshot and dull with fatigue.

"It's good to see you," he said, clasping a heavy arm around Felix's shoulders.

They entered his study, sat down facing each other and began to talk in the faltering way of friends who have long been separated and are trying to recapture their former intimacy. Yes, Clara was well, but away on another of her concert tours. No, he no longer went with her. Someone had to look after the children . . . She was the breadwinner now that he had foolishly crippled his finger and couldn't give concerts any more . . . Oh, yes, he was writing music. More than ever, despite his doctor's advice.

"This idiot doesn't want me even to listen to music!" he scoffed with an intense, disquieting laugh. "As if I could stop, when music's going on in my head all the time!"

To Felix's questions he replied in muffled, jerky sentences, as though it cost him an effort to speak. His opera, was it finished? . . . Yes, *Genoveva* was completed. Along, uneasy pause. Any new compositions? . . . Yes, a few things. There was another morose, embarrassed silence, then suddenly he seemed to come to life. Counterpoint! There was something fascinating. Especially when you began getting into really intricate combinations. "Look, Felix, suppose you have a double fugue and you want to reverse the first theme . . ." Now he was waving his arms, tossing his dishevelled blond hair, launching into impassioned tirades. For a moment he was again the man Felix had known, the impetuous young genius who would burst into his study, sit down at the piano and play his new compositions. But now his excitement had a new disquieting quality of frenzy, no longer the ebullience of a creative artist but the feverish ratiocinations of a recluse losing himself in billows of oratory after weeks of silence. As he ranted over the beauties of *sestupla* and *septupla* and eight-voice counterpoint, he reminded Felix of a mathematician gone mad.

He broke off as suddenly as he had started. "This blasted counterpoint will drive me crazy one of these days," he said, a sheepish smile on his bloated, bristly face.

He raked his hand through his thick blond hair and asked softly, "And you, Felix, how are you? You don't look any too well."

"I have painful headaches now and then, but except for that I am all right."

Again they attempted to bridge the chasm in an exchange of desultory information. How was Cécile—beautiful as ever? . . . Yes, Cécile was fine. She had gone to Frankfurt to stay with her mother for a while . . . And the children? . . . They were fine, too. Growing up . . . And dear old Hermann Schmidt, and the Gewandhaus and the Conservatorium? . . . All about the same . . . And what was he doing in Dresden?

"The trustees sent me to look into the question of an opera season for next year."

Schumann let out a derisive chuckle. "Are they still talking about that!" he said, rubbing his lids. "I lived in Leipzig fourteen years and each year I heard about the wonderful opera season they were going to have—next year. Always next year."

"Our chances are about nil. I've sent my report to the board, recommending that they keep away from operatic production. But they'll do what they like. I don't care. I'm more interested in finding a composition teacher to take your place at the Conservatorium. I've been thinking of that fellow Richard Wagner. What do you think of him?"

"I don't know," said Schumann with a noncommittal gesture. "I've just read the score of his *Tannhäuser*. One moment his music is pompous and trivial, the next it is magnificent. I can't decide whether he is a genius or a charlatan."

"He could be both. It's happened before."

"He is a strange little man. About as high as a stein of beer with an enormous head. Vain as a peacock. Talks your arm off and always about himself. Up to his eyes in debts. Treats his wife shamefully. Fancies himself as a writer, a poet, a philosopher and a statesman. Meddles in politics. Makes speeches in political clubs and is going to wake up in jail one of these days."

"Good." Felix smiled. "He may find it advisable to change towns and move to Leipzig."

They talked a while longer, but the strangeness between them remained. They parted with the usual assurances of friendship, the usual promises to meet again which they knew they wouldn't keep.

Outside, the grey November afternoon was decaying into night. A cold eastern wind blew in hissing gusts down the empty street, announcing the snows from Poland. The breath of winter was upon Dresden. Felix made his way back to the hotel in a dispirited mood. His visit to Schumann had left him with a feeling of discouragement. Poor Robert, poor Clara! They had fought so long and valiantly for their love, and now what did they have? A penurious, difficult marriage, strained by long separations and madness looming in the future* . . . And what about Cécile and himself? Had there ever been a more auspicious wedding? Had two people ever started the journey through life with greater chances of success —and now look at them! Apart, embittered, each entangled in his own net. She of her self-righteousness; he, of his pride and sin. Oh, God, wasn't there any enduring happiness in this world? Must everything that once was bright and joyous turn to dust and ashes before our eyes?

When he entered his room he did not immediately see Maria. He hung up his hat, unfastened his cape and was about to light the candle on the nightstand when he noticed her, lying on the red plush lounge chair near the window, still dressed in street clothes. She was watching him quietly, her face an oval blur of whiteness.

"Darling!" he cried joyously, rushing to her. "I didn't expect you so soon."

He leaned down to kiss her. Her lips were cold, her cheeks tear-wet.

"What's the matter?" he asked with tender concern, sitting down on the edge of the chair and taking her hands.

She did not reply.

"Why are you crying?" he asked, his voice low and anxious.

"Because of you," she murmured, a smiling wretchedness in her eyes. "Because of you and me."

He knew what she meant but pretended not to understand. "Why should you be crying about us?" he said with feigned lightness. "We're happy, aren't we? We love each other. In ten days we'll be leaving for Paris. You'll see, we'll have a little house all by ourselves on some quiet side street near the Boulevard Saint Germain. It will have a garden. You'll meet my friends. I have

* A few years later unmistakable symptoms of insanity declared themselves in Robert Schumann. One afternoon, in Düsseldorf, he threw himself from a bridge into the Rhine. Rescued, he was carried into a private asylum, where he died two years later.

wonderful friends in Paris. Writers, artists, even a few musicians. We'll dine at Larue's and I'll take you to a little *gargotte* I know on Quai Voltaire where they make the finest *boeuf en daube* in the world. After the theatre we'll have supper at the Café Anglais. Have you ever been there?"

He spoke with strained eagerness, trying to kindle her enthusiasm, but she looked at him smiling, not listening, scanning his face as if she were seeing it for the first time.

"Why I love you so?" she said under her breath with a bewildered shake of her head. She sat up, pulled away one of her hands, lovingly trailed her fingers down his cheek. "All these years I think of you I tell myself I am a stupid woman. I tell myself many men have more beauty and richness than you, no? They give me diamonds and the money to me. Everything. But all the time I think only of you."

She was not addressing him but merely thinking aloud, barely moving her lips, gazing at him with a sort of baffled perplexity.

"Why I love you so much I cannot understand," she went on in the same monotonous drone. "Even now I cannot understand. When you say the good wife says you go and she had finished loving you, I know you tell big lies. But I love you, I don't want you to go, so I pretend and I make believe you tell the truth because in such ways I think I don't lose you and maybe we stay together always."

She let out a long, desolate sigh. "But now the Madonna has much anger against you because you tell lies about the wife. Also against me because I want to take you from the wife, and that is the greatest *peccato*, the greatest sin, no? And so she punishes you and me and she puts the poison in our love and the love is no good any more and we are unhappy."

"But we aren't!" Fiercely he grasped her arms, squeezed them hard. "We are not unhappy. I am happy, I am the happiest——"

The slow shake of her head cut short his protests.

"No, *carino*, you are not happy," she said with gentle patience. "I see the sadness in your eyes. Often, when you don't look I watch and I know you are sad and think of the good wife and the *bambini*."

Angrily he pushed her away and sprang to his feet.

"The good wife, the good wife!" he shouted. "I'm glad you approve of my wife, but I happen to know her better than you do. She was cold and selfish and righteous and——"

"I think you talk loud but say only lies," she interrupted with unruffled indulgence. "I see her only one time in Paris but I watch and I know she makes fine wife for you. Very beautiful and genteel.

Never sell flowers in the street, no? Never go with men in the hotels, like me. Always good girl."

She saw him open his mouth, but before he could speak, she went on, "Another thing I watch. Each time when she looks at you I see the love come into her face. Then I know she is the good wife for you."

"You saw all that in a moment in a room full of people," he scoffed, "but I lived with her many years."

She ignored his sarcasm. "A man can live with a woman many years and not have the understanding of such a woman. Love, yes—but not the understanding."

Again he sat down and bent forward, his voice an urgent whisper. "Please, darling, believe me. I do understand her and she isn't the woman you think. Yes, she is a lady and very 'genteel,' as you say, but it takes more than that to make a happy marriage. Inwardly she was selfish. For instance, she knew I wanted to leave Leipzig and move to Berlin, but she never——"

"Why you want to go to Berlin?" she cut in aggressively. "Berlin's no different from Leipzig. Same people, same houses. In Leipzig you have the good home, the *bambini* are happy. Why you want to go to Berlin?"

The sudden petulance of her tone, the directness of her question unsaddled him for a second. "Because—because it offered much greater opportunities for my work. Do you know that the King of Prussia wanted me to be general music direktor of the Kingdom with the rank of minister?"

She wasn't impressed. "Happiness is more important than big post."

The calmness of her voice exasperated him. "Well, then, if you think she is so wonderful why did you sneak into my room the night I arrived?"

He knew he had struck low, and the blow had hurt this time. For an instant she looked at him in silence through the liquid lens of unshed tears.

"I come to your room because I am a bad woman and I love you," she said with abject humility. "Because all these years I pray the Madonna she make a miracle and let me kiss you again, and when you say you stay in Dresden a week I think the Madonna has done the *miracolo* for me, because she sees I love you so. But now I know you don't go back to the good wife because I give you many kisses and I make love to you and I do everything so you forget her and stay with me. For this the Madonna punishes me one day and for this I burn in the inferno when I die."

He knew her too well to try to shake her beliefs. To her, the Virgin, miracles, the everlasting fire were incontrovertible realities.

To her, every kiss she gave him, every caress, meant literally a step towards eternal damnation. In its pitiful, almost ludicrous naïveté, Maria's torment suddenly assumed a Faustian grandeur. She truly was selling her soul for love.

"Do you want me to return to Cécile?" he asked softly. "Is that what you want?"

She nodded, and the expression on her face was one of complete despair.

"I don't want, but I know it is good for you, *carino*," she said, still nodding. "You go to her and you tell everything. Yes, you tell how I come to your room with nothing under my dress, like a *puttana*, and how I give you many kisses. You tell her how you feel much shame and you love only her and not me, and after a while she gives you the kiss of forgiveness."

"And you?"

She shrugged. "What matters about me? When you go my heart dies, and it matters not where I go. I sing at the opera and I give much money to the priests for the *bambini*, I pray the Madonna and I don't go with the men any more. And so, when I die, perhaps God gives the kiss of forgiveness to me also."

He looked at her, as overwhelmed by her capacity for self-sacrifice as he had been by the greatness of her charity. There was something holy about her, detached, almost unearthly. Saint Mary Magdalene must have been that sort of woman . . .

For a second he hesitated between pity, anger and derision. He chose tenderness.

"Nothing would be accomplished but to make us both miserable," he said, drawing her to him. "Don't you see, Maria, that we love each other? We need each other, we'll always be together. And you'll see, we'll be happy . . . very happy . . ."

She did not argue, did not resist his embrace. She cuddled into his arms, limp as a sleepy child. He went on talking in lulling whispers, his lips on her hair. But he knew he would never convince her, that some day she would try to escape, as she had done in England.

He would watch, and this time he wouldn't let her go.

During the following days Maria appeared to have silenced her religious qualms. She did not mention Cécile any more or make any further attempt to send her husband back to her. She seemed content to be Felix's mistress and accepted their liaison without protests or reservations. She talked a great deal about the things they would do in Paris. Her behaviour, however, did not improve. She smoked more and more, her language grew worse and she even began to drink. Unused to alcohol she rapidly got drunk and obnoxious. Her love-making became, if possible, more abandoned than before and she lost whatever modesty she had possessed.

Felix endured these new developments with patience, knowing full well they were the outward expressions of her inner conflict. At times he read in her dilated eyes a terror and hatred that were beyond description. He would have liked to assuage her fears, but no reasoning would dent her convictions. She was beyond help. Helpless and broken hearted, he watched her stumbling, struggling descent into Hell. He told himself that a crisis of such violence could not last. In Paris she would regain control of herself. Meanwhile he would increase his vigilance.

Fortunately, he calculated, the odds were on his side. She wouldn't be able to vanish as easily as she had in England. First, he was on his guard, no longer the naïve lover who had conveniently walked out of the thatch-roofed cottage at her request. Also, she was being watched by Herr von Wierling. The wily direktor intended to have her fulfil her engagement, even if, as he said, she was bankrupting the opera house. Finally, she had all her belongings at the hotel, and most important of all, Romola. He knew she would never leave town without Romola or without the little plaster statue of the Madonna. Of that he was sure. He decided he would keep his eye on both.

The figurine was in his room, on the chest of drawers where Maria had placed it herself in the first ecstatic days of their reunion. The old servant was upstairs. From his room he could hear the tired shuffling of her footsteps. His position, he assured himself, was strategically ideal.

He purchased a mountain of books and the scores of Mozart symphonies and almost never left the hotel. The weather facilitated his decision. Long spells of icy rain followed sieges of howling wind, ending up in squalls of lashing snow. The sun had given up and did not even attempt to pierce through the thick slab of clouds. Dresden was plunged into a perennial twilight which by mid afternoon crumpled into a woolly darkness. Stretched out on the lounge chair, a three-armed candelabra at his elbow, a book or a score opened on his raised knees, Felix enjoyed the comforts of indoor living while doing sentry duty. At times the thought brought a smile of sly amusement to his gaunt face.

One afternoon, however, a sharp jab of conscience prodded him out of his comfort and sent him, reluctant and grumbling, on a long trek through unfamiliar and dingy streets in search of Richard Wagner. Having finally located the composer's lodgings, he entered the nauseous entrance hallway, climbed four flights of creaking stairs and rang the hand bell.

After a long and pregnant silence the door opened a crack, and a woman's eye, brown and apprehensive, appeared.

"He isn't in. Come to-morrow."

The words were spoken in haste behind the door, and the door itself was about to be shut without further ado. Swiftly Felix inserted the tip of his boot in the slim opening.

"I come to talk to Herr Wagner about a position," he said quickly and with a most promising smile.

The effect of this announcement was immediate. The door opened wide, and Frau Wagner came into view. She was young and pretty, but the discouraged curve of her mouth and the disarray of her coiffure made her look plain and older, almost middle-aged.

"I thought you were coming for the rent," she said with the dispirited frankness of one who has long given up pride. "Richard's out, but he should be back soon. If you don't mind waiting in the kitchen, you can sit down till he comes." As a humble inducement she added, "It's warm in there."

He groped in her wake through an unlit and winding corridor and followed her into the kitchen, dim and cheerless in the November gloom. Although daylight was almost gone she didn't make any attempt to light the stub of candle set in a pewter holder over the water pump.

"Perhaps you'd like something to drink?" she asked uncertainly as he sat down at the kitchen table in the middle of the room.

He caught her expression of relief when he courteously declined and he felt a surge of sympathy for this care-worn, prematurely aged woman.

"Haven't I seen you somewhere?" she said, scanning his face. "You look familiar."

Of course she'd seen his lithographed portrait that was sold throughout Germany in stationery and music shops . . . "My name is Felix Mendelssohn."

"Now I remember. You're a composer, like my husband. I've heard about you." She started towards her stool near the window and resumed the peeling of potatoes lying in a green earthenware basin. "You've written a lot of songs, haven't you? I saw them in stores. You're lucky to get them published." A note of bitterness crept into her voice. "Richard's written a stack of songs, but he can't get anybody to publish them."

"Perhaps I could be of some help," he offered with genuine warmth as well as the desire to win her confidence. "I know several publishers."

"If you could, I'd so appreciate it," she said with her characteristic frankness. "We need the money."

Yes, no doubt, they could, he reflected. When you fell to saving on candlelight, you were scraping the financial bottom . . . Among the poor the kitchen, he had noticed, was the brightest, cheeriest room, but this one only revealed their desperate poverty and their unhappiness. Its very air, chilly and damp despite the meagre fire in the wood stove, smelled of despair and discontent and told of their acrimonious quarrels, their mutual disappointment.

"Even great musical talent is often slow to assure material security," he said, to make conversation. "You may like to know that the position I've come to discuss with your husband commands a steady and comfortable salary."

She turned to him, wearily pushed back a loose strand of hair with her wrist. "It's nice of you to climb all those steps to offer him a position."

Gratitude shone in her eyes, melting away her previous aloofness. She was relaxing, enjoying the diversion that his visit brought into her dreary and lonely life, happy to have someone to talk to, someone who hadn't come to threaten or ask for money.

For a moment she was silent, gazing at him through the increasing dimness, her face tense with longing. "You don't know how it feels to live from hand to mouth, never knowing where the next thaler will come from. Ten years now—it was ten years ago last April that I married Richard, and things don't ever seem to get any better. Before I married him I was doing all right. I was an actress. My name's Minna Planer." With the pathetic and indestructible vanity of former actresses she asked hopefully, "Perhaps you've heard of me?"

"Of course," he lied blithely. "Your name is well known."

Her eyes shone with reminiscent pride and her face was young again. "I was leading lady at the Magdeburg Theatre when I married him."

In her mouth the dingy provincial theatre became a place of wonders. a scene of glamorous artistic triumphs.

"Richard was conducting the orchestra. He was only twenty-three and I didn't pay any attention to him. But he wouldn't leave me alone. He got sick and I felt sorry for him and nursed him. I think he got sick just to get me to say yes. He is that kind of man. When he gets something into his head he must finish it—even if he regrets it later."

Words came out of her in an even flow, but the brief accent of pride had gone out.

"The moment we were married everything went wrong. I don't say it's his fault, but everywhere he goes trouble goes with him. Two months later the theatre closed and Bethmann, the manager, left the town, and there we were stranded in the street without a thaler between us. Well, somehow we found work. In Koenigsberg, this

time, and it looked so good we even took my sister Thérèse, who
played second lead, with us. We stayed there one year and then
the same thing happened. One night the manager took French leave,
as they say, and we were back in the street. We slept in the public
park and I sold the only fur piece I ever had, a little necklet I'd
bought at the time of our wedding. Then we went to Riga."

For the first time she raised her eyes and looked at Felix.

"Have you ever been to Riga?" she asked.

He sensed he had arrived at the precise moment when this forlorn
and neglected wife must talk to someone—anyone—unburden her
soul or die . . . "I'm afraid I haven't. It's in Russia, isn't it?"

She nodded and went back to her work. "On the Russian side
of the Baltic. A nice town, except you die of the cold. Well, everything was fine for a while. Good pay, good food. Richard wasn't
gambling any more, he was working on a comic opera. A sort of
operetta, you might say. But he wasn't happy. He wanted to go
to Paris. Only in Paris they'd appreciate his music. That's what he
said."

She gave out a throttled sound that was half snort and half sob.

"They certainly did! . . . We stayed three years in Paris and how
we lived through those three years I'll never know. Not that he
didn't try. Nobody wanted to look at his opera, so he tried writing
songs, he made arrangements for music publishers, he even gave
a few lessons. But we never had enough to eat. Then all of a sudden
everything was wonderful. The direktor of the Théâtre de la
Renaissance, his name was Monsieur Joli, took his opera. He even
gave him an advance. Well, that's all he needed! Right away he
must buy new clothes, new furniture, new everything. We must
move to a fine new house so people would be impressed. And then
you know what happened?"

Again she looked up at Felix. "The theatre closed the very same
day we moved into the fine new house."

She paused to give Felix time to savour the full irony of the
coincidence. Then, with that peculiar throttled sound of hers, she
hunched back over her potatoes again.

"Well, after that I don't know why we didn't starve. The only
people we ever saw were the landlord or bill collectors. My heart
stopped each time the bell rang. Poor Richard, he did whatever
he could. He even tried to become a chorister in one of those little
local theatres they have in Paris. He even grew a beard to escape
his creditors, but they caught him and clamped him in jail for debts.
To show you how bad things were . . . We had a dog, a great big
Newfoundland dog Richard adored. Well he left us. And when a
dog leaves you, let me tell you, things are pretty bad."

Felix nodded sympathetically, but Minna did not see him. For a moment she peeled a potato, her delicate profile a hazy silhouette in the encroaching dusk.

"Somehow he had finished his opera *Rienzi*. Don't ask me how, but he had. Naturally, nobody wanted to look at it in Paris. So he got the idea of coming here. I liked that because this is my home town. My father was a mechanic with a little shop two streets away from here. Well, we get here, and everything seems wonderful. They give his *Rienzi* at the opera house and it's a big success, though the scenery keeps on falling down during the performance. It lasts six hours but the public loves it. And to crown it all they give him the post of assistant music direktor at twelve hundred thalers a year."

She pronounced the figure in a tone of wonder, as though she couldn't believe that such a sum was ever within her reach.

"Another man would be happy, don't you think ? But you don't know him . . . Right away he starts squandering money as if he was a banker. The same as in Paris—new clothes, new furniture, new everything. He buys himself a quilted silk bathrobe. Then he gets the idea of having the whole score of *Rienzi* lithographed. And since he is at it, that of *Tannhäuser* too, which he had just finished. He tells me of the money he's going to make and how every opera house is going to play his operas, and I already see us living in a palace like that of the King. Well, they give *Tannhäuser* and nobody likes it much. Nobody buys his beautiful scores either. Pretty soon the money's gone and we have to sell the furniture and even the silk bathrobe. But you know how much you get when you try selling things, and soon we have more debts than a dog has fleas."

She let out a sigh, not of discontent but of resigned hopelessness.

"And so, here we are. We haven't had a piece of meat for a month. I have no money for candles. The rent hasn't been paid for three months. And you know what he's doing?"

She looked at Felix with a smile of amused despair.

"He meddles in politics! . . . Yes, he's going to start the revolution, and the revolution is going to make him rich. He'll take over the post of Herr von Wierling and produce his operas!"

She did not speak for a moment. Her face sagged with lassitude. "I'd like to know how it's all going to end," she said under her breath, gazing out of the window. "But I expect I won't be there to see it."

"Perhaps he will accept my proposition," Felix said to cheer her up. "It would mean steady employment and later the chance to conduct a fine orchestra."

She turned around. "Anyone else would leap at the chance, but he . . . I don't know. I've been living with him for ten years and I still don't know what goes on in that head of his. I only wish he'd settle down so we could pay our rent and eat regularly, like other people."

Silence fell between them once more.

"Do you think he'll be here soon?" asked Felix. "I am afraid I have to go back to my hotel."

"I don't know," she sighed discouragedly. "He said he'd be here, but with him you never can tell."

She pursed her lips in thoughtful perplexity, then with sudden decision, she went on. "If it were anyone else I'd never tell, but I can see you don't come from the police and he does need the work." Her voice dwindled to a whisper. "He is at the little tavern down the street. You go through the garden at the back and you see a green door. You knock and give the password and the man will let you in."

She went on giving him instructions while she escorted him to the door.

"I hope he takes the position," she said as he was leaving. "And please tell him to come home, will you? It's lonely in here all day by yourself."

Felix had no difficulty in locating the conspirators' meeting place. He pushed open a rusty iron gate and found himself in a narrow unkempt backyard. A single denuded linden tree stood in the centre, a circle of soggy dead leaves at its base. Dutifully he knocked on the green weather-beaten door, gave the password and was ushered into a hot, smoke-filled room. Ten or twelve men were sitting at a table, their faces bathed in the soft amber glow from an oil lantern hanging from a nail on the wall.

He recognised Wagner and walked to him.

"Please forgive me for coming here," he said with a smile, "but I am most anxious to have a few words with you."*

After a few minutes the conspirators slipped furtively out of the tavern, and Felix found himself closeted and sipping beer with an astonishing little man.

In the course of his career he had met a multitude of artists and was familiar with their vanity, their sensitivity, their everlasting complaints against a stupid public who failed to acclaim their masterpieces, but never, never had he encountered such vitriolic hatred and colossal conceit as Wagner's. For one solid hour he watched the snarling, shouting gnome bang his fist on the table and proclaim that he was an immortal genius and would force the world to recognise it—if it took a revolution to do it. With understanding pity he listened to the ravings of this brilliant but em-

* When less than two years later revolution broke out in Dresden, Wagner took an active but unedifying part in it, fleeing to Switzerland and leaving his followers to pay for their naïve faith in his leadership. He was banned from Saxony for many years.

bittered man who, after years of privation and failure, had pinned his hopes on the reckless and the catastrophic. He sensed that this selfish and desperate artist, this hungry, debt-ridden agitator, saw nothing in the revolution but a chance to impose his operas, hear the ovations that haunted his sleepness nights and earn huge sums of money to satisfy his oriental craving for display and ostentation.*

Taking advantage of a break in Wagner's verbal torrent, Felix quickly pushed back his chair and rose to his feet.

" I understand your reasons for not accepting the humdrum position I had come to offer you, and please accept my thanks for your most interesting conversation. Your servant."

Wagner remained seated to conceal his short stature. " Your servant," he said gruffly.

With uncanny timing the proprietor appeared in the doorway. Felix paid for the drinks and walked to the door.

" By the way," he said, turning around, with his hand on the knob, " Frau Wagner asked me to tell you that she is lonely and waiting for you at home."

Wagner did not reply and Felix went out.

He rapidly forgot the Wagner episode in his growing anxiety over Maria's behaviour. As the end of her engagement at the opera house approached, her fretfulness increased. Her moods became more unpredictable than ever. Like a dog biting its chain, she tried to break the bond that tied her to him. Again she begged him to return to his wife, only to rush into his arms and with gasping sobs make him swear never to go away. She quarrelled with him for no reason, merely to relieve the tension of her nerves. She shouted at him that she didn't love him, never had. At other times she would cuddle in his arms and dream aloud. "Maybe I do not sing in the opera any more and we go to Italy, no? . . . No, not Venice. Too many sad memories in Venice. Also much rain and snow in winter . . . Maybe we go to Taormina, *si*? They say the sky is always blue in Taormina . . ." Once when he was suffering

* According to eye-witnesses, Wagner carried a red flag during the Dresden revolution against the Saxon monarchy, but became a fulsome panegyrist of royalty when Ludwig II, the Mad King of Bavaria, began financing his operatic ventures out of the Public Treasury. He renounced his native citizenship and was naturalised as a Bavarian subject in 1864.

As for his passion for bizarre personal adornment, it was almost beyond belief. In his later, more prosperous years, his favourite working attire consisted of a pair of pastel-shade silk pantaloons and a bathrobe of yellow quilted silk, ermine lined at the neck and wrists, embellished with a sprinkling of pearls. And, of course, the inevitable black velvet beret. He never outgrew his taste of extravagant decor. The room in which he died at the Palazzo Vendramin in Venice had been transformed under his direction into a blue silk replica of Capri's Blue Grotto.

Mendelssohn never knew of Wagner's virulent anti-Semitism. The notorious pamphlet, *Das Judentum in der Musik* was published in 1850—three years after Mendelssohn's death— under the pseudonym K. Freigedank.

from one of his headaches she knelt by his side with tears in her eyes, and for the first time in a long while he saw her cross herself and pray to the Madonna to make him well.

In one of their quiet moments he asked if he could attend her farewell performance at the opera house. Her response was immediate, almost violent.

"No," she said. "If you come I don't sing."

Gently he argued with her. Was he to be the only man in Dresden who couldn't go to hear her?

"If you like my singing I sing for you now. Just for you. I sing all day, no?"

But she did not want him to come to the opera. "Also," she added triumphantly, "you cannot buy the *biglietto*. Even a small mouse cannot squeeze in the opera the last night I sing."

He did not insist, but the emphasis of her refusal confirmed his suspicions. She might well try to run away that night after his performance. Or even before—anything was possible with her. Plainly, the confusion of her farewell night would give her the best opportunities.

He decided he would attend that night. But, as she had said, every ticket had long been sold. This was to be the night of nights. The King and the Court were to attend. No amount of money would get him a seat that evening. Somewhat reluctantly he paid a call, ostensibly a farewell call, on his friend Herr von Wierling.

The opera direktor was genial and courteous as ever.

"So you haven't left yet, have you?" he said, greeting Felix at the door with a hearty smile. "I knew you'd discover the charms of our fair city. Of course the weather's awful these days, but then the weather isn't everything, and if one is lucky, one can find many diversions indoors."

This while filling the inevitable sherry glasses. He turned around and glanced at Felix over his shoulder, a gleam of teasing in his eye. "Can't one?"

Felix agreed that one could indeed find pleasant diversions indoors. "But it's easier at home than in a hotel." To change the subject he went on. "I've finally dispatched my business and I've come to express my gratitude for your gracious co-operation." He took a sip from his glass and went on with what he hoped was proper casualness. "I'm planning to leave in four or five days."

"What a distressing coincidence!" The direktor's face expressed a well-simulated dismay. "Our city will lose at the same time its two most distinguished guests. You and Miss Salla. And His Majesty is leaving the day after her farewell performance for a state visit to the King of Bavaria. Dresden will be a mere hulk. *Un corps sans âme*, as the French say."

He glanced at Felix across the desk to judge the effect of his little performance. " At least," he went on more cheerfully, " have you had a chance to hear Miss Salla?"

It was Felix's turn to engage in a bit of acting. " Alas, no! I had hoped to attend her farewell performance, but no ticket is to be had at any price."

From then on the conversation turned into a sly game of hide-and-seek, each one pretending an innocence that his eyes belied. What, the famous Doktor Mendelssohn unable to attend the opera! This was unthinkable.

" Ordinarily I'd suggest we have dinner together. It'd give you a chance to know her better and see how very beautiful she is. But, as I told you, she's become a recluse. She enjoys solitude to an unusual degree."

But at least Felix would be able to attend the farewell performance " Unfortunately it will have to be in my box and my wife insists on coming that night. She is the kind of woman who talks during performances. . . ."

Felix would have preferred some unobtrusive seat at the rear of the house, far from the stage, but this, he realised, was impossible.

Again he thanked the direktor and promptly departed.

And now it was mid-afternoon of the following day, and he was lounging on the red plush chaise longue, reading a letter from Christoph Muller that had arrived that morning.

His Lordship wrote that the board of trustees had approved a motion of thanks (his own, incidentally) for his brilliant report on the operatic question. The vote had been unanimous, even Kruger joining in it. Which meant that whatever animosities had arisen in the past had now vanished. Pastor Hagen had similarly abstained from any more personal allusions in his sermons. In short, the tempest in a teapot had calmed down. The unpleasant Passion incident was forgotten, and on his return Felix would find nothing but friendly smiles and open arms. The Mayor ended on a personal note, saying that he for one was anxious that Felix would decide to come back before long, as he missed his good friend.

Felix rested the letter in his lap and gazed unseeingly at Maria's little statue of the Virgin. The Mayor's message had awakened memories, stirred old feelings. He hadn't thought much about Leipzig since his arrival in Dresden. Now it was coming back in a procession of little tableaux, familiar daily scenes of his prosaic, well-regulated life. His classes at the Conservatorium, the orchestra rehearsals in Gewandhaus Hall, Hermann Schmidt puffing on his flute, the board meetings, the leisurely walks back to the house in the late afternoon, Gustav opening the door and taking his feet

and cape, the visits to the nursery with the children running to
him, tugging at his coat, telling him the breathless events of the
day . . .

And Cécile . . . Her exquisite face, the golden sheen of her hair,
her calm eyes that could be like two windows opening on a blue
cloudless sky. The quiet evening in the study with her on the green
sofa knitting, sewing—always busy. The perfect wife, the perfect
lady, the perfect hostess at dull gatherings, the vice-president of the
Leipzig Ladies' Charitable Society for Succour to the Poor . . .

Yes, it had been a peaceful life, happy in many ways. Why
then didn't he want to return to it? Because—because it had become
a meaningless routine, a sequence of acts, gestures and words culminating in a total of nothingness. It wasn't enough to live, you
had to be alive . . . He was willing to forget about Berlin, his
aspirations to a brilliant, stimulating social life. He was willing
to eat the grey porridge of Leipzig, but he must have love, the love
they had known in Düsseldorf. Warm, joyous, tender and
passionate, not this polite, sexless, empty charade . . .

Not now, not after the Passion. Strange how this old music had
affected his life. If he had never found it he might have resigned
himself to the peaceful somnolence of his life. At least he would
have been at peace with himself, waited for death in tranquillity.
But he was not at peace with himself, couldn't face the coming of
death knowing he had failed his duty to give this music to the world,
refused his father's last wish to do one great and good deed. It
would have been the ransom for all the privileges he had enjoyed—
wealth, talent, success. But he hadn't paid for them, he had slunk
away when the test had come. And because of that, silence was
unendurable. Why did thieves carouse in taverns and get drunk?
Because they couldn't stand silence or their own company. Well,
he too was afraid of solitude, and that was why he clung to Maria,
why he didn't want her to run away . . . Of course she was foolish,
irresponsible, illiterate, even vulgar, but at least she loved him.
And he needed someone to love him, for love brought pain and joy
and anger and delight—and it kept you from thinking . . .

He was jolted out of his reverie by a loud and insistent pounding
on the door. As he had left strict orders not to be disturbed, his
reaction was one of distinct annoyance which changed to distinct
irritation when the importunate caller, impatient at not receiving
any answer, turned the knob and flung the door open.

Karl Klingemann stood on the threshold, legs apart, looking
formidable in his ruffled beaver and travelling cloak.

"Don't ask any questions," he said before Felix could utter a
word. "I am too hungry to argue. Get into your coat and come
with me."

A moment later they were sitting at a secluded table in Dresden's most fashionable restaurant, deserted at this late hour. The diplomat had opposed a stony silence to Felix's inquiries, speaking only to the waiter to order a copious and discriminating lunch. It wasn't until he had disposed of the third course that he appeared to become aware of his friend's presence across the table.

He ran his bulging eyes over him with an expression of acute distaste.

" Friendship," he began at last with smouldering resentment, " has all the drawbacks of love and none of its rewards. If I had another friend like you I'd shoot myself."

Having delivered himself of these two statements, he took a long draught of excellent Tokay and dabbed his lips with his napkin while glancing over his shoulder at the rain which was now coming down in solid curtains of water.

" You might be interested to learn why I find myself in this God-forsaken town in this revolting weather," he went on, turning back to Felix.

" Yes, I would," said Felix, sensing that these preliminaries were leading to an unpleasant climax. " I'd like very much to know why you're here."

" Because of you," said Karl accusingly. " All the way down from London I've been cursing the day when our paths met."

" Well," said Felix with false cheeriness, " now that you've got that off your chest you may go back. Or have you come all this way to deliver a sermon? Believe me, it would be quite useless."

" Quite right," nodded Karl. " I have no faith in sermons, having myself endured an immense number without any profit whatever. My father—God rest his penny-pinching soul!—died in the midst of one. No, I merely came here to judge for myself whether or not you've gone crazy."

Felix did not reply and went on fingering his glass of cognac.

" Before leaving Leipzig," Karl went on, " you wrote to me, if you remember, a long and despondent letter which worried me enormously. In it you mentioned your intention of separating from Cécile. At once I asked for a leave of absence and I would have been here much sooner if our minister hadn't fallen in love with a twelve-year-old girl. Since he was writing sonnets and in no position to run the legation, I had to run it for him until he came to his senses."

In Leipzig a pale and forlorn Gustav had informed him that Felix had left for Dresden and Cécile for Frankfurt. " So I took the first train and drove straight to the Hanoverian Embassy. Yes, foolish as it is, there is a Hanoverian Embassy in this town."

"How did you find my hotel and how did they let you come up and pound on my door?"

"My good friend Baron von Stulenheim provided me with your address. Like all diplomatic chiefs he receives daily police reports on important arrivals, on the remote assumption that some distinguished Hanoverian might visit this miserable town. For the second part of your question the hotel manager himself gave me the number of your room."

"How? I'd given strict orders——"

"I know," said Karl, raising a fleshy hand. "But I scared him. I told him I was from the police. You'd be surprised how many people believe you when you tell them you are from the police. You can show them any sort of credentials. I flashed an old club membership card. He was satisfied and told me all I wanted to know."

"Well," said Felix with challenging irony, "now that you've found me and learned everything, what are you going to do?"

"It depends," said Karl noncommittally. "I'd prefer that you tell me what *you're* going to do."

"I expect to leave with Maria for Paris in a few days. She has an engagement there." For the first time the two friends were facing each other with open hostility, preparing for the clash. "Anything else you'd like to know? Or will you flash your card and make me confess?"

Karl ignored the jibe. "And what will you do after her Paris engagement?"

"I don't know exactly. She mentioned another engagement in Vienna."

"And then?" Karl's voice trembled with anger. "Another one in Milano. Or Berlin, or London, or St. Petersburg . . . And everywhere she goes you'll go. You'll roam through Europe in draughty coaches, keep her company, attend to the luggage and the details of travelling. A sort of secretary-lady's companion-manager-lover all rolled into one. In every city you'll receive the invitations and flowers that her former lovers will send and hear the gossip about her previous affairs. During rehearsals you'll wait patiently in her dressing-room or at the hotel and you will attend every performance—from the wings, of course—until you've heard *Il Barbiere*, *Lucia* and *Norma* two hundred times and can't stand a single bar of them. And for that you, you, Moses Mendelssohn's grandson and a great musician in your own right, will abandon wife and children!"

He stopped abruptly.

"You fool!" he blurted out. "Can you see yourself leading this sort of life? Don't you see you'd be a hundred times more miserable than you were ever in Leipzig?"

Felix was startled by the violence of his friend's outburst. Never had he seen Karl angry. It was an awesome sight. He seemed to grow taller, broader. His heavy jaws were locked in pugnacious determination. It was easy to understand how he could have terrified the hotel manager. And he was telling the truth . . . Felix knew it, and that was the worst of it, for truth was the last thing he wanted to hear.

"Perhaps," he flung back, "perhaps you're right, but at least she'll give me love."

"Sex, you mean."

"Call it what you want." He shrugged wearily. "Love has many faces. I think it's the Chinese who call it ' the tree with many branches.' Who can tell how much sex goes into love? Too much sex is supposed to kill love, but I know damn well that not enough sex does kill it." The aggressiveness returned. "Anyway, what do you know about love? You've never been in love."

"But I've had plenty of sex, and one thing I've learned about it. It doesn't last. Who builds on sex builds on sand."

He broke off abruptly and looked at Felix with a cool, almost clinical detachment. "You know, Felix, I don't think you even love Maria."

The remark caught him unprepared. He always had analysed her feelings, never probed his own. Perhaps Karl was right, but this was no time to debate the question. "Don't you think this is for me to decide?" he scoffed, seeking refuge in irony.

Karl ignored the sarcasm and went on, pressing his advantage. "You know I am right. You think you love her because you need her, and you need her because you're lost, confused and afraid and you want someone to soothe your remorse and your fears with kisses and caresses; because you don't want to be alone and can't face yourself. And you——"

There it was in the open—the truth. "At least she loves me," he almost shouted to stop his friend's inexorable drilling.

"Yes," conceded Karl with skilful calmness. "Yes, she does love you. She loves you as this type of woman does, with every nerve, every gland, in her body. The kind of love that is a chain, a disease. She knows you aren't made for each other, that you will destroy each other. That sort of love doesn't make for happiness."

"It's better than no love at all."

"How do you know Cécile doesn't love you just as deeply, just as intensely as Maria?"

"Cécile!" The name came out in a snort. "She has a strange way of showing it."

"That also is true," admitted Karl, "but for God's sake don't you understand she is the product of her education? Since childhood she's been trained to be a lady, repress her feelings. But the fire is there just the same. Love, real love this time. And if you'd only give her a chance——"

"A chance to be noble?" scoffed Felix. "To be charitable? Open her arms and forgive her repentant husband?"

Suddenly there was nothing in him but anger, a black, sputtering resentment against the bulky, red-faced man before him, this former friend who was too blunt, too clear-sighted, who denied his sympathy and refused to accept his flimsy, insincere arguments. "Why don't you go back to London?" he flung, pushing back his chair and springing to his feet. "Who gave you the right to meddle in my affairs?"

"Our friendship!" Karl slammed his heavy fist on the table. "I am not going to let you wreck your life."

Felix's reply was a cruel, derisive laugh. "You can bang your fist and shout all you want. I'm leaving with Maria and there's nothing you or anyone else can do about it. I don't ever want to see you again."

With unbelieving eyes the diplomat watched his childhood friend stride out of the restaurant. He saw him stand in the rain, scanning the empty street for a carriage, then with a hunching of shoulders plunge ahead and out of sight. He felt his throat tighten and for an instant he longed to run after him, plead with him and make him see reason. But Felix, he knew, was past reasoning. It would do no good.

To hide his emotions he took a leisurely pinch of snuff. Then, brushing the specks of tobacco from his lapels, he signalled to the waiter, asked him to call a cab.

A moment later he ducked into a dilapidated hackney.

"To the Hanoverian Embassy," he cried to the driver.

Felix did not mention Karl's visit to Maria. They talked about their departure and decided they would leave early in the morning after her farewell performance. She spent much time in her suite and he increased his vigilence. Stretched out on the bed, his eyes on the ceiling, he would listen to the clumping of heavy boots upstairs as her trunks were being brought in, and later on to the scurrying of her light footsteps as she began packing. Now and then her voice would seep down to him as she shrieked at Romola.

He felt tired, vaguely angry, despondent and lost. His rupture with Karl filled him with remorse. He had lost his friend, severed the last mooring to the past. Now his life assumed a quality of nebulous aimlessness. Perhaps he was a fool to go with Maria, perhaps their life together would be a wandering hell, as Karl had said. Perhaps . . . perhaps . . . He no longer knew how he felt or what he wanted. He was tired of thinking, trying to peer into the troubled mirror of the future. His head ached, and at times he pressed his knuckles against his temples as if he wanted to crush his skull. Oh, why couldn't he stop thinking? But he couldn't. No one could. You didn't give orders to your brain any more than you could stop your heart from beating. You could feel as you pleased, be sad or gay, in the throes of despair or on wings of rapture, but your body didn't care. The machinery of living went on. Your heart kept on beating, your lungs went on pumping air, and even after you were dead, your hair and nails went on growing. Your body outlived your mind.

On the day of Maria's farewell performance it started snowing in the afternoon. By evening the streets were white. On Theater Platz the opera house had become a structure of fantasy, the baroque handiwork of some giant pastry cook.

In the sitting-room of his suite a fire had been lit, and Maria, reclining on the sofa, was watching it in silence. He was looking at her, holding her hands in his own, but without pressure, only to feel the blended warmth of their flesh. They had said all there was to say. Everything had been agreed upon. He was to wait for her at the hotel, she would join him as soon as she could.

" But maybe to-night I come a little late," she said suddenly, without taking her gaze from the fire, as though her thoughts had turned into words of their own accord. " Many people come to say good-bye after the performance."

" I understand," he said. nodding quietly.

There was a long pause. Then, suddenly, she spoke again, her eyes still on the fire.

" Maybe you think I go away to-night like I do in England, no? So I leave Romola at the hotel and you wait with her."

He held his breath, stunned by the sharpness of her intuition. How complex was the simplest human being! . . . She wanted to let him know that she had been aware of his suspicions and was leaving a hostage in his hands.

Before he could say anything, she went on. " Also the statue of the Madonna."

He protested that he had never entertained any doubt. Gently he teased her for the crafty deviousness of her Italian mind. " A regular little Machiavelli, that's what you are," he said, leaning down to kiss her brow. " You think everyone's mind is like yours, full of clever little tricks."

She did not say anything and went on looking at the fire, her face salmon-coloured from the glow of the flames.

"I'll be glad to get away from this hotel," he declared after a while.

"We have much happiness in this hotel, no?" she murmured with tender reproach. "I never forget this hotel."

Under her breath she repeated, "Never."

There was a timid knock on the door. Romola announced that the carriage had arrived.

With supple languor Maria sat up, and Felix helped her rise from the sofa. She yawned and said to Romola, "You wait here with *il signore*."

Gallantly he wrapped her long sable cloak around her shoulders, insisted on fastening the bow knot. Together they walked to the door. Under the archway she rose on her toes to kiss his lips.

And suddenly she was gone, hurrying down the long red-carpeted corridor, in a waning rustle of white taffeta.

He returned to the sitting-room, sat down and stretched his legs to the fire. Perhaps he'd been wrong to think she wanted to run away? Perhaps it was he who was the Machiavelli?

He turned to Romola, who was still standing. "Sit down, Romola. We have a long wait before us." While the old woman took the other seat by the fire, he asked, "Have you finished packing?"

"Yes, Your Illustrious Lordship. Everything it is finished."

It was then that he noticed she was crying. At first she refused to explain her tears, took refuge in vague allusions to "much sadness in the heart."

"Aren't you glad to come with us to Paris?" he asked.

She shrugged. "To me every place is the same. Always hotel, always the opera." All at once she broke into a wailing sob. "Now we never go to Italy, never buy the fine house."

What was she talking about? What house? . . . In halting, gasping words she told him how Maria had promised her that some day they'd return to Italy, buy a fine villa near the sea and spend the rest of their lives together. To this end each time Maria received her salary, she would hand a sizeable part to Romola, who would hide it and save fiercely.

"Yesterday she asks the money and I do not give to her because it is our understanding I always keep it, even if she asks it. But she speaks to me with much anger and she says she beats me if I don't give the money. She shakes me like the tempest shakes the tree. So with death in the heart I give it to her."

"What did she want it for?"

"This, Your Illustrious Lordship, is the most remarkable part. She takes the money and goes away. When she comes back I ask, and she says she gives away for the little *bambini*." She let out a groan of pure desolation. " So now we never go back to Italy, never buy the fine house. Always on the road, always hotels, always opera. . . ."

The conversation died. After a while he saw that she was dozing, her chin resting on her chest.

" You'd better go upstairs and lie down," he said, gently shaking her.

He accompanied her to Maria's suite, saw the trunks locked and ready to go. Obediently Romola stretched out on the lounge chair and was asleep at once For a moment he watched her breathing the short rattling breath of the old, her wrinkled face peaceful, her brown, bony hands lying at her sides.

On tiptoe he walked out of the room, softly closing the door after him.

Less than an hour later, in silk-lined cape and full evening dress, he was entering the director's box at the opera. The performance was in progress. With appropriate expressions of dismay he apologised for his delay and took his place behind Frau von Wierling, using her generous, naked shoulders as a screen.

At once he spied Maria on the stage, dressed in fetching Spanish costume, saucily waving her little fan, flirting with blushing impudence behind the black lace of her mantilla. She was singing the part of Rosina in *Il Barbiere*, and never had she sung as she did to-night. Each one of her arias sent the spectators into galvanic transports with the King himself, resplendent in gala uniform, giving the signal of applause The performance over, a breath of madness seemed to rock the old opera house and the ovation soared to a paroxysm of enthusiasm. Abruptly the stately glittering audience turned into a shouting, stamping, unmanageable mob. In the red plush royal box, His Majesty stood, calling her name, clapping his hands.

Cautiously Felix remained behind the protective bulk of the director's wife. With beating heart he watched Maria return before the lowered curtain, her arms laden with flowers. She dropped a bowing curtsy to the King, blew kisses to her admirers. Tirelessly the public clamoured for her presence. As she was being recalled for the fifteenth time she lifted her head in the direction of the von Wierling box with such purposefulness that Felix felt she knew he was there. Her eyes searched his gaze as if to say, " You see, *carino*, I keep the promise." With a pang he remembered the happy hour when she had sworn to beat Jenny Lind's record. For a trembling instant they were alone among the delirious crowd.

At last the acclaim died out. People streamed out of the theatre.

" Isn't she wonderful?" exclaimed Herr von Wierling. " You

must come with us to her dressing-room. I've ordered champagne to be served. To-morrow, when she's gone and taken all our money with her, I'll cry over my ledgers, but to-night I don't want to think. Let's go and enjoy ourselves."

Politely Felix declined the invitation, pleading a sudden headache. He bent over Frau von Wierling's hand and quickly took his leave.

In the pale candlelight his hotel room seemed very dim and silent after the brightness and hubbub of a moment ago. He sat down on the bed, his elbows on his knees, listening to the sound of applause lingering in his ears. Yes, it had been a triumph. She was indeed a great artist . . . It would be hours before she could join him. By now her dressing-room must be crowded with ruffle-shirted gentlemen in evening clothes, officers in dashing uniforms, ladies in silk dresses and pearl necklaces. His Majesty would probably be there, toasting her health in champagne.

He saw her in his mind moving about among the heaps of flowers, smiling, chatting in her faulty and charming German, holding out her hand to be kissed. And he—he was here in this gloomy hotel room waiting for her. Perhaps that's what his new life would be. Waiting, always waiting. Other opera houses, other farewell performances, other dressing-room receptions. And he somewhere about, out of sight or standing unobtrusively in the background, waiting . . .

His lids felt heavy. The silence of the room was getting on his nerves. The flicker of the candle rippled his own enormous shadow on the wall like an eerie, airless breeze. Tiredly he ran his hand over his eyes. Why didn't she come? Why didn't those people leave her alone? They had heard her—must they also have her? Didn't they know she belonged to him . . . to no one else but him . . .?

An irresistible lassitude was blurring his thoughts, engulfing his mind. Unconsciously he stretched out on the bed and fell asleep.

He awoke with a start as if a bell were ringing in his ears. A sudden chilling fear clutched his heart. In its porcelain holder the candle had guttered down into a lumpy stub. It was still night, but late, very late, and Maria wasn't here . . . She had run away. No, this was impossible. Her luggage was still upstairs, he'd seen it. It couldn't have been removed without waking him. No, she hadn't gone. She had come, seen him asleep and gone upstairs to her room.

In a flash he was upstairs, knocking on her door. Gently at first, then louder, angrily rattling the knob and calling her name. No answer came and he ran down to the lobby.

"Where is she?" he shouted, shaking the night clerk out of his doze. "Where's the *signorina?*" The man blinked dazedly. "Damn you, where is she?"

At last the clerk came to life. "Your Excellency——"

"Never mind. Where is she? Didn't she come?"

"The *signorina*? . . . She's gone." He spoke as if everyone knew that except the haggard, wild-eyed man before him. "A few hours ago."

"What about her trunks?"

"She sent for them after you left for the theatre. Three men came——"

Felix didn't wait for details. He raced through the lobby, pushed open the bolts and ran into the snowy night. Across Theater Platz the opera house, spangled with lights a few hours ago, now stood black and lifeless like a charred ruin. His heart tolled in his chest as he groped his way towards the stage entrance. It, too, was dark and locked.

"Maria! . . . Maria! . . ." he called, pounding on the door with his fists. The name dissolved in the darkness, melted into the texture of the night.

For a long time he hammered on the door, shouting her name. A black, murderous anger surged through him. The slut! She'd tricked him again, run away again . . . How carefully she had pre-pared her escape! How she must've laughed when he was teasing her about her mind full of clever little tricks! She had guessed he'd come to the theatre, known he'd try to outwit her, make sure she wouldn't leave. And he'd given her her chance . . .

At last he gave up, walked back to the hotel, unaware of the snow piling up on his shoulders. Like some dazed automaton, he crossed the lobby again, climbed to his room and flung himself on the bed. His anger had exhausted itself. He felt too numb, too spent to grieve or even to focus his thoughts. She was gone . . .

"She's gone," he said aloud to himself. His voice was calm, impersonal, with only a faint undertone of incredulity. "She is gone . . ."

How simple and final it sounded. Simple and final as death . . . He sank into exhausted sleep.

It was late afternoon when he awoke again, and this time the pain did set in with lancing acuteness. His eyes fell on the small statue of the Virgin. Gently he took it in his trembling hands. How much it must have cost her to leave this behind . . . It meant so much to her. It was her talisman, the confidant of her most secret thoughts. She kissed it before every performance. She had left it to him as a reminder of her love.

Gradually his mind was taking fire. Once again she had sacri-ficed herself, but this time he wouldn't accept her sacrifice. There was a train in a few hours. He would be in Paris before she arrived, for she, too, like Cécile, was afraid of locomotives. He would give her back her little statue . . .

Already he was changing into travelling clothes, pulling the bell rope, asking for his bill, giving instructions for his luggage to be taken to the station. Impatience made him restless. He wouldn't wait another minute in this room.

He was about to leave the room when there was a knock on the door.

"Come in," he cried irritably.

A tubby well-dressed stranger in a puce double-breasted coat removed his beaver, revealing a pink bald pate.

"Yes?" asked Felix with a frown. "What is it?"

"Your servant, sir. Allow me to introduce myself. I am Baron von Stulenheim, of the Hanoverian Embassy. Here is my card. May I come in?"

"I am afraid I'll have to postpone the pleasure of your acquaintance. I am in a great hurry and, as you see, I am about to leave."

"It is my turn to be afraid you may have to postpone your departure," said the ambassador with unruffled graciousness. "You see, my dear Herr Mendelssohn, you are not leaving."

Before Felix could utter a word he went on in the same tone of bland courtesy. "May I suggest that we sit down? It is easier to converse on one's buttocks than on one's feet."

"Is this some sort of practical joke?" asked Felix through clenched teeth.

The baron flashed him a benevolent smile. "It does look like it, doesn't it? Let me assure you that it is not." His cold, beady eyes belied the merry dimples in his smooth-shaven rosy cheeks. "Do not trouble to pull the bell rope. No one will come, I've seen to it. Don't try to bolt either. Two hulky and very stupid men are on guard in the corridor. Of course," he added, letting himself down on a chair, "you could hurl yourself through the window, but I have too high an opinion of your common sense to believe you would attempt such a ludicrous escape. No woman is worth suicide. Again may I suggest you sit down? I feel embarrassed to be the only one comfortable."

"I will not sit down," Felix blurted out, "and I demand——"

"An explanation." The baron nodded with sympathetic understanding. He leaned back and crossed his pudgy hands over his sizeable paunch. "Here it is. I have in my pocket a letter signed by me demanding your immediate arrest. Would you care to look at it?"

"Arrest?" Felix's tone became threatening. "This farce has lasted too long already. I must ask you to leave at once, or——"

" Or what?" asked the visitor with infuriating calm. There was something granite-like in this roly-poly, baby-faced man. For a while he kept his beady eyes on Felix. When no reply came, he proceeded. " As I was saying I have a letter demanding your arrest."

" On what grounds?"

" The most terrible of all, the most difficult to disprove—suspicion."

In his placid tone of voice he enumerated his charges. Felix was suspected of revolutionary leanings and possible intent to foment political unrest in Hanover. As he expected, his words were greeted with hoots of derision and threats of reprisal. Patiently, with his debonair smile and his hands locked over his stomach, he let Felix vent his feelings.

Then he said, " You are absolutely right. These charges are unfounded and ridiculous. But coming from me they cannot be ignored—this is one of the few advantages of being an ambassador, and it will take quite some time—let's say three weeks at least—to prove them erroneous. You see, my dear sir, you have made the mistake of hobnobbing with well-known political agitators in the back room of a certain out-of-the-way tavern."

With stupor Felix realised the possible implications of his innocent visit to Wagner. If one musician could indulge in political activities, why not the other? Who would believe he had gone into a dingy tavern through a back door, given the password merely to discuss musical matters?

The baron had been silent to give him time to think. After a lengthy pause he resumed his discourse. " The trouble with revolutionists is that they always meet in cafés. And café proprietors are born informers. Those who aren't are induced to become such —or they cease being café proprietors."

A look at Felix told him that the stage of threats and recriminations was about over. Again he urged Felix to sit down and this time with success.

" Perhaps you are thinking of calling on His Majesty?" he proceeded with dulcet thoroughness. " Everyone knows his high regard for you. Unfortunately His Majesty, as you know, left this morning for Munich."

" All right," said Felix, admitting defeat. " What do you want?"

" Give me your word you won't try to leave Dresden for ten days and come to dinner with me. I am a lonely man and I'll greatly enjoy your company."

As Felix seemed to hesitate, the diplomat added with genuine, almost fatherly affection, " Believe me, my dear sir, you have no choice but to accept. As a last inducement, may I add that I have a superb cook and that I think you will enjoy your dinner."

The strange part of it—and it annoyed Felix to admit it—was that he did. Dinner was served in the ambassador's private dining-room, a dainty cheerful room in the rococo style of so many Dresden mansions. Tousled cupids cavorted on the ceiling in an azure and improbable sky while above the door graceful nymphs gambolled in an even more improbable forest. The table had been set before the fire and the lambent flames brought out ruby or amber sparkles from the wine goblets.

At first Felix had taken refuge in churlish untalkativeness, a surly attitude of prisoner under duress, but as the meal progressed he found it increasingly difficult to remain ungracious towards an amiable and courteous warden. Anger is a tiring emotion if maintained for long, and he was getting tired of being angry. The ambassador's superlative wines were having their mellowing effect. A sort of helpless resignation was stealing over him. In ten days Maria would still be in Paris . . .

"May I compliment Your Excellency on a most delicious dinner," he said as a peace offering.

The baron received this remark with a disarming, almost childlike pleasure. "You see, my dear sir, in an embassy such as this there is practically nothing to do and a swarm of people to do it. An Ambassador would go out of his mind if he did not invent some way to exercise his mind and occupy his leisure. I spend most of my waking hours in preparing my meals, then in digesting them."

He took an appreciative sip from his glass, held the wine an instant in his mouth and regretfully gulped it down.

"The pleasures of the table are the last," he went on with a wistful sigh, "but alas they are the only ones still permitted to me. Unlike love and other such youthful and turbulent emotions, they do not bring transient ecstasies or agonies of mind, but a sense of well-being and an inclination towards philosophy. All worthwhile philosophers from Plato to Montaigne have been gourmets."

In the course of the exquisite dinner Felix learned his host's views on various national cuisines, the correct way of tasting a vintage bouquet and the French people as a whole. "They have a flair for all the charming and useless things that make life enjoyable. They produce the finest wines, paint the nudest nudes, write beautiful poetry. If only they would stop producing Napoleons, having revolutions and hating their neighbours, they would be the most delightful people on earth."

Over the crêpe suzette the baron imparted the information that he was married. "My wife is an adorable woman with the mind of a child, the body of a grenadier and a voice like a bird's twitter. She never says anything worth listening to and says it in a thousand charming words. She has the heart of an angel and about as much wit. There was a time when we were passionately in love with each other. Marriage cured us both of this dangerous state of mind."

Again he raised his glass to his small mouth and took a thoughtful sip of champagne.

"In fact," he went on, dabbing his lips, "I'd say marriage is about the surest cure for love. If you cannot get a woman out of your mind, if the mere touch of her hand makes your heart capsize in your chest, if the sight of her bosom sends you into transports of carnal frenzy, I'd strongly advise you to marry her. You see, my dear friend, love is a disease of the optical nerve. It makes us see things that simply are not there. A few months, at most a few years, of marriage and the scales will fall from your eyes. You'll see her as she really is and be appalled at your own stupidity. By then she will have gone through the same process of gradual disappointment and you'll then be ready to talk sense. My wife does me the favour of taking frequent and protracted trips. When she returns she finds me the most devoted and attentive of husbands. A few days later I discover urgent reasons for me to report to my illustrious master, His Majesty the King of Hanover. We take tearful leave of each other, and I am off. In this way our marriage has a good chance to last our lifetime."

They were sitting by the fire, discoursing and enjoying their after-dinner brandy when Felix turned abruptly to the baron.

"Why did you do it?" he asked. "Why did you go to all this trouble to stop me from leaving Dresden?"

The ambassador pondered the question a moment. "Because of our common friend Karl Klingemann."

"I suspected he was behind all this."

"You were right. I know him well enough to trust that his reasons were good. When he did me the honour of explaining them to me I was certain of it."

"Why ten days?" There was no longer resentment but only curiosity in his voice.

"He felt that ten days of reflection would be enough to bring you back to your senses."

Felix rose, preparing to leave.

"When you write to him will you please tell him that I hate him, feel nothing but contempt for him and hope never to see him again."

He had tried to say it with appropriate feeling of hatefulness, but the jovial face of his friend danced before his eyes. His rancour was melting away. No, he didn't believe in sermons, he would act. The scoundrel . . .

"On second thoughts, I think I'll write him myself," he said.

"Yes. Why don't you?" The baron smiled as he escorted his prisoner to the door.

Felix spent the next few days alone. He had become used to solitude while waiting for Maria, but now it was a different kind of solitude. He wasn't waiting for anyone or for anything. He lived through time in suspension. A curious lethargy had descended upon him, the reaction from weeks of excessive feeling and emotional chaos. All desire to leave town had left him. He had given his word and found it easy to keep. He went out for long walks. He read. He even prayed. Not ardently, whisperingly. In the secret of his heart he was calling for help.

In the evenings he went to the embassy sensing that the baron was expecting him. "I've come to report to my jailer," he would say with a smile. "I understand this is the thing to do." The diplomat would protest he was not expecting him, but Felix would discover he had ordered the table set for two in anticipation of his visit.

Soon these evenings in the dainty rococo dining-room proved a genuine diversion for both of them. Baron von Stulenheim was an educated and intelligent man. Like most intelligent men he had started life as an idealist, turned cynic in his maturity and mellowed into a benign philosopher in his old age.

"One of the sadnesses of life," he mused wistfully one evening, as they were enjoying a superb pheasant *en gelantine,* "is that you have so much time to see yourself die. It is a melancholy sight, like following your own funeral. Just when you are beginning to know how to play the game of Life, you are too old to enjoy your knowledge or put it to use." He washed down a mouthful of pheasant with a velvety old wine and let out a sigh. "The truth is that you are a vertical corpse for many years before becoming a horizontal one. This is most depressing."

Felix tried to cheer him up, but the baron raised his hand. "Thank God, I still have a few vices to keep me company. The old age of virtuous people must be dreary indeed. Imagine yourself waiting for an eternity in a Christian Heaven. The mere thought of it makes me shudder. Mohammed had much more attractive ideas on this subject. The four virgin *houris* that await each believer on his entrance to Paradise were an idea of genius. What a welcoming committee! This is why, unlike Christians, his followers are, if I may put it this way, simply dying to die."

Usually, however, the rotund little man did not indulge in such despondent table talk. His spirits were high. He was full of pungent anecdotes about the people he had known and the places he had seen. The evenings went swiftly by.

One day he stopped in the middle of a sentence, looked at his guest over the rim of his glass and remarked, " I'm pleased to notice that you look much better."

His eyes softened in a wistful, understanding smile. For an instant his round ageless face reflected the secret longing of an old and lonely man for affection and confidence. " What have you been doing to-day, Felix?" he asked gently.

Felix shrugged, " Nothing much. Thinking mostly."

" A distinctly painful process, don't you think? That's why most people avoid it at all costs. And what, may I ask, have you been thinking about?"

Felix hesitated an instant, staring at his glass. " If you must know, I've been thinking about my wife," he said at last. " Wondering whether I've been fair to her."

" You miss her, don't you?"

Felix nodded, and the diplomat urged him on. " Go on, Felix. Confession is good for the soul. This is what the Catholics have so well understood. They have doubled the pleasure of sinning by giving an opportunity of speaking about it."

" Yes, I do miss her," said Felix very low. " I miss her terribly."

They didn't go further that evening. The baron sensed that Felix was undergoing a profound change, taking stock of himself, slowly fulfilling Karl's prediction that he would come to his senses. He felt that a bond of confidence had begun to form between them and did not want to strain it unduly. He launched into an oration on the complexities of the human heart and their distressing influences on human behaviour.

It was late when Felix returned to his hotel. In the silence of the wintry night Dresden had become a fairy town of moonlit snow and lunar stillness. In the purple-black sky stars blinked very bright, like frozen fireflies. The snow crackled softly under his boots as he crossed the deserted Theater Platz.

He entered his room, undressed mechanically and went to bed. But sleep wouldn't come. For hours he lay motionless, his hands crossed behind his head. Again his eyes fell on the little statue of the Virgin. It was now eight days since Maria had gone, without a word, leaving the pious figure as a token of her love. But had it really been love?

At last he dared face thoughts he had desperately avoided. Yes, it had been love. A certain kind of love . . . Burning, exhausting and in the end destructive. Only real love could stand the acid test of time, and they had only spent, all told, a few weeks. What turmoils, what conflicts in these few weeks! No, it wouldn't have lasted. It couldn't have lasted. Already her lovely face had begun to blur in his mind while that of Cécile became ever clearer. Passion was the hurricane of the heart. It shook, it tormented—but it did not last. They had merely desired each other and like numberless lovers before them, they had lied to themselves and called their desire love . . . But beyond desire there was another love. A love that was not only of the flesh but of the mind, heart and soul. Beyond desire, like a sun behind a veil of clouds, shone the true, everlasting love that fused two human beings into one not only for this life but for eternity . . .

Suddenly he was thinking of a Cécile he had almost forgotten. The prim Frankfurt maiden, the apprentice *Hausfrau* who diligently poked her finger into the cakes of cheese . . . The proper young débutante who maimed Mozart's Minuet . . . the bride who had brought him a pure heart and a pure body . . . The joyous bargain hunter of the Düsseldorf days who had hung the curtains in his white study overlooking the Rhine . . . The wife who had sat with his head on her lap in the Swiss meadow and heard the mysterious call to Leipzig . . .

And now he had lost her.

Baron von Stulenheim was not overly surprised when Felix burst into his office, a spacious green-brocaded room with a marble bust of some long-deceased beak-nosed princess on the marble mantelpiece. A flowery Aubusson carpet lay on the marquetry floor and faded pastel portraits hung on the walls.

"Come in, Felix, come in and sit down." The ambassador waved from behind his sumptuous desk. "I've just finished giving orders for to-night's dinner and I was wondering how on earth I was going to spend the rest of the day."

While talking, his sharp little eyes scanned Felix's tired face. "You look as though you hadn't slept a wink. What's the matter, my boy?" Cautiously he ventured, "Cécile?"

"I can't get her out of my mind." Felix nodded miserably.

"You won't," said the baron soberly, "simply because you love her." In the cold morning light he looked unusually pale, his round face a criss-crossing maze of fine wrinkles. With a start Felix realised that his friend was a very old man. "You've never been out of love," he went on. "Karl Klingemann told me so and he was right."

"Then how could I shamefully betray her as I did?" blurted Felix, lashing himself with his words.

The ambassador smiled his wise, indulgent smile. "Only the heart can betray, and your heart never did."

"What about Maria?" asked Felix angrily, his voice shaking with remorse. "What about her?"

"A mere incident, as we say in diplomacy," said the baron with a casual wave of his hand. "That's all she was. An unimportant episode, a fleeting indiscretion. The French aptly call it a *bagatelle*. You merely kissed the wrong woman and slept in the wrong bed for a few weeks. No great harm in that. Regret it, of course, regret it to your heart's content, but please don't forget it. It'll give you something pleasant to remember when you are an old man like me."

His hand went to his chin, and for a while he rubbed it in thoughtful ponderousness. "In fact, you should thank Providence for this brief adventure. First, it brought you a good deal of pleasure. Second, it made you realise something you were on the way to forget. That your wife is a fine woman and you love her very much. Sin has occasionally such beneficial results."

He leaned forward and rested his elbow on his desk. "What are you going to do when you leave Dresden?"

"I'm going back to Leipzig," said Felix with calm finality, "and perform the Passion."

"Passion?" exclaimed the baron. "What Passion? Please tell me about it."

When Felix finished telling the story of his discovery of the Passion and the opposition he had aroused over its performance, he paused and glanced at the ice-frosted window panes. "Frankly, I don't know how I'll go about it," he said. "I may well fail again. But I'm going to dedicate the rest of my life to this work. I could not live with myself if I did otherwise."

He looked up at the ambassador with tormented intensity. "Tell me, Your Excellency, what should I do about Cécile? Do you think she'll ever forgive me?"

The anguish in his voice brought a smile to the old man's eyes. "My dear friend, women love nothing better than to forgive. This trait is so strong in their nature that some of them attach themselves to scoundrels and incorrigible drunkards for the sheer pleasure of forgiving them indefinitely."

"What should I do?" cried Felix in a spasm of dismay. "Go to Frankfurt, tell her the truth and beg her to forgive me?"

The baron received this suggestion with noncommittal reserve. "It is always imprudent to tell the truth to a woman, especially one's wife. But then," he added with a sigh, "you are an impulsive, undiplomatic sort of man and you will tell her anyway. Do not, however, demean yourself and beg her forgiveness. Don't ever beg a woman for anything. It is undignified. Besides, being a creature of contrariness, she may refuse. Merely to do the contrary of what you're begging her to do."

He went on caressing his chin. "No. My suggestion would be to write her a long and affectionate letter, with few details and many protestations of love. She will see in it what she's been dying to see and rush back to you. Mark my word, she'll actually force her forgiveness upon you."

A short time later Felix returned to his hotel. He went into his sitting-room, sat down at the desk and began to write:

> My dearest,
>   With shame and despair I come to tell you how much I love and need and long for you. I've done wrong. I beg you to forgive me——

He paused. It was undignified to beg, the ambassador had warned. To the devil with dignity! . . . He would tell her the truth, the whole truth, and beg her to forgive him. Page after page he unburdened his heart, telling her his doubts, his longings, his regrets. All the things he had so often wanted to tell her and hadn't:

> To-day I am like a man waking up from a bad dream. I can't believe the things I've done, the words I've said. I don't know whether or not you will forgive me. If you don't, I shan't complain. I shall walk alone to the end of my journey. But one thing I shall do. I shall return to Leipzig and try again——

He stopped, startled by a rush of footsteps in the room. He turned around and saw Cécile in her travelling clothes, running to him.

" Please, Felix, forgive me . . . I didn't know, didn't understand."

For a while she couldn't say more and clutched him, sobbing in his arms like a child.

He tried to lift her face, ask her to forgive him, but she wouldn't listen and went on, her face pressed against his chest, in a mumble of words. " No, it wasn't you, it was me . . . It took our separation to make me see it. And also that I can't live without you . . . You'll see, darling, I'll be a good wife, the kind of wife you need. We'll never part again. Wherever you want to go we'll go, whatever you want to do we'll do together . . . This time, darling, it's really for better or worse. This time it's forever . . ."

BOOK THREE

The End of the Journey

Chapter 9

IT WAS a bright, snapping cold Sunday afternoon with the December sky as blue as in July and the snow on Saint Thomas's steeple sparkling like cut glass. On the floor of the study the sunshine made a slanting yellow rug. The house was very still and lifeless with the peculiar Sunday stillness, as if time did not move.

They sat quietly on the green baize sofa, side by side, almost touching. She, sewing, her face in repose, a matronly white shawl crossed over the brown bodice of her dress; he, in his smoking jacket, looking alternately at her and at the fire, still doubting the wonder of being at home with her.

"Do you realise we've been back four days already?" he said, breaking the silence.

She nodded without glancing at him, and after a pause, he went on, "I wish the children were here. I miss them."

"We'll get them as soon as this thing is over," she said, going on with her work. "They're better off there."

"And so perhaps would you be," he said, his voice low and apprehensive. "Are you absolutely sure, darling, you want to come with me into this brawl? It's going to be a long, hard fight, and there's no telling how it will end. I tried once and failed."

"But this time you have me." She bit her thread. "You're strong when you're two."

"And what if we fall flat on our faces?"

Placidly she threaded her needle. "We'll pick ourselves up and try somewhere else. Berlin, perhaps."

He shook his head. "No, Cilette. If we fail we'll be so tired we'll want to crawl into a hole and forget everything. I thought of Berlin for a while. It wouldn't do. The obstacles would be just as great, even greater. My family would be drawn into the fight. A lot of people would get hurt. No, darling, it's Leipzig or nothing."

"You're right," she said, resuming her sewing. "Here it is just

269

the two of us. We know the place and we still have a few friends."

"Not many, I'm afraid, and we'll probably lose those, too, before we're through."

He knew that for her the cruellest side of the coming dispute would be the loss of many friends. She had enjoyed being "popular," going on shopping tours with Elsa, the Mayor's wife, attending the meetings of the Ladies' Charitable Association.

"That's why," he went on, placing his hand on her knee, "you must be absolutely sure you want to come with me into this fight."

She didn't let him finish. "If you say that once again I'll—I won't love you any more," she threatened, her eyes full of love. "I told you I want to be with you in all this. Not just near you—with you. If we go down, well "—again there was the brave little shrug—" we'll go down with our guns blazing."

He grinned at the martial metaphor. "You make it sound like the Battle of Trafalgar."

She flared up. "A fight is a fight, and we're going to win this one. And I don't want you to laugh at me."

"I am not laughing at you," he protested, the lines at the corners of his eyes belying his words.

"Then what are you laughing at?"

"Nothing. I wasn't laughing at all . . . Come and sit down on my lap."

She rested her sewing on the sofa and sat down on his knees. "That's what Grandfather used to say, 'If the worst comes to the worst we'll go down with our guns blazing'."

In a flash he saw her a little girl in pigtails and pantalets listening to her grandfather, memorising the expression . . . "I don't think it'll come to that." He laughed openly this time. "I don't think we'll shoot one another. But it's going to be a bad fight, just the same, I can feel it."

"Perhaps it won't," she said with forced hope. "People have been very nice since we came back."

"It's true. Very nice."

He had been surprised by the warmth of his welcome and found that no one is so popular as a prodigal son. Hermann Schmidt had been beside himself with joy. "The place wasn't the same without you, Herr Direktor. And the orchestra didn't sound like when you conduct . . ." The members of the Gewandhaus Orchestra had risen in ovation on the first morning of rehearsal. But it was his students' tribute that had touched him most. On his desk he had found flowers and a thin velvet-lined case containing a conductor's baton. "Even the trustees seemed almost friendly," he said, "except Kruger, who still hates me as much as ever."

"He hates everybody. Elsa told me that one day at dinner he said all Jews and Catholics should be run out of Leipzig."

"I know. Christoph told me. He thinks Kruger is a little mad. There are people like that everywhere. But the trustees seemed very pleased to have me back. Christoph made one of his flowery little speeches." His chuckle ended in a sigh. "But I'm afraid it's going to change when it becomes known that I intend to go ahead with the Passion. They won't like that at all."

"It can't be helped. You can't please everybody."

"In fact," he said, the smile returning to his eyes, "there are people whose disapproval is a badge of distinction."

"Meanwhile, how are you going to go about it? What's the first thing you're going to do?"

He looked at her, struck once again by her grasp of realities. She might be the daughter of a saintly, day-dreaming pastor, but she was also the granddaughter of a hard-fisted, clear-thinking merchant prince . . . "To be frank, I don't exactly know," he confessed somewhat sheepishly. "The more I think about the Passion the more I am appalled at the difficulties of performance. We need an orchestra, soloists, singers, people to train them. It's going to be a colossal task."

"That's why we must discuss things and make plans, if we want to win."

"And not go down with our guns blazing." His teasing had no effect. She remained thoughtful, her brows knit in concentration. "I had an idea," he went on hesitantly. "I thought I might play some excerpts of the Passion to the members of the orchestra during recesses. We break rehearsals with little ten-minute recesses. I thought I'd play them the score of the Passion. As musicians they couldn't fail to see the beauty of this music. They might sign a petition asking the board to——"

He broke off, stopped by her emphatic head-shaking. "What's wrong with that?"

"Everything, my darling," she said, turning to him and running her fingers through his hair. "You forget those people are poor. They need their salaries to buy food, shoes for the children. You never think of money because you have it. The poor think of nothing else. They'd listen to your playing and think about their jobs. They'd never dare to go against the board if the Passion had been written by God Himself. All you'd accomplish would be to get the board against you right away."

"Perhaps you're right."

She *was* right, and he had to admit it with a mixture of delight and annoyance. Delight at finding her a realistic, cautious ally ;

annoyance at revealing himself as impractical and thoughtless.
" What do you suggest then?" he asked.

" I don't know yet." She spoke without looking at him. She
pulled back her hand from his hair and pressed a finger against her
chin, a familiar gesture of deep meditation with her. " For the
moment just go about your business. Be friendly with everybody.
Don't say a word about the Passion till after Monsieur Chopin's
concert."

" That's next week."

She nodded. " By then we'll think of something. Or something
will turn up."

" What makes you think it will?"

" Because God's with us."

She said it with devastating simplicity, and again he envied
her unquestioning faith. " Let's hope so," he said with wishful
fervour.

" It will, you'll see," she assured him with blissful confidence.
" Meanwhile I'd like to start doing something." She turned on him
the full impact of her blue eyes. " There must be something I
could do to help. I'd do anything."

He was moved by her eagerness, her self-abasement for a cause
which meant so little to her. " You're sweet," he said with tender
condescension, as one declines the eager but useless services of a
child. " I do appreciate your wanting to help, but I'm afraid——"

" I can read notes and I could copy music, couldn't I?" she
suggested, a little breathless at her daring. " You'd show me and
I'd be very careful and go very slowly at first."

How could he tell her that music copying was a craft, that she
would get lost in this galaxy of sharps and flats and minims and
quavers and semiquavers? . . . How could he resist the appeal of
those blue eyes, now so humble and pleading? . . . " It'd be
wonderful," he said, mustering all the enthusiasm at his command.
" Simply wonderful . . . There's going to be a lot of music to
copy. Parts for the singers, for the musicians. Reams and reams."

" Perhaps to-morrow before you leave for the Conservatorium
you can give me two or three pages, not too difficult, and when
you come back I'll show you what I've done."

In spite of himself some of her confidence broke through the
wall of his doubts. He was no longer alone. He had an ally now,
wise, laborious, devoted unto death . . . The first trembling step
was taken towards a performance of the Passion. Johann
Sebastian Bach had made his first convert . . .

" You know something?" he whispered in her ear. " I love
you."

She nestled against him in a gesture that was both defenceless and victorious. A gesture of helpless abandon that had behind it centuries of Woman's conquering surrender.

"By the way," he said later that evening, "I don't know if I ever told you, but before I went to Dresden, Schmidt asked me to give him one of the choruses of the Passion. He is president of some sort of vocal society. They have practised it during my absence, and next week he wants me to come and hear them."

"Can't I go, too?"

"You?"

"And why not?"

"Well——"

He lifted her in his arms. "I warn you it's a rather motley crew."

"The world is a motley crew, too, isn't it?"

She couldn't go any further, for his lips were upon hers.

Chopin's concert was a great success. The rumours about his affair with the famous novelist George Sand—a horrible lady who smoked, went about in men's clothes and wrote books about women's right to love—had created around him a delicious fragrance of sin and caused a rush to the ticket office. When he appeared on the Gewandhaus stage, melancholy and elegant in his ruffled shirt front and swallow-tail coat, he confirmed everyone's suspicions. Leipzig's buxom matrons heard in his music veiled undertones of caressing wickedness and responded with enthusiasm.

He began with the playing of his exquisite variations on Mozart's theme, *Là ci darem*, and proceeded with a number of his piano compositions. The audience fell under a spell. Listening to his whispering nocturnes middle-aged spinsters dreamed behind closed lids of romances they would never know and applauded with passion, their eyes moist with tears. The second part of the concert was dedicated to his Concerto in F minor. Felix was conducting the orchestra, and the two friends shared the ovation that greeted the end of the performance.

As an encore they played the two-piano duet Liszt had written on one of Felix's melodies.* Another pianoforte was rolled on to the stage. Once again, as in the dim and distant days in Chopin's Paris garret, they found themselves facing each other across the length of their enormous concert grands. Their eyes met and Chopin smiled his dolorous smile as memories of their joyous and foolish youth flashed through their minds.

After that there was nothing but the ripple of arpeggios, the racing of chromatics and the pounding of chords—the familiar

* The manuscript of this Liszt composition has been lost.

Lisztian pianistic frenzy that thrilled audiences as no other music did. The piece ended in a thunder of applause.

Since Chopin was leaving in the morning, Cécile excused herself after dinner, and the two men remained alone in the study, relaxing in their chairs, the tension of the concert gone. They spoke little, sensing the futility of words between them. It was enough to be together again. Silence doesn't weaken friendship.

After a while Chopin told Felix about the end of his affair with George Sand.

"It was horrible," he said in his muffled tone of voice. "When lovers break up after a long affair it seems they want to bury their love in mud."

"What are your plans?" asked Felix, to change his train of thought.

The Pole shrugged with Slavic fatalism. "I don't know. Things are very bad in Paris. There are rumours of revolution and many of my pupils have already fled abroad. I am about as poor as when I arrived. Miss Stirling, one of my few remaining students, has offered to arrange a series of private concerts in England. I'll probably go—if I have the strength."

After a long pause he added, "Have you noticed that in the end it's always the English who come to the rescue of distressed musicians?"

Felix nodded. "Even Beethoven had to beg an advance from the London Philharmonic."

"Strangest of all, he got it," Chopin said, and smiled.

Silence fell between them. A moment later they went upstairs to their rooms.

Next morning Felix escorted him to the stage. As the coach rumbled away on its way back to Paris, Chopin waved from the window, and suddenly Felix felt that the disappearing carriage was taking his friend out of his life.

He remained in low spirits that day, but Cécile cheered him up by showing him her work. With antlike patience and infinite care she tackled the colossal task of copying the Passion. To his surprise her work was excellent. His compliments brought a gleam of pleasure to her eyes. "I like copying music," she said. "It makes me feel useful."

That evening, as she was rising from the table, he seized her hand and drew her to him.

"No work to-night, darling. To-night we're going to hear Hermann Schmidt's singers. And don't blame me if you are shocked. I warned you they weren't your kind of people."

"We'll see."

It was a clear, cold night, and they decided to walk. Half an hour later they were tramping through snow on the outskirts of the town. Finally they stumbled upon it, a long brick structure, its windows yellow in the night, at the end of a large courtyard.

"I see why they've chosen this place," he remarked as they passed through the snow-crusted iron gate. "They can sing their lungs out without disturbing anyone."

In the workshop about fifty men and women, their faces softened in the amber glow of lanterns and coach lamps fastened to soot-blackened walls, were standing in small groups, waiting amidst a jumble of heavy iron tools, chains, pulleys, axle shafts and wheels of all sizes. Hermann Schmidt sat on the anvil, warming his back at the heap of ash-covered embers in the hooded forge, addressing a semi-circle of listeners while keeping an eye on the door for the arrival of the two distinguished guests. Conversations stopped and heads swivelled around as Cécile and Felix made their entrance.

Hermann rushed to greet them, his bushy eyebrows bobbing with excitement. "It's a great honour to welcome you at the Cecilia Vocal Society, Herr Direktor," he recited all in one breath, bowing up and down and making little nervous gestures with his hands. "You, too, Frau Mendelssohn."

With agitated solemnity he led them through the length of the shed to two ornate gilt-and-plush arm-chairs which had been set side by side on a small platform, looking strangely out of place in such surroundings. He fussed and fretted while Cécile and Felix sat down, insisted on relieving Felix of his hat and cape, which he handed with many admonitions to a tow-headed youngster who appeared to be his assistant. Meanwhile the singers had gathered their music and grouped around the home-made conductor's stand, the women standing in front of the men.

"With your permission we will now begin," said Hermann with punctilious protocol.

Feeling like royalty on display, the two guests smiled their assent, and Schmidt climbed on to the podium, a few feet in front of the platform. He rapped with his flute, which he used as a baton, and dramatically stretched out his arms. At his signal the choir of women's voices rose in the tide-like crescendo of the opening chorus, soon reinforced by the ensemble of the men's chesty baritones.

Felix held his breath. A prickling shudder coursed along his spine, and his hands gripped the arms of his chair, as slowly the Passion came to life. Even without the support of organ and orchestra, despite the singers' shortcomings and Schmidt's inexpert conducting, its splendour grew with each successive bar, swelling, spreading with the irresistibleness of a rising sun inflaming the whole morning sky. He had been right. This was the greatest music ever written, and he would give it to the world, if it cost him his life.

He felt Cécile's hand creeping over his own, and his heart throbbed with love. Yes, she was there, at his side, in this wheelwright's shed, among this alien crowd. Better than words her gesture told him she knew what he was thinking and she would be with him in his task, come what may, for better or for worse and forever, as she had said that day in Dresden when their love had been reborn.

During the interval they met the singers, shook the men's leathery, calloused hands, responded with smiles and compliments to their proud and embarrassed smiles. Hermann Schmidt, living his hour of glory, performed the introductions. This was Hans Muller, this was Otto Reinbeck and this was Karl Ritter. Most of them were factory workers, short-necked and broad of shoulders, with stubbly chins and deeply lined faces—tanners in the Grimma Gate dyeing plants, brewery vat men, or coopers or teamsters, masons with mortar-caked nails, livery-stable men faintly stinking of manure. Here and there a modest craftsman—watchmaker, doll painter, cabinetmaker. And occasionally a neighbourhood shopkeeper.

" And this is Franz Tanzen. He owns this place." Hermann Schmidt turned to a grinning colossus with curly grey hair, his eyes sparkling in a brick-coloured face.

" I've admired your beautiful carriages," lied Felix, feeling an instant sympathy for the bashful giant.

" And to-night we've admired your beautiful voice," Cécile chimed in, giving him one of her devastating smiles.

The wheelwright gulped, nodded shyly and shook hands with a back-throat mumble of words.

The women also belonged to the working class They wore shapeless and voluminous clothes, wood-soled shoes and heavy woollen scarfs. Most of them were middle-aged and wobbly-breasted with years of washing, scrubbing, water-pumping imprinted on their jowled faces. A few, however, were young and comely, apple-cheeked and flaxen-haired, dressed in home-made versions of the current fashions.

" And this "—Hermann cleared his throat and waved uneasily at a plump red-haired woman in her late thirties—" is Magdalena Klupp."

Felix looked at her with a frown of perplexity. He'd seen that woman somewhere, but where? . . . She was dressed with pitiful flamboyance in a rainbow of vivid and conflicting colours. Unlike the others who contented themselves with bashful grins and awkward nods she exuded worldliness and self-assurance.

"At your service, Madame," she minced, dropping a sketchy curtsy to Cécile.

Then, under the awe-struck gaze of her fellow members she raised her white and limp hand with almost unbearable graciousness to the level of Felix's lips and he had no choice but to place on it a perfunctory kiss.

"Magdalena has a fine voice," said Hermann hastily. "She is our soprano leader."

"That's because I'm a professional," she explained with ebullient good humour. "Have been practically all my life. Name any theatre you want—Lauenstedt, Magdeburg, Baden—makes no difference, I've played in it." She looked straight at Felix. "Many years ago I used to sing at the Friedrich Theatre in Berlin——"

The noisy smoke-filled tavern-theatre . . . Anna Skrumpnagel . . . and he, the spoiled young man-about-town in cashmere cravat and yellow gloves . . .

"That's fine, Magdalena," interrupted Schmidt, "but the Herr Direktor——"

Magdalena simply ignored him. "Of course it wasn't the same kind of singing, like what we've just done for you, because you see at the Friedrich they didn't care what you sang so long as you——"

Fiercely this time Schmidt cut short Magdalena's reminiscences with the remark that the Herr Direktor and his lady were tired and anxious to go home.

Again Felix congratulated the singers on their performance. "Some day the Passion will be heard in all the concert halls of the world, but you'll be able to say you were the first to sing it."

On their way home Cécile clung to Felix's arm and walked by his side in thoughtful silence. As they were approaching the house she suddenly declared, "I'll never forget this evening. Why, these people are nice!"

The wonder of discovery still rang in her voice. To her the trip to Tanzen's shed had been a daring expedition into some social Dark Africa. For the first time she had ventured out of her social circle, mingled on a "calling" basis so to speak, and not as the basket-bearing Lady Bountiful, with humble people and found them likeable and altogether human.

Gently he squeezed her arm. "Cilette, I'm going to tell you a great and profound secret. There is absolutely no difference between a poor man and a millionaire, except that only one has money."

Later, as they were undressing for the night, and she was methodically brushing her long blonde hair, she came out of her reverie and observed, "I thought their singing was very good." She glanced at him over her shoulder. "Didn't you?"

"I thought it was excellent. Much better than I had hoped. Of course they need training, especially the group leaders. They don't keep accurate time, they attack too late or too soon."

"Perhaps you could help them?" she said softly.

"I?"

"Yes. Couldn't you train them, teach them how to keep time?"

Her suggestion caught him unprepared. Whenever he had envisaged the performance of the Passion it had always been in terms of professional vocal ensembles painstakingly trained in regular rehearsal halls by professional chorus masters. Instinctively he had the indulgent, faintly snobbish, condescension of the expert for the amateur.

"Couldn't you?" she repeated, as she slipped into bed.

"I suppose so," he said uncertainly.

"It would be a beginning," she murmured. "It would be better than nothing."

But already objections were crowding his mind. "It would be extremely difficult work. These people can't read the music. I'd have to teach them the score, bar by bar. I'd need a piano. And where would I train them? I don't quite see myself playing the choirmaster in Tanzen's shed. Do you?"

She didn't answer, didn't press the point and remained silent even after he had come to bed. For a while they lay side by side, their heads on the same pillow. It was a new habit of theirs these last few minutes at the end of the day, face to face, lips almost touching. It was a moment of oneness, of absolute frankness, in which their eyes said the things too complex or fragile to be put into words. Sometimes their hands joined beneath the covers and from the quality of their touch—an imperceptible pressure, a caress of fingertips—they knew whether they were hungry for love or ready to sleep.

To-night she looked at him, her eyes clear and unblinking. "This girl Magdalena," she murmured suddenly, "you knew her in Berlin, didn't you? Was she your—mistress?" She forced the sinful word through her lips.

"Good God, no! I never saw her before."

"Then how does she happen to know you? Did she go a lot to the Friedrich Theatre?"

There was no escaping those eyes . . . "Well, you see, Karl

had a girl who worked there. Her name was Anna Skrumpnagel . . ."

"Was she pretty?"

He didn't remember, it was so long ago . . . And it meant nothing to him. Karl had begged him to keep an eye on her . . .

"Did you?"

Well, yes, in a manner of speaking . . . He had to, he owed it to Karl . . . It was the kind of service one renders to a friend when one is young. But absolutely innocent, nothing in it at all . . . A chore, in fact.

For a while she let him expatiate on the tediousness of his visits to the Friedrich Theatre, then she said quietly, "But she became your mistress, this Anna, didn't she?"

Dammit . . . There was no use being clever with her. A wife found out everything about a man's past if she wanted to . . .

"Yes," he muttered, lowering his lids.

"Did you love her?"

"Me?" Vigorous protestations. "Not at all, not in the——"

"Did she love you?"

"Of course not!" With much fervour in the denial. "Didn't care a pfennig about me. I tell you it was nothing . . . I heard she's now respectably married."

"And this Magdalena?"

There he was on solid ground, he could be both emphatic and truthful. Never! Never saw her before . . . "I give my solemn word of honour . . ."

She believed him. For a moment she remained silent, paying no heed to his proclamations of innocence.

"Then I think it's all right," she said softly under her breath. "She could come here, I suppose."

"Here? What for?"

"You're going to help those people, aren't you? You said they needed training."

"Here?"

"I'm afraid it's about the only place. You have a piano, and the trustees couldn't possibly object to what you're doing in your home."

His eyes clouded with tenderness. He knew what effort these words cost her. Home was the sanctum of privacy, the family shrine rarely opened and only to carefully selected friends . . . "You really wouldn't mind having those people here?"

She swallowed hard. "No. Really I wouldn't. They're nice when you get to know them."

They kissed each other good night. As she was about to fall asleep she turned to him, a drowsy smile in her half-shut eyes.

"I told you God was with us and something would turn up, didn't I?"

And so Felix began leading a double life. During the day he fulfilled his official duties. In the evening he coached the four group leaders of the Cecilia Vocal Society. Hermann Schmidt came also, as a matter of course. He made himself useful, stood at the piano and turned the pages while Felix played, repeated his instructions. During breaks Cécile brought in refreshments and an assortment of *Würste*, sausages and cheese cakes. Tactfully she kept Catherine, Gustav and the other servants out of sight to lower the social barriers and create an atmosphere of ease and informality. She poured large cups of coffee or steins of beer, asked the singers about their work, their families. Gradually Schmidt and Tanzen lost their bashfulness. Tanzen even began telling her about his four children and conceived for her a sentiment akin to adoration.

To Magdalena, these evenings in high society were the most exciting things that had happened to her since coming to Leipzig. Ignoring Schmidt's attempts to hush her up, she would recall her years on the stage, the numberless misfortunes—usually the bankruptcy of the manager or the jealousy of her colleagues—that had buffeted her career and, with buoyant complacence and mouth full, the men of exalted rank who had pursued her favours. "A blessed miracle it is," she would say, munching daintily on a sausage, "I didn't wind up a princess in one of those damned turreted castles."

Magdalena's prestige, however, stemmed from another source. She was the only known friend of Olga Becker, the Mayor's mistress. Olga was Leipzig's woman of mystery. Ostracised by the local aristocracy, rarely seen in the streets, she almost never left the small house behind the Saint Joseph Catholic Church which Muller had provided for her. Everyone knew and talked about her, but no one knew her. Magdalena did. "Why, me and Olga are practically sisters," she would say, slightly straining the truth.

She had met Olga in the course of her perennial wanderings, and somehow their friendship had endured. Like herself, Olga was an actress. They were living together in Wiesbaden, scrimping along, sharing their sauerkraut, when Christoph Muller had dropped from Heaven into Olga's life and solved forever the aching problem of a regular diet. When Olga had departed for Leipzig to become His Lordship's Madame de Pompadour, Magdalena had come with her. "She wanted me to live with her," she would expatiate, "and keep her company." But Magdalena was proud. Besides she was a dedicated artist while Olga, well . . . Sure, she had a nice little voice and a heart of gold. Would cut off her right arm to oblige a friend, but no real artistic talent, except after working hours. And so, although they saw each other constantly, Magdalena had kept her independence.

Strangely, Cécile grew rather fond of Magdalena Klupp. She was fascinated by this itinerant trouper as by a denizen of some other planet. The legend Magdalena had woven about herself and and come to believe concealed a loyal and generous nature, a brave acceptance of a hard and lonely life.

" How do you think she lives?" Cécile asked Felix one day at dinner.

" Hermann mentioned that she ekes out some sort of pittance by singing at weddings or in beer gardens during the summer or filling some extra part whenever a road company happens to land in Leipzig. I fear she has a pretty difficult time, the poor girl."

" She's made me realise how fortunate I've been. I'd like to help her. Do you think I could slip some money in an envelope and send it to her?"

" She would guess where it comes from and feel embarrassed. Some poor people are very touchy about money. I'll ask Schmidt to give her privately some regular salary on the grounds that, as a professional, she can't be expected to sing without remuneration. It'll save her pride."

Christmas was approaching. Already the Yuletide joyousness was bursting out in the displays of toys in shop windows, the carolling of poor students in the street. Every family was preparing for the coming of the *Jesuskind,* the Infant Jesus, on Christmas Eve in His tiny golden sleigh drawn by winged ponies.

" Have the trustees made any remark about your going to Tanzen's shed and training the singers?" Cécile asked one evening, after a coaching session.

" I don't think they know about it yet."

" Perhaps they won't say anything."

" Perhaps."

They had decided to go to Frankfurt for Christmas and spend the holidays there with the children. Lulled by the calm, Felix began forming cautious hopes. The singing in Tanzen's shed had greatly improved. Everyone was practising with diligence and tireless good will. Cécile, now assisted occasionally by Schmidt, had almost finished copying the Passion. Perhaps, after the Christmas holidays, some other vocal ensemble might be persuaded to join the Cecilia singers. With luck and hard work they might be ready for a performance on Palm Sunday, in April. Of course, there was still the question of the orchestra, but as Cécile said, God was with them and something would turn up. Perhaps he might be able to hire privately some of the Gewandhaus musicians. He himself would sit at the organ—if they could find an organ. If they couldn't, he would have one installed in the house. No, it wouldn't be perfect by any means, but it would be something. A modest victory, if not a triumph. People, on hearing the thrilling Passion music, would lose their antagonism. Other, better performances, would be arranged. Little by little the Passion would be heard.

" You know, Cilette," he said one Sunday afternoon as they were sitting by the fire on the green baize sofa, " it may not be as hard as I feared. I'm beginning to have hopes. We won't have to go down with our guns blazing, after all."

Two days later, with the swiftness and violence of summer storm, it struck.

By tradition the last board meeting before Christmas was an informal, cheerful affair. Serious business was set aside. After a brief review of the year's memorable Gewandhaus concerts, Christoph Muller would proceed to compliment everyone, tossing bouquets right and left: to the trustees for their civic spirit, to the Herr Direktor for his tireless diligence, to the members of the Gewandhaus Orchestra for their musicianship, to the Conservatorium professors and employees for their devotion to duty and finally to the invisible but ever-present people of Athens-on-the-Pleiss for their love of culture ; the whole performance ending in an emotional exchange of Christmas greetings and wishes for the New Year.

The moment Felix entered the board room, he felt that this was going to be no ordinary Christmas meeting. The trustees avoided him, some ostentatiously turning their backs on him as he took his place at the table. In his red damask chair Christoph Muller looked flushed and disgruntled. The atmosphere was one of impending catastrophe.

Nervously the chairman pounded his gavel and declared the meeting open.

" I am sure I express the unanimous opinion of this honourable board," he began in a grave, appropriately solemn tone of voice, " in saying that this year ends for us on a note of bitter disappointment." He rested his heavy eyes on Felix with a mixture of anger and discouragement. " Information has reached us that you intend to persist in your ill-inspired project of performing that music. Is this true?"

Felix remained silent for an instant. It had come . . . Deep in his heart he'd known it would some time. Well, let it come . . . " Yes, Your Lordship."

" And this," Muller went on with rising irritation, " in defiance of this board, the Church authorities and the disapproval of the entire population."

Felix looked slowly at the row of stony faces at the table. "Yes, Your Lordship," he said quietly.

"I, for one, intend to stop you," Kruger hissed, barely moving his lips, "and make it impossible for you to proceed with your plans."

"So will I," blurted out another trustee at the end of the table.

After that the meeting degenerated into a verbal free-for-all. Speaking at the same time several board members declared they would discharge any employee of theirs belonging to the Cecilia Vocal Society.

"That will stop you," one of them sneered. "You can't very well perform it by yourself."

All had a go at him, like hounds at a cornered stag. Where would he perform this precious masterpiece? And how would he find the necessary singers and musicians? Would he import an orchestra at his own expense and give a performance on Saint Thomas's Square? This sally was received with guffaws of derision. Muller, instead, pleaded with him. He appealed to his feelings, his standing in the community. How could he—he who had been called Saxony's First Citizen by the King—how could he engage in such a ridiculous venture, stir up animosity in a town that had befriended him?

"I'm sorry, Christoph," said Felix sadly. "It's something I have to do."

"Yes," Kruger rasped, "why don't you go back to your own town to launch your crusades. We don't like foreigners in Leipzig."

"Whom do you like, Herr Kruger?" asked Felix with cutting irony.

His words were lost in the hubbub of angry voices. Some trustees suggested that his sole interest in the matter was personal advertisement. "You don't deceive us with your talk about the beauties of this old music . . ." Others, self-appointed champions of the Church, decried his meddling in a question of sacred music.

"Christian sacred music," stressed Kruger, his pale eyes darting with venom.

Of course, there were righteous outcries at the social status and morals of the rabble with which he surrounded himself. Common labourers, brewery teamsters, scrub-women, a so-called actress . . . The idea of this prostitute singing the Passion was intolerable.

"Yet there was one at the foot of the Cross," Felix said over his shoulder.

But most of all they were outraged at his disregard of their prestige, his defiance of their authority. Hadn't they ruled against the performance of the Passion?

"Yes," Kruger shouted, leading the attack, "how do you dare to defy this board?"

"I'm not defying anybody," Felix snapped. "I'm doing something I want to do, and since I'm doing it on my own time and without taking a pfennig of the board's money, I don't see what you have to say about it."

"You'll find out." Kruger's eyes narrowed into slits of brimming vindictiveness. "I intend to ruin you, and compel you to leave this town."

"I know," Felix said with a contemptuous snort. "You already sent me a note to that effect. Anonymous of course."

Rage had turned Kruger's gaunt face a blotchy grey. He looked like a vituperative corpse. "I'll make you pay for your insults."

"When did I insult you?"

"When I made some remarks about your friend Chopin——"

"Oh, yes, I remember! . . . Well, I repeat them."

"You won then, but you won't win this time, Mendelssohn," Kruger said ominously. "You'll find out I am a very powerful man in this town." He was shaking, and the veins in his hollow temples stood out in throbbing relief.

"Go ahead," Felix said with icy scorn, "but stop talking or you'll have an attack."

Finally the chairman pounded his gavel and re-established a semblance of order.

"The whole incident is most regrettable." He spoke fast, like a man anxious to close a futile and acrimonious debate. "But since the Herr Direktor fulfils his functions and doesn't use any of the board's funds, the trustees cannot legally enforce any disciplinary measure and will therefore refrain from discussing this painful subject any further."

Again he slammed down his gavel and added hurriedly, "The meeting is adjourned."

When Felix returned home that evening he found Cécile hunched at his desk copying music. Hermann Schmidt on the opposite side was doing the same.

"Look, Felix," she cried happily. "We've almost finished. We'll be through by Christmas. Won't we, Herr Schmidt?"

She stopped abruptly. "What's wrong, darling?"

"The war is on," he said tonelessly. He ran his hand over his eyes in a gesture of weariness. "Really on, this time."

Gently he drew her to him. "My poor darling!" he murmured.

She led him to the sofa and made him sit down. He gave them an account of the meeting.

There was a long silence after he finished. For a while he said nothing, absently rubbing his chin.

"I'm afraid things are going to start happening soon," he said at last.

"What things?"

"I don't know, Cilette," he said, pulling her down at his side on the sofa. "But we must prepare for the worst. Kruger wants to ruin me."

"He's a very rich and powerful man," said Schmidt, sadly clucking his tongue, his jovial face a study in distress. "He owns the Grimma Gate Dyeing Works. If he learns that some of his men belong to the society, he'll discharge them. Sure as snow comes in winter. I'd better go and warn them not to come to the shed."

"That's right," nodded Felix. "Tell them not to come till they hear from me." As the old flute player was crossing to the door, he called after him. "Sorry to bring you all this trouble, Hermann. I'll try to make up for it somehow."

"You don't worry about me, Herr Direktor," said Hermann, with concern. "Go to bed and try to sleep. You look as if you could do with some rest."

With a sigh and an anxious shake of his head he hurried out of the study.

Neither Felix nor Cécile spoke after Hermann had gone. They sat, side by side, gazing unseeingly at the fire, each lost in his thoughts. After a while she cupped her hand over his, waiting for him to come out of his reverie.

At last he let out a sigh, ran his free hand through his hair and looked at her deep and long.

"This time it's going to be serious," he said calmly. "You see, darling, it's not only Kruger who is against me, but the whole board, including my good friend Christoph."

He turned to her, grasped her hand in both his own, and his tone became urgent. "Are you absolutely sure you want to be in this thing? It's going to be an ugly fight. I can feel it. You should've seen Kruger's eyes when he was talking to me. He reminded me of a snake. Why don't you go to Frankfurt, spend Christmas with the children?"

His words trailed off as she slowly shook her head. Nothing he could say would make her change her mind, he knew that. Again they fell into silence, both staring at the logs that glowed pink under their moss of ashes.

"What are we going to do?" she said suddenly in a faraway voice, without looking at him. "What are we going to do?"

"I don't know," he said, also without looking at her. "We'll first have to see what they're going to do. It won't be long." He ran the palms of his hands over his knees and swayed his torso a few times. " But I'll tell you something," he said with some abruptness. " I am almost glad it happened. It was too easy. And then I couldn't stand the deceit. Chatting with the trustees at the meetings, joking with Muller when I knew all the time I was doing something of which they disapproved. I am glad it's in the open. At least now we know where everybody stands. On one side there are the two of us and poor Hermann and Tanzen and a handful of amateur singers. On the other—well, on the other there's everybody else." He gave a brave, unconvincing little chuckle. " Not very encouraging, is it?"

She turned to him. " But don't forget God is with us," she said quietly.

Again he was startled by her indomitable faith. As long as she was at his side there would be hope . . .

He slipped his arm around her shoulders. " You'd better have a talk with Him," he whispered in her ear. " We're going to need Him."

Next morning when he came down into the dining-room for breakfast he saw the newspaper neatly folded over his napkin as usual. He rustled it open, cheerfully greeted Gustav. Then his eyes fell on a two-column headline on the first page: " A Blasphemous Christmas."

The article was short and well written. It told how a rabble of amateur singers calling themselves the Cecilia Vocal Society met in a wheelwright's shed at night to profane the spirit of Christmas by bellowing an old piece of Church music, under the personal direction of a certain well-known musical personality of the town, born himself in a non-Christian faith. It ended on an ominous note: " We hope that the municipal authorities will promptly put an end to this sacrilege."

" Don't you feel well, Master Felix?" asked Gustav, noticing that Felix had turned white.

Felix looked at the old servant, and a softness came to his eyes. " Gustav, do you remember when something went wrong at the bank and Father would come home grumbling, ' By Moses, we are in trouble '?"

" Yes, Master Felix."

" Well, now it's my turn. For your information, we are in trouble."

It had stopped snowing, and he decided to walk to the Conservatorium. The doorman at the Gewandhaus Building gave him a chilly nod instead of his usual expansive " Good morning, Herr

Direktor." Even the professors he met in the corridors of the Conservatorium hastened their steps at the sight of him and hurriedly ducked into their classes. Only his composition students had not changed. If anything, their eyes shone with greater affection, as if to reassure him of their loyalty.

He returned home early that afternoon and found Cécile in the study, sobbing.

"The landlord came to see me," she said.

"About the singing?"

She nodded. "That—and something else."

The "something else" concerned the sort of people who frequented the house, especially at night. Common labourers, undesirable women—one of them an actress . . . There was a clause in the lease forbidding the entertainment of immoral persons in the house . . .

He listened, choked with remorse, a muscle twitching in his jaw. That also had come . . . For years she had pleaded with him to buy the house. But no, he had been mulish about it. He hadn't wanted to own a house in Leipzig because he'd still hoped to move to Berlin. Well, now he had no home, he couldn't receive his friends. This was the end of the coaching sessions.

"What is he going to do?" he asked. "Dispossess us?"

"No. But we'll have to be careful."

"What did you tell him?"

She looked at him, her lovely face misshapen by tears. "That we wouldn't have the singers any more. What else could I say?"

"Nothing, of course," he admitted dolefully. "You had no choice. And it's all my fault. Forgive me, darling."

He moved closer to her and she to him as if they were attracted to each other by some mysterious magnet.

"When it's all over," she said in a small coaxing voice, "do you think we could buy this house? I love it so . . . and the garden is so nice for the children."

"When it's all over I'm going to take up gardening and I'll stay in all day and never let you out of my sight." His lips brushed her cheek. "Have you noticed we always seem to be in each other's arms these days?"

She nodded without speaking.

There was still another little piece of bad news, but she waited till they were in bed, their faces on the same pillow, to tell it to him.

"This afternoon, before the landlord came, I went to the Ladies' Association," she said in a barely audible whisper. "They almost shunned me, except Elsa Muller. They had read the article in the paper and passed a resolution not to give any Christmas basket to families belonging to the Cecilia Society."

"What did you do?" he asked calmly.

"I told them they made me feel ashamed to be a Christian and I resigned."

Normally an announcement of this importance would have been discussed at great length; now they didn't even want to comment upon it. He merely said, "You did right," and they went on looking into each other's eyes, feeling their oneness, their breaths mingling in the short span between their lips.

"What are we going to do, Felix?" she asked, barely forming the words.

"I just don't know, darling." A feeble smile trembled at the corners of his mouth. "To-morrow is Sunday, and we'll have another of our strategy meetings. Perhaps something will turn up, as you say." The smile spread over his face, reached his eyes. "We always seem to be doing our thinking on Sunday—have you noticed?"

"It's a good day, it's God's day."

Next afternoon they did hold a strategy meeting, but not the kind they had anticipated.

"Well, let's have our meeting," he announced, smacking his lips and leaning aside to rest his brandy glass on the small round table. "I've been racking my brain and the more I think the more hopeless it gets."

With a vestige of his old bantering ways, he added, "We are in a hole, my darling, and have about as much chance to perform the Passion by Palm Sunday as to grow wheat in my hat."

"Why Palm Sunday?"

"Because that's the service for which it was written. You see, darling, in the old days almost every organist wrote at least one or two Passions. There must be as many of them as there are paintings of the cruxifixion. When I was studying music with Zelter he made me study the Passion of Hobrecht and that of Joachim von Burgk."

She was listening attentively, her eyes fastened on him full of love and awe of his knowledge. He found a strange and new pleasure in speaking about music to her. It was one of the things he had dreamed about. And so he went on, warming up to his subject, "There have been all kinds of Passion music: choral Passion, motet Passion, scenic Passion, oratorio Passion. There are even different Passions for the various days of the Holy Week."

He was extolling the merits of the Passion by Johann Walther, who had written the first Lutheran Passion, when Gustav knocked on the door and announced that Schmidt and Tanzen were waiting outside in the hallway.

"What can they want?" he asked, looking apprehensively at Cécile. Only a matter of the utmost gravity would prompt them to call on him uninvited and on Sunday.

"Ask them in," he said to Gustav.

The two men entered, the wheelwright towering over the flute player, their faces set in lines of dismay.

"Excuse us for calling on you like this, Herr Direktor," Schmidt began. "We come from the City Hall. His Lordship sent for us."

"On a Sunday?"

Both men nodded in unison.

"He received us right away," Schmidt went on, "and for a moment he just looked at us as if we were criminals. Then he banged his fist on his desk and said the whole thing was our fault, that the city was up in arms and he had had enough of it. He was so mad he couldn't stay on his chair and started pacing up and down, talking louder and louder. First he turned to Franz and he said he would have his guild licence revoked so that he couldn't work. Then he came to me, waggled his finger in my face and said I must disband the Cecilia Society at once or he would fine us a thousand thalers for illegal gathering. He walked again and came back to me, and I swear I've never seen anyone so angry in my life. He told me I was a disgrace to my profession, a disgrace to the Gewandhaus Orchestra and he was giving me two choices. Resign now or wait till the next board meeting and be discharged. So I resigned."

He had spoken without a break, hardly taking time to breathe, and Felix and Cécile had been too stunned by the news to notice that the two men were still standing.

"Please be seated," said Cécile, who was the first to recover. Without hesitation she walked to the brandy decanter and filled two glasses. "Here," she said, handing each one a glass. "Drink this. You need it."

Felix's eyes followed Schmidt as the old man lowered himself into a chair.

"So you're no longer with the Gewandhaus?" he asked absently, not as a question but as the reiteration of an unbelievable fact.

"That's right, Herr Direktor. I won't play the flute any more."

Felix looked at him unseeingly through eyes remote with thought. So, that's how they were going to fight . . . Starve a working man, dismiss Schmidt . . . Like a lackey, after twenty-nine years of devoted and competent service . . . Schmidt the dean of

B.D.   K the Gewandhaus Orchestra . . . Who had travelled to Düsseldorf to watch him conduct the Rhine Festival . . . Who had sung his praises to the board . . . His friend . . .

"It's all right," Schmidt went on with a brave unconvincing shrug. His flabby face twisted into a grimace, piteous and comical, as he fought back the tears. "I was planning to retire next year, anyway. Gertrude and I, we'd been talking about moving to the farm for good."

"I think it's a shame," Cécile said with ladylike violence.

Felix did not make any comment. He went on nibbling his underlip, his eyes lifeless and unblinking. He seemed to have withdrawn into some deep and compelling meditation and forgotten the people in the room.

For a while no one spoke.

All at once, life returned to him. "Hermann," he said sharply, "how far is your farm from the city?"

"Four and a half miles, Herr Direktor. About forty minutes from Saint Thomas's Square, depending on what kind of a horse——"

"Where do you pay your taxes? . . . Leipzig?"

"No, Herr Direktor. At the Reudnitz City Hall."

"Reudnitz?" he repeated, his face tense, his tone urgent. "You're sure?"

"Of course, I'm sure," retorted Schmidt in a huff. "After all, I——"

"Hallelujah!" Felix gave a sigh of relief. "Then your farm is outside the city limits, and Muller can't do anything." He felt their questioning gaze, caught a glimpse of Cécile watching him with lips parted, her bosom heaving with excitement, but didn't take time to explain. "Would you be willing to lease me the farm for a few months?"

"Lease it! What for, Herr Direktor?" Astonishment shot his curled eyebrows midway up his forehead.

"We'll need it for rehearsals, and it'll be wiser to have the place in my name. I'll explain later." Leaving the flautist to his conjectures, he turned to the wheelwright. "Tell me, Franz, how long would it take you to build me a coach?"

"Depends on what kind, Herr Direktor," Tanzen said, slowly stirring himself out of his thoughts.

"A big travelling coach."

"I'd say four months. Perhaps five." He droned the words with pathetic, almost childlike despondency of very strong men suddenly helpless. "But without my guild licence I couldn't even build you a wheelbarrow."

"You couldn't in Leipzig, but you could in Reudnitz," said

Felix quickly. "If you moved to the farm, turned one of the sheds into——"

He stopped, seeing the veil of incomprehension in Tanzen's eyes.

Slowly he repeated, "If you moved your equipment and your tools to the farm, turned one of the sheds into a workshop, you could build me a coach, couldn't you?"

For a while the wheelwright's eyebrows knitted in laboured mulling. Then abruptly comprehension came, breaking into a flashing smile on his red leathery face.

"Of course I could!" he exclaimed, slamming his enormous hand on his leg. Life was rushing back into him. His blue eyes were sparkling with new hope. "I could build you anything, any kind of coach you want."

"Good. Come early in the morning. With Hermann," he added, glancing over his shoulder at the still-bemused flautist.

With a wave he dismissed the matter and leaned forward, his gaze encompassing the two men. "Now listen to me." His voice lowered to a confidential rumble. "This is what I want you to do."

Cécile was watching him, bewildered by his talk and even more by his manner. This was a new man, a man she didn't know . . . Soft-spoken, yet brisk and commanding. Giving orders, telling people what to do, expecting to be obeyed and—she saw it in the way Schmidt and Tanzen were looking at him, nodding to him— being obeyed . . . It was strange and startling, this discovery of an entirely unsuspected trait in a man you thought you knew completely. Like finding a secret stairway in your home . . .

His tenderness, his sensuality, his moodiness she knew. Also his fits of teasing and bantering, which she used to regard as signs of immaturity and shallow-mindedness because all the important grown-ups she'd known had been dull and pompous. His fabulous capacity for work, his deep kindness, his pride and complete lack of vanity . . . But this commanding tone, this sudden affirmation of authority—that was new. Perhaps it took a terrible shock to uncover the core of a man? . . . If this were true then she was glad he'd been shocked, for she liked this new order-giving husband of hers, this Felix in a fighting mood. Virile and strong and unafraid.

With an effort she pulled herself out of her musings as she heard him say, "Is this all clear?"

The two men nodded. "Yes, Herr Direktor."

They got up, and Schmidt said, still a little groggy but ready to bounce into action, "I feel much better than when we came in. Don't you, Franz?"

Tanzen didn't say anything, but his grin was eloquent. He too had regained hope.

With the punctilious courtesy of the poor, the two men thanked Cécile for the glass of brandy, gingerly shook her hand and took their leave. Felix escorted them to the door.

" As I was telling you, there are various kinds of Passions," he said as he returned to the study. " Those written according to the Saint Matthew text were always played on Palm Sundays. The Passion by Johann Sebastian Bach is one of them. Have you noticed how he wrote the Saint Matthew text in red ink as a sign of reverence?"

He resumed his seat by the fire and with studied casualness filled himself another glass of brandy. " The Passions written on Saint Mark's text were performed on Tuesdays of Holy Week. On Wednesdays, the Passions according to Saint Luke. And on Good Friday——"

" Aren't you going to tell me what you said to them?" she interrupted in a small injured voice, coming to sit at his side. " What's all this about renting the farm and ordering a travelling coach?"

He looked at her, a pensive smile in his brown eyes.

" When those two men came in they were two very frightened people," he said quietly. " They'd just lived through what for them must have been a harrowing, shattering experience. Imagine Muller sending for them, shouting at them, wagging his finger in their faces and taking their livelihood away . . . Can you realise what it meant to them? Schmidt may have a few thalers, but Tanzen has only his work. And so they were panic-stricken, didn't know where to turn or what to do, and they turned to us, their only friends who could help them. I just couldn't let them go empty-handed, without some sort of hope."

" You were right."

" And you know what happened? I was so angry at Muller for taking revenge on those two poor defenceless people that I decided to go ahead with a plan I'd entertained at one time and discarded."

" Why?"

" Many reasons. For one thing, it is melodramatic and I don't like melodrama. It has many weaknesses and it is full of risks. And in the end there isn't the slightest guarantee that it will work. Incidentally, it will also be very expensive."

" What is it?"

Gently he pulled her to him. " Don't ask me to explain it to you now. You would point out all the things that are wrong with it, and I'd probably get discouraged before we started. It's a pretty desperate plan, but then we are in a pretty desperate situation."

"At least it's a plan," she said. "I tried to find a way out and I couldn't think of anything."

"Well—we're going to try this one," he said with a rueful sigh. "It's going to bring many changes and upset our whole life." He felt her stiffen and hugged her more tightly. "I'm afraid it can't be helped. Darling, we're going to move to Schmidt's farm."

She gasped and her eyes filled with tears.

"Forgive me, darling," he murmured, his voice furry with sadness, "but we've got to do it. You'll see, it won't be so bad . . . The Schmidts are fine people."

They didn't speak for a moment then she said, "When are we moving?"

He hesitated before striking the other blow. "During the Christmas holidays."

He felt her body tremble against his. "I know you're thinking of the children. It will be hard spending Christmas away from them. But try to think of the kind of Christmas Schmidt and Tanzen would have had."

She wiped her tears with her wrists, even tried to smile. "You're right. To-morrow I'll start packing."

Much later that evening, as they lay quiet and thoughtful with their heads on the same pillow, gazing at each other, savouring the moment they called "the last-minute summing-up," he asked in a whisper, "Cilette, do you still want to come with me into this thing?"

She looked at him, then slowly lowered her lids. And her gesture was one of sadness and surrender—the lowering of a human being's flag . . . Yes, she would follow him wherever he went, wherever he wanted, happy that he was a good man but not caring much any more, for now she no longer could help herself and would follow him anyway, right or wrong, anywhere . . .

In a rush of fear, tenderness and accepted defeat she flung herself into his arms, kissing his lips, pressing her hungry flesh against his. And that night they too, like so many before and after them, found refuge from their troubled thoughts in the reassurance of their caresses.

Chapter 10

THEY SPENT a melancholy but not unhappy Christmas at the farm, where they had moved three days before.

Cécile helped Gertrude, Schmidt's wife, with the setting of the table. And, indeed, it looked inviting and festive with its decorations of holly and red berries, its pewter candlesticks and hand-painted faïence plates. They were six at dinner that night—if Gertrude, who kept running back to her stove, could be counted as a guest. Felix presided, smiling now and then at Cécile across the table. Franz Tanzen also was there, uncomfortable in a stiff collar and Sunday clothes. He, too, had moved to the farm, bringing with him most of his equipment, and installed a combination blacksmith and wheelwright shop in one of the farm's empty barns. At Cécile's suggestion Magdalena Klupp, who had no family, had been invited. She added considerably to the allure of the occasion by the flashing elegance of her attire—a golden-frogged green velvet court dress she had worn as Anne Boleyn's faithful lady-in-waiting and which she had kept as a memento of her artistic triumph and as security for her unpaid salary when the manager had absconded with the troupe's funds.

Although the guests did their best and the conversation was animated, there was too much underlying apprehension of the future in everyone's mind for genuine jollity. Cécile was thinking of her children in Frankfurt and her Leipzig home, always so bright and cheerful at this time of the year, now lifeless and dark under its snow-laden roof. Tanzen recalled his workshop, now closed; Schmidt, his long years with the Gewandhaus Orchestra. Felix thought of the strange adventure he had embarked upon. All felt they had burned their bridges, and this Christmas dinner marked for them the end of a period in their lives and the beginning of a new hazardous one.

" Yesterday I went to Lindenau," said Schmidt, as the dinner was coming to an end. " They've got a nice choral society there and I told them your proposition."

" What did they say?" asked Felix.

" They were very much interested. You see, Herr Direktor, they've never been paid for singing and they just couldn't believe it when I told them you were offering professional musicians' wages. That appealed to them, because there's a good deal of poverty in Lindenau right now."

Cécile glanced at Felix across the table. So, that's why he'd said it would cost a lot of money . . . He was trying to raise a chorus out of the various vocal ensembles in Leipzig's vicinity and was using the simplest, oldest, most convincing argument in the world— money. His own.

" Naturally," Schmidt went on, " some were scared. They said, " Look what happened to you and Tanzen. You lost your job and they've shut his shop, and now neither of you can work, and maybe the same will happen to us."

" So what did you tell them?"

" I explained to them nothing like that could happen to them because they didn't live in Leipzig and His Lordship couldn't do a damn' thing."

" *Ach,* such swearing in this house!" wailed Frau Schmidt from the stove. " And on Christmas night!"

The old flautist assumed a brief expression of contrition and proceeded, " Finally they said some of them would come to our next rehearsal and then decide if their group would join."

" Good. At least they didn't turn us down."

" I think they'll come, Herr Direktor, and that'll give us seventy-five singers. Good ones too."

" Let's hope so."

Already Magdalena, who had been silent too long, was taking the floor. " Me, too, I've been to see some of my sopranos. Naturally there were some that were scared——"

" Just like those people in Lindenau I was telling about."

Anne Boleyn's lady-in-waiting gave Schmidt a withering frown. " Is it you that's talking or is it me?"

He crumpled under her gaze, and with a toss of her red hair she went on. " As I was saying, there were some that were scared because they'd heard rumours they'd be attacked, or their taxes would be raised, or their husbands would lose their jobs if they came here. So I asked them if it was turnip juice they had instead of blood and said probably their mothers had been leeches judging by the fine strong backbones they had, and in this way I answered all their objections. In the end they said they were sorry and would come."

She accompanied her last words with a gesture that seemed to deliver her whole flock of erring sopranos right there on the dinner table. There was a ripple of amusement at Magdalena's missionary technique.

" Fine work," Felix said. " But I'm afraid those threats are real and you'd better be careful. I don't like your living alone in Leipzig and it might be safer for you to live here for a while."

" Plenty of room," suggested Schmidt invitingly, trying to regain her good graces.

Magdalena wouldn't hear of it. " How do you think it'd look if I stayed here when I keep telling them there's nothing to be scared about?"

" Perhaps you're right," admitted Felix, " but be prudent."

" What can they do to me, Herr Direktor? They can't raise my taxes, since I've got nothing. I can't lose my job because I haven't even got one. Not even a husband they can take it out on, for the reason I am what you call an unmarried *Fräulein*. And they won't beat me up because everybody knows me in the Saint Joseph district where I live and they know I am a friend of the Chief Marshal and practically a sister to Olga."

" All right," nodded Felix, " but be careful."

For a while they lingered at the table in a mood of timid hope, making plans, discussing various problems. Many people might have to live at the farm. Thank God there was plenty of space in the various barns, stables and haylofts scattered over the farm. It was decided that the rehearsals would be held in the main barn across the courtyard. Schmidt and Tanzen promised to have it ready in a day or two. Then Schmidt said that a number of the neighbourhood farmers and their wives had offered their services but would prefer to rehearse in the afternoon.

" You see, Herr Direktor, they aren't like us city people. They're used to going to bed by sundown. Come six o'clock and they're sleepy. So I thought maybe with your permission you might let me train them, since you'll be in Leipzig all day."

Felix nodded absently. Poor Hermann, he missed the evenings in Tanzen's shop. He missed his podium, his baton . . . The enormity and difficulty of the task became more apparent every hour. How could a competent vocal ensemble be fused from all these various elements? And what about an orchestra, soloists, an organ? What about the management, the administrative details, the bookkeeping? No one around was capable of attending to these things. Tanzen, Schmidt, Magdalena—they were full of courage and good will. But courage and good will weren't enough.

Wearily he ran his hand over his eyes, and across the table, Cécile understood the meaning of his gesture.

" You're worried, aren't you, darling?" she asked later that evening.

They had excused themselves, left the others discussing and planning among themselves and had repaired to their bedroom— the same ceiling-beamed oak-floored room he had slept in on his previous visit to the farm.

" Yes," he said in a low voice, sitting down on the rustic straw-bottomed chair. "Worried—and a little frightened. No, not by the rumours, the absurd things they say about me in town. I've been expecting that. What frightens me is the details, the complexities, the thousand and one little problems that are bound to arise every day. I just don't know how I'll be able to do all the things I shall have to do and still drive every morning to Leipzig, hold my classes at the Conservatorium, rehearse the orchestra, attend the board meetings, conduct the regular concerts."

He looked at her with pleading anguish. "Darling, why don't you let me resign? Then I could give all my time here, at the farm."

She crouched on the floor at his feet, her face raised to him. "Please don't Felix. I know it's too much for one person, but so long as you are director of the Conservatorium and conductor of the Gewandhaus you are an important official. They can't ignore you. Your personal prestige gives weight to the cause you're fighting for. If you resign, you lose all that. You become a troublemaker, a rabble rouser."

He saw the soundness of her argument. "As usual you're right," he said gently, running his hand over her blonde head.

"Have faith, darling," she murmured. "Please have faith. You'll see——"

"I know." He smiled ruefully. "Something will turn up. God is with us and therefore everything's going to be all right."

"It'll be all right," she insisted in whispered vehemence. "You must believe it, darling."

"I'd like to, but frankly if the Passion is performed on Palm Sunday it'll be the greatest miracle since Joshua stopped the sun."

She caught his look of dubiousness. "I know how you feel. Sometimes it looks as if there just were no hope and God didn't pay attention, and you don't know where to turn and feel lost inside. But He's watching all the time and in the end——"

"Something turns up." For an instant he smiled down into her blue eyes. "Darling, you have the faith that moves mountains. And we're going to need all of it."

They went on looking at each other in silence, feeling their love in the stillness of the candle-lit room.

"*Fröhliche Weihnachten*, dearest," he murmured.

"Merry Christmas, my love."

Strangely, something did turn up the following afternoon in the shape of a tall elderly gentleman in a well-cut double-breasted grey coat. He introduced himself to Hermann as Herr Jakob Meyer Howlitz and demanded to see the Herr Direktor.

" I am glad to see you again, Herr Howlitz," said Felix, greeting the visitor at the door of his " office."

This was a rather long and narrow room. It opened on the hallway and through an inner door into the bedroom. Like the bedroom it was low of ceiling, bare-floored and white-walled, with a small deeply-recessed window at one end. Felix had transformed it into a semblance of an office by the presence of a desk which had been brought in from the Leipzig house, together with his small pianoforte, his father's portrait and one of Cécile's contrived water-colours.

" Even," he went on, waving the banker to an easy-chair which also came from Leipzig, " if you've driven all this way to tell me that the Leipzig Jewish community is furious at me and invoking Jehovah's wrath upon my head."

For an instant the old gentleman watched him in silence, his slender bony hands folded over the gold knob of his cane. At last a faint approving smile skidded from the corners of his eyes down his lean clean-shaven cheeks. " To be frank, you aren't exactly popular in the Jewish district at the moment."

" I am not exactly popular with the Christians either, if this can be any consolation to them. In fact, I don't seem to be popular with anyone."

" You are with me," said the banker slowly and distinctly.

" What did you say?"

" I said you're quite popular with me." Again the smile rippled down his cheeks. " I am here strictly on my own initiative this time. As a matter of fact, I am prepared to be severely criticised for what I am about to say, but I've been watching you for some time. I think I understand what you're trying to do. I am in full sympathy with you and I am here to offer you my services."

He paused for a second, then went on. " I should like to take a small share in this venture of yours."

He spoke in the same tone he would have used to signify his intention to purchase a small block of shares in one of the Roths-child railway companies.

Felix looked at the elderly financier with mystified gratitude. " No need to tell you that your services are being accepted with enthusiasm. But perhaps I should warn you that this venture of mine, as you call it, announces itself as distinctly unprofitable, hazardous and unlikely to succeed."

" I am aware of that," said the banker quietly. " I've weighed the chances before making up my mind. I am not acting on an impulse."

For the first time Felix permitted himself a small chuckle.

" May I say, Herr Howlitz, that you do not strike me as the sort of man who would do anything on an impulse."

" I can't afford impulses, Herr Mendelssohn. I am a banker."

" So was my father, and I wish I were more like him. For, alas, I am a man of impulses. It was on an impulse that I came here and placed myself in my present unenviable and melodramatic situation. But even in the light of cold reason, I can't for the life of me see how I could have acted differently than I have. As you know, all this confusion and agitation is about a certain piece of church music which I feel should be performed. Somehow, I've managed to antagonise just about everybody and arouse unanimous resentment and condemnation. Finally I was forbidden to receive whomever I wanted in my house and threatened with ruin. When a group of innocent singers was disbanded by the Mayor and two defenceless men lost their livelihood because of me, I felt I had no choice but to respond in kind. And well—here I am."

A smile drifted across the old man's face. " A remarkable man once said something somewhat similar. He said, ' I cannot, I will not recant. Here I stand.' His name was Martin Luther. The point I wish to make is that it requires courage to take a stand on anything, and very few people are capable of it. Again I wish to offer my services."

" How much time would you be willing to give?"

" My full time," said the banker with calm. " My bank has long ceased to need me and I've left it in the hands of my head cashier, a most competent man. I'm entitled to a holiday and I can't think of any place I'd rather spend it than here. You may use me in any capacity you wish. Being a banker I am therefore an administrator and may try to make myself useful in this manner. I am also a violinist of sorts." Back came the downward furrows of his smile. " Frankly, I am a better banker than I am a violinist."

Felix sprang to his feet. " My dear Herr Howlitz, you've just been appointed administrator, treasurer, bookkeeper and executive manager to this organisation."

He struck his forehead, and his expression became one of extreme perplexity. " There's a delicate matter I've forgotten to mention," he said, plucking the lobe of his ear. " Everyone is supposed to receive a salary. This, you must understand, is to avoid any possible——"

" You needn't explain," said the banker. " This decision of yours proves merely that you are a banker's son as well as a sensible man and realise that very few important things—even in the spiritual realm—can be achieved without money. Churchmen of all persuasions understand this better than anyone. That's why they are always asking for it. My rabbi, for instance, is a remarkably persistent man in this matter."

He shifted the position of his hands on the knob of his cane and went on. "When I learned you were offering regular musicians' wages instead of depending on people's ideals and good will, I decided to come here. Therefore, with your approval, I shall put myself down on the ledger as a violinist temporarily delegated to administrative duties."

Methodically he unbuttoned his frock-coat and pulled an envelope from his inside pocket. "Now, does your organisation have any rule against anonymous donations?"

"The possibility hadn't even been contemplated," said Felix with a chuckle.

"Here is a cheque for five thousand thalers on a Berlin bank." He handed the envelope to Felix. "It cannot be traced to any one person, least of all to me."

With a thoughtful smile Felix considered the envelope in his hand. This was exactly what his father would have done . . . . "If the financial burden proves too heavy for me," he said, handing back the cheque, "I'll ask you for it. Meanwhile, permit me to express my deep appreciation of your generosity."

There was a knock on the door.

Cécile peered in. "Lunch is ready, darling."

He beckoned to her. "This is Herr Howlitz, our new business manager." He turned to the old gentleman, who was rising from his chair. "This, Herr Howlitz, is my——"

But already she was grasping the banker's blue-veined hands. "I know we're going to become great friends," she said with emotion. "You may not know it, but you came directly in answer to my prayers."

Since Felix had moved out of Leipzig, rumours had run high about him. When it became known that he had sent an appeal to amateur vocal societies in neighbouring towns and offered regular musicians' wages, there was much indignation. Pastor Hagen climbed into Saint Thomas's pulpit and spoke loftily about "the evil-doer who buys poor men's consciences to do the devil's work." In a statement from City Hall, Mayor Muller declared that the whole thing was "a gauntlet flung into Leipzig's face." Meanwhile, Kruger's affiliates went about whispering that a dangerous rabble was being trained at the farm under the pretext of music by a vague but sinister non-Christian conspiracy. There was some talk of retaliation. In the Jewish district a candle shop was sacked. Dr. Hurbach revealed that Felix had visited his office complaining of severe recurrent headaches. Now everyone knew that such headaches were the sure symptoms of incipient madness. Before long, people said that the Herr Direktor had gone mad. Some, better informed, asserted that he had sent in his resignation and had been committed to some unnamed private sanatorium.

Thus, on a morning in early January, there was extreme surprise and much speculation when Felix was seen alighting from his carriage in front of the Gewandhaus Building. Henceforth, every morning he was observed doing the same thing, leaving promptly after four every afternoon, in a brougham and occasionally in a closed sleigh. He went about his business, apparently unaware of the gossip circulating about him. He attended to his various duties with all the evidence of a well-balanced mind.

Only his face seemed to have grown paler. His manner, never familiar, became distant. He was unapproachable, except on strictly business matters. At board meetings he took little part in the discussions, ignored taunts and parried leading questions. When Muller inquired why he had moved to Reudnitz, Felix replied that the country air was distinctly cleaner than that of Leipzig.

For a while his daily presence in town, his apparent unconcern, spurred the rumourmongers into a last flurry of absurd or ominous fabrications. Then, all of a sudden, like a pricked balloon, the charges against him collapsed. The non-Christian conspiracy was first to fall by the wayside, choked to death by its own absurdity. The madness theory promptly followed suit, daily refuted by his presence and behaviour. As to his sacrilegious meddling into Church affairs, people were getting tired of that, too. What was so blasphemous about getting people together to sing some old Church music? Certainly he was using farmers and workers. Who else could he get, if His Reverence refused him the Saint Thomas choirs and the trustees didn't let him use the singers of the Leipzig Choral Society?

But the final sweeping argument was his irreproachable private life. Never a breath of scandal about that. A fine, respectable man, that's what he was. A good husband, a good father. Everyone had seen him on Sunday afternoons in spring walking on the Promenade with his wife and children. Now a man like that wouldn't do anything wrong. And what about his wife? A real lady if there ever was one. Pretty as a picture and charitable, always prompt with her bills. And a Christian, too, even though she was the daughter of some strange kind of parson in Frankfurt. Now why should a lady like that keep her children away and move out of her beautiful house and go to live with her husband on some farm? Because she believed he was right. And, who could tell, maybe he was . . .

By the end of January the tension had subsided.

"I'm beginning to think it was a good idea to come here," he told Cécile one evening. " Perhaps things are going to work out after all."

" I told you God was with us."

" He may well be. But I know what's changed people's minds more than anything else."

" What?"

" You. The fact that you are with me. You have no idea the effect your presence at my side has had. You see, my darling, people in Leipzig think you are rather a wonderful person. And I sail on your popularity."

Gently he lifted her chin. " Perhaps we're going to perform this confounded Passion after all. Things are going pretty well here."

" I'm praying all the time."

He smiled into her eyes. " You know, darling, I really believe you're going to nag God into doing that miracle."

It seemed in fact that the miracle had already begun. The farm had become a beehive of activity, a combination of hostelry and singing school with the atmosphere of a guerrilla camp. A number of people now lived in the various farms and sheds. Dormitories had been organised. Newcomers sometimes had to sleep in haylofts until accommodations could be made for them.

Some sort of pattern of daily living had established itself. Schmidt was recognised as Felix's lieutenant in musical matters. He conducted afternoon rehearsals, examined applicants, tended the huge stove in the rehearsal barn. He never had been so busy, and he no longer regretted losing his position with the Gewandhaus Orchestra. Tanzen, when not working on Felix's coach, had become a one-man police force whose arrival quelled disputes and whatever arguments threatened to degenerate into fights. Cécile, assisted by Gertrude, supervised the kitchen and all domestic arrangements. Gustav, back from Frankfurt, where he had gone to deliver the Christmas toys Felix and Cécile had hoped to bring themselves, made himself useful. Supper was served early, because of the evening rehearsal, and eaten in common in the huge kitchen, with Felix presiding and Cécile sitting opposite him at the end of the table.

Felix was, of course, the supreme head of the entire organisation, but since he was away most of the day, the burden of management fell on Herr Howlitz's stooped but very solid shoulders. The elderly banker now spent all his time at the farm and apparently enjoyed himself very much. Promptly at eight every morning he alighted from his carriage and began the day's work. His tall and slender silhouette was by now familiar to everyone, and the gentle tapping of his gold-knobbed cane announced his approach as he meandered through the farm's various structures. A small desk had been brought in from the bank and set in Felix's office under the recessed window. There, in his calm and methodical way, he accomplished an enormous amount of work. Gradually he had brought order and economy where before there had been none. Food was now purchased wholesale. He asked Tanzen to turn carpenter and build a chicken shed capable of accommodating a large flock. On Gertrude's birthday he presented her with three prize milk cows and henceforth milk was plentiful.

"I don't know how you do it," Cécile told him one afternoon as he was showing her his books. "Do you know what Felix said the other day? He said that if you don't watch out you're going to run this place at a profit."

But the most astonishing of all was the fact that out of all this makeshift, this jumble of humanity, a genuine vocal ensemble was coming to life. More than two hundred singers had responded to Felix's appeal. Small vocal groups from various small towns, many former members of the disbanded Cecilia Vocal Society who sneaked out of the town at dusk, farmers from the neighbourhood, even itinerant field hands, piteous vagabonds attracted by the tales of this miraculous money to be had just for singing. Most of them arrived in groups, early after supper, in processions of squeaky yellow-lanterned carts or sleighs, bundled in blankets, singing to keep warm, cheeks red and lips blue from the cold. In the courtyard they tumbled out, ran to the rehearsal barn and gathered around the purring stove, holding out their frozen hands, shivering and laughing. Cécile served hot punch, chatted with them, asked about their children and listened to their troubles.

And, of course, Magdalena was there, tireless of limb and tongue, flitting from group to group, a rainbow of good cheer, tossing saucy remarks and making people laugh. She had become an integral part of the venture. Although still living in Leipzig, she arrived early at the farm, often walking all the way. She was in a class by herself, belonging to all groups, at ease with everyone. She coached backward singers with unexpected patience and obtained surprising results. Pursuing her missionary work among her wide and varied acquaintances, she brought more recruits than anyone else. Waitresses, beer-garden entertainers, ladies of uncertain calling. All great chums of hers and like her out of work. Her ultimate ambition was to "convert" Olga, the Mayor's mistress. Up to now she had failed. "But don't worry," she would say, "I'll bring her yet."

To Felix, the greatest wonder of all was the fever of enthusiasm that had descended upon all these people. A collective fervour of work had seized men and women alike. On Sunday afternoon rehearsals, as he strolled among the groups during recesses, he would feel their genuine love for the Passion and their devotion to him. Compliments from his lips brought blushes of pride to their cheeks. Those who first had come for money, now came for pleasure, eager to please him, determined to do their best for him on the great day when the Passion would be performed in public. When and where that would be—they didn't know. But they had faith in him. He was a great musician and a kindly man. He would not fail them and they wouldn't fail him.

"They're getting really good," he told Cécile one evening. "It's extraordinary how much they have accomplished in one short month."

"It's because they love you," she said. "You'll see, darling, everything's going to be all right."

Even Herr Howlitz began showing signs of cautious optimism.

"I might as well confess I entertained little hope for the success of your venture when I came to offer you my services," he told Felix one Sunday afternoon before rehearsal.

"Then why did you come?"

They had been talking in a relaxed digestive mood, calmly computing the chances of the "venture," as Herr Howlitz still called it with an ominous undertone of imminent collapse, sipping with guilty relish a furtive thimbleful of brandy in violation of the strict ruling at the farm against beverages of high alcoholic content. The office's small wood stove spread a pleasant somnolent warmth. In the window the snow-laden branches of a nearby elm traced a delicate network of wintry peace against the light grey sky.

"Because I felt you were doing something worthwhile and I wanted to help, even if we were heading into defeat. Once in a lifetime a man should allow himself the luxury of a noble lost cause."

"And now what is your opinion? Are we still noble and lost?"

"Now," said the banker, gazing speculatively at his glass, "I think we have a slim chance. Our greatest problem, in my opinion, is that we are confronted with the opposition of a madman and an honest fanatic."

"I suppose you are referring to Kruger and Pastor Hagen. I don't think anything can be done about Kruger, but I've been thinking a great deal about the pastor lately. Perhaps if I went to see him, apologised for my behaviour, explain——"

He stopped, discouraged by the old man's quiet shake of the head. "You think it would be useless?"

"I am afraid so. There are two kinds of people who are impervious to reason. Madmen, of course, and honest fanatics. A crook is always ready to compromise. Not so an honest man. And I am afraid Pastor Hagen is one of them. I've asked my head cashier about him."

"Why should your head cashier be an authority on Pastor Hagen?"

"Because he happens to be a staunch Lutheran." For an instant he enjoyed Felix's surprise. "It's a curious story. Paul was born somewhere in eastern Saxony—Kamenz, I think. Both his parents were Lutherans and both died in an epidemic of cholera when he was four or five years old. It seems that his father had befriended a poor Jewish family of the town and when he and his wife died almost at the same time, they adopted Paul. What is more remarkable is that out of respect for his parents' memory they raised him as a Lutheran. When they moved to Leipzig thirty years ago Paul went to work in my bank. He's been with me ever since. Since he has taken his foster parents' name, I was for many years unaware that he wasn't Jewish. We've become great friends. It is he who has introduced me to the beauties of Martin Luther's prose. On one of my birthdays he gave me a beautifully tooled set of Luther's works."

"And I suppose you gave him a beautifully bound copy of the Talmud?"

"No—Spinoza," said the banker. "Paul is, like me, a bachelor. He plays the 'cello well and, confound him, chess even better. Anyway, I asked him about Pastor Hagen, and I regret to say that all the information about him is excellent. He is really a godly man and does God's work as he sees it."

"Which is most discouraging," said Felix.

"I am afraid it would be very difficult to show him the error of his ways."

They were silent for an instant. Then Felix drained his glass and rose from his chair. "By the way, Kruger has gone away. Nobody seems to know where he is. Good riddance."

The banker, who was putting the bottle of brandy back into a drawer of his desk, looked sharply over his shoulder. "I don't agree. I like to know where my enemy is, and what he is doing."

"Well," said Felix, starting towards the door, "we'll see what he has up his sleeve. And now, back to work."

These rare moments of relaxation were for him a welcome diversion in the gruelling routine of his life. With delight he had discovered that Herr Howlitz was a man of culture as well as an efficient administrator. Together they would discuss many things —art, literature, philosophy and the baffling complexities of Man— finding pleasure in the exchange, and sometimes the conflict, of their ideas. Occasionally, the banker would read aloud excerpts

from Martin Luther's works, for which he had an enormous literary
admiration. " Of course his subject is somewhat tedious. It can
grow wearisome to read about God and sin and Hell and how
easy it is to get there. But for sheer mastery of words, robust
earthiness and at times lyrical grandeur he is without peer. Until
you've read him you can't suspect to what peaks of beauty the
German language can attain. His pages about music, for instance,
are among the most beautiful ever written on the subject. There is
a man who would have loved the Passion . . .!"

And before they knew it they would be discussing the Passion
itself. Happy to find an intelligent and appreciative listener, Felix
would point out the beauties hidden in these time-yellowed pages.
He would sit at the piano, play some melodic theme or explain the
superlative craftsmanship of the work. " Take the opening chorus,
for instance. Listen how well the 12-8 captures the mood of turmoil
of the scene, the vehemence of the text . . ." A few pages further:
" Notice these few bars given to the oboe without any orchestral
support. Like a distant alarm signal, a premonition of tragedy . . ."
Deeper still into the score: " This is the magnificent scene of Peter's
repudiation of his master. Listen to the gasping rhythm of the
Apostle's sobs . . . And this long aria for violins only on the text
'And bitterly he wept.' And in this bar the faint crowing of the
cock . . . How it all comes to life, how it all becomes dramatic
and poignant . . ." And reaching the last pages of the score, " Listen
to this wonderful melody describing Christ's advance, His staggering
steps under the weight of the cross . . . I tell you no greater music
was ever written. And that's why we must, we simply must give it
to the world. . . ."

And for the hundredth time they would be peering into the
future, wondering what were the chances of their " venture " . . .

To Cécile, Herr Howlitz also gave a much-needed companionship, discreet guidance and complete devotion. As she had
predicted, they had become great friends. She liked his ceremonious old-fashioned courtesy. Sometimes in the afternoon she
would come and knit by his desk. Gently she would chide him for
being a bachelor. " When I wanted to marry I couldn't," he
would explain, " and later when I could I didn't want to any
longer." She would rebuke him for his selfishness. " Think how
happy you could make some woman, especially with all that
money," and his eyes would light up with malice: " But Madame,
I am not sure at all she would make me happy." One of her
favourite grievances was his habit of taking snuff and she would
lecture him on his lack of will-power. " But, Madame," he would
protest lamely, " I take snuff for medicinal purposes. It clears the
brain of toxic vapours." She would give a small ladylike sniff

and expatiate on men's duplicity. "Tut, Herr Howlitz. You know perfectly well there isn't a speck of truth in what you say. Grandfather used to say it purifies the blood, Uncle Theodore swears that it stimulates the digestion. You men are all the same. Always finding excuses for your vices. Even Felix declares that his brandy after dinner is good for his nerves . . ." And again the glint of mischief would come to his eyes. " But, my dear Madame, if we ever listened to you ladies, and became what you wanted, you couldn't endure the sight of us . . ."

At other times she would knit in brooding silence, her lovely face bathed in the grey window light. He wouldn't ask questions. Patiently he'd wait for her mood to change. Before long she would begin to speak. Of her children, of her home. With blurred eyes she would confess how much she missed them, how much she missed the quiet orderly life she had woven for Felix and herself. She even pined for the simple social amenities she had forsaken. The decorous afternoon receptions, the formal dinners, the meetings of the Leipzig Ladies' Charitable Association . . .

But mostly she would confide her anxieties over Felix's health. " He looks so tired!" she would sigh. " Do you think I was wrong to stop him from resigning? At the time it seemed to be the right thing for him to keep his official position, but now I am not sure. I wonder how long he'll be able to go on like this . . . And those headaches of his, they frighten me. He doesn't speak about them, but I see the pain in his eyes . . . How do you think it's all going to end, this Passion business? Tell me, Herr Howlitz, do you really think this music is worth all that Felix is going through for it . . .?"

The old gentleman would shake his head. " Yes, I've noticed how tired he looks. But, please don't torment yourself. Nothing anyone could do would make him stop. He feels it is his duty to give the Passion to the world and he will do it or die trying. He is like that. One of these men who must do what their consciences tell them to do at whatever the cost. There are very few like him . . . And perhaps it's just as well. As to your question how it will end, nobody knows."

Thus January ended. At the farm life went on, crowded with work, heavy with anxiety but brightened with hope.

Abruptly the weather turned brutally cold. It stopped snowing, but an icy wind arose that wouldn't stop but went on and on, day and night, with howling, unrelenting fury. Sleep became impossible. In their stalls the cows bellowed like wounded beasts. During the day people went about the farm puffy-eyed and with jaws clenched, not daring to open their mouths for fear of snapping at one another. Cécile caught a cold and began coughing at night. Felix still went to Leipzig every morning.

One day, shortly after he had left, Cécile entered the office. Her face was peaked from fatigue and lack of sleep.

" Felix's birthday is next week, on the ninth," she told Herr Howlitz. " He'll be thirty-eight. I came to see if we could arrange——"

She buried her face in her palms and broke into nervous, uncontrollable sobs.

" Please don't cry, my child."

Gently he led her to the chair and for a little while watched her cry. She was beginning to break up under the strain, he thought. Another month and she would be dangerously ill . . . " You are tired, Cécile," he said softly. " Try to lie down and get some rest."

It was the first time he had called her by her first name and she gazed at him with a start of surprise over her trembling hands. " How long—how long is it going to last?" she asked. " I tell you he won't be able to go on like this much longer . . . Since that wind began, his headaches have been getting worse. He almost doesn't eat any more, have you noticed?"

" Yes, I have noticed," murmured the old man. " This double life he's living under is beginning to tell on him. Frankly, I wish——"

" What?"

He shrugged helplessly. " I was going to say, ' I wish he would suspend the rehearsals for a while, take a few days of rest,' but I know he won't."

" You're right, he won't," she echoed dully. " If this thing doesn't stop soon, he——"

She pressed her fingers to her lips as if to stop the words. For a moment she stared unseeingly, terrified by her thoughts. Then, abruptly she sprang to her feet and ran out of the office. For a long time he heard the muffled sound of her sobs through the bedroom door.

That morning when Felix entered the Gewandhaus office he saw a man standing in front of the fireplace, his back to him, still in his travelling cloak.

At the sound of Felix's footsteps the stranger whirled around. It was Herr Kruger.

" I have just arrived from Dresden," he said.

Chapter 11

FELIX STOPPED, rooted to the floor by a jab of sudden, withering pain. His brain seemed to swell, crash through the bony dome of his skull. In a wincing reflex his hand flashed to his brow. For a few seconds he stood motionless in a vortex of blackness spangled with blistering sparks.

Then it passed. As swiftly as it had come. The image of the room and the man standing before the fireplace shuddered before his blinking eyes. With a feeling of miraculous achievement he reached his desk and slumped into his chair. For a while he held his face in his cupped hands, dimly aware of Kruger's voice wafting to him in ululating waves of meaningless sound.

At last air returned to his lungs in a long gasping draught. He lowered his hands, wiped the sweat from his face. " Excuse me," he heard himself say, " I must have had a fainting spell."

" Startled, aren't you?" Kruger was now standing across the desk, a leer of exultant jubilation on his face. " Gave you quite a jolt, didn't I?"

Infuriated by Felix's look of incomprehension, he leaned forward, barking the words. " Still pretending, aren't you? Fooling everybody with that handsome face and lofty air of yours, aren't you? But not me! I've been to Dresden. Understand? Dresden!"

Suddenly, like a wound-up watch, Felix's brain was clicking again, giving meaning to sound, flashing thoughts, ringing alarm bells. Oh, my God! Kruger has found out about Maria!

Yes, he had. And he couldn't control his joy at the thought of it; he was wallowing in triumph, his lips drawn over his yellow teeth in a sneer of victory. The great Herr Direktor! . . . Such a famous musician and such a fine man. Until now people hadn't really believed the rumours against him because he was personally irreproachable. But wait till they learned a few things about this paragon of husbands, this devoted father. Wait till they learned about what had gone on in a certain hotel on Theater Platz . . .

" And this time they will have to believe what I want them to believe because I have proof. Signed affidavits. Proof!"

" Why did you come here?" asked Felix quietly.

" Why?" Kruger's eyes narrowed into slits of hatred. " To tell you what I'm going to do to you. I'm going to get the people so much aroused against you that you won't dare to come here any more."

"Tell me, Herr Kruger, why do you hate me so? Because I was born a Jew?"

"Yes! Because you are the most famous among them. Because your music is being played everywhere. Because you've received the highest German decoration. Because the King called you Saxony's First Citizen and your portrait is in shop windows. Because you have built the Conservatorium and your name has brought glory to your entire race. But I'll get you out of this town, you and the other Jews. And after that I'll go after the Catholics of the Saint Joseph district. And I'll get them out also because I am rich, I am powerful, I have men who will do anything I tell them to do!"

The words tumbled out of his distorted mouth in a panting frenzy. He was addressing some imaginary crowd, conjuring some confused vision of power and violence. Suddenly Felix realised that Kruger was insane. Muller had been right. The man was really mad.

"Get out," he said without anger. "Go ahead. Do what you want, but get out."

As Kruger was looking at him, open-mouthed, as though he hadn't heard, he made a sweeping gesture of anger, fatigue and disgust and shouted, "Get out!"

When he returned to the farm that evening, Cécile immediately sensed that something was wrong.

"Please, darling, what is it?"

He looked at her strangely. "I'll tell you later—after the rehearsal."

She watched him during the rehearsal but, unable to endure the sight of his worn, haggard face, returned to their room. At last, very late, she heard his heavy steps on the wooden stairs. They stopped an instant and she knew he was catching his breath. He, who used to swim a mile and climb mountains . . .

At last he shuffled into the room, sat down as though his whole body had sagged. For a few seconds he gazed at her, his elbows on his knees.

"We're lost, Cécile," he said in a toneless voice. "Really lost this time. And through my fault."

He told her about Kruger's visit and saw the blood drain out of her face.

"You must resign," she said. "Resign immediately."

He shook his head. "No, Cécile. Not now." She knew he wouldn't change his mind.

After a pause, he said, "I wish you'd go to Frankfurt."

"Please don't send me away now," she said in a whisper.

He did not insist, sensing that anguish would be more cruel away from him than at his side. Silence fell between them, a speechlessness of consternation that made them look at each other in a sort of dumb, helpless despair.

"What are we going to do, Felix?" she asked in a small frightened voice.

He smiled wanly. "My poor Cilette, it's no longer a question of what we are going to do, but what they are going to do to us."

Outside, the wind howled and rattled the shutters.

Groups had formed around the Gewandhaus Building when he arrived next morning. He saw the hatred on their faces, the brandished fists, and he heard their threatening rumble. All day he went about feeling the hostility around him. When he left that afternoon the knots of people had formed again around his carriage, and Tanzen had his hand on his whip. Cécile was waiting on the Reudnitz Road, almost a mile from the farm, a shawled figure in the dusk, shivering from cold and anguish.

"Please don't scold me," she said, snuggling to him. "I couldn't wait any longer."

Gently he stroked her hair. There was no use trying to reason with her. She was afraid, and you didn't reason with fear.

"And perhaps she is right," said Herr Howlitz late that evening. In the soft glow of the two candles on his desk his face was grave, tense with thought. "Perhaps you should resign." As Felix did not speak, the old man went on. "What do you expect to achieve by facing an angry mob twice a day?"

"I don't know," said Felix dully. "Perhaps they will disperse in a day or so when the novelty has passed."

The banker shook his head. "They won't, Felix. They'll be there to-morrow and the day after and the day after that, until you break up and give up. That's what they're being paid for. Kruger may be mad but he is an extremely intelligent man."

"I am afraid so," admitted Felix with a rueful sigh. "He certainly seems to be winning this game."

"Twice he has proved his cleverness. First, like you and me he knows the power of money. He has seen how you've raised a vocal ensemble by offering musicians' wages. He is paying ruffians to get rid of you. The ends are different, but the technique is the same. Second, he found and forged the only weapon that could defeat you. Until now people wouldn't believe the rumours against you because they thought you irreproachable. He's shown that you are not, and now they hate you and want to hurt you for having deceived them. They want to take their revenge for having admired you. It's the story of the savage who must trample on the fallen idol. You will see that the entire population are going to compete with each other for the privilege of hurting and reviling you."

Herr Howlitz's predictions proved right. Each day the groups of people waiting for him in front of the Gewandhaus Building grew more threatening and audacious. Now he felt grimy hands tugging at his clothes when he walked up the wide entrance stairs. No marshal of police was to be seen. Instead of abating, the temper of the town was growing worse. An eloquent sermon by Pastor Hagen on " those who betrayed the sanctity of marriage " had produced considerable effect. Newspaper articles, a swarm of rumours, old and new, kept churning public opinion into a mood of incipient violence. There was no longer any attempt at fairness or understanding. Nothing was too absurd to be believed.

The Dresden episode had been repeated, enlarged and distorted into one of many. After all, he had often gone to Dresden before, hadn't he? And what about his trips to England and Paris. He probably had women there, too. And because he was such a wicked man, everything he stood for was wicked, too. That Passion for instance. After all he wasn't even born a Christian, how did he dare to conduct a work that was all about the Passion of Our Lord Jesus Christ. Even the old discredited fable about the non-Christian conspiracy was rearing its hoary head and finding adherents.

At the farm Herr Howlitz was becoming alarmed.

" I don't understand why you don't resign," he said discouragedly.

" I don't understand it myself. But they can't make me resign and I won't."

That was true. In a doleful statement from City Hall the Mayor had deplored that the statutes of the Gewandhaus Association contained no provision for a situation of this kind and therefore it would be illegal for the board of trustees to discharge the Herr Direktor from his high office. " No doubt, however," Muller had added with unctuous reprobation, " that he will see his unfitness and resign of his own accord."

But somehow the Herr Direktor did not or would not see his unfitness and the hopelessness of his predicament, and Herr Howlitz grew every day more distressed. " Please, Felix, resign," he urged. " Your obstinacy may well push Kruger into doing something desperate. You are not only endangering yourself but many innocent people. Remember, the man is mad, he is going to do something crazy."

Felix nodded. " You're right," he said. He admitted the sound-ness of the banker's arguments. Yet every morning, like an exhausted prize fighter staggering into the ring at the sound of the bell, he returned to Leipzig, his head throbbing, his ears ringing with Herr Howlitz's warnings, leaving behind a trembling, white-faced Cécile.

She, too, tormented him, but in another way. By her silence, her uncomplaining obedience and the signs of her own torment. Unlike the banker, she did not attempt to show him the unreason-ableness of his behaviour. Instead, he felt that in some deep recess of her mind she admired his useless courage, as one may admire a gallant and futile gesture. But she was afraid, living in unrelenting dread of what might happen to him and what he was doing to himself. She knew he was close to exhaustion, morally and physically, and it distracted her to see him squander his last reserves of strength and nervous energy. At times she almost hated him for loving his duty more than herself. " Doesn't he care about me at all?" she would ask Herr Howlitz in a sob. " Doesn't he care how I feel and what will happen to me if something happens to him?"

She was breaking under the strain, and Felix knew it. The sight of her lovely face, pinched and distraught with fear, sent him into a panic of self-reproach. He had had to forbid her to come and fetch him at the Gewandhaus in the afternoon. But he couldn't stop her from waiting for him on the road, half frozen and haggard from anguish.

" Cilette, my poor Cilette," he murmured one day as he pulled her to him on the carriage seat and wrapped his cloak over her shoulders, " what have I done to you! I should never have let you come into this thing."

She lifted her blue eyes to him. " I would have hated you if you hadn't," she said, smiling at him with heartrending love and relief that at least for a few hours he was safe and she was in his arms.

Thus a week passed, a week that seemed an eternity. The icy February wind did not relent. On and on it blew in long hissing, nerve-shattering gusts over the farm's snow-thatched roofs, tearing through the naked trees, rattling windows, sweeping a dust of snow under the doors, whirling into chimneys in a sort of senseless monotonous rage.

The evening rehearsals were still held but a mood of sullen restlessness had settled over the singers. Why they still came was a puzzle to Felix. Their faith had gone, they knew that the " venture " was doomed, swaying like a mortally axed tree before the final collapse. Yet they still came, out of some obscure loyalty which they couldn't explain to themselves, as soldiers rally around a general who has led them to defeat.

Towards him their feelings were complex. They didn't really care about what had happened in Dresden. If his wife was willing to forgive and forget, they were ready to do the same. No doubt he was a victim of some conspiracy against him and they felt sorry for him. But victims did not win and they brought disaster upon their followers. With troubled hearts they reflected that they had been wrong to put their faith in him. When retaliation came, it would fall most heavily upon them. They were afraid and because they no longer had faith in the ultimate success, their performance had deteriorated. Expecting dismissal, they no longer practised. Gloom now hung over the rehearsal hall, so joyous and confident a few days ago.

Only Magdalena had not surrendered to the atmosphere of debacle. She still went from group to group, sharp of tongue and unvanquished in spirit, berating them for their cowardice, her generous bosom heaving with her stinging rebukes. " Milk and turnip juice, that's what must come out of your veins when the doctor cups you! . . . Blind as bats and with the brains of fleas you must be to believe those Leipzig hypocrites! Yes, hypocrites, that's what they are, down to the last of them. You'd think they were blessed little angels the way they talk. How about His Lordship? Why didn't the newspaper write about him, why didn't the pastor give a little speech about him? Olga herself was telling me she was disgusted the way they're hounding the poor Herr Direktor. But you wait, I'll still bring her here one of these days. That'll give them something to talk about." Her puny challenge fell on deaf ears. They shrugged wearily. What did they care about Olga or His Lordship? They were poor people, defenceless and afraid.

Dinners at the farm were now silent and forlorn affairs. Schmidt had been warned that his doubtful title to the farm would soon be investigated. Gertrude's jowels sagged despondently. On Tanzen's good and simple face there was anxiety and bewilderment at finding himself up to his neck in this ill-starred adventure. A few days before he had found his Leipzig workshop ransacked, its windows smashed, the half-unhinged door flapping in the wind. What would become of him and his family when it was all over?

" I know the end has come," Felix told Cécile one evening as they were about to go to sleep. " I know I'm beaten and there isn't a chance in the world to perform the Passion on Palm Sunday. I know you are unhappy and Herr Howlitz is right, and it is absurd for me to keep on going to Leipzig."

"Then why do you?" she murmured. "Why don't you resign, disband the singers and put an end to the whole thing?"

He looked at her for a long time through the brown sadness of his eyes. "Cilette," he said at last, "do you remember the day in Switzerland when you said I should come to Leipzig, and I was angry at you because I wanted to go to Berlin and you couldn't give me any reason, except that you had a 'feeling?' Well, it's the same now, I have a feeling . . . I'll be hanged if I know what it is. But something tells me I must hold on a little longer. Just a little longer."

"Perhaps God will come to our help," she said, and her voice was low and muffled with doubt. For the first time she was wavering in her faith. "Sometimes I feel He has forsaken us."

"Don't darling," he said quietly, and it was her turn to be surprised. "He hasn't forsaken us. It certainly looks like it, but somehow He'll make it right. Don't ask me how. I can't even imagine how He can help us, even with a miracle. But He will, you'll see."

A pale echo of his old bantering moods returned an instant, and he smiled. "I only wish He would hurry a bit."

And so, next morning he drove again to Leipzig. He no longer tried to explain his actions to himself. Perhaps, he reflected with wan amusement, he had reached the stage where he could no longer form a decision, even that of stopping. His reason told him there was no hope and his struggle was hopeless. Like the reeling prize fighter he longed for the hard mattress of the floor under his back that would tell him that the end had come at last and he could give up and sleep and try to forget. But not yet . . . Until then there was nothing to do but go on, groping blindly ahead, trusting that secret "feeling" that told him to hold on a little longer. Just a little longer . . .

It was during dinner one evening that he noticed an ugly bruise on Magdalena's cheek. She had tried to conceal it under a thick layer of unguent and face powder, but with little success. The blotch of purplish flesh showed through, and she was now pointing at it, describing to Tanzen how she had acquired it by slipping down the stairs of her house. The lie was so palpable that even the wheelwright, who wasn't very astute, was pinching the lobe of his ear in frank disbelief.

"You'd better take care of it," he said at last. "If you got that bruise by slipping down the stairs, unless you were walking down on your hands, I'd hate to see the bruises you must have on your back."

Dinner over, Felix asked her to meet him in his office, and a moment later there was a timid knock on the door.

"Sit down, Magdalena," he said gently. "Now tell me the truth."

Her bravado collapsed. "A man attacked me last night when I came home from the rehearsal. He was waiting for me behind the door."

"Did you make a complaint to the district marshal?"

She smiled ruefully, gazing at the flame of the candle in the pewter holder. "If I went to Hans, you know what he'd say? He'd shake me by the shoulders till my tonsils were down to my stomach and he'd say, 'You damn' fool, I told you something like that would happen.' That is what Hans Polden would say, and he would be right, because he warned me to be careful."

She turned her plump saucy face to Felix and a melancholy smile hesitated on her lips. "You see, Herr Direktor, me and Hans, we used to go together. That was two years ago and I was younger then. More slender, too. He said he wanted to marry me, but you know what people think of actresses, and I knew it would be bad for his career. So I told him I was already married, which was a lie. So that was the end of it, and last year they made him chief marshal and I didn't see him so much any more. Though he still lives in the same district, and now and then he comes to see me in the evening and I give him something to eat. Now you understand, Herr Direktor, why I can't go to him and make a complaint. He'd kill me."

"You're going to stay here from now on, understand?" said Felix with affectionate sternness. "Frau Mendelssohn will take care of you, she's very good at this sort of thing. If necessary, she will call a doctor. And please, don't come to rehearsals for a while. The singers are frightened enough as it is."

She nodded meekly, apologised for the trouble she was giving. "I'll do whatever you say, Herr Direktor. Remember, at Christmas you already told me I should stay here. But I wasn't scared then. Now I am, I really am." A tremulousness came into her voice. "You, too, Herr Direktor, you'd better be careful. They're in real earnest this time."

She got up, took a few steps towards the door, then turned around, an odd smile on her lips. "Strange, our meeting like this, isn't it, after all those years. I see you don't remember, but one night at the Friedrich you were standing in the wings watching Anna and I was waiting for my turn. I gave you a quick nudge but you didn't even glance at me . . . God, you were handsome! We all envied Anna. But then she always was a lucky one. She even found herself a husband . . ."

She sighed and with a shrug opened the door. "Well, good night, Herr Direktor."

" Good night, Magdalena."

For a moment he stared unseeingly at the wavering flame of the candle. Memories stirred dimly in his mind. The Friedrich Theatre . . . Anna Skrumpnagel . . . Leipzigerstrasse . . . That life so carefree and confident, had it really been his? And that handsome young man waiting in the wings, had it really been he?

With a heave he pushed himself up to his feet and went to the rehearsal barn.

When he returned to the office that evening he found Herr Howlitz still working at his desk. " I thought you had gone home," he said.

" I wanted to close a few odds and ends," he said, shutting his ledger, " but I am about ready to go. How was the rehearsal? "

" Hardly fifty people turned up," said Felix with a sort of detached hopelessness. " They still sing, but their heart is not in it. The flame is out, it's the end. By the way, Magdalena was beaten up last night."

" I noticed her bruise at dinner." There was a hint of reproach in the banker's voice, but he refrained from comment.

He rose from his chair and Felix helped him into his heavy winter coat. They went downstairs in silence. Felix took a lantern at the door, and they crossed the courtyard, holding their hats, bending against the unrelenting wind.

" I wonder how it's all going to end," said Felix, as he closed the carriage door. " Please be careful, Herr Howlitz."

The banker pushed his wizened face into the frame of the window. " My dear Felix, at my age nothing matters much any more. Go and get some sleep. You need it."

Lantern in hand, Felix returned to the house and climbed the wooden stairs to the first floor. As he trudged towards the bedroom, he noticed that the candle on his desk was still burning. He was leaning down to blow out the light when he noticed a letter. Recognising Karl Klingemann's elegant script, he broke open the wax seals and began to read.

His mouth slackened and his arm slipped down at his side.

" She is dead," he said softly to himself.

He gazed ahead at his own shadow on the wall. Yes, she was dead . . . Thank God she'd been killed instantly when her coach had overturned on the Edinburgh road and tumbled down a ravine . . . Somehow it was fitting that she would die on the road, like the wanderer that she was. Romola, who was accompanying her, had died a few hours later. Poor Romola, grumbling, loving, loyal to the end . . . " Your Illustrious Lordship . . . This I swear on the Madonna della Salute . . ."

He tried to recall Carrington Castle, the thatch-roofed cottage by the brook, Dresden, their first night when she had been waiting in his room. Images barely coalesced in his mind. He was too tired to feel deeply. You must be in health to suffer.

He walked to the piano, softly pressed a key. She had laughed in that key . . . He had noted it that day—only three months ago but it seemed like years—when they were driving through the Vogelwiese Woods.

Faintly her laughter throbbed in his ears and her face floated before his eyes. Then they faded—the laughter and the face . . . Receding into space, growing dimmer, dissolving into the nothingness from which they had emerged for an instant.

Then they were gone.

Now there was nothing but his shadow on the wall, and on the table at the end of the wick the drop of yellow light swaying in melancholy and tender farewell.

One afternoon, two days later Cécile and Herr Howlitz were sitting in the office, both pretending to be absorbed in their task.

" Do you think this wind will ever stop?" she asked without raising her eyes from her knitting.

" I doubt it," he replied fitfully.

As usual, he was writing in his ledgers; but not in his usual placid, methodical way. He kept on glancing out of the window, nibbling the tip of his quill, pushing pinches of snuff up his nostrils.

" Having trouble with those toxic vapours?" she teased.

He growled an answer and snapped shut the lid of his snuff box. For a while he seemed absorbed in his work, but soon his nervousness betrayed itself again.

" What's the matter?" This time she rested her hands in her lap and looked at him. " Since this morning you've been fretting and behaving most peculiarly. Are you by any chance beginning to crack up, like everyone around here? Come on, tell me what it is."

" I might as well," he said, deliberately turning to her. " This morning I received a disturbing message from my head cashier. Felix has been hurt."

He saw her face go white and added hastily, " Nothing serious. Someone threw a stone at him as he was entering the Gewandhaus."

She sprang to her feet, ran towards the bedroom door. He still had time to call after her, " Please, Cécile, don't go . . ." but already she was out of the office.

A few minutes later Tanzen, his green scarf flapping in the wind, was cracking his whip over his two galloping horses, and Cécile was speeding over the Reudnitz Road. Huddled in a corner, her eyes stone-hard in her taut, white face, she watched the trees flash across the window as the big yellow wheels jostled and leaped over the frozen ruts.

At the same moment Felix was sitting in his Gewandhaus office, gazing out of the window. The stone gash in his cheek had stopped bleeding but still throbbed dully. Now and then a wince of pain creased his face. Well, it had begun . . . After threats, the blows. First Magdalena, now himself. To-morrow . . .

He heard the knob turn. His Lordship slipped swiftly into the room, latched the door. Only then did he seem to relax.

" May I sit down, Felix? " he asked thickly.

Felix was startled by his appearance. Muller was one of those men who conceal their true age under the truculence of their manner. But there was no truculence in him now. Only fatigue and fear. He had lost much weight. Flesh hung down his face in flabby, tallowy jowls. His florid complexion had turned a blotchy magenta. Suddenly he looked old.

He slumped down on a chair and stared down at the carpet for an instant, his mouth slack. " You know, of course, I had nothing to do with that stone, don't you? "

" I know that."

" I know who did it. If you want I can try to have him arrested."

" What's the use? To-morrow there'll be another one."

Muller lifted his bulging bloodshot eyes. " You wouldn't have a drink, would you? Schnapps or brandy? "

" Only port. I'm sorry."

" Never mind." He ran the tip of his tongue over his lips. " Olga's leaving me. If she does, I'm finished in this town."

He spoke in hurried gasps, rushing words between breaths. " She's learned about Magdalena. She wants me to arrest the man who beat her up. She doesn't know I can't. Kruger would be in my office in five minutes and have him released. She says I am a coward and a hypocrite. She wants to go to your side."

Felix looked at the wheezing, frightened man before him. Only a few months ago they had been friends. Almost . . . Now they were in enemy camps and by an irony of fate, both in desperate situations. " Why don't you send her away? "

" She won't go. You don't know her. She'll barricade herself in the house, make a scandal."

He paused and again ran the tip of his tongue over his lips. Then, like a man playing his last card he blurted out, " Look, Felix, I'll make a bargain with you. When she comes you send her away, and in exchange I'll tell you a secret. A really big one."

" You don't have to. I'm thinking of your wife and children.

There's been enough grief. If Olga comes, I'll send her away. You have my word."

A gleam of incredulousness flashed through Muller's eyes. How easy it had been . . . "Thank you," he mumbled.

"You'd better go now. Someone may come in."

The Mayor stirred uneasily on his chair, swaying his bulk in response to some anxious dilemma. "I'm going to tell you just the same," he said at last. He leaned forward, lowered his voice to a whisper. "Kruger's planning to send a gang of ruffians into the Jewish district some night next week. They'll be armed."

"Are you sure?"

"The chief marshal told me. He saw the shipment of arms Kruger received from Bavaria. I told you the man's crazy."

"Why can't you arrest him?"

"On what grounds? Madness doesn't show like smallpox. And how can I prove what these arms are for? If I had a sworn statement, some papers, I could try——"

He got up.

"Anyway now you know. Do whatever you want."

"Thank you, Christoph."

Muller stopped in front of the desk. "I don't know how it's all going to end up," he said in a muffled, almost sobbing voice. "But I want to tell you I'm sorry for all that's happened. Perhaps some day we'll be friends again . . ."

"Perhaps." He opened the door, peered into the hallway. "It's all right. Now you can go."

After the Mayor had slipped out, Felix closed the door and returned to his desk.

Well, he thought, leaning back in his chair, it had come at last. This was the end, the hard-floor mattress he had longed for. Now he could give up. This time there was no doubt, no hesitation. He must give up. To-morrow he would write his resignation——

With a start he glanced over his shoulder and saw Cécile rushing into the room.

"I want to see it," she said.

Before he could speak she was bending over the crimson gash. "Felix, I want you to resign," she said, straightening up, "or this thing will kill us both."

"Yes, darling. To-morrow . . . I wish you hadn't come," he said, hurrying to the wall and snatching his hat and cape from the hanger. "I told you I——"

He froze in mid motion as a rumble of voices rose from the square below. "Oh, my God!"

"What's that?"

"Nothing. Let's go."

But already she was fleeing to the window. She had just time to get a glimpse of a mob gathering downstairs and Tanzen reaching for his whip. "Who are those people?"

Roughly he jerked her away from the window. "Come on," he said, pulling her by the wrist. "You go down the back way and wait at the rear gate. They can't collect there, the street is too narrow. We'll come and fetch you."

"I won't."

"Do as I say."

"I want to go down with you."

"I don't want you to."

"Then I stay here."

She spoke with the senseless, unshakable defiance of a child. For a second or two his jaws clenched in anger and he thought he was going to strike her. She cowered and nestled against him. "Please, I want to go with you."

"You can't," he flung impatiently. "Don't you see——"

"Please!"

"I tell you——"

"Please, darling!"

"All right." He grabbed her wrist. "You can be the most aggravating, the most——"

In the midst of a running stream of words he propelled her through the room with such force that she had to steady her flying bonnet with her free hand.

As he was closing the door, a rock crashed through the window with a glittering shower of broken glass.

"You see why I don't want you to come down," he said, gripping her shoulders.

She shook her head. "Remember Dresden, darling? For better or for worse."

Nothing he could say would make her change her mind. "All right, Cécile. Hold on to my arm."

They walked in silence through the deserted corridor. He flung open the entrance door, and for a moment they stood side by side in full view. Her hand was trembling on his arm but her face showed no fear. Her appearance created a commotion. They hadn't expected to see her. Her beauty bemused them, made them forget their purpose. They gaped at her, not knowing what to do as she walked slowly down the wide stairs leaning on Felix's arm. Inadvertently a man raised his hat as they passed by.

The spell broke as soon as they disappeared into the carriage. Grimacing faces pressed against the windows. A lanky, bristly-faced man held the champing horses by their bits. Tanzen leaned forward and with an angler's gesture unfurled his whip. The man loosened his grip and let out a howl of pain as the twine cut a scalding red streak across his face. With flaring nostrils and charging hoofs the horses strained in the harness and plunged into the crowd. In less than a minute the brougham was half-way down the square.

"Felix, let's go away," she said, looking at the yelling mob out of the rear window. "I'm afraid."

He took her limp cold hand. "You are a brave girl, Cilette. By the end of the week we'll be on our way. To-morrow at the rehearsal I'll disband the singers."

He spoke quietly, but she was not deceived by his calm. It was an admission of defeat, the end of his hopes. The long struggle was ending in surrender.

"I am so sorry," she whispered, pressing herself to him in a rush of compassion. "I so much wanted it to succeed for your sake. It meant so much to you."

Gently he patted her hand, but she saw the mist in his eyes and read his heartbreak in the pallor of his tight-lipped face.

"It's all right," he said, swallowing hard. "I thought it could be done and I was wrong. We've done our best, but they're stronger." He looked at her and forced a semblance of a smile on his lips. "We'll have a long holiday and forget the whole thing."

"I just don't understand. I prayed so hard . . ."

Like a broken stem she toppled against his chest, limp with grief. He put his arm around her. And like this they drove back to the farm without speaking.

In the office Herr Howlitz was waiting for their return, pacing the floor, anxiously tapping with his gold-knobbed cane.

"Is Cécile all right?" he exclaimed the moment Felix entered the room. "I haven't had a minute of peace since she left. This wife of yours will be the death of me."

"Of us both," Felix said with a weary grin.

With a mixture of admiration and exasperation, he told the banker about her behaviour at the Gewandhaus, and the old man shook his head at women's boundless capacity for love and contrariness.

Then Felix gave him an account of Muller's visit and Kruger's plans.

"The man is really mad," said Herr Howlitz, aghast. Then, after a pause, "I can never thank you enough for the warning. We'll be ready when they come."

"They won't," said Felix quietly. "I'm sending my resignation and disbanding the singers."

For a while the banker remained silent. "You're right," he said sadly, at last. "There is nothing else to do. It is the only thing that will break the spine of Kruger's project. When it is known that you have resigned and disbanded the singers, people will no longer tolerate violence. Things will calm down rapidly. Everybody is tired."

To conceal his emotion he pressed a pinch of snuff to his nostrils. "I am sorry it had to end like this. Truly sorry."

Felix did not reply. A moment later he escorted Herr Howlitz to his carriage and bade him good night.

"By the way," said the banker, lowering the window, "let me attend to the dismissal of the singers and the closing of the 'venture.' Go away with Cécile as soon as you can. You are both on the verge of collapse."

Felix watched the carriage disappear, its side lanterns glowing in the night. With a start he noticed that the wind had stopped. He lifted his face to the sky. With infinite gentleness a snowflake alighted on the tip of his nose. He smiled to himself and went back to the farmhouse.

Cécile was already in bed when he entered the room. She was waiting for him, torn between her relief that the end had come at last and her distress that it all had ended in failure and disappointment.

He sat down on the chair, looking at her in silence.

"Well," he said at last, "it just wasn't meant to be. You know, Cilette, I can't get used to the idea that we are beaten. Really, completely, irrevocably beaten." A pale smile hovered on his lips. "We won't even go down with our guns blazing, as you used to say, remember? We're just going down, that's all. I suppose you die as best you can."

"I am sorry, darling," she said softly.

He shrugged, got up and began to undress. "By the way, how's Magdalena?"

"She was fine this morning. Her bruises are healing, but it will take some time for her to be all right. We've become great friends. She still talks about bringing Olga to our camp."

"You must tell her to stop asking Olga to come here. I promised Muller I wouldn't accept her if she came. I certainly owe him that."

"All right. I'll tell her in the morning."

He slipped into bed and they lay side by side.

"I love you," she murmured.

"Then everything is all right," he said softly. "Go to sleep, darling."

He kissed her, and she fell asleep instantly. He turned on his back, his eyes opened in the darkness. He felt Cécile move closer to him in her sleep. She did love him, and that made everything all right. That, as Shakespeare said, paid for all . . .

His lids closed.

Outside it had begun to snow.

Chapter 12

PASTOR HAGEN ran his hand over his tired eyes and looked up at the paleness in the window that was dawn. The soul-searching night had not brought peace. In vain he had asked for reassurance that he had been right in doing what he had done. The reassurance had not come. Only the feeble testimony that he had meant well. To him, that wasn't enough. Only too well did he know that half the evil deeds in the history of the world had been committed by well-meaning people who had called their pride righteousness and their opinions God's justice. Now, in the stillness of his book-lined study, he raised his sleep-tormented eyes, begging for a moment of rest. As if in answer to this prayer, a merciful overwhelming lassitude engulfed his mind. He toppled forward on the open Bible and fell asleep, his head buried in his arms.

At that moment an old woman bundled in rags and bent over a pauper's stick was plodding through a vacant lot in the Saint Joseph district on her way to early Mass. She noticed something jutting out of the snow, stopped, looked again and let out a long piercing yell.

Night-capped heads appeared in windows of the surrounding houses, shouting questions at the crone, who ignored them and went on yelping with the unabated shrillness of an alarm clock. Soon disgruntled figures, shivering in hastily donned robes, trickled out across the snowy field, intent on finding out what this unseemly racket was about. Before long a group of people, their teeth chattering from cold and horror, circled Katherina Pleck, who had finally stopped her howling and stood pointing down at a woman's hand that lay open skywards, frozen and flowerlike, in an agonised gesture of appeal. Someone more callous or daring or curious than the rest bent down, gave a swift push to the body lying on its side beneath a shroud of snow. The corpse tumbled lifelessly on its back, revealing, amidst a shuddering gasp of recognition, a bloody clod of broken flesh which, only a few hours ago, had been Magdalena's plump and vivacious face.

It was then that Olga Becker appeared on the scene. She too had been awakened by the old woman's yells, the vacant lot being at the rear of her house. She gave one glance at Magdalena's face and screamed, " He killed her!" and lifting her hands to her face she broke into uncontrollable sobs. Everyone in the Saint Joseph district was aware of Olga's status with His Lordship, and her

325

words jarred the onlookers into a rush of questions. Who was he? Who'd killed her?

In a stammer of hysteria Olga revealed that the Mayor had forbidden her to see Magdalena, who had been urging her to join the Passion singers. Last night Magdalena had visited her and shown her the still visible marks of her bruises. In a fit of indignation Olga had promised to go to the farm with her this very morning.

"That's why he made someone kill her!" she cried, her words ending in a fresh outburst of sobbing.

"Now what's going on around here?" said a gruff voice behind her. It was Chief Marshal Polden, who lived in the neighbourhood. "And you," he went on, addressing Olga, "you'd better stop talking nonsense and go back to your house."

He elbowed his way through the crowd and his eyes fell on Magdalena's dishevelled red hair and shattered face. His handsome features froze into a mask of wincing pain which turned almost immediately into one of frightening anger. Clenching his fists he looked up at the sky in a wordless oath of revenge, then plunged into action. He ordered people back to their houses. The group scattered and scurried away, each bursting with news. He dispatched a youngster to police headquarters at the City Hall and he himself darted in the direction of Markt Platz. Katherina Pleck was the last to leave. Once again she looked at the form lying on the ground, slowly made the sign of the cross over it and resumed her laborious stooping progress towards the church. Only Magdalena remained, her piteous face turned to the sky, her glassy eyes unblinking in the falling snow.

Less than an hour later Chief Marshal Polden was being received in informal emergency audience by an extremely ill-tempered and sleep-befuddled Mayor in slippers and dressing-gown.

"Look here, Marshal, I'll have you demoted for this," His Lordship began from behind his desk, as the police official entered the cold study. "I won't be routed out of bed because some fool woman's been killed. What do you expect me to do? Catch the murderer and throw him in jail?"

"You don't understand, Your Lordship," said Polden with strained patience. "The woman is Magdalena Klupp and people are saying you had her murdered."

"Me!" gasped the Mayor.

"That's what your—your friend, Fräulein Becker, said herself."

"I never saw the woman before——" Then in a searing flash of comprehension, "Oh, my God! What did you say?"

The police official gave him a brief account of the morning's event. When he finished repeating Olga's version of the crime, the

Mayor's face was purple with rage. "Stupid fool! Blundering slut!" He looked at Polden with sudden anxiety. "You don't believe her, do you?"

"No, Your Lordship. I know you had nothing to do with it because I've already arrested the man who did it and he confessed."

"Who is he?"

"The same one who threw the stone at the Herr Direktor. I caught him in bed, still drunk and snoring away. By the time I got through with him, he wasn't drunk any more."

"Where is he now?"

"In jail." Meaningfully he added, "And he's going to stay there until the hangman comes for him."

Despite the coldness of the room, sweat was gathering in the hollow of the Mayor's throat. The thing he had dreaded had happened: one of Kruger's thugs had gone too far and Kruger would insist that he be released or given a chance to escape, and it could not be done.

"Besides," Polden went on as if reading the Mayor's thoughts, "if we let him escape the people will go after you, Your Lordship. They are in an ugly mood."

Muller pulled out his handkerchief and wiped his face. Abruptly he stopped, his arm in mid-air. "Who, besides yourself, knows he's been arrested?"

"Nobody. I took him to prison myself and came directly here."

The Mayor sprang to his feet. "Wait for me. We're going to see him. This may be our chance."

Pastor Hagen responded at last to his servant's respectful but insistent shaking. With a wrenching effort he lifted his head, forced open his gritty, bloodshot eyes upon Gottfried standing before the desk in a state of panting excitement.

"Your Reverence! Your Reverence!"

"What is it?" asked the pastor from the depth of his weariness.

In faltering words the sexton informed him that he had just returned from the milk shop where he had learned from agitated housewives that a woman had been murdered in the Saint Joseph district and that the murderer was none other but His Lordship himself.

"But it isn't his mistress that's been killed. No, Your Reverence, it isn't that strumpet, that Jezebel, that hell-spawn harlot he keeps for the satisfaction of his sinful lechery." In his years of association with the pastor the old menial had acquired some of his master's Biblical imagery.

"Who is it then?" asked the churchman with an edge of impatience.

"A friend of hers, Your Reverence. As bad as herself. An actress. A fallen creature, a daughter of Satan, a painted woman . . ."

The pastor listened to the ancient, maledictory epithets. Each one fell upon his ears with the sickening impact of a stone hurled at an unknown, defenceless woman. Was this the voice of Righteousness? The old Pharisees, righteous and hypocritical, had used those words. Now the new Pharisees, the Christian Pharisees used them, too. Nothing had changed. What had become of Christ's Law of Love and Charity? What had become of His example when He had shielded the adultress with His mantle? Did He have to die on the Cross if His Passion had taught nothing to those who called themselves Christians, followers of Christ?

"Get the carriage ready," he said. "And please, hurry."

It was still early when the pastor's carriage stole noiselessly into the farm's courtyard, snowbound and deserted in the morning's stillness. It was Schmidt's wife who answered his timid knock on the door and led him to the office, where Felix was writing his resignation and announcing that he no longer intended to perform the Passion.

For an instant Pastor Hagen stood in the doorway. His face was ashen and he held the gold cross on his chest as if for support.

"May I come in?" he asked with the humbleness of a wanderer begging shelter for one night.

Felix stared at him.

The tall tragic-faced churchman standing motionless on the threshold was a new man, reborn in grief and humility. The little vanities, the complacency, the unctuous pomposity had washed away. Only the godliness remained, glowing about him like an aura.

"I have come to tell you how sorry, how very sorry——"

His voice broke and he was unable to proceed.

"Your Reverence," said Felix, rushing to him, "it is you who must forgive my behaviour on the occasion of my visit to you." Gently he took his arm and led him to a chair. "Let us be friends."

In a tone hushed with grief the pastor told Felix about Magdalena's murder.

"I understand she had come to urge a friend to join your singers. You may like to know she had finally succeeded. They were coming here together this morning."

Felix remained silent, aghast at the news. It seemed impossible that she was dead, that she would no longer flit from group to group during the rehearsals, saucy and defiant in her flamboyant clothes. Poor Magdalena Klupp, her wanderings had finally come to an end—on that vacant lot, on a snowy night. She had been warned and then beaten up, yet she had gone back, despite her fears, to plead once more with Olga and bring her to the farm to divert the cruel gossip about him, grant him a little respite . . .

"Who could do such a thing . . .!" he said at last.

The pastor shook his head disconsolately. "This morning I have seen the lowest in cowardly abjection and the ultimate in evil pride."

He then described the scene he had witnessed in the prison before coming to the farm. Magdalena's murderer, teeth chattering and wild-eyed from fear, confessing his crime, betraying Kruger's plan, shouting the names of his confederates in a rage of vindictiveness . . . And a moment later the scene, more harrowing still, when with the Mayor and the chief marshal he had entered Kruger's study and watched the crumbling of the man who had thought himself so powerful.

"It was horrible," he said, his voice still shaking. "But Magdalena Klupp has not died in vain, Herr Direktor. Her death has opened my eyes and brought the population back to its senses. Like myself, the people have at last seen the truth and understand the meaning of the cause for which you've endured so much and for which she has died. I, for one, want to do everything in my power to help you. Saint Thomas is open to you, Herr Mendelssohn. Its organ and its choirs are at your disposal. I shall also endeavour to bring you other choirs from neighbouring towns."

Felix looked at him, not daring to believe his ears. His dream was coming true. Hundreds of trained singers ready to bring the Passion to life. The organ on which Johann Sebastian Bach himself had played . . . It was too grand, too wonderful, too much. A banquet to a starving man . . .

And it came too late. There were only six weeks before Palm Sunday. The task was too big and the time too short. If he were strong and calm it might still be done. But the strain of these last weeks had sapped his energy. The long-accumulated lassitude had finally caught up with his will-power, descending upon him in swirling waves of drowsiness and brutal unrelenting headaches. He was exhausted in soul and body. He wanted only to sleep, sleep and forget. Like Moses he would die in sight of the Promised Land. Someone else would have to perform the Passion, give this immortal music to the world.

And then there was Cécile. She, too, had reached the breaking point. He had no right to ask her this new sacrifice. She, too, needed rest . . .

Sadly he looked at the pastor. " Some miracles arrive too late."
" I understand."

A few minutes later Felix escorted him to his carriage. Then
with slow, thoughtful steps he returned to the house.

He went into the bedroom and the moment he opened the
door he knew he shouldn't have come. A board in the oak floor
creaked under his foot. Cécile awoke with a start.

" What is it, Felix?"

Her voice was tense, apprehensive—the voice of someone who
has lost confidence in life and expects only bad news. She had
raised herself on her elbows, clutching the sheet with one hand,
her eyes wide open.

" Nothing, darling," he said lamely. " I just came——"

" But there's something. I can see it on your face. What is it?
Please, tell me."

How did one break the news that someone had been murdered?
He sat down on the edge of the bed, gently unloosened her fingers
from the bed sheet and drew her to him. " You haven't even said
good morning. What kind of wife is that?"

His piteous effort at banter did not deceive her. She knew him
too well. With him banter started with the eyes, in gleams of
teasing light. His eyes were heavy and dull.

" Good morning, my darling," she said, kissing him. " I didn't
hear you get up."

" I couldn't sleep, so I thought I might as well get up."

She nestled against him. " You will soon," she cajoled. " As
soon as we get away from here." Then, with repressed urgency,
" When can we leave?" She mistook his silence for calculation,
became eager. " I can be packed in no time. Do you—do you
think we could leave to-morrow? Let's go to Italy. It'll be too cold
in Switzerland. You know, that place you mentioned, where lemon
trees grow on top of a cliff——"

" Sorrento," he mumbled without looking at her.

" We'll go there. We'll take a house with a garden so the
children can play, and we can lie in the sun all day. Is there a
beach?"

" Oh, yes. A beautiful one."

" Fine. We'll lie on the beach all day, and sometimes I'll let you
take me fishing in a little boat. And if you mention the Passion
or write a note—even a little note, I'll shoot you."

He did not answer and she jerked herself away from him,
looking at him with a mixture of anguish and anger. " You
haven't changed your mind, have you, about the Passion? . . .
We're going, aren't we? . . . I don't want you to stay here."

Panic was creeping into her voice and he knew she was thinking about the evening before in Leipzig, the grimacing faces in the carriage window.

"I know something will happen to you if we stay here," she went on. "I know it. You'll get sick and I don't want you to be sick." Her eyes did not leave his face, pleading yet imperious. "I want you to get well, to have a long rest. Then "—now she lied to soothe his qualms—"in a few months, when you are well, we'll get the Passion performed."

She paused and saw he was not listening. "What is it, Felix?" she cried in a rush of fear. "I know there's something wrong. What is it?"

"There's been an accident."

"Who? . . . Where? . . . Tell me, tell me."

He could feel her nails through the velvet of his smoking jacket. "Magdalena . . . She's been——" The pressure of her fingers relaxed. She waited open-mouthed, holding her breath. "She's been killed," he blurted out, angry at his own clumsiness.

She said "Oh!" and the word came in a soft exhalation. Then she clung to him in a gesture of fear—and also with some obscure shameful relief that it wasn't he who had been killed.

She asked no questions, made no comments. He did not know whether he should say more or not, and said nothing, gazing down at the floor, his arm circled around her shoulder.

For a long time they did not speak.

Then she asked quietly, "Who told you?"

"Pastor Hagen. He was here a moment ago."

She wrenched herself away from him. "What does he want, that one?" She flung the words with an intensity of resentment that shocked him. "To tell you he was sorry, I suppose? Tell you he had nothing to do with her being killed?"

This was a new Cécile, a Cécile with drawn lips over her teeth, brimming with hatred. And of course the pastor had just said that, how sorry he was . . . And there was no use trying to make her understand the grandeur, the poignancy of the scene of a moment ago . . .

"And what else did he have to say?"

"He offered me Saint Thomas. The organ, the choirs—everything."

"I suppose he thinks that will make up for everything," she snorted, back in her mood of anger. "I suppose he expects you to go down on your knees and thank him . . . Did you accept?"

"No."

"Good. Then we can leave to-morrow." There was no other thought but flight in her mind. "I'll start packing at once."

Already she was struggling out of the sheets, squeezing herself out of bed. "You can let Herr Howlitz attend to everything." With thoughtless candour she added, "He'll do things better than you would. He is a businessman, he is good at this sort of thing."

"No doubt," he said coldly, getting up from the bed. "But I think we should first attend Magdalena's funeral. Or do we also forget about her in our haste to be off? I intend to go to-morrow to Leipzig and make arrangements for her burial."

He had taken that tone of command which she had learned to respect and sometimes to fear. She knew he would do exactly what he wanted, and that they would leave only when he decided they should do so. For an instant she hesitated, about to run into his arms, but he did not wait and without another word walked out of the room.

"You must forgive her," Herr Howlitz told him a moment later. "She isn't herself these days. She lives in a constant terror that something may happen to you. The shock of Magdalena's death snapped her nerves and intensified her fears a hundredfold."

The crow's-feet of wrinkles at the corners of his eyes trembled in the suggestion of a smile. "At this moment she probably hates you with a passion and wishes she had never set eyes on you. The tears will come later. Then it will be all right."

He had arrived at the farm knowing about the morning's events and was relieved to see that Felix had already been informed. "I dreaded to have to break the news to you. There is one thing, however, that you probably do not know. I learned it from my cashier who, I told you, is a staunch Lutheran and a fervent churchgoer. Pastor Hagen has delivered this morning a magnificent sermon. It certainly was the first unprepared sermon in his career, but it moved his flock to tears and touched their hearts. I admire that man. It takes great courage to recognise one's faults, and heroism to do so in public. Humility in public is as rare as courage in private."

For a while they talked about Kruger's mental collapse. "I understand that a physician is attending him," remarked the banker, "and preparations are being made for his transfer to some private *maison de santé*."

"Just the same," remarked Felix, absently looking down at his hands, "It is frightening to think of the ravages a madman can inflict."

The old man nodded. "Yes," he said in a sigh of long-suffering patience. "There will be others, but they too will pass. Perhaps some day there will finally be peace and understanding." He paused and rested his eyes on Felix. "That's why it is such a pity that you must abandon your task when you are so near the goal. It would have been more than a memorable artistic event, it would have been a forward step in the conscience of Man."

Felix did not reply and avoided his friend's gaze. He went on cracking the joints of his fingers, which was one of his ways of releasing his nervous tension.

The following day he called at the City Hall and found His Lordship in exultant spirits.

"I was just about to come and see you," he cried, before Felix could say a word, and rushed to greet him, effusively pumped his hand. "You'll never know what I've been through. Please, sit down," he went on, plopping himself heavily into his ornate mayoral chair.

He puffed his cheeks, blew a long visible plume of air through his small puckered lips. "Thank God, it's over! But believe me, I had a few uncomfortable moments. I'll never forget my last interview with Kruger. As a precaution I had Pastor Hagen and my chief constable with me. The moment Kruger saw us entering his study he felt the game was up. But I didn't give him time to speak. I pounced on him, shoved the confession in his face, charged him with intent of sedition and complicity in murder and declared him under arrest before he could say Athens-on-the-Pleiss. Well, you should have seen him! Foam came to his lips and he started shaking as though he had the ague. He began ranting and raving that we were all traitors—including poor Pastor Hagen!—and shrieking at us that he would take his revenge some day. Then, all of a sudden, he crumpled into a heap on his chair and, though his mouth kept on moving, he couldn't speak any more. Last night they took him to a private asylum."

Unable to bear his jubilation he sprang to his feet and took a few steps towards Felix. "When you came in I was just composing an announcement about his retirement because of illness, and what a fine public servant and all that. After all, one must always speak well of the dead," he added piously.

His bombast was as embarrassing to watch as his recent cowardice had been. Felix sensed that he would like to let out a yell of victory, trample his victim, hop and skip with delight. After yesterday morning's terror, he still revelled in ecstasy at finding himself in this impressive office with the portrait of King Friedrich Augustus over the mantel and on the opposite wall that of his great ancestor Karl Wilhelm Müller, who had founded the Gewandhaus Association.* He just couldn't believe he still was His Lordship the Oberbürgermeister of Leipzig, entitled to the heavy

* A statue to Burgomaster Karl Wilhelm Müller was erected in later years on the promenade facing the Dresdner Railway Station in Leipzig.

gold chain of office. And this time with no one around to make him squirm and sweat. What a difference, Felix reflected, between the noble, tragic figure of Pastor Hagen bending under his remorse, humbling himself to regain his peace of soul, and that of the red-cheeked braggart swelling his chest underneath his gaudy waistcoat. Remorse? Remorse for what? Muller would have said. He hadn't been caught, had he? He still was the Mayor, wasn't he? He was the sort of man to whom self-reproach came only with adversity, like those people who remembered their prayers only when they were sick.

"Well, that's the end of that!" he puffed complacently.

He stood before Felix, waiting for some mark of approval, some sign of admiration, like an actor waiting for applause. "Let me tell you I had to think quickly," he said, inviting congratulations.

"You must feel quite relieved," Felix said quietly.

It wasn't much of a compliment. In fact it was no compliment at all, yet it delighted the Mayor. "Certainly I do! I feel ten years younger."

He lowered his voice to a confidential whisper. "But I've learned my lesson. Women talk too much. In politics you can't have that. That fool Olga almost cost me my gold chain with her blabbering."

"If she hadn't blabbered, as you say, you'd still be trembling before Kruger."

"*Ach, mein Gott,* I never thought of it! Just the same, one can't be too prudent. I'm sending her away. After all, I must think of my good wife and my children." He gave Felix a sly twinkle. "I'm sending her to Dresden. And of course I have to go to Dresden quite often—on business."

He was so pleased with himself that he wanted to sow happiness around. "Now, let's talk business," he said, propping himself against the ledge of his desk. "Don't you need an orchestra for that Passion of yours? How about the Gewandhaus?"

"It would be wonderful, but I won't be performing the Passion."

"What! You can't do that. We've got to give people something to get their minds off all this past trouble and confusion."

He was off. The people wanted Felix to perform the Passion. His Reverence wanted it. He, the burgomaster, wanted it. Athens-on-the-Pleiss would never pardon him if he didn't. It was his duty. As an artist. As the First Citizen of Saxony. As a German . . .

Felix let him speak, listening absently, his lids half closed. Yes, it would be wonderful to perform the Passion with a really great orchestra, a splendid choir in Saint Thomas's Church, for which it had been written. This would really be the ceremony as he had dreamed it, the consecration of Johann Sebastian Bach worthy of his genius. But Cécile——

"You aren't listening!" trumpeted the Mayor. "Here I am telling you you can have the Gewandhaus, the Leipzig Choral Society, all the money you want and you are half asleep! What's the matter with you?"

"I am very tired," said Felix, rising. "I'll let you know. What I came to see you about was Magdalena. She had no family. I want to claim her body and arrange for her funeral."

The Mayor waved an impatient hand. "Anything you want," he said, returning to his desk. "You can do anything you want." He caught himself. "But have the funeral late in the afternoon. And only a few people. After all, she was a nobody . . ."

With a shrug he returned to his panegyric of the Honourable Herr Wilhelm Kruger, First Councilman of the City of Leipzig, that civic-spirited public servant whose sudden illness had shocked and distressed all those who knew and loved him . . .

"And so, what did he say?" Cécile asked.

"I could have the Gewandhaus and all the money I need."

It was their last-minute-of-the-day ritual. Their lips were almost touching, but she was tense, still hostile. A performance of the Passion would entail six weeks of unbroken, superhuman effort. It would kill Felix.

"What did you say?"

"I'd let him know."

A long pause.

"You'd like to do it, wouldn't you? Tell the truth."

"That is not the question, Cécile."

"What is it, then?"

"Whether I should or not."

"What do you think?"

"I won't do it unless you are with me, and I don't feel I have the right to ask you to stand by me if you feel you shouldn't."

Another pause.

"It'll kill you, I know."

"There is no guarantee that it will. But even if it did, I'd die happy."

"You would, wouldn't you? And the children? And me? Don't we mean anything?"

"You know you do. But I would have done my work and you'd be proud."

"Well, I won't let you! I don't want to be a proud widow. I want to be a happy wife." Tears welled up in her eyes. "Even a miserable one." Then, with the helpless fury of those who love too much, " I hate you, I hate that music, I hate everybody. Good night, darling."

A grudging wifely kiss.

" Good night, sweetheart."

A soft loving kiss on the tip of her nose.

According to the Mayor's wishes, Magdalena's funeral was at dusk in the Saint John Cemetery. Pastor Hagen officiated. There were no speeches; only a handful of people who left as soon as the coffin was in the ground.

Felix and Cécile were the last to leave. They walked slowly side by side in silence past the snow-shrouded graves. Very far in the slate-grey sky a long saffron-coloured gash bared the flesh of twilight. Somewhere behind the clouds the sun was setting in a splendour of molten light.

Now they were passing through the " poor " section, nearest the gate.

" Look, Felix," she said, stooping.

" What is it?" It was just another grave with an inexpensive oak cross at the head.

" Read. On the cross."

Some of the letters had blurred beyond recognition. Some could still be deciphered.

" Johann Sebastian Bach."

They stood a moment in the deepening dusk. Even the snow was turning grey.

She raised her face to him, and he saw that it was streaked with tears.

" He's been waiting so long," she murmured.

They looked at each other, nodded at each other.

" I can't fight you both," she said softly, under her breath.

Chapter 13

HE LAY in bed, not quite awake yet no longer asleep, slowly adjusting himself to the breathtaking, unbelievable fact that it was Palm Sunday and he was still alive.

For more than an hour the bells of Saint Thomas, each swung by twelve strong ear-muffed men, had been booming away, shattering the April sky with their clamour of humming bronze. Across the Pleiss, Saint John's answered with clapperfuls of brassy noise, while in the distance, little Neue Temple, the poor's church, sprinkled its own neighbourhood with drops of high-pitched joyful tinkle.

Still he did not move.

It really was Palm Sunday. That was the most astonishing of all. At times during the last six weeks it had seemed that it would never come. At others, that it was coming much too fast. And all the time it was on its way, just like any other day, neither fast nor slow, simply waiting for the hours, minutes, seconds of the previous days to tumble down into the ocean of spent time. Now its turn had come. And it was a lovely spring day, in spite of those confounded pounding bells, with a gentle breeze floating through the window, and the house full of people and the children excited as if it were Christmas, and Cécile somewhere, probably busy as a bee. And he, slothful and happy, lying in bed when everybody in Leipzig had been up for hours, enjoying these last moments of quiet before it all began and there would be no more time to breathe, let alone think. Just as astounding, in a few hours it would all be over. Already this remarkable, unique Palm Sunday was moving, advancing with irresistible flowing force. By to-night it would have nearly rolled over the brink of the cataract and by midnight it would have dissolved into nothingness. Just another Sunday gone by. But not to him . . . To him it would never die simply because he would never forget it. It belonged to him. He would take it with him when he died.

Strange how important a single day could be in a man's life. Of course, it was ridiculous to start imagining things, seeing portents and secret meanings in the sequence of episodes that led to an important event in one's life. Just the same, ridiculous or not, it did look as if it had all been decided way, way back by some power, some sovereign force. Maybe God? . . . Anyway, by Someone Who might have said, " Jakob Ludwig Felix Mendelssohn

. . . Now, let's see . . . He will be born in Hamburg in 1809, raised in Berlin by a wealthy, wonderful family. He will be a musician and write some superlative music—and some not so good. He will become very famous, marry one of the loveliest girls in Germany and have fine children. He will direct the Gewandhaus Orchestra, give the first performance of Schubert's Unfinished Symphony, found and direct the Leipzig Conservatorium. But none of these things will be his main purpose in life, his reason for being on earth. His mission will be to perform a certain piece of old church music by an obscure eighteen-century choirmaster named Johann Sebastian Bach. That's all. Nothing more will be expected of him. Others will take up from there . . ."

Whereupon some Invisible Hand had gone to work and arranged it all. But so skilfully, so deviously that no one could possibly have guessed what it meant or where it would lead. For instance, what if old Herr Zelter hadn't found those last four pages in some second-hand music store? . . . What if he hadn't been his music teacher? After all, there were other music teachers in Berlin . . . If—if—You could go on like this indefinitely up to the moment when Pastor Hagen had come into his office at the farm, ashen-faced, holding his gold cross . . . It was like a slowly unfolding fugue of people and events, each falling into its place, each fulfilling some definite purpose, bringing nearer the ultimate resolution.

He himself had done very little about it all, groping through a maze of conflicting emotions, stumbling along, wondering what it all meant, grasping the full meaning only very late . . . But the Hand had kept him on the path and prodded him along. And he had been the chosen one. And for this he thanked God. Thanked Him for allotting him this noble task, offering him—a musician—the chance to render a great service to the master of all musicians. And finally, for granting him—born in another faith—the honour of returning to Christians their greatest music. This amply justified whatever it had cost—the struggle, the discouragements, the back-breaking strain of those last weeks. For this it had been worth living.

Where on earth was Cécile? . . . Would she mind very much if he had breakfast in bed? After all, this was a special day. Although deep inside she disapproved of it, felt it was hedonistic, sybaritic, vaguely sinful. He would dedicate the rest of his life to converting her to the delicate and much-maligned pleasure of breakfast in bed . . . Meanwhile, with a house full of people, she probably was trotting about, supervising everything, attending to everything, making everyone comfortable. The perfect *Hausfrau* in her hour of glory. Sweet, wonderful Cilette . . .

Her mother had arrived yesterday, looking fresh and unbearably refined after a long and tiring coach journey. With her was her brother, Senator Souchay, looking puzzled and wondering why she had dragged him out of his bank. Forceful creatures, those Jeanrenaud women . . . His sister Fanny was here, bless her! She had come all the way from Berlin with her husband to attend the performance. She was the *chatelaine* of 3, Leipzigerstrasse, now that Mother was dead. Even Paul had come. He was probably downstairs having breakfast in the dining-room, chatting with Gustav or reading the financial news. The nursery was a bedlam. Now and then, when someone opened the door, a waft of children's voices floated up to him. They were bursting with excitement without having the faintest idea what they were so excited about. Perhaps that's what childhood was—a capacity for being happy without any reason . . . Outside, the streets were already buzzing with people. He recognised this peculiar humming sound that crowds make. Now, where . . . ? Düsseldorf, of course. At the time of the Rhine Festival. Oh, if only Father were here! How proud he'd be! He would clear his throat and say, " Jakob, I am rather pleased with you. Now your grandfather Moses . . ."

And thank God, it wasn't raining as it had been all week. To-day was clear and breezy, as a Palm Sunday should be. Cécile had probably prayed for that, too. She looked upon God as on some sort of rich and grumpy uncle who could be coaxed into doing almost anything—and usually did.

So much had happened in the last six weeks that nothing had left a deep imprint on his mind. To him it was a swirling blur of rows of singers with mouths open watching him for signals, instruments in motion, rappings of baton on the edge of the music desk, orders given, Schmidt rushing about, dinners dispatched in haste. Cécile looking at him with a mixture of pride and anguish, wondering how much longer he would bear the strain . . . A sort of collective fever had descended upon the town. Everyone had tried to make amends. Ladies calling at the house, telling Cécile how glad they were she was back. Elsa Muller, of course. A real friend . . . Councilmen's wives, trustees' wives. Even Amelia Dossenbach, bringing a half-thaler's worth of flowers . . .

And, of course, His Lordship. A week after Magdalena's murder he had annexed the Passion. It was his project. Why, everyone knew he'd always been for it . . . Overnight he had become a musicologist, tossing technical terms right and left. He delivered pronouncements from the fastness of his City Hall office, exhorted the population to greater and still greater diligence. He had even volunteered to go to Dresden—at great inconvenience to himself, he avowed—to persuade Herr von Wierling to grant leave to three opera singers to fill important solo parts. Athens-on-the-Pleiss had never known anything like it, and he, Muller, was at the head of it! He really had come to believe his own oratory. How fortunate the man with the gift of self-delusion . . .

One who had genuinely made amends was Pastor Hagen. Without hesitation he had suspended the school's curriculum so that the Saint Thomas boys could be trained intensively. He had granted permission to use the church's great organ at any hour, day or night. He had allowed orchestral rehearsals in church. He had brought several vocal ensembles from neighbouring towns. No man could have done more. And a measure of peace had returned to him. Not the complacency of the self-righteous, but the humble, tremulous peace of the penitent fulfilling his penance.

But strangest of all was that everything had begun with that puddle of blood in the snow, Magdalena's murder. Some things defied logic. Man's behaviour, for instance. Why should the murder of a middle-aged provincial actress rock a city like Leipzig? Shatter a churchman's complacency and lead him into the path of humble charity? One could not fathom such things. Perhaps that's why it was written that God moved in mysterious ways.

He heard the door open and the muffled tread of Cécile's footsteps on the rug.

As he had expected, she bent down and said, " Darling, you must get up." Through slitted lids he watched her, pretending to sleep. Her voice became urgent. " Please, darling. I know you're very tired, but you must——"

He felt the cool pressure of her lips on his cheek and opened his eyes. " I was waiting for that kiss," he said, propping himself up on the pillows. " Sit down and let me look at you."

She looked a little better, not very much. Those few weeks at home, the presence of her children had helped. But her cheeks were still pale and those purple shadows under her eyes hadn't gone. Also, that cold she had contracted at the farm hung on. Often at night he heard her cough in her sleep. Switzerland would do her good.

" Forgive me for taking such a long time," he said with the pretence of banter which lately often disguised his real thoughts, " but I was wondering how a Calvinist pastor ever begot such a ravishing creature."

She smiled, touched but not deceived by the undeserved compliment. A woman knew how she looked better than anyone, because she knew better than anyone how she felt, and beauty started inside . . . As for him, she could only too well see how he looked. His face carved in wax. Skin tight over the bridge of the nose, showing the bone beneath. Nostrils pinched, eyes sunken deep in dark shadowy sockets, blue veins protruding in the hollow temples. The scar left by the stone an ugly purple on his right cheek. Furrows of pain and fatigue and overwork at the corners of his mouth. And he thirty-eight not even two months ago. And she still in her twenties . . .

"I think I know what you're thinking," he said with a rueful smile.

"What?"

"That we both look like an attractive pair of ghosts." She nodded in piteous assent and he went on. "But you'll see, two months of Switzerland and we'll be so full of health we'll shame those hardy villagers. By the way, aren't you anxious to try our new——"

"How do you feel?" she asked, trying to hide her concern. "Did you sleep well?"

"Like a child or like the dead, you can take your pick."

"I'm all packed up. We can leave at any time."

She had been packed up for days, ready to leave on an instant's notice. Those last few weeks, so busy for him, had been an eternity of waiting for her.

"To-morrow, if you want," she suggested cautiously. "By to-night everybody will be gone."

"Do you think so? How about your mother?"

She and the senator were leaving early in the afternoon; Uncle Theodore had important business in Frankfurt. As for Fanny, her husband and Paul Mendelssohn, they were leaving immediately after dinner, by train.

"Then to-morrow is fine." he said. He really was impatient to leave. So long as he remained in Leipzig there always would be things for him to do, people to see. And he was about done in. One more week of it and he would have cracked up. His head had been hurting savagely these last weeks. Especially in the evenings, after a long gruelling day. "The sooner the better."

"Good. What did you ask me a minute ago? If I was anxious about something?"

"Our new coach. It's even more beautiful than the one Father had."

She nodded. "And I am glad Tanzen's going to be our coachman. Gustav's getting old."

"A bad habit a great many people have," he said, smiling. "Except us, of course."

Only then did he notice the breakfast tray on a corner of the chest of drawers, and because he was weak from fatigue and his nerves were wrought, the sight moved him out of all proportion.

" You're spoiling me, Cilette," he said, feeling the prickling of tears.

" Darling, I'm going to spoil you so much, so very——" She couldn't finish. Her lower lip quivered and her voice broke into a sob. In a gust of love and fear she flung her arms around his neck.

Until you die . . . That's what she'd been thinking, he told himself while patting her back and mumbling piteous assurances that deceived neither of them. " Now, now . . . What sort of wife have I got here! You'll see, everything's going to be all right . . . Everything's going to be fine . . ."

Both knew it wasn't true. The last few weeks had drained out his last resources of strength, taken the few more years he still might have had. She had guessed about the true nature of his headaches. He had caught her glances of fright, seen the trembling of her lips when he raised his hand to his brow. " I expect we're both tired," he admitted at last. " Very tired."

Gently he untangled her arms and pulled her away. She would be, he told her, the ugliest woman in Saint Thomas's if she didn't stop crying. She nodded and wanly smiled, wiping the tears with the back of her hand. Then, with assumed briskness, he pretended to be famished. " What good does that tray do me over there?" he said, pointing to the chest of drawers.

" You weren't even awake when I came in," she protested, fetching the tray and setting it on the bed.

" Now tell me how everything is," he said with a flourish of napkin. " How's everybody? Where's dear *Maman?*"

Despite the fatigue of journey *Maman* had been up since the crack of dawn and taken a tour of inspection through the house. Cupboard, linen closets, storage room, kitchen—she had looked in everywhere.

" Even in the attic," said Cécile with the indulgent smile of grown-up children for the foibles of their parents. " To see if I keep house as she taught me."

" And does she approve?"

" Everything, except "—she smiled embarrassedly—" the little Greek statue in the study."

" Oh, my God! We forgot to hide it. What did she say?"

" She said it was immodest and undignified."

" Well, I'm afraid we're just a pair of undignified and immodest people."

" She's getting old," Cécile said lovingly. " She has old-fashioned ideas."

" On the contrary. Her ideals are eternal. There'll always be ladies like her, so long as there are mothers-in-law. Where is she now?"

" She's already left for church with Uncle Theodore. I tried to tell her the service wouldn't begin for at least two hours, but she said she wanted to get good seats and couldn't think of a better place to wait than God's house. Even if it was a Lutheran church."

"Wonderful *Maman!* I simply love her," he exclaimed, his mouth full. "Wouldn't she be dumbfounded if she found on arriving in Heaven that God was a Mohammedan or an Ana-baptist?"

Softly she clucked her tongue. "Don't make fun of these things, Felix. People have to believe in something. It helps them to live and it helps them to die. And you'd better hurry and get dressed. A lot of people are already downstairs and more are coming in all the time."

"What do they want?"

"To see you. People I've never seen. From Berlin, Hamburg, Paris. Even a gentleman from London. Sir Somebody-or-other . . . Gustav didn't know what to do, so I told him to let anyone in. The town's bursting with visitors. They say in hotels people are sleeping three to a bed. Come on, hurry up."

There was a light knock on the door and Fanny Mendelssohn-Hensel came in.

"Breakfast in bed!" She laughed. "He hasn't changed. My poor Cécile, I knew he'd break your spirit and get his way in the end." She kissed her brother on the cheek.

"You, too, have vices," he flung back with typical younger-brother petulance. "I'll tell Cécile about those."

Fanny ignored the threat. "He's always had a passion for breakfast in bed. Father used to say it was the sure sign he would come to a bad end."

"I have." He dabbed his lips with his napkin. "And if you have any more calumnies to spread about me I wish you'd do it behind my back and not to my face."

While talking he gazed at his sister with smiling eyes. "For an old matriarch you look surprisingly well." He turned to Cécile. "It's a family trait. We Mendelssohns grow more and more handsome with the years."

He tossed his crumpled napkin on the tray and let out a sigh of satisfaction. "This was very good. I am now ready to face the hardships of the day."

Cécile slipped down from the edge of the bed. "And I'd better go down and see how things are," she said, removing the tray. "And you'd better get up. Please, Fanny, make him get up."

"I'll try."

"Remind me to take you down in the garden before we go to church," he called after Cécile as she was going out. "I want to show you something."

As soon as she was gone, Felix looked at his sister in thoughtful silence. For a while they gazed at each other with memory-clouded eyes, wistful smiles forgotten on their lips. Episodes of their youth swirled through their minds like dead leaves in an autumn wind. Their pranks, the four-hand duets, the Sunday musicales, the sumptuous dinners, the picnics, the first whispered love confidences . . . Now they held each other's hands in an instinctive bond against their common, nameless fears, a foreboding of imminent and final separation.

"Happy, Fan?" he asked at last. "How's that husband of yours?"

"More wonderful every year. He's had an exhibition in London and the Queen bought one of his paintings. And the children are wonderful, too. I went into the nursery a moment ago and played with your little ones. Strange, they are all blonde, like their mother. Incidentally, Cécile looks very tired."

"I know. I'm worried about her. I'm anxious to get her to Switzerland." He felt her tender searching eyes on him and he guessed her thoughts. "I look pretty bad, don't I?"

"You, too, need rest. A long rest." Then she said unexpectedly, "Those headaches are terrible, aren't they?"

He frowned sharply. How had she guessed? "I also have them," she said in a whisper. "They start here, don't they?" She touched the back of her neck. "The doctor says there isn't much to be done. The usual thing—rest, no emotion, plenty of milk . . ."

With an effort she forced a smile, and before he could say anything she pulled the blankets away from him, as she had done so often in the old days. "Now, get up, or Cécile will be angry with me."

He was in process of shaving when Cécile burst in, bubbling with excitement.

"There's a crowd downstairs! Herr Muller has arrived with all the councilmen. All in their robes of office. They look beautiful."

"I'm sure they do." He grinned, glancing at her while running the razor under his chin. "Christoph especially."

"You should see him with his gold chain and red velvet mantle! He looks like—" No apt simile presenting itself, she babbled on. "And the name of that English gentleman is Sir George Smart."

He stopped, razor in mid air. "Oh, my God! All the way from England . . ."

"Who is he?"

"Just the conductor of the London Philharmonic Orchestra, that's all. And that, my darling, is what I call an orchestra. He gave me my first chance." For a few seconds he was back in Sir George's office and Maria, flashing-eyed, was crashing in. *Signor*

Smart, you are a big bugiardo . . . Quickly he resumed his shaving.
" I tell you, Cilette, the British are wonderful people."

" Oh, you and your British," she teased, knowing his admiration
for British character and customs. " They're just like everybody
else. Some good, some bad."

" Yes, but when they're good, they——"

" Oh, I forgot. A lady, Frau Riemann called. Very pretty, too."

" Yes?" He was studying his face in the mirror. " And what
did Frau Friemann want?"

" Not Friemann, darling. Riemann. She said to tell you she was
very proud of you."

He ran his fingers up his cheek. " Very kind of her."

" She also mentioned she used to know you very well."

He let out a groan. " She, too! Will my past ever lose track of
me? Don't believe her, Cécile. She is an impostor. I never saw
her in my life."

" You almost married her, you goose. If I hadn't come
along——"

" Riemann?" he repeated under his breath.   Remembrance
came in a flash. " Of course, Nina . . . Is she here?"

" Yes, with her husband. He is here on business. She told me
he was going to build the new railway station."

Expertly he wiped the razor blade. " Ah, Nina! That was the
woman for me. A shame she jilted me and I had to be content
with a pastor's daughter."

She smiled. This was genuine banter, the kind that brought
impish glints into his eyes. " If you don't hurry, the pastor's
daughter is going to——"

She was interrupted by the sound of striding footsteps accompanied by heavy panting. They turned around in time to see Karl
Klingemann charging through the doorway of the *cabinet de
toilette*.

" I swear, Madame," he puffed, ignoring Felix, " my friendship
for your husband will bring my early and untimely demise." From
his pocket he pulled a large handkerchief and mopped his broad,
jovial face. " Why doesn't he lead a placid, uneventful life like me?
I never know whether I must pay him a tribute or put him under
arrest."

" When did you arrive?" cut in Felix hastily, honing the razor
with murderous swipes.

" What was that, Herr Klingemann?" asked Cécile. " About
putting him under arrest?"

" Nothing," Felix snorted with the emphasis of insincerity.
" Karl's always boasting about diplomats' privileges. Why, if he
ever did that to me "—he waved the razor blade meaningfully be-

fore his friend's face—" I'd slice his throat." To change the subject, he repeated, " When did you arrive?"

" Last night. And this confounded village is so full of people I had to sleep on a billiard table."

" It's good for your soul," said Felix with unction. " Also keeps you in trim."

Cécile excused herself. As she was passing through the doorway she flung over her shoulder at Karl one of her devastating smiles. " I should like to hear more about those diplomatic privileges."

" If you ever tell her——" began Felix when he was alone with his friend.

" I won't." Gingerly he lowered his bulk on the edge of the bathtub. He took a pinch of snuff and while brushing specks of tobacco from his ruffled shirt he looked at his childhood friend. " You miserable *Musiker*," he said, a suspicious moist gleam in his bulging eyes, " you finally made it, didn't you? I am proud of you, Felix. I knew you were a great musician, now I know you're also a great man." His familiar mocking smile returned and he added, " Infinitely too much for one single individual."

" And you've been the best friend a man could have." Felix said, emotion piercing through his voice in spite of himself.

" By the way," said Karl, who like many sentimental people detested emotional display, " I have a bit of news for you. Having now reached the distressing age of forty and tottering into senility I've decided to get married."

" Wonderful!"

" It's the only imprudence I haven't yet committed, but I can't help myself. I am like a mountain climber hypnotised by the sight of the Matterhorn. He knows that almost everyone who tries to climb falls into a precipice, yet he's got to try. Even more astonishing, I have found a woman willing to marry me. Some women will do anything."

They talked in this vein for a moment while Felix went on dressing. Karl told him about his fiancée, announced that the marriage would take place shortly before Christmas. " The Yuletide cheer provides an atmosphere of hope distinctly encouraging for two people embarking on such a hazardous journey," he explained.

Abruptly his manner changed. He reached for his hat and took a few steps towards the door. " *Auf Wiedersehen,* Felix. Take a long rest. You are about done in. I won't see you after the performance. You'll be surrounded by people and I'm taking the first train back to Paris." He paused, looked very intently at his friend. " It's been a great honour knowing a man like you."

Already he was out of the room. Felix heard him exchange a

few laughing remarks with Cécile in the corridor. Then the heavy tread of his footsteps faded.

"What are you doing, staring at yourself in the mirror?" she asked, hurrying into the room. "Aren't you ready yet?"

"I'm fussing with those confounded decorations. I wish they'd find something more practical."

While she helped him fasten his decorations on his coat he watched her reflection in the mirror. She was dressed for church, the strings of her bonnet knotted under her chin. "You look much too attractive," he remarked. "I don't know whether I should let you sit by yourself in church. Especially when you seem much smitten with Christoph and his gold chain."

She paid no attention. This was his way and he would never change. Even with the ribbon of the highest decoration on his shirt front he remained natural and said foolish things. Perhaps only superior people could permit themselves to be natural and say foolish things; the others had first to stress their importance by being pompous.

"Let me look at you," she said, giving a final appraising glance. "You look most handsome."

She raised herself on her toes to reach his lips. "And I love you very much."

Before going downstairs they stopped in the nursery. His entrance created a sensation. Karl and Marie were old enough to maintain their poise at the sight of their father, resplendent in full dress at this hour of the morning. They greeted him formally, kissed his hand, very self-conscious in their own finery. But the others gaped openly in speechless wonder.

"You see, they don't recognise me," he said to Cécile. "It's those decorations. I told you they frighten people."

Soon, however, the ice was broken. He squatted down and they circled around him, clapped their hands when he told them that to-morrow they'd all be leaving together in their beautiful coach, and in Switzerland they would do nothing but play, climb mountains and go fishing. They kissed him for that, asked more questions. He would have liked to linger among them but Cécile wouldn't hear of it.

"What is the thing you want to show me in the garden?" she asked as they came out of the nursery.

"I can't tell you. It won't take long."

They climbed down the stairs at the rear of the house and found themselves in the verdant stillness of the garden. He took her hand and slowly they walked down the sun-flecked alley, their blended shadow gliding behind, long and blue, over the sand. Spring was at work everywhere—in the white-bloomed apple trees, the sprouting grass, the glossy leaves of the rose bushes, the swelling buds.

A mood of silence had come over him. She walked at his side, sensing the remoteness of his thoughts, covertly watching his profile, still strikingly handsome even in its tragic gauntness. His nostrils flared at the scent of the earth in travail. He felt the morning breeze waft in cool waves over his face, inhaled deeply the fragrance of new foliage and returning life. Yes, he thought, another spring has come. The most beautiful because the last. He knew and no longer rebelled. He had had a good, happy, wonderful life. And he hadn't lived in vain. What more could a man want?

Abruptly they came upon it, as they reached the end of the garden. In the mossy stone basin the sky trembled on ripples of water. Somewhere nearby a bird twittered softly, as if talking to itself. And there it was. A bench. An ordinary public bench.

He had feared she wouldn't recognise it, but she did and at once. She gulped and squeezed his hand. They stood side by side, gazing at it.

"You'll never know the trouble I had stealing this bench," he said. "Cities simply hate to part with their public benches. They watch them, count them, rivet them into blocks of cement. They don't want to sell them, they don't want to give them. Finally Tanzen had to bribe the policeman—the same one, I suppose, who first told me your name. Together they dismantled it at night and carted it away. Fine police you have in Frankfurt," he added with a twinkle.

"I still see you sitting on it," she said dreamily.

"You said I looked supercilious."

"No. Just silly and—touching. The day you got drenched in the rain I fell in love with you. I've never been out of it."

"Two people in love can fill a world," he said softly.

They stood in silence for a little while, each lost in his thoughts. Then quietly they moved away and returned to the house.

Again they climbed up the service stairs and found themselves on the first floor. As they were approaching the staircase landing, he stopped, looked deep into her eyes and gently kissed her lips.

"And now, we must go," he said.

His hands spread over the organ keyboards, he gave a last look at the orchestra, the soloists, the masses of singers, eager and orderly, all looking at him, waiting for his signal. He spied Hermann Schmidt, flute in hand, his curled eyebrows bobbing with excitement; Tanzen, towering among the men's choir. The sopranos had a fine new leader, but somehow Magdalena had waved her off and taken her place . . .

He gave the signal.

In waves of grief the opening chords of the Passion flowed through the church. Slowly it swelled in a steady, throbbing crescendo. Then on an upward sweep it burst through Saint Thomas's nave, and like an eagle taking flight, the immortal music soared into the blue, higher and still higher, beyond the pointed spire into the Infinite.

Epilogue

SIX WEEKS after that Palm Sunday—on May 17, 1847— Felix Mendelssohn received the news that his sister Fanny had died suddenly while playing the piano; he fell to the floor in a faint and remained unconscious for hours.

He never fully recovered from that shock. When he was well enough to travel, he took Cécile and the children to Switzerland, where he spent the summer, trying to regain his strength; but letters and documents from that time show that he thought constantly of death. A daguerreotype of him exists—the only one ever made of him—showing him as he looked then, standing in his long cape, his handsome face hollowed and lined by illness and overwork. Once during the summer he walked to the nearby village of Riggenberg, on the lake of Brienz, and there for the last time in his life he played the organ.

The Mendelssohns returned to Leipzig in the fall, and Felix's health grew steadily worse. On the night of November 4th at the age of thirty-eight, he died in Cécile's arms—six months after the death of his sister. What illness they both had would be difficult to say with assurance, but some authorities have asserted, on the basis of the evidence, that Felix and Fanny died from cerebral hæmorrhages.

Cécile devoted the rest of her life to the children, but she lived for less than six years after Felix's death. She died on September 25, 1853.

Some lives leave a deep and lasting impression on the world, and Felix Mendelssohn's was such a life. Immediately after his death a movement was originated to set up a musical scholarship fund in his memory. In London a committee was formed with Sir George Smart as chairman and Karl Klingemann as secretary. With the generous assistance of Jenny Lind the necessary funds were raised, and the first promising composer to be awarded the Mendelssohn Scholarship was Arthur Sullivan.

The impetus given by Mendelssohn to the recognition of Johann Sebastian Bach's towering genius was decisive. No greater service was ever rendered by one artist to another. Much of Bach's work has not yet been found; more than one hundred of the cantatas he is known to have written are still missing. But Mendelssohn's

351

performance, after nearly one hundred years of neglect, of the immortal Saint Matthew Passion, and the subsequent search for Bach's manuscripts, have already brought the humble choirmaster to the place in music which is rightfully his—the highest.

THE END